ANTELUCAN

Artorian's Archives Book Thirteen

DENNIS VANDERKERKEN
DAKOTA KROUT

ACKNOWLEDGMENTS

From Dennis:

There are many people who have made this book possible. First is Dakota himself, for without whom this entire series would never have come about. In addition to letting me write in his universe, he has taken it upon himself to be the most glorious senior editor and keep straight all the madness for which I am responsible, with resulting hilarity therein.

An eternal thank you to my late grandfather, after whom a significant chunk of Artorian's personality is indebted. He was a man of mighty strides, and is missed dearly.

A special thank you to my parents, for being ever supportive in my odd endeavors, Mountaindale Press for being a fantastic publisher, and all the fans of Artorian's Archives, Divine Dungeon, and Completionist Chronicles who are responsible for the popularity allowing this to come to pass. May your affinity channels be strong and plentiful!

Last of all, thank you. Thank you for picking this up and giving it a read. Avalon is the continuation of a multi-book series, and I dearly hope you will enjoy them as the story keeps progressing. Artorian's Archives may start before Divine Dungeon, but don't worry! It's going all the way past the end of Completionist Chronicles! So if you liked this, keep an eye out for more things from Mountaindale Press!

Please consider giving us five stars on Amazon, Audible, and anywhere else you'd like to spread the word!

CHAPTER ONE

"It's all different." A child-sized Artorian gawked at Avalon in wonder. His new, barely teenaged body squeezed an arm tight around Ember's slightly taller shoulder, relying on her to support him to the point of being his actual legs.

Regardless of him having real ones once more.

The reborn Incarnate who had both a year or two and several inches of stature on him quietly felt very smug about this as the stumbling foal struggled, her boy vividly overwhelmed by all the sights as she kept him steady while his mouth moved faster than his feet did. "Somehow, it all feels the same."

Ember stopped in the middle of the street when he grunted and held his head. She'd gone through these same paces, having learned that a momentary pause could soothe this ailment. When he was about to apologize for stopping again, she curled her bronze arm around his head to hold him close. She cared for no apology. Only his health.

The uncanny familiarity of the bustling city still didn't sit right with young Artorian. After wandering through a few main arteries, the constant hustle of activity became too much for his fresh senses. He grumbled his words when Ember made a

1

prompting noise. "Boisterous, busy, too many people. Too much to pay attention to."

He closed his eyes and hid his face in Ember's neck to let the world be dark, planning to take in Avalon one measure at a time. She didn't eschew the role of primary support pillar, her hands covering his ears to give him a moment of muffled silence before she kissed his temple.

In the middle of the busy street, the adorable sight of the two children was provided a wide berth as foot traffic passed them by.

His ears tuned to the environment when the protective shields moved away, the details trickling in. The shuffling of feet over cobblestone. The murmuring and banter of people. Half-apologies from individuals needing to brush by. Laughter.

Laughter was a good sign. A child screeched, chased by another, who was chased by another. They all collided into a hencoop and then ran for their lives as the poultry took offense. The hens were guided by the calls of a moonlight rooster with shining spurs, masterfully stroking his wattles with a wing while surveying the situation from a tall perch that no nyan cat dared assail.

Classic village antics, on a larger scale.

He heard the gobble-gobble circus of livestock roaming. The dinging bell on a Dire Cow that moseyed by and snuffled the top of his head on the way. Without a care in Caltopia, the vast beast bellowed while trudging along. "Mooooo!"

There was the grunting of labor and stoking of fire, the rustling of wood being thrown into hearths. The plinking of hammer to metal, as metal met anvil. The fussing of villagers and the secret hush hush that lived behind every corner. Gossip? Yes! Delicious gossip. His favorite. There was some scheming about... mead, where the voices of men whispered. Some early cache they would be breaking into. Then there was... the ladies being aware, and plotting to ambush them, war-ladles at the ready. "War-ladles? Ah, yes. Soup for the soup god. How could I forget?"

"Mortality. Forgetting is healthy." Ember chuckled while working her fingers through his hair with a short-lived smirk as her eyes shot towards the conversation in question. Her face remained still, but she did gain a smile. Her attention shifted to the sensation under her digits, curious how a leftward riff of her hand made his short hair seem blond, while a stroke to the right made it brown. Like that set of dresses that were actually blue and black, though most people saw them as white and gold. Ember did not repress her grin as she recalled burning that warehouse to the ground with Rosewood handing her ever more torches to chuck.

Ember continued her quiet affection when Artorian stopped talking, taking the time to rest. He felt so frail under her fingers, knowing it would take time for him to grow.

She didn't mind this. She would be there, and she was but one of many who would blindly stride forth to protect him. In his many adventures as a kindly grandfather, he had adopted many souls into his hearts. Now that he needed them, regardless of him not having thought to ask for help, the backstage and scaffolding were rife with activity.

Ember held her boy, glad he was allowing the pounding in the brain to subside. Unlike Artorian, who would remain small in stature a few years longer, she grew up quickly. As an Elven child of the Yaran family, she was the walking example of stronger, better, faster. Her current mortal form did not deviate from those parameters. In part, purely to survive a bothersome side effect that she would always have to contend with.

As if to serve as a poetic reminder, the wind turned to blow some strands of hair into her face.

Her own locks were a long, feisty, burning red. Courtesy of an Elemental Affinity Channel that traveled with a person, regardless of body. Even as a non-cultivator for now, that Elemental Fire Affinity manifested itself with obvious markers. The connection had sparked into existence during the exact moment of her mind and soul transferring into her own, new, young mortal form. Then *wham*, her hair took the brunt of the immediate Affinity effects. She'd been self-conscious about the extreme red at first, but a mid-sleep mumble from a curled up Small-torian on how nice it was had made that thought flee, never to return.

He'd half-asleep mentioned a dream where she'd made him a bracelet from it, and the other people in the room had needed to restrain her from getting her hands on a blade. She thought that'd be a wonderful idea! Why did Lunella have to sit on her to stop her? *Phah.* She'd promised to find an alternative before Lunella had gotten up. That smug Matron.

It bothered her, slightly, that the Affinity channel had such a strong influence on her. A strong quality Fire channel had swayed her to anger and brute force often, yet she'd controlled that. The choice had been made hers, with practice and time. An Elemental Channel was an entirely different beast, one far more difficult to wrangle. Time with the Volcano Dungeon had helped her control most of her own volcanic tendencies, so she had it handled. Mostly.

She pressed her cheek to Artorian's head, repeating the phrase to soothe both him and herself. "Practice and time, sugar. Practice and time."

A deep breath followed, Artorian's nose freeing itself from the crook of Ember's neck. The smell of fresh, clean air, mixed with hints of brioche and other fresh breads came first. He liked how Ember smelled of mint and honey. Hints of spice from the merchants were pleasant, before his tongue curled from a sudden wave of salty wind that slid in from stage left like a dirty jester with a dirty joke.

He hadn't merely smelled the salt; the flavor had jumped right into his mouth.

Taste kicked open the door, demanding to come join the fray as Young-torian made a face and groaned in distaste. A happy cow, and not a whiff of cheese pontiff? Fantastic news. A breeze so salty that you felt like you just ate a mouthful of sand? Less so. He smacked his mouth to wet it, trying to get the unwelcome flavor out as he looked up at a pleasantly cloudy sky. "Dear, I may need some…"

A thick, short-cut, bamboo pole filled with water sloshed into his hands. Ember was at the ready with supplies. "Twist the cork while you pull. Big, slow gulps. Then re-cork the opposite way. Lefty-loosey, righty-tighty. If you forget, look at the grooves in the cork."

Artorian popped the proverbial lid, drank the clear Nidav-ellir spring water as instructed, then had the bamboo water bottle stubbornly tied around his waist when he tried to hand it back.

Ember herself carried four. "Keep that one. Any time a draft from the Salt Flats comes in, everyone makes that face. Last I heard, they were still working on the scent problem. We have a few of those this iteration. I know iteration isn't the right word anymore, but work with me. Some materials have bonded with synesthesia effects while Cal was trying to fix some core materials and covalent bonds. Salts are one of the affected crys-talline structures."

"It wasn't a problem indoors." Artorian grumbled while refitting the bottle so it didn't whack him in the thigh with each step.

"Wind doesn't tend to be with the shutters closed, no." Ember grinned back, her tone full of cheek and mischief. "Are you going to insist on acting like a fussy old man in body number… What are you on? Three? Four? Maybe indulge in being a kid some, while you are one again."

Artorian huffed, playing at being difficult. "There isn't enough honey on toast to bribe me to be something I don't want to be. I'm just this for now. I will get back to it! I was fussy to Cal when he turned me into an adult, thinking it a kindness. I will be fussy about this as well! No matter how thankful I am to have the form at all."

Ember laughed a good, deep, childlike belly laugh. She then poked his cheek with a big grin. "You're cute. So much fire! Did

I mention I have a thing for fire? Don't burn too hot or Shaka will show up."

"We'd need a cat cafe for that, according to him." Artorian turned beet red as her earlier words registered, his free hand pressing to his hip as he feistily snapped his head away like he wasn't affected. "You incorrigible flirt. I thought we weren't doing that?"

"No." Ember teased, completely delighted. *"You're* not doing that, because you're a sweet sugar pop that considers my feelings, and I asked you not to. That does not mean that I will not be taking every opportunity to turn you into a blushing wreck. Do you know how hard that is to do with you? Fussy old man version naught point four?"

Ember comedically mimicked him from the old days. Waddling forwards and dragging him with her as she copied his grandfatherly gait and antics in a mocking tone. "Ah yes, look at me. Wise and dastardly. Fu. Fu. Fu. I shall plot and plan and secretly tappy-tap my nose while pretending I had nothing to do with a whole string of coincidences. Yes. Fu. Fu. Fu. I shall be stoic, and play strong for everyone, and love them as my own, but never will I make myself happy beyond living vicariously through theirs. Fu! I shall groom my beard and look upon the horizon, a thousand answers in my eyes, and then when someone takes my attention, I shall gaze upon them as if they were the stars themselves. Fu!"

She then—without warning—straight up bit his ear like an upset C'towl having been giving exactly half a tummy rub too much. "Consider yourself more, brat! Or else everyone else gets up in arms on your behalf."

"Ow!" He yelped in retort, pulling away and holding the side of his face while looking utterly accosted. "Excuse you!"

"I am excused." She glared at him, growling like a beast before peering straight ahead and preparing to resume the march. "You are not!"

A sudden peck to her cheek froze her solid before he looked away with another 'I didn't do anything' tsun-tsun huff. This startled Ember, making her mouth and face squeeze together as the sensation of the smooch spread over her cheek like ice melting. A tiny hint of pink flushed her cheeks, while the gears in her brain were grinding between, 'Yes, we liked that,' and, 'Boy, you better reel it in,' moderated by a healthy modicum of, 'Only one? How dare there be only one! You cheapskate miser!'

Her eyes slowly narrowed while he whistled dreadfully off-key, so very interested in all the trees sprinkled along the road. "Oh, you think you're clever?"

"I am!" His finger rose to point at something, drawing her gaze away from the glare she was digging into his temple, and coming face to face with an entire tavern of people collectively melting into their tables with a '*dawwwww*,' and shooting Ember's cheek flush up from a concealable rosy to an embarrassed cherry red.

Ember dragged him out of the public eye at speed, while Artorian grinned and imagined a cloud of steam venting up from her head with how red her face had become! Ha-ha! One did not need strength to win snappy little argum—

Don! His back ended up against a brick wall as Ember's hand slapped into the facade, colliding with the brick right next to his face. She leaned in to be threatening, but the obvious red blush still vivid on her face was making that terribly difficult to accomplish. "In *public*?!"

Young-torian really shouldn't be grinning like a fool right now, but he did not have the capacity to stop. It was too good, and he was no Mage. He leaned into his cheeky mood, doing what she told him. "*Ah*, to be mortal and young."

Sharp encouragement whistled from behind Ember made her tense, feel like a cornered animal, and turn only to hiss over her shoulder at whoever *dared*.

Her hackle-raised discomfort was answered with a tight hug from her 'Torian, the squeeze added in for emphasis as he rubbed the back of her head. "Did it bother you so, dear? Would you rather I didn't?"

Growling, she slowly lost tension in her shoulders. Her arms reflexively curled around her boy when feelings of intensive possessiveness kicked in. She exhaled sharply and dropped her face onto his shoulder, hiding her flush while mumbling out a dejected, but honest response. "...No. I'm fussy, but I liked it and I wanted another, but I don't want to admit I wanted another, and people seeing made my skin crawl, and now I feel awkward and embarrassed."

She went quiet, the squeeze increasing.

"Do you want another?" Artorian, with soft finesse, whispered the request. His cheek grinding up and down against her face like a cat giving attention.

She nodded into his shoulder, then immediately hissed afterward, shushed him for no reason, then turned the squeeze into a crush. One *hrk* from Artorian later, and a smile took the place of where uncertainty had laid. "Okay, I feel better."

Wheezing and seeing stars as he had neither breath nor footing, Ember patted his back until he stumbled properly upright. She bumped foreheads when he was stable and put a finger on his mouth. "I'll tell you when. I want! But I'll tell you when. Otherwise, *I* become a blushing wreck, and I'm the one attacking!"

CHAPTER TWO

"Alright, dear." Artorian conceded with a tiny conciliatory smile.

Ember helped his arm back around her neck, grinding her cheek into his face to aggressively cat-nuzzle him back. When content, she dragged him back into the middle of the street for more walking. A preventative tactical move! Before he could slide in any more of his commentary. Or snark. Or quips. Or whatever else he kept in his sleeves that was going to cause the color on her face to catch actual fire.

She liked... things. Just... Hush! Shut up!

Emotions were a lot easier for her as an Incarnate! When she had the power to step on anything she truly disliked, and her look could both silence a whole council and unanimously clench the butt cheeks of a national army? That did something special for morale, feeling like she had a handle on life, and the forces that could oppose her.

Now it was just her as a mortal again, and the distinct sensations of that non-cultivator mortality was a step too far over the discomfort line. If a step was a wild, uncontrollable tumble down a steep grassy hill.

Reverting from a Mage to a mortal was... probably doable for the newer Mages. The older Mages would definitely have Eternia-like acclimation side-effects. With nausea, stomach sickness, the horror of helplessness. Some suffered The Full Chandra, as they were calling it. As the recorded effects of her initial Eternia entries had required seed core sleep to heal.

Going from a double-S-ranked Incarnate to a non-cultivator? Ember had been physically ill for months and would never tell Artorian that she'd barely gotten to her feet in time before the news came down that he was likely to wake soon. Nor would she divulge the abyss-show of a volcanic cat that she'd been, trying to get there with haste.

A whole underground economy of potions existed due to her belligerent need to sprint headlong towards her goal. She had been thankful for the reprieve when it took an additional few weeks for her boy to safely be able to get up and get going, with immediate Old-Fringe antics tacked on from Tibbins, Lunella, Wuxius, Tarrean, Irene, Jiivra, Astrea, and Blanket. Tychus kept his book of a brother company in the Library, where he retained a running tally of Anansi flirting with Alexandria, and who was winning the snappy comeback war.

Lunella had whole new stories about noodle dragons, which she referred to as 'blasted longs.' A detail some traveling Dwarves heard once and kept forever. There was an entire litany of Lunella trying to broom-beat a noodle dragon out of the pantry like an oversized cookie thief, bits of its nose sticking from the pantry door. The rest of the dragon haphazardly floated outside, coiled through an open window.

Erusturm, that broom-beaten troublemaker, was part of a group of pleasant—if a bit overly self-assured and unwittingly destructive—noodles that had all smelled the honey pie and were attempting in their own way to abscond with some.

Luckily, it turned out that the fluffy noodles were passionately fond of head rubs and were all convinced to wait until more pies were ready so they could each have one. To the great delight of the hordes of children all using the landed noodles like playsets. According to the footnotes, this convincing had nothing at all to do with Jormungandr showing up above the broom-swept lot. Causing them all to tangle up like a fearful ball of yarn, as Jorm was the noodliest of them all, and ever so slightly bigger. By a category or twelve.

Ember found the sight of the yarn ball rolling away to flee, particularly cathartic.

Her own mortal being was still a swirl of uncommon experiences, and the ability to separate oneself from rogue thoughts and senses was not a convenient luxury that a mortal simply had.

First-order thought was a difficult beast to wrestle. When she got hungry, she ate, only realizing afterwards that she had solved the immediate problem without considering the consequences. When she was angry, that was an all-consuming emotion. Jealousy? Affection? Same boat, different oars. Second-order thinking was as difficult as breathing in the Mage ranks, if you wanted to do it. The skill was so helpful to have. To know the reason for your feelings. To have the ability to distance yourself from them before acting without effort.

Ember had no such conveniences now as, much like Artorian, she was swallowed by the whorl.

She clung to her boy equally as much as he needed her for support, working on it as she went through her days. Ember then grit her teeth, reminded herself that she wasn't going to have this any other way, and blew out a gust of air while Artorian darted over the place with his eyes. Ogling the architecture, buildings, trees, a few potted houseplants.

In what seemed like no time at all, he appeared once more overwhelmed by the general idea of being in an actual city that could be called home.

Ember didn't notice that the majority of her attention fell on Artorian, but all the passersby giving them a healthy berth did. The populace suppressed hidden grins until they'd passed, some ducking a detour into a barbershop, or tavern, or anywhere open for poking one's nose in so they could join the gushing and gossip.

The passerby who had whistled and stirred up a storm— Lucky Luca, a B-ranked Mage of Art—did just that! The Viking with Ratatoskr the squirrel napping on his shoulder couldn't help but involve himself and dove into Eri's Oni Emporium and Fabric Shop as his gossip-laden corner of choice.

The fabric shop was a front for the true goods that Eri peddled, but that wasn't important when there was news! Luca's voice was excited and incensed when the door closed behind him, his accent a blocky Finnish. "Did you see them? They're so small, and *adorable!*"

"I knowwww." The artsy seamstress slapped down her yarn. Eri, a red Oni fond of flowers and fancy outfits, hungrily made 'come here' motions while pulling out a chair. The fashion-inclined Oni instantly made herself cozy by flinging a fat, fluffy white boa around her neck before leaning her elbows on the table. There was gossip to be had! "They're precious. It's darling. I heard from Osha herself that the Saintess turned beet red right in front of her tavern? Because she'd gotten one snuck to the cheek in the middle of the street, and everyone *puddled.*"

The visitor's behind quickly connected his butt to the offered chair, Luca surprised at the name drop. "Osha of the Steel Cable? How in Cal did you get a line of birds to her?! Her tavern is busier than her safety regulation department. That ant's nest is incessantly trying to make everyone wear P.P.E."

Eri locked gazes with Luca like she was about to spill state secrets. "That's nothing! Blue the Axolotl, Piano the Evanescent, and Raillery the Cheeky dropped by earlier! All starry-eyed, with some hot gossip about this *thing* that happened against Smith Ullard's wall? I hear it was you who whistled? Tell me it was you; I *need* a first-hand account of the kabedon story. There's already a rumor that her handprint is embedded on the stone."

Tea and cups were swiftly stirred, more chairs filled in haste as other gossipers flocked into Eri's Emporium, accompanied by birds tittering for another good tweet, including a Corvus named Coraxi, and a Pylon-loving Arachnid that only ever went by Mr. Webb.

Nobody in Avalon was making it *obvious* that there were a lot of eyes on their reborn little celebrities.

There were strict, furious orders from Lunella that the duo should traverse unaccosted. If they came to you, then there was no problem. If you got in their way with more than a polite nod? Then the woodworks would explode with critters, and every mandible-clicking shadow and veiled-dagger spot of night in the dark would descend upon you with incredible hostility.

Not that anyone in Avalon needed to be told, save perhaps some of the roaming Heavenlies playing tourist who nobody could stop anyway. Outside Avalon was a different story, but for everyone within the walls, the rules were ironclad.

Mortals, Mages, and humanized Beasts alike had found homes, purpose, and a sense of belonging in Avalon. With Father Richard in tow, Caesar and his Faithful had visited in force from their own chosen corner of the world, aiding existing construction efforts. Nidavellir Dwarves had the same idea but pitched the stoniest of fits about regulations when multiple outside groups couldn't come to an agreement on how tall something could be. Particularly after a Goblin tower, which reportedly had been made from little more than toothpicks and moxie, had collapsed on a brewery and somehow caused the entire building to catch fire.

That day, Avalon had turned from a modest village into the aftermath of a Lawful and Good Dwarven rampage. People woke in tears, finding their abodes were not only upgraded, but perfectly up to code.

To oversee that no further disasters to brewery-related locations could occur, the Dwarven perfectionist, Osha of the Steel Cable, had chosen to stay behind should her kin ever need a proper tavern to return to, or to raise a solemn mug in their attempt to understand how every individual brick of that brewery had self-immolated after contact with Goblin architecture. Like the brewery had chosen death by the mere brush of such haphazardly built nonsense.

Goblin architecture had been banned. If they wanted to build, it had to be in their specifically assigned segment or zone, otherwise there would be war.

Roamers of all kinds, from far and wide, were welcome. Whether injured or broken or whole or just fine, all found a spot in Lunella's haven. For here they had been considered, their trials and troubles deemed important. There were whole groups dedicated to the worries of their minds. The struggles of the self. All were greeted and wanted by wide open arms.

Many found mundane jobs, and in finding a goal and the hints of a new passion, had turned their gifts and powers to making something of those crafts. A fond notable sight was the growing occurrence of Mages turning their sizable might to the matters of mortals. For what took a hundred men weeks in the field, a sole Mage did in a day. Jin of the Earth Vein, master of the moonlight rooster, and farmer most casual, was particularly famous for this.

The movement had begun small.

A dare here. A comment there. An 'I'm pretty sure I can do that better than you' sniped past the ear. A couple of Dwarven boasts and laughter to up the blood pressure. A few pieces of Dark Elven craftsmanship on display to show what they were working on to spur strong opinions.

That one had caused mixed reactions. A few 'I'm not going to let them show me up' jealous mumbles joined cries of 'you did that without tools?' Only for a few Mages to join the bickering pile of non-Mages, resulting in a two-evening long discussion on the functions and forms of a basic cabinet.

There was much heat about shelves, and even more ado about nothing. Plus, two wrestling matches on the amount of hinges one should apply to a door, including at least one tussle concerning the best wood, and why it was mahogany.

Newcomers to Avalon were swiftly given a drive if they

lacked one. A nudge of 'what are you good at?' coupled with a sudden comment of 'Really? This other guy I was talking to earlier said that what you said is wrong and his way is better. He's over there. Working. Go prove him wrong.'"

Many sleeves were pushed to the elbow in response to such words.

Slippery suggestions from the shadows about 'just showing him the right way to do it and having the crowd decide' curtailed fervor, letting the engineers-to-be stride towards the action without matters devolving into fights.

Fights happened anyway, but there was a general consensus that the end-result should include both people making the things their way, to then present it for discussion and critique. This resulted in a rapid rise of smithies, carpenters, cobblers, seamstresses, farmers, and more.

With housing aplenty, and facilities long ready to receive them, there wasn't a new arrival to Avalon that rejected the sudden gift of a place to rest their head, a home to call theirs, and a time for when meals were had. With a very welcoming, open invitation that 'they better be there!' Or there would be a horde of mothers coming to drag them from their dreary bed. Plus, of course, their rival got to claim that they were correct, since the newcomer was absent *anyway*.

Cabinets were clearly better if shaped *oval*.

Or any such claim that made the newcomer loudly throw off their blanket with a 'What?!' and storm through the door towards whatever fool was making such baseless, ungrounded claims. "The best shape for a cabinet is a trapezoid. Trapezoid!"

Lunella had wiped her hands off after that one. "Another successful addition."

Astrea kneaded the bridge of her nose. "I have no idea what half of all these people are on about? What is a trapezoid?"

"Don't care!" Lunella was already on her way out. "Don't matter!"

The Matron strode forth powerfully.

"I was warned years ago that I should expect people with all kinds of difficulties, and all my old man asked was if I could help them. Make a place for them. I have those letters framed in my house! Just like the success we had with Jillian, Kinnan, and Pollard, I shall make it so!" Her declaration was swift and to the point. "They're here, they're part of the group, and we will keep making space for more until there's nobody left to look with big, pleading, puppy eyes at our door. We take everyone! For this is Avalon!"

Astrea snickered at her sister. "You picked up Grandpa's flair for the dramatic, Lu."

Lunella, garbed in Village Matron robes of finest Lapis spider silks, sporting no less than three scarves of various affiliations that had recognized her sovereignty, and wearing the most comfortable sandals in existence, posed in a ray of sunlight that broke through the limited clouds. A mysterious breeze perfectly fluttered by to make her hand on hip pose appear both heroic and magnanimous, her elderly face pointed to the sky. She narrowed her gaze, and Astrea could swear she heard a wooden recorder as Lunella spoke.

"This is the way."

CHAPTER THREE

Ember and Artorian walked until they were tired. The duo wandered outward through the winding alleys of the Avalon, roaming a district set aside for kittens, C'towl, and the humanized variants thereof.

Planting his butt into a claw-carved chair, Artorian inspected the seat two whole times to cope with how such a flimsy, thin thing was not cracking to splinters under his weight. He looked up at Ember, who was leaning her elbow on the table, smirking as she carried her chin on her palm.

She schmoozed out her words, grasping his current struggle. "Not a Mage, bunny boy. Normal weight. Normal density. A chair that can handle a C-ranker can handle you. Cedarwood, before you ask. Just like the big beams in all the homes of the district we just left."

Artorian, placated, shifted to sit like a normal human being, his eyes and hands consuming the world with ravenous intent. He simply could not stop brushing his palms over the table. "It's soft. Emby, they made the table *soft.*"

"Well, yes." She grinned, pawing at the table herself. "What better to catnap on? Have you seen the humanized C'towl population in this section of Avalon? Every little nook, cranny, and sun-bleached spot is a place for them to lounge like lizards. Soaking up the heat."

"We're in C'towl territory?" Artorian appeared to have missed that clue, his blue eyes snapping back to the ridges in all the wooden buildings that did appear to have claw marks. "That explains why all the architecture here looks like one massive play-park."

The previously strange protrusions of wooden beams, platforms, and cylindrical pathways crisscrossing the area, as every building had to be connected to another in some convoluted way, now made much more sense.

They were in cat land!

"What's a Nyan-derthal?" Artorian moved a hand to gain additional cover from the sun, spotting one of the hanging signs showing a ball of yarn being toyed with. Now that he was looking for signs, he spotted artwork carved into the walls. Much motivational work too! He read some off while Ember thought of how to answer him. "Silver memories: Go be your favorite self. Not your best self."

"Nyanderthals are..." Ember struggled in her attempt to be correct. "I have a lot of problems understanding how they portray themselves, because there was a bad territory war with other cats of different names, and they did not win. Giant explosions and lots of fallout. That's the part I understand easily. War? War never changes."

She raised her hand for the attention of a person lingering by an open window, who'd been trying not to smirk at them while keeping a respectful distance. "Nyanderthals are an affiliation of cats, not necessarily a species, that all subscribe to a mantra of neutrality. Think of a Hidden Race? They got slapped down and now they want to stay out of the spotlight. Aligning with none, conflicting with none. Accumulating wealth in the shadows for 'fun.'"

Ember narrowed her eyes in a scowl. "This means they gain possession of some knowledge and toys that they really shouldn't have, but since they delight in shoving those toys into the pockets of people who they think could cause the biggest catastrophes with them... It honestly helps us find the actual troublemakers more easily."

She tapped her fingers together, annoyed at a different aspect of Nyan society. "Unfortunately, Nyans have these massive swaths of complex and irritating rules that they all know and abide by? While everyone else must play guess-guess at what's going on, making us think that they're actually making some of the rules up as they go."

She quickly pointed at the motivational line on the wall that her boy had just rattled off. "That? Silver memories? That's a way of life here. To Cat folk, all actions that are not required in order to live are a game. Commerce? A game. If you so much as walk up to some humanized kittens wanting to buy a handful of chalk, they will indulge you, but it's a game to them. When you look over your shoulder, they will suddenly all be gone, with whatever money you gave them. They will appear, disappear, and do only what is good and fun to them as they pursue being their favorite selves. Not their best selves. Don't expect morality lessons here."

Artorian laced his fingers, chewing on that detail as a tall, lanky man with a big smile approached. One deviously curled cat tail swayed behind him until the man halted at two feet from the table, stopping on some invisible line and placing a hand to his outfit for a light bow. "Welcome to Crème de la Crème à la Edgar. I am C'towl O'Malley, I shall be your server today."

Ember smiled, showing her teeth. "Purrfect."

O'Malley turned to the lady and recreated his small bowing motion. "Thank you, mademoiselle, I have been practicing. Your consideration is most gracious, Grand Saintess."

Artorian stole a glance at his dearest from the titles being dropped, regardless of her current mortality and distinct lack of S-rankery. The C'towl introducing himself by both species and name also piqued his interest, but he put all those puzzle pieces in his pocket for now. Artorian didn't have enough for a clear picture. Instead, he waited for Ember to take the lead. She clearly had a grip on the social rules.

"We would like two hot honey milks, and some Nidavellir noodles, please." Ember commanded the cat delicately, her comfort rapidly increasing as she got snug in her chair and looked around to spot a few details Artorian didn't know to look for. "Thank you, C'towl O'Malley. I shall remember this."

Those words straightened the C'towl's tail, his human features breaking and fraying as whiskers sprouted from his face, followed by the floppiest set of cat ears Artorian had ever witnessed. "You honor me, Grand Saintess. I shall inform the Clowder of your presence and request."

A short nod from Ember sent O'Malley on a beeline path into the Crème de la Crème à la Edgar, where mad meowing instantly kicked up like orders being yelled to the chef, and the chefs yelling back indignantly. Then there was a moment of silence, cut open by a single, questioning mewl, as if to ask: '*Who* did you say was here?' A myriad of catlike faces populated all the open spaces of that building seconds later, followed by the heads pulling away and a rapid rustling happening inside. The meowing turned far more organized and militant.

"You herded cats." Artorian's expression was pure bafflement. He turned to her, hands flat on the table. "You can herd *cats*."

"C'towl, precious." She winked back with pride and enjoyment. "I can herd C'towl. That half-cat, half-owl distinction is important."

Artorian blinked as he thought of a social interaction step that had been missed, taking a second look at the opening of the door and Ember's smug face. "Do... Do we not need to pay them?"

"I have. However, you bring up a good point I needed to address." She reached her hand into empty space... but nothing happened. She then inhaled sharply, dropped her head at having forgotten she could not do that right now, and instead pulled two Silverwood bracelets out of the satchel hanging from her hip. That… shouldn't have reasonably fit in there? "Not being able to reach directly into warehouses at will is a thorn in my side."

Artorian was too engrossed in the satchel she was wearing to pay attention to the ones in her hand. "Spatial bag! Do they work now? I remember rings were a convoluted backup."

"Same convoluted backup, just with a bag. The rings work better. These are special." Ember clarified while she held out her hand, expectant. "Arm."

"What, dear?" Artorian leaned forward, not sure what she meant as his eyebrows furrowed.

"Arm!" She dropped her open hand again, firmly repeating herself.

Confused, Artorian reached his left arm forward, fully encapsulated by the glowing, growing smile on her flushed face as she slid the Silverwood bracelet onto his wrist. When understanding snapped into place, he matched her expression and stole the other Silverwood bracelet from her grip!

"Hey!" Ember instantly complained, trying to reach for it while distracted by butterflies.

"Nuh-uh!" Artorian joyfully rebuked her request, his smile widening as he leaned back to keep it out of her reach. "If you get to do the sweet thing, I get to do the sweet thing! Arm!"

Ember snatched at empty air where the item had been, the bracelet suddenly no longer between Young-torian's fingers. She blinked at his open hands when he twirled them like a street magician to show they were vacant, confused as to where he'd disappeared an entire bracelet off to. He didn't have Mana! He couldn't make it vanish? But it was gone! That was not possible! She claimed his entire arm in both her hands instantly thereafter, searching for where he'd put it. There must be some kind of secret, hidden sleeve. "Give that back!"

Artorian's face was one massive smile, his words soft and sweet when the reply came. "I already did."

She squinted at him, demanding answers.

Artorian's response was to move his left arm to her left arm, and clink Silverwood bracelets together. "Sleight of hand needs no extra magic. It's magic all by itself, dear."

Ember was too busy gawking at the bracelet that had appeared on her arm to ask for an explanation. How... how had he pulled that off? She hadn't even felt it. "Well, that's... impressive. Since when are you so good at thievery and tricks?"

Artorian beamed, equal measure amused and proud that he'd gotten away with it. Incarnates couldn't be fooled. But the normal folks? The eye can only see so fast, and only so much when it's looking exactly where you want it to look. "Classic misdirection? That comes with a story about a thief girl that I met in a tavern. I tricked her into pickpocketing a note out of my pocket, wrapped around some iron shards. I let her see me put the coins in my pocket, but I never really put them in my pocket. Instead of coins, she had a lovely evening with me at the lake."

"I don't know much about your life before you were Artorian, sugar." Ember tastefully pulled his attention back to her as the jealousy crept in. Talking about another girl when she was right there? She'd get him for that! "Or was that a preamble for how you'd like to take me to a lake?"

"Of course!" Artorian swiftly backpedaled, recognizing his mistake and the hole he'd begun to dig by reminiscing. His hand quickly pressed into hers. "T'was just a memory of olden times. I would much rather the new memories. These are better."

"*Mhm.*" Ember didn't drop her eyes from her boy, her hand poised to flick the abyss out of his forehead. Lucky for the loquacious little trickster, he'd said the smart thing, and she agreed with him right away. "Yes. Yes, they are. I am, indeed, better."

Artorian beamed. Crisis averted!

CHAPTER FOUR

"Hot Tristram milk with El Dorado honey, and Nidavellir noodles, Grand Saintess." O'Malley slid smooth as silk into the scene while the chefs lurking in the doorway shook their paws with pinched fingers. The server carefully injected himself at a very calculated time, his tail flicking away their comments of 'Che vuoi?' as the chefs bickered about his pickiness. O'Malley chose the very moment when the potential strife of his customers was over and buried, arriving with his arms piled full of fat, steaming plates of deliciousness.

Artorian ogled the food; the smell sensational, the visuals divine. The sauce... orange? "There's more meat than noodles in there! Just how much protein do my Dwarven friends eat?"

He then picked up a single bow-tie noodle, checking the consistency to find it decently firm. The quality was far above what he remembered noodles to be, though the design was foreign to him. Perhaps it was something else? With his meal, he received a personal scribble from Chef Al Dente, stating that they were out of linguine, and farfalle was used. "This is a noodle, right?"

O'Malley choked on his stifled laugh, then politely nodded.

"Yes, Monseigneur. That is, indeed, a noodle. I would have thought you an expert on the matter, given the stories."

"*What* stories?" Artorian's entire stomach fell down a pit. O'Malley fled like the wind as Artorian yelled at his afterimages. "*What* stories, O'Malley?!"

Troubled, his attention wrenched to a shrieking, red with laughter, falling out of her chair Ember. Observing her laughter caused it to double in intensity when she could see the full extent of his facial turmoil. She was bashing the bottom of her fork on the ground, tears rolling down her cheeks while she heaved in breaths.

She wiped her tears away and clambered back into her chair when the look became too much. Allowing the occasional sputter to escape her lips, she tried very hard to twirl her noodles as a distraction. In vain, of course. Ember secretly enjoyed the heavy glare she was receiving from Artorian. Who staunchly refused to let up, since there were clearly whole books worth of shenanigans at play, and he wanted to dig seven layers deep into this gossip dessert.

He was about to address it when a familiar heat swept in from stage left.

"Don't fault a child of **Fire** for burning, my **Loving** young friend." Shaka clicked as he swaggered onto the scene with a flaming **vmumph**. Hands nested in his pockets as the grin on his face spread harmlessly from ear to ear, Shaka greeted them by spreading his arms wide open. He adjusted his colorful dashiki after a slam-hug from Ember, grasped the extra chair, and claimed it with his rear when she sat back down as well.

The shadows visibly bristled at his doing so, distorting from their assigned, sensible locations as demanded by physics. They begrudgingly settled. There was little the hidden mandibles and dagger-wielding dervishes could do against a Heavenly, and Shaka was whitelisted as welcome company.

"I still want to know!" Artorian snapped his head toward the visitor, Shaka's sudden appearance accepted in stride. His own fork stabbed into the meatier portion of the noodles before shoveling a fistful into his face. Artorian then angrily mumbled with food in his mouth, words replaced by noises, pointing motions, and chewing. '*Hmllmmlm*' sounded like a fish trying to speak above water, but Shaka merely grinned wider as Ember looked away to drink her milk so she wouldn't spray it all over her food when the laughter overtook her. One instance of hot milk up the sniffer was enough for a lifetime.

Shaka waved a 'no, I don't need anything' motion to a C'towl's head poking out from the open window of the Crème de la Crème à la Edgar. The cat vanished right after, the indoors mewling turning subdued, like the conspiratorial whispering of an undercover acquisitions operation doing its best not to be brought to the light. Especially right now. The people in power that were able to book them sitting right outside of said very legal operation? What a fantastic time to keep one's nose out of the milk bowl.

Ember smirked hard; her cheeks squeezed while she put effort in trying to keep it together. A distraction from the pain in her cheeks was welcome, even if she very much still wanted Artorian's attention all to herself, his blue eyes spending more time on Shaka than on the food. "What brings you, Shaka? Random roaming? Or are you here on business?"

The Heavenly slapped the table. "I am—"

Shaka paused, opening and closing his digits. "One moment. This table is very soft."

The dark man rubbed his palm across the surface with intrigue, nodding in approval as Artorian also slapped the table and pointed at him. Swallowing a mouth full of farfalle, the youth got out his words. "That's what I said!"

The Heavenly pawed his digits across the surface in full agreement. "Business first. Then fun. Artorian? I informed and conversed with some of the other Heavenlies that have managed to fully manifest a physical form. Please do not mistake Heavenlies for being happy about that. Manifesting means things are bad up in our rung of reality. Aside from that, I have spoken at length with others per your comment on the structure of the Tower not being very efficient or well-designed. You should have seen Somnum's Cheshire grin when that particular cup was pushed from the table. Ah, Somnum is the **Sleep** node, and she sends her half-awake but mostly asleep regards."

Artorian froze with a fork in his mouth, turning pale as his shoulders bunched together. His entire form tensed like a cold front had just slammed into him, thoughts stuck on the idea of multiple Heavenlies being informed that he had strong opinions on their Tower, and that they discussed it. "Ohno."

"Oh yes!" Shaka laced his fingers mid-confirmation. "*At length.*"

Artorian shrunk into his chair, his voice that of a mouse. "*Ohno.*"

"We also spoke about your many, many accomplishments." Shaka raised a brow as he sank into his chair for comfort, the cedar creaking until he adjusted his own weight so he could enjoy the chair, rather than the chair suffering. "During my movement to this locale, my senses developed in time to hear the C'towl mention... stories?"

Artorian attempted to be one with the chair. Both his hands covered his face and head as tiny groans escaped the hunched-up, boy-shaped ball. "You're going to keep them from me too, aren't you? You dangle them only to smirk and giggle."

The Heavenly broke into laughter, his accent carefully restrained. "Not at all! The stories of little Artorian are vast and plentiful. Each embellished and confused over the ages. I had a great time debating the River Styx of events in your pre-Cal days. In truth, there is a vast, massive list. Shaka shall indulge you with snippets!"

The Heavenly tapped a drumbeat onto the table, a scrolling ledger of solidified fire entering existence to list notable events. One at a time, he verbally crossed off current popular topics. "Blowing up the clockwork sun. Demon genocides. The Forky crusade. Shark dental hygiene. Becoming a Long flag. Outrunning Wagner on a racer. Cow-a-geddon and the cheese fondue, also called the Pontification Elimination. Can't sing but can Dance. Spreading and gathering Iridium. The Crown that smacked the abyss out of a usurper's face. Then, finally, some ancient tale concerning Dark Elves with Brianna being assigned nap time puts this cheeky waffle of a grin on Ulam's face, yet he won't tell us why."

Artorian made a truly unpleasant noise when the burning ledger doused itself. "I think I would rather be told about how I'm going to be killed by Heavenlies for making commentary about their Tower. Thank you."

Shaka leaned into the opening.

"We came to the conclusion that you reached that statement because you couldn't see... certain truths about the Tower, as we didn't want you to see them. This is common consensus for many of the Tower's aspects." Shaka attempted to be helpful, reaching over to first pat, and then rub Artorian's sullen back. "I am of the group that shares the opinion that you should see these truths. Then, perhaps, you will amend your statement."

Artorian shot upright like a piece of rubber snapping back into shape. "I hunger for this. Are you serious or are you being the most incorrigible of teases? Don't do that to me, Shaka. Don't put that plate of pie in front of my nose and expect me not to crave it."

"Eat your actual meal, **Love**'s disciple." Shaka enjoyed this far too much, his dark fingers pleasantly drumming on the soft table. "I shall speak, only if you eat. You require nutrition. Alternatively, I would gladly continue the topic of Tales D'Artorian. Or perhaps stories of Tuatha dé Danann? Well, more, Tuatha dé Dani."

Shaka slid into the role of an amateur bard, hands strumming a burning lute that formed from vacant space as he continued on the topic of Artorian's deeds. "He finds the lost and broken. Whether by his choice, coincidence, or smoke of the Oaken. By the will of the universe, traveling bards love you and make you this verse. The story of the giant crab is also amusing. I think I needed to rhyme here with the word bruising."

Squinting at the sky, Shaka dismissed the stringed instrument. "No. This is not for me. Shaka has tried. Shaka does not like the flavor of this sound. Shaka does the drums."

Adjusting in his seat, the Heavenly returned to petting Artorian's head. "The size of that crab gets embellished to the point that people start to believe Jotunheim was actually the shell of said dead crab, who you launched into space... or something. I'll have to ask them to tell me again. There's just books and books worth of—"

"I'm eating!" Artorian quickly begged the Heavenly to stop, Nidavellir noodles inhaled at speed. "I'm eating!"

"I award you one leaf of smartness." Shaka cackled, his beaming expression oozing with delight at all the rib-poking he was getting in at **Love**'s disciple. He even copied the pose of pointing both his hands to the top of his head, complete with a silly grin.

Artorian, mouth full of food, attempted a poor man's rebuke as Shaka had clearly gotten someone to talk. The guess went to Wux living the life on honey mead, blabbing. "You know that one as well? Is nothing sacred?!"

Seeing that Artorian had made the capital mistake to stop eating, Shaka launched into a serenade of continued bardic dramatics. His hands drummed a jaunty tune onto the table, his singing dreadfully off-key, devoid of any attempts at rhyme. "During Cal's worldly timeline: Artorian becometh the sandman. The maker of happy dreams. The prince of tricks and the bane of tricksters! The only things that can stop him are angry women and nap time!"

Young-torian wept while eating, his face buried in his hands as he begged the Heavenly to stop with whimpers, and a mouth full of noodles. He deeply understood the woes of Kere Nolsen now. This was awful.

"That's enough, Shaka." Ember calmly, flatly, and coldly

stated her demand like it was a law of the land. "A little was fine. Now you're overdoing it, and I'm getting upset. Stop."

Shaka took a breath, as if he would dare one more jest. Then he caught something in Ember's eye and dropped the topic like a rock. "I apologize, Artorian. I assure you that they are all good stories, and I am merely enjoying myself. I shall cease. Instead, why do I not tell you Tower secrets? This would cheer you up as well as a wild drum circle pleases my heart, yes?"

Still whining, his eyes wet, Artorian pathetically swallowed his noodles and nodded his head. He wiped his mouth free from sauce when Ember provided him with a miniature towel. She hummed a supportive note, Shaka's jaunty tune stuck in her head. "Never go anywhere without a good towel."

With his face clean, Artorian contemplated vengeance. Bulging his bottom lip out like an injured child, he hammed up his expression before aiming it squarely up at the Heavenly. Shaka felt the pain stab right through that heart of his as the youth attacked him with the attack known as: the big, wet eyes.

The Heavenly gripped his chest, defeated by a mere child. "You win, **Love**, you win! Release me from that gaze! I yield!"

Shaka knew he'd been played when Artorian smugly wiped his face with his sleeve afterwards, easily returning to a neutral expression while slurping from his mug of milk. Artorian maintained eye-contact while shooting the Heavenly that patented over-the-glasses look of expectation.

Shaka dramatically posed; the back of his hand held to his forehead. "You fiend! Retribution for mere gossip. Whatever shall Shaka tell the drum circle?"

"Gossip is good, yes." Artorian conceded, remaining serious. "Knowledge is better. What did I get wrong, and is there a visual aid? I love visual aids, and I can't make my orbs right now."

Shaka threw his head back to release a belly laugh. "Ha! Never change!"

The Heavenly then motioned above the table, a detailed

model of the Tower starting to manifest from the lower levels. A crystalline, see-through version of the real thing that could be touched growing from a single point. "I am aware that Dawn provided you with prior memories, so that will cut my explanation down significantly, as you already know many basics. The first floor of the Cultivator Tower holds the basic six nodes."

Celestial

Infernal

Fire

Water

Air

Earth

When Shaka noticed that Artorian was squinting at the nodes on the second floor, mouthing their names as the tiny text floating above those motes was fit only for ants, he created a proper, floating list next to the Tower as he built the replica. "Here, let Shaka teach you properly. Take in the updated hierarchy of main concepts that are currently held by each floor. The order has changed since your diplomacy with Henry and Marie. By which I do not mean that the Cultivator Tower suddenly has more than six nodes per floor. It does not, so relax."

His eyes momentarily flicked to Ember, who was posing as the picture of innocence. "I am aware that you both are aware that there are more than three Towers around this sphere. Knowledge of *one* is already too much for Incarnates, as far as Heavenlies are concerned. So do not go *blab*. They do not all love you as Shaka does, and as there is some rivalry at play between us, and Heavenlies occupying Towers in other spheres, this will cause tension. *Do not blab.* If you need to find comfort on the topic, find and ask your Wo'ah the Wise about Lagrange Points."

The Heavenly reached over to grasp Artorian's head, turning the youth's gaze so his blue eyes faced the list. "I have always liked his name. The best parts combining 'Wo': something explodes, and you go *whoa*! Then 'Ah': when you understand what happened and you go *aaaah*!"

Shaka laced his fingers, then sat back like an army recruiter looking at fresh starship troopers. The stars were already sparkling in their eyes. He motioned at the crystalline Tower. "Would you like to know more?"

CHAPTER FIVE

"I want the lists!" Artorian peppered Shaka with his answer, speaking quickly while also tapping on the table with both his hands, and bouncing in his seat like an impatient child currently on all of the sugar. "I want all the lists!"

Shaka laughed and didn't make it difficult. Completing both the visual representation of the crystalline replica Tower and adding clean outlines to each in order to detail what the main floors contained. "Will this cover my transgression? Very well, here. Enjoy your lists."

Tower Tier Two
Lightning
Metal
Effervescence
Plant
Acid
Disenchantment

Artorian wiped his face with the towel when he realized his mouth had been open this whole time. His eyes consumed the list of the second floor's currently reigning concepts. He immediately motioned to the side panels as Shaka formed them, before paying attention to the third tier. "What are those?"

"Skipping steps?" Shaka chuckled, having somewhat expected this. "The Tower, or its main trunk? It's just that. A straight pole, or the middle of a tree. However, why must it be the case that only a single instance of space can exist within that pole? We have many layers and those all get along... for the most part."

Shaka reached into his replica, grasped the node of **Lightning** between his fingers, and pulled it like the knob on a cupboard. As his hand moved, the Tower shifted, turning into more of a pole shaped like a cabinet with shelves. A wedge representing exactly one sixth of the floor slid free. Shaka then twiddled his fingers to be cute, revealing a whole host of secondary meanings, the concepts floating like motes of light within the crystalline shelf. "Two instances of space can exist in one location. More than two is fine as well, it just becomes a problem of energy cost."

He motioned at the see-through shelf. "This is the simplistic example of how secondary meanings are stored under a single node. Think of marbles in a box? There is a more correct example, but I am terrible at growing trees. This must do."

To be helpful, he pointed to one marble and poked it. "This mote of light is **Remembrance**."

The eyes of the ancients in children's form filled with wonder. Neither of them had seen this before, engrossed and entranced by the visuals.

Shaka then took hold of the Tier Two **Effervescence** node and pulled that section out as well, revealing another wedge-shaped container. He pointed at a rogue node within the confines of this new shelf. "**Cloud**."

Seeing as that earned wild nodding, with a clear hunger for more, Shaka continued. He pulled out the **Plant** node, then pointed at a few concepts, one after the other. Each marble bounced away as he poked it. "**Fungus, Quicksand,** and **Mud**."

Lastly, he tugged on the **Acid** node, then flicked a particularly moody mote within its extended shelf. "This snooty little heathen is **Hel-fire**. Or **Hell-fire**. Honestly, they're the same concept with a spelling difference; it's only wrong if you add a third L. The concept is what matters, not the spelling. Making this node the butt of many jokes! Particularly mine! As it could have chosen to come home, but *noooo*."

The Heavenly rolled his wrists above his head dramatically. "Look at me, I have a fancy infernal affinity. Oh, I'm so special. I am going to flaunt my fancy new skirt and *leave the house for several eons without telling anyone where I went.* Hella can make everyone else worried so long as Hella isn't worried."

Shaka glared at the rebellious marble like a disappointed father. "I swear on my favorite bonfire, my children are responsible for all my white hair. **Heck-fire** has to do with a very particular kind of fire, and functionally? The end result of what the different spellings of this concept produces is the same. This is going to come up again in the future, as different people, and different languages, will have different ways of grasping concepts."

He cleared his threat, stealing a sip of Artorian's mug. "That is good milk! **Hel-fire** used to exist on the third tier, but Heavenlies have been forced to make some compromises. Hella is a touch sore about this, so should you ever encounter her and need to make her hiss and flee, add a third L to her name. It is Hellla entertaining to see the cold shiver crawl up her spine. May it one day teach her not to make those who care for her worry sick. Though, I fear it is too late."

Shaka motioned at the list.

Tower Tier Three
Poison
Steam
Curse
Arrogance
Holy Fire
Eruption

Shaka pulled **Steam's** node out, purely so he could point at **Force** before his audience continued to enjoy the information. He figured he should detail a secondary meaning in a wedge here and there. Shaka then made it a point to unveil **Cursed Weapon** as a secondary meaning that lived in the box of **Curse**. "I will comment that I am not as upset at **Holy Fire** as I am at its sibling. Urtu, at least, sat down with me to speak about their plans. **Holy Fire** is the definition of a good child, and I am most proud. Wish he would learn to chill, but proud nonetheless."

> *Tower Tier Four*
> *Nature*
> *Portals*
> *Ice*
> *Shadows*
> *Darkness*
> *Light*

For this floor, Shaka pulled the **Nature** node out, opening the wedge-shaped room so he could note the existence of **Wood**, **Animals**, and **Flowers**. "A special note, if I may? **Nature** has been thriving, and now has a considerably higher spot on the Tower as well. **Nature** is currently one of the few primary concept nodes with multiple such prestigious spots. I will get into this more later if you wish, but given how the environment on Caltopia flourishes, I believe you already know why that might be."

> *Tower Tier Five*
> *Annoyance*
> *Ambiguity*
> *Recursion*
> *Sardonicism*
> *Argumentation*
> *Contradiction*

Shaka pulled his nose up at the fifth tier, saying nothing on any of the nodes. He didn't even want to touch it, based on how his fingers recoiled from that floor. "We don't speak of this one. I'm not on good terms with them."

Tower Tier Six
Pedantry
Pride
Snark
Spite
Laws
Cultivation

The Heavenly deeply exhaled through his nose. "Floor six has... complications. Still, here, let me pull **Pride's** wedge out. There are some cute ones in here."

Shaka gleefully flicked around **Rainbow** and **Illusion**. "Shame that they are relegated to secondary meanings in the **Pride** node; these are fun-loving people. **Rainbow** is technically a secondary node of **Light**, but they spend so much time here that we all simply accepted it. **Rainbow** adores Artorian, by the way, should you ever have the chance to meet Prism and cause havoc together. Prism is their name, short for Prismatic. Speaking of! I should make sure you are aware of this one particular troublemaker!"

His aggressive poke at the **Snark** node happened with a growl. The mote refused to be solid enough to be touched or bounced. "This one and I are going to have *words* when he can manifest. Though I believe he is purposefully being **Pedantic** alongside his friend. I can imagine the 'I don't wanna' mockery. **Spite** will get them both."

Ember and Artorian both snickered, but kept commentary to themselves, refusing to pull away from the available information while it was so very graciously being supplied! The lists could vanish at any time, and if this was the current up to date Tower, they both eagerly craved that knowledge.

Tower Tier Seven
Calibration
Barrier
Disease

Metrology
Corrosion
Onion

Shaka was about to speak, but a rapid motion from Ember made him skip the **Onion** explanation. Ember instead pointed at the next list. "**Pylon**? How is **Pylon** a **Law**?"

The heavenly skipped to level eight.

Tower Tier Eight
Sound
Magnetism
Gemstone
Pylon
Color
Refraction

"Do you not wish to be told a fun story about how **Gemstone** also holds **Swamp** as a secondary meaning?" Shaka glanced at her with a degree of worry. "Or have I done enough dredging up of the old stories?"

"Enough dredging." Artorian apologized. "Please."

"As you wish." Shaka motioned to the **Pylon** node. "This concept has been so used and invested upon that it outright consumed the prior node that was there, because *someone* keeps making more of them. In the billions. Can't say I'm at all surprised with a concept getting that much use. **Pylon** was going to get a main branch spot with so much activity. That's how it works when there's no Mages to guide the organization. Let us move on."

Tower Tier Nine
Cheese
Bread
Beer
Sword
Games
Wine

"Well, someone had fun. This must have been a great Era. No butter? With decadence like that, I'd expect butter." Ember freshly picked up her noodles again to munch while studying. "All the fun things for a starting civilization. I swear, no matter where humans go, someone will figure out how to ferment things and someone else will make a poky stick. Every time, and without fail. I don't know of any other animal that cooks their food or spends so much time preparing it."

"Says the Lady Saintess as she shovels butterfly noodles into her pretty face." Artorian's joke, his attempt to be coy, fell on deaf ears as Ember countered with a wink, skewering his heart and making him the recipient of all the damage. "*Ghah*! I am bested!"

Shaka giggled, tapping the table as he indulged in watching these two be painfully adorable. The gossip leading him to this location had both been correct, and completely worth it. He couldn't wait to return to his own gossip circles and indulge even more! "Shall we have another?"

Powerful, enthusiastic nodding in tandem was enough of an answer.

Tower Tier Ten
Analysis
Mathematics
Binary
Geometry
Topology
Nuts

Silence filled their little table as all the eyes came to a full stop on the last item in the list. Ember and Artorian quietly shot furtive glances at Shaka, who was grumbling to himself while leaning on his elbows and kneading both his eyebrows with the full width of his hands. "Give… give Shaka a moment."

They did, inhaling their food in peace as the Heavenly collected himself so he could explain why **Nuts** was present on a list of universal **Laws** and great conceptual powers in the cosmos.

CHAPTER SIX

"So there is this *squirrel.*" Shaka began cautiously, clapping his hands together as his lips pursed and popped. "This single, unstoppable, nuisance of a creature is a Beast that jumped ship onto the cultivator track due to some Pylon nonsense, causing the most unholy of havoc. Breaking a continental ice shelf would not be out of character, because *this* little..."

Shaka stopped his words cold, composing himself and making gripping hand motions in empty air as a coping mechanism. "Look at the bottom of list eleven."

Tower Tier Eleven
Algorithm
Logarithm
Exponential
Engineering
Statistics
Bolts

Ember wheezed and fell off her chair. Artorian squinted at the list instead, not fully grasping why the **Nuts** and **Bolts** in two tiers worth of mathematical **Laws** were the outlier. They were the only two that made any kind of sense! "I'm not seeing the problem. Go squirrel go?"

"Go squirrel go, indeed. **Nuts** takes on disciples like they are to be hoarded for winter, and by the power of squeakums-squee, both he and **Bolts** *will* find a way to fatten them up with power. Ratatoskr is around here somewhere. I know it!" Shaka complained dryly, his tone devoid of fun as he regarded Artorian. "Just because we made sure it was possible, and nothing would horribly break if it happened, doesn't mean I'm feeling particularly hot about it."

"Ha, hot!" Artorian chuckled at the Heavenly of **Fire**. "Good pun. Very smooth."

Shaka resumed holding his face while making a 'please move on' motion.

Tower Tier Twelve
Sleep
Empyreal
Knock
Sonder
Zeal
Kenopsia

"Well, this all looks familiar!" Artorian happily chirped out like an excited songbird, his hands clapping together. "There's Yuki, Father Richard, Ellis the door, Wo'ah the Wise, and the most glorious of sandy cats. Even if Somnus looked at me like a cup on the table and couldn't help herself."

O'Malley outright apparated at the table. "My most profound apologies, Monseigneur. Could I please be informed which one of these wonderful **Laws** carries the grand standard of El Gato?"

Artorian pointed at the **Sleep** node without considering why that may not have been the smartest idea. O'Malley bowed again and disappeared as if he were standing in a tiny pool of tepid water, having just noticed his paws had become wet.

Shaka chuckled as he leaned on his chair to look over the

shoulder. "Certainly, nothing terrible will come of that. Yes...
certainly not."

Ember had gotten back on her feet, trying and failing to
grab the **Violence** node in the next tier to make the wedge
appear. Sadly, it was to no avail. She whined out her displea-
sure. "Shakaaaaaa."

Tower Tier Thirteen
Hunger
Bone
Violence
Sand
Annoyance
Greed

The Heavenly shook his head, leaning back in his chair to
peer into the distance, spotting something his very mortal counterparts had no hope of detecting. His face betrayed his irritation, but he hid that well enough when turning to speak to
them. "No, no, my dear Precursor of the **Sun**. I know what you
seek, but it shall remain a mystery until you can speak to
Violence directly. I will give you up to floor fifteen, but I fear
we may not get that far. Finish your meals and take in the last
few lists. Our time is swiftly coming to an end. An M.F.B.T. is
almost here to disrupt us."

Artorian didn't know what that abbreviation was short for,
but since Ember suddenly devoted all her energy to finishing
her noodles, he quickly followed suit while stealing glances at
floor fourteen.

Tower Tier Fourteen
Redemption
Compassion
Devotion
Retribution
Empathy
Sympathy

Artorian knew that Tier. He'd met the Paladin round table
in person. Feeling no need to comment, Artorian moved on to

tier fifteen, where he was glad to have held his tongue, because now he had nothing but questions. This tier clashed terribly with both his preconceptions, and information he'd been told beforehand. His spoon hit the table hard as he sat upright. "Okay, what?"

Tower Tier Fifteen
Apathy
Sorrow
Death
Force
Blood
Grief

Shaka preemptively kneaded the bridge of his nose. "I knew I should've stopped at fourteen."

Artorian spared him a look, but dropped his open hand towards the list, because… so many things were wrong. "Shaka, where do I even start?"

The Heavenly being held up both hands like he was trying to stop a flood with his palms, then finger wagged at the top, his accent bleeding through. "I knew this was comin', work ya way down."

Apathy and **Sorrow** were not what had Artorian by his currently nonexistent beard. **Death** was strange to see. "Bob was a tier fifteen Mage? Or **Death** is a tier fifteen **Law** *now*?"

"The second one." Shaka made a 'let's keep it moving' motion.

Artorian pointed sharply at **Force**, then immediately pointed to Tier Three's list. "We clearly saw that one when you pulled out the wedge of the **Steam** node. You even verbally mentioned it. *What?* How does this node have two spots?"

Shaka helpfully, and with the patience of a saint handling children, pulled the **Steam** wedge back out after it had closed by itself. He poked the secondary meaning in the **Steam** node representing **Force**.

A most helpful projection evolved out of the secondary **Force** node on the second floor, showing a far deeper layer of information. Including the two-type Essence mixture, its exact, balanced particle amount, and whole charts worth of data that Artorian did not have the education to understand. Shaka moved his hand to tier fifteen and poked the main node of **Force** occupying a central tower slot.

To Artorian's bulging eyes as his copper dropped, *three* Essence types became visible. He slapped his forehead like a student slow on the uptake. "I'm dumb."

"You are *not.*" Ember's head snapped up from her mouthful of noodles as she wasn't going to accept any measure of that kind of talk. Swallowing hard, she waggled her fork between both points. "Just because the two-Essence variant is insufficient for a main tower spot, and the three-Essence-variant version is, does not mean you are dumb for not catching that right away. **Force** had to be explained to me, and you figured it out at a glance."

Artorian perked up, picked himself up, and offered her his mini towel. Ember used it to clean her face, having more to say. "I was told that it works like the **Nature** node... sort of."

Artorian turned his head to Shaka, who nodded at first, then leaned left and right with uncertainty as he picked up the thread. "Yes and no. **Nature** is special because she takes up multiple *main* node slots in the Tower, with each tier where she takes up that slot being another stable version of what **Nature** could be, with more essence types. Tier four now holds the three-Essence combination version of **Nature**. Tier one-hundred and four holds the four-Essence version. Tier *three*-hundred and four holds the five-Essence-variant version, and as you can guess by the pattern, tier *six*-hundred and four holds the all-Essence variant. All six affinity types of the local sphere."

Artorian grasped the explanation, and wasted no time pointing at the **Blood** node, because he had, in his prior Administrator iteration of life, read a whole treatise by Emilia Nerys on her **Law**. Detailing how **Blood** used a bunch of secondary nodes as a hive mind, rather than having a grip on a single, true and proper main-Tower node. There had even been notations by Alexandria! A truth that no longer appeared to be true, as the **Blood Law** was front and center on the listed display.

His affronted expression needed no additional words.

"She earned it." Shaka stated his opinion with a flat smile, and a clearly repressed bundle of amusement. "Emilia, yes? She is responsible for getting her **Law** a proper spot, having brought a vast number of cultivators into the fold under that **Law**. In addition, she is partially responsible for the exacerbated issue of vampirism in... uhh..."

Shaka turned his attention to the Silverwood Tree taking up a significant portion of the horizon, tracing a path with his finger until appearing to find what he was looking for. "Ah, there. The **Order** child, Eternium. The one with a Soul Space large enough to play host to that game Calcite desires. I, too, wish to play this when possible. I hear there are some difficulties before I can, but if that is merely a matter of time? Then I have nothing but."

Gaining a full smirk, Shaka returned from the path of the segue. "I admit, I do not have a full grasp on what 'Vampires' are, but the end result is the same. The spot was earned. The secondary nodes are all incredibly proud of her, and still function as they did prior. They can simply sit at the main table now. I'm certain it will make conversation... sanguine."

Artorian blinked at the smirking Heavenly. Very slowly. "I need no explanation why **Grief** is on this tier. All you pun-loving monsters seem *compelled* to give it to me."

CHAPTER SEVEN

The time for lists ended when the screech of an engine powered by Gnomish madness and Dwarven engineering roared around the corner of the C'towl city section. The sound of its approach steadily rose as Ember and Artorian's attention diverted.

Shaka dismissed his crystalline creation. "Our time is up. The M.F.B.T. is here."

"What's that short for?" Ember squinted while keeping her attention on the large racer drifting onto the scene like a clumsy, hurried predator about to stumble over its own front paws.

"Move fast, break things." Shaka growled quietly, already getting up to leave. "May you both have a most blessed outing. Shaka does not get along with the machines."

He swirled his hips, performing a dance jig. The Heavenly vanished in a puff of heat, and an upturned nose, to some slight applause from his young audience. "Dashiki, dashiki, dashiki. *Out!*"

The shadows pulled their knives out when the Dwarves piloting the racer got enough control of their machine to putter towards the Crème de la Crème à la Edgar. Not even traces remained of Shaka's heat as they arrived. Unlike the activity that once more bristled in the shadows, and the yowling of upset residents who had needed to yeet themselves out of the way.

"Don!" Artorian's small arms shot upright, his smile widening as the somewhat older version of the Patriarch he knew screamed his vehicle to a halt within nose-touching distance of their table. The massive contraption appeared to bend so the front bumper didn't touch anything.

The shadows had been poised to lurch and wash over the intrusion immediately, but stayed their fangs after Artorian's welcoming motion. For now.

"Safe!" The Dwarf howled to the sky with a brutal grin, his teeth the only part of his face not covered in soot. Peeling the goggles off his face, Don Modsognir held them up and shook them like a gift from the heavens, exposing his eyes as the only other clean part of him. "These darn pyrite-blessed things are the best! A whole tour through the mines, and I'm clean as a wee whistle!"

Artorian meekly pursed his lips and pointed at Don until he had the man's attention. When the Dwarven Patriarch checked himself over, he threw the goggles into his seat. He clearly hadn't noticed that he was cosplaying Torgue the Heavenly. "Pyrite! I be blasted sooty! Sunneh! Swat me with a cleanse!"

"I can't!" Artorian got up from his chair with a towel to carry over, laughing the event off as he wadded the cloth into a ball and hurled it upwards. "Here you go, old friend. Best I can do right now."

"Ayyy... Ah forgot! Right. Ya be all newly reborn and what-not." Don caught the towel, doing his best to wipe some of the filth off from having taken the deep mine route. "It be good to see ya, old friend. Or mah young friend? I don't know what to call ya. Is Sunny fine?"

"Sunny's great, Don." Artorian nodded to approve and appreciated the ask. "Thank you."

Patriarch Modsognir pulled several levers, the contraption concealed as a racer releasing several upset whistles and whines before simmering down and lowering closer and closer to the ground. Backing up, the janky racing platform straightened out its curved appearance now that it was no longer threatening to nudge a table.

Don slapped the roof and looked over his shoulder at a tarp. "Ya wanna say the thing, or for it to be a surprise?"

Artorian couldn't crane his neck far back enough to see who Don was talking to, but Dimi-tree threw off the back cover and heaved himself from the trunk platform to make a grand entrance. Landing to pose with a heavy thud, the half-giant half-dwarf boomed out a sonorous "Surpriiiiiise!"

"Poultice man!" Artorian copied the silly pose without thinking, up and off his cedar chair in record time. Zipping in front of the massive dwarf and copying his pose a second time, he faltered before completing the stance. Artorian momentarily felt strange, reached out to a random piece of nearby air to stroke and rub it like the head of a cat, and said, to the confusion of those watching. "That is right."

He then returned his attention to Dimi as if nothing had happened, completely oblivious to the fact that he'd just given a random chunk of air some affirmation and a health check. Don frowned but was too busy with the levers, Dimi burst out with laughter, Ember held her face, and the Air Elemental that could have sworn it was completely hidden felt incredibly validated about the consistency of its form.

"Good to see you again!" Artorian chimed as if starting the conversation fresh. "Last I saw... or heard? It gets muddled. The distinct lack of Seed Core and Mage mind is rapidly making me forgetful. You were a tree! A metal tree! With metal in it."

The half-giant snorted with a big grin, speaking in complete dry deadpan. "Yes, Artorian, that's how metal trees work. There's metal in them. Good job."

The flat tone cracked Ember's facade, her hand repeatedly slapping the table as she tried not to laugh.

Don leaned out from the operator seat, giving Dimi a look,

while the oversized dwarf's face slowly and with certainty broadened into an ever-wider smile. Don knew what Dimi had done. Artorian was blinking; his mental gears were turning but not catching the hidden joke. Which made it extra funny to Ember as his open-mouthed stare combined with the blinking made it clear that he didn't grasp that there had been no hidden joke, and he'd been made the joke.

"Yer gonna turn his head into fried mush." Don grumbled, working his way out of the exceptionally large racer. "Oy, Sunny! Eyes on me!"

Artorian blinked once more, returned to reality, and saw Don descend. "Yes?"

Don then clambered to the middle of the racer and threw off the other tarp. "Ta-dah!"

A sole, massive, crystalline Pylon sat wedged right in the middle of the speedy platform. Snug and easy! If snug and easy was code for a bug that had been turned into a feature. The glowing crystal looked suspiciously like… it had fallen on the racer from a great height? Pierced the craft straight through the middle. Then someone had the bright idea to continue building the rest of the racer around the Pylon anyway, because the chassis looked a little crooked. Like the impact had not been clean, the construction both hurried and haphazard.

This was no Gnomish art piece, so Artorian focused on the crystal. A single acorn was housed in the very center of that Pylon. Like some holy Artifact that it would forever refuse to let go of.

Artorian glanced at Don, then the Pylon, then at Don again. "I don't get it."

The Patriarch blew out air from bulged cheeks. "Non-cultivator averages are setting ye back, Sunny. It's the Pylon! From Eternia! The one that calculated everything in nuts? We stole it! Miffed the pyrite out of the Task Manager, but that rusty one-eyed triangle can choke on a damp rag doused in nitroglycerin, freshly lit. If ever ye're able? Please set that sodding drab pyramid on fire. A biggun! A funeral pyre tha' would do meh proud."

"Big Mo, isn't that *why* we stole it? Because that triangle can sod right off?" Dimi addressed Don for his own clarity as he looked back at the Patriarch, now that the man was no longer buried deep in the operator seat.

A displeased passerby detoured to wave a hand over both Dwarves, cleaning them up completely before bowing in light apology, and making himself scarce. The hungry shadows let Axon the Chronomancer go in peace, the timely intrusion forgiven.

This provided Artorian a clear view of their outfits! Both were dressed in half of a Modsognir suit. The jackets were missing. Their button up shirts and cashmere pants sang of wealth but were secretly nothing but comfort. He noted metal adornments on the pockets, matching cufflinks, with a large golden 'N' embroidered on the shoulders. Likely short for Nidavellir.

"T'was one of the reasons, aye." Don agreed, making 'get up here' motions to Young-torian as he unfolded a step ladder out from the side of the racer and worked it down. Unwilling to continue conversation about his most disliked rusty triangle, he instead helped Artorian clamber up, revealing the true and proper mess of the control system.

The youth needed to stop and stare.

"It's nothing but levers. There are only levers. A world of levers." Artorian chuckled in a half-mocking, half disbelieving tone. "How is it even possible to operate this thing?"

Ember's face shoved in next to his, having whisked her way up the steps with catlike grace to mush herself into the scene. Her eyes flicked from lever to lever, frowning deep as she too didn't get it. "Don? This... has no rhyme or reason to it. Explain."

With Artorian, the Patriarch responsible for half of all the Dwarves in existence had some leeway. The old sod in child form could take a good ribbing and get him back for it later.

The Incarnate currently in child form might as well have Grandmama poking her head out of the kitchen with an expectant glare in the eyes, and slippers already in hand. The explosive potential building in the chancla.

Don slapped the racer's roof in distraction. "This beastie can fit so much speed in it!"

It was Artorian's turn to hold his face.

Ember clicked her tongue, making the Patriarch sweat and swiftly keep gabbing. He motioned to the Pylon, which had once been some kind of apocalyptic squirrel obsessed with counting only in nuts. "By which I mean, this is Kronk! The racer is lever operated! You do it with feeling. Yell out: 'Pull the lever, Kronk!'"

The dwarf reached out to grasp at air and make an example motion. "Then, ya yank one!"

Don's enthusiasm doubled. "If all goes well, great! If suddenly a hole appears in the ground and you fall, or anything else goes wrong that shouldn't have, ya yell: 'Wrong leverrrr!'"

Dimi nodded, experienced in the matter. "You may then complain and question why we even have that lever. Just remember to remain seated and keep your arms and legs in at all times. She's a roller coaster!"

The half-giant motioned from the racer up to the crystal. "You have to feel the power, or rather, Kronk must feel it."

Don picked the thread up. "Kronk speaks at times, so don't be surprised. It's a very deep and sultry voice for a squirrel. Think of a large human man with very good manners that is more in it to make you happy than to have a good time. Not the brightest Nixie tube in the box, but means well. Will also, at complete random, have the brightest of ideas, but will never be able to explain to you how you arrived at a location before someone else when it was clearly unreasonable and shouldn't have happened."

Ember realized what was going on and released a wild groan. Rather than interrupt the duo, she held her face and hoped Artorian wouldn't be entranced to take this death trap for a spin.

"Kronk is the speaker of great wisdom. Particularly in the face of great enemies." Dimi stuck a digit into the air while taking up an official pose, one hand behind the small of his back while keeping his spine straight. "Remember, from above, the wicked shall receive their just reward."

"So we landed on 'em! Then did donuts on his face." Don tried so hard not to break apart in laughter, but the giggling had a mind of its own. "*Ahhh...* good times. Still hate that ruttin' triangle."

Ember rubbed her temples with both hands, trying to get back into the swing of conversation. "So this racer is operated by haphazard idiocy and a complete disregard for the sensical?"

"She is operated not by skill, but by intent!" Don clarified with vigor, as if that helped at all, giving Ember the full and proper breakdown of the formula. "Ten percent luck. Twenty percent skill. Fifteen percent concentrated power of will. Five percent pure accidents. Fifty percent squirrel gain. Somehow, we reached a hundred, the gnomes are surely to blame."

Ember leaned dangerously on the side panel and clicked her tongue a second time, turning her head towards the Pylon as she completely disregarded the Gnomish pish that Don was giving her.

She addressed the nutcase directly. "Kronk? I accept pure concentrated power of will, or the name you'll remember is what will make you wish you could drink swill."

Ember then reached for a lever while maintaining dangerous eye contact with the Pylon, yanking it hard enough for the contraption to complain, squeal, and promptly rumble back to life as the underlying colorations in the racer illuminated.

Kronk the Pylon had calculated, in nuts, the chances of survival for being a cheeky brat. Upon receipt of the most unbelievable result, Kronk had run the nut numbers again. The nuttelator was never wrong, since it was a perfect calculator. So why the number said zero percent simply didn't compute.

When the number came back a second time, this time underlined, Kronk re-evaluated all its life choices, wished it could have been a chef, and adhered to the will of she who wields the lever. Pure concentrated power of will it was! A whistle in the racer played a victory chime, which was enough for Ember to finally let go.

Kronk thought this a wise decision.

The nuttelator was never wrong.

Trust the nuttelator.

CHAPTER EIGHT

"Out. Standing." Ember coldly growled out pure frustration, her eyes flicking to the dwarves as the shadows in their vicinity began to leak out of their confines. "I was enjoying walking my boy through Avalon. Taking quality time. Planning to go on a cozy trip through each of the segments. Try some food. See some sights. Then, on leg two of my trip, while I can forgive Shaka for his whims, you and your contraption scream in and steal my thunder."

Don held his own hands nervously, trying to laugh the problem away with an ever-growing wince, and ever-less-convincing expression.

Her voice adopted the same disappointing tone Shaka had possessed earlier. "I was going to spoil him by showing him the new college, but *noooo*."

She turned enough to see the stars in Artorian's eyes, and the big lower lip. He had already clearly fallen in love with the speed machine, and its most ridiculous operating procedures. Ember grit her teeth, stabbing her deadly gaze into an innocently whistling Patriarch. "You just *had* to mention the speed."

Scratching her wild red hair, she hopped off the racer,

stomped back to her table, and threw the last of her milk down her throat before slamming the mug down and taking a big breath. Now her boy was going to go off on crazy adventures again, and her mood both dropped into her stomach and caught fire at the very thought.

She was surprised when the legs of a chair next to her loudly scraped as it was pulled from under the table, and Artorian plopped down with her. "*Hmn?* Aren't you going to go wild about all the levers?"

"It can wait." He reached out a hand for one of hers to hold, his expression changing from neutral to affectionate as his eyes trained on her with the same starry expression that the racer had received. "Don's laugh took a moment to register, but it snapped me from the trance and dream of speed, made me frown, and allowed me to hear your frustration. The racer can wait."

Ember looked at her chair, then at her boy, then at the racer that was currently being used as a wall that two non-innocent Dwarves were hiding behind, their eyes barely poking out above the protective metal monstrosity as a frankly frightening number of bleach-white Arachnids and ominously dressed Dark Elves bled their way out from every corner of available blackness.

Seeing this and feeling no intent to grant either of the Dwarves a reprieve, her decisions became snappy, made on instinct. She abandoned her own chair and dropped herself into Artorian's lap, draping herself over him like a protective cat. Her arms swung around his neck as she hissed at Don and Dimi, who were hurriedly clambering back into the racer to gain the illusion of protection.

Only when her cheek rested on his shoulder did she mutter words. "Are you sure? I know that you don't like mortal speed that much. It's always been obvious."

Artorian wasn't sure how to feel about that comment, so he addressed his thoughts in order. First, his hands went to Ember's head, applying gratuitous attention. Then his head turned to Don, hiding with Dimi in the cockpit.

Both of them were developing an equally meek shade of pale as the swarm of Arachnids took their sweet time advancing on the trapped duo. He held his gaze with Don's. "You brought a very neat toy, but all things have an order, and you skipped the line."

Artorian then pointed at an empty table. "Sit. Let me come back to you. My dearest is my priority."

Dimi and Don shared a glance, then crept from their protective seats as the Arachnids clicked mandibles together before begrudgingly making way for them. The Dwarves hustled their way to the assigned seating, not wanting to chance a dagger in the butt.

Dimi stuck two fingers in his mouth and whistled, the entire racer turning into a squirrel-sized monster with a pop! The little rascal with a crystal sticking out of his chest hustled along to them, finding a spot on the table since he was far too small for a chair. Dimi opted to be cross-legged on the ground due to being too girthy for a chair, while Don opted to be civil and sit like a commonplace adventurer.

The local shadows sharpened as the Dark Elves and Arachnids bled back into the darkness from which they'd come, and Don didn't want to push his luck past what he'd accomplished. The racer was now a known variable! His task was seen to. The sacrifice made.

Dev owed him buckets of money!

Ember ogled Artorian with the largest eyes, her words sappy and wet as she retained the grip of her arms around his neck. "I'm your priority?"

"Of course you are, dear." Artorian pressed his forehead to hers adoringly. She made a truly precious sound, then squeezed him so tight that Artorian choked and flailed, bapping her shoulder to tap out as he turned blue and red within seconds.

Breath was heaved, treated as the most precious act when he was once more able to inhale. Artorian half-collapsed on release, but was already sandwiched between a chair and a cherished one, so the movement was minimal.

When he could talk again, he emphasized the support. "Talk to me, Ember. You had things planned. Events aren't going according to plan. I don't know the real plan. Did you even tell me? I already can't seem to remember, and I blame all these flashy bright spots in my vision."

Ember replied by running her nails through his hair. "Sorry, sugar. It's… very difficult, as a mortal. The feelings seem to have almost complete control over my actions, and all the control I thought I had built up is nowhere to be found. Like I have no muscle memory. I have mechanisms for this, but they take practice."

Artorian pondered that detail. "Well, aren't these brand-new bodies? Skip answering that, dear. Let's talk about what's bothering you. Or perhaps why there's a small army of spiders lurking in every conceivable corner? There's not a cat in sight, but plenty of the sharp acrid smell that tells me they fled like the wind."

Ember spared a glance at the terrified Dwarves, politely sitting at the table. No waiter was coming to attend them, and judging by the breeze moving through the building, the back door hung wide open, and all the staff had fled. She exhaled through her nose, failing to relax. "Don, Dimi?"

The Dwarves shot to their feet; salutes snapped to foreheads.

Ember found this response acceptable. "You did good sitting when Artorian suggested you to, but I do not want you here. I call foul on this Gnomish contraption, because I *know* Nidavellir is about Sugar Glider Racing. Not this palanquin pedantry that I expect someone to put you up to. You will wait your turn for when we get to Nidavellir. Then you get to show off. Understood?"

"Ma'am, yes, ma'am!" Both Dwarves moved with military-grade unison. Snatching Kronk the Squirrel off the table, as he too had snapped a salute. With all the might of a stout Dwarven sprint, they ran for their lives as all the glowing eyes in the shadows followed them.

Ember buried her face into her boy's neck, kneading his back with her hands. "Now I am stressed."

Artorian thought only of how to help, softly humming the tune from Shaka's drumming that was now stuck in his head as well. "Would telling me about the city segments in Avalon give you comfort? A platform to start from, if your feelings are difficult to translate into words. You mentioned something about a tour."

Ember grumbled from the throat as she fished a piece of vellum from her satchel. When her fingers pulled free what she was looking for, she pressed it right into his hands before reclaiming her prior relaxation spot. Artorian suddenly understood, placed the vellum on the table, and slid his hands over her ears.

Not sensory overload, but experience overload.

Based on the breathing of the person playing at being a cat vastly improving, darkness and silence was helping her as much as it helped him. He pecked a kiss on her forehead and got a reprimanding shoulder-slap for his trouble. The act had no force in it whatsoever, so it only made him smile. He released her ears when she stopped kneading his back. That seemed like a good enough marker.

Ember didn't budge, but she had given him something to inspect. He might as well read it. Unfurling the vellum, Artorian discovered that the contents included a crude, handwritten copy of the Avalon organizational system.

Pushing up nonexistent glasses, Artorian read the contents out loud, attempting to be soothing for the overburdened girl. "Avalon segment structure: while the major subdivisions are actually squares, all these squares make a circle."

He had to immediately pause and pinch the bridge of his nose while Ember stifled amusement, keeping her vision dark against his neck. Inhaling deep after a moment of silence, he proceeded as if that line hadn't just happened. "There are three major zoning features in Avalon, not considering landscape."

Artorian noted the scribbled map detailing three rings that extended from the center of Avalon. "One: the center contains Lunella's original village. Two: the inner ring is a space dedicated to non-cultivators. Three: distinct and separate 'pie slices' divide up the outer ring, referred to as districts or sections."

He rattled them off while turning the vellum in his hands, as they appeared to be listed in a clockwise direction.

C'towls

Bashers

Faith

Goblins

Wood Elves

Wisps

Gnomes

Dwarves

Dark Elves

College

Mages

Cultivators

Humanized Beasts

Beasts

He proceeded to scratch his head, once again feeling sincere surprise at the sensation of hair. Artorian really wanted to ask Ember for some clarity on this list. Faith? Beasts? Wisps? Wisps kept to the Silverwood Tree, so why a section? Reading over the list again, it dawned on him just how quiet his surroundings were without the bustle, mewling background noise, or constant interruptions. "Have to admit, the quiet moment is nice."

Tracing his finger over the crude map, Artorian discerned the route. Ember had led him from Lu's patch, through the non-cultivator ring, and into the Cat's Meow. "You must have wanted to circle around with me. Enter from the C'towl gate, cut through the Basher section, then keep going around."

Ember made an animalistic sound that translated to

'headache,' prompting Artorian to hold the back of her head. A sound of approval instantly followed, so he supposed that was where that hand lived now. Continuing his jaunty reading, he tried not to make a sudden movement when discovering some handwritten notes!

Artorian picked up a hum to conceal his spoken words. "Master Plan: take Artorian through Avalon. He does not like mortal speed, but as a non-cultivator, there is no going whee, or nyooooom, or zoom."

Artorian stifled the laughter that built in his nose. Ember was another convert to the language of sounds! Eeeeexcellent. The once most stoic of statues was a hilarious image to keep in mind as he thought of early age Dawn trying to explain concepts to him with noises and hand motions. He liked it! Very preferable over the laconic speech pattern that she was working her way out from.

Returning to read more of the notes, his elation turned into a frown. Since Ember was making soft sleeping sounds against his neck, and her arms had loosened, he whispered the next section to himself. "Everyone else, on the other hand, likes that he will be slow. Exploring the details. Not flying through things. Being part of daily life."

That turned him contemplative.

Lowering the note, he stared at a random patch of table, for no reason other than to have something for his eyes to lock on to as some regret gripped him by the shoulder. He quietly drummed his fingers on the table as the cold, creeping, dastardly feeling spread. There was no way to be everywhere at once. To see everyone as often as he liked. To avoid the... choices he had made in order to be where he was today.

Massive amounts of life had passed and gone unseen.

Years of being a gaping hole in the life of people where he would have been happier to become pillar and staple. Would anyone resent him for his choices? There was no way someone out there wasn't unhappy at the truth that he had not been there as a constant fixture. His thoughts flashed to countless months spent on Zephyr, toiling away at paperwork, needing Decorum to drag him out of that office. "To work on the balance."

He squeezed his forehead. "Balance in all things. Beyond stumbling over my own feet. If that classy monster was trying to teach me a double-edged lesson with wordplay all this time, it flew over my head like a coconut-laden swallow."

Dropping his hand to perform the sacred act of the head rub, he pondered his regrets, and if he would have done differently. Artorian shook his head. "If I could erase all the mistakes of my past, then I would also erase the wisdom of my present. Remember the lesson, not the cost."

CHAPTER NINE

Artorian sighed, combing his fingers through Ember's fiery hair. He focused on his breathing. The feeling had come, but the feeling would pass. It all always passed, with time. That was the way of the mortal. Life happened to you more than you happened to life. A truth that flipped around during Magehood.

However, he was a Mage no longer, and his incessant need for speed had encountered unstoppable brakes. He reminded himself that, as a common mortal, he would need to sleep daily. Eat daily. Cleanse daily. There was no leeway to vanish to some obscure corner for weeks to months on end and return without a wink of a nap, or single bite of a snack, in all that time.

A thought struck that... he could... walk Lunella's path? Refuse the route of the cultivator. Live out a normal, simple, mundane life. He would miss out on no details this way. He'd be able to stay entrenched deep in a tight community of people. He would miss out on events in the greater world, but he would gain no further regrets concerning holes in his closer circles. The thought was... tempting. Very tempting.

The ideological standpoint of his adopted girl from the Fringe, who was now an elderly Matron, world-wise and weary, held merit. She had chosen not to branch out into all the wider problems. She had rooted herself as a tree and spread her branches to all she could reach from the hill she had chosen to fight and die on.

The hill of being the stable face and voice of Avalon.

He remembered that feeling fondly as it occurred to him. The Elder of the Fringe, in his own pre-cultivator days. How he missed it. To know the details of every heart. To be the pillar people ran to in their hour of need. To be the voice people sought. It was... enthralling, in a way. Warming, as a memory. Then, as warm as the memory was, it turned cold just as easily.

A hand on his jaw returned him to his senses.

Also where had the brightness gone? It was night.

Ember rubbed her thumb over his cheek. "Sugar? You've had that vacant look in your eyes for two hours now, and I don't know when it began. I had a good, healthy nap. Are you well?"

Artorian blinked. He looked around, feeling confused as he had no idea where the time had gone, and didn't remember zoning out. "Maybe?"

"I see this happens to you as a mortal, as well? Some things about you never change." Ember ground her forehead into his other cheek like a cat bumping another. "Do you want to talk about it?"

"Yes." Artorian was firm about his feelings, the world gaining steadiness. "Yes, I think I would rather get this out of my head, while it's fresh. Otherwise I'll forget, and it will become that buzzing in the brain, always in the background. Do you ever feel like you have missed out? On life? On time with people? You've got, what, fifty-thousand years on me? Multiple ages of technology and events?"

"No." Ember's clear verdict startled Artorian, whose face did a double take to look down at hers. She merely shrugged and returned her hand to his jaw, so her thumb could rub his cheek. "No matter how you cut it, I don't flow through life with the same priorities that you do. You cherish people and minds. You love them. Every single silly one. From the most cinnamon roll eucalyptus tree to the most burdened eternal dungeon. You see people, and you take them in your hands, and you place them on this... pedestal."

She fished a different scroll out of her satchel, but this one was a refined, amber- and ivory-encrusted object. The scroll itself was paper at the core, but some laminate glossy sheen that made it slick to the touch covered the original text, the work compressed and protected within. He unfurled one part of the scroll into the other, pausing at a particular snippet when Ember stopped him to point at a quote. "I feel that this is how you see people? As beacons of possibility who blaze and shine bright. They are stars in your eyes, whose lives create constellations."

Artorian read the words on the amber and ivory scroll.

Human progress is not measured by industry.

It's measured by the value you place on a life.

That is what defines an age.

That is what defines a species.

She stole the scroll from his fingers after Artorian had time to digest the words, furling it back up. "This scroll is by one of those ancient scholars you like so much. Professor Capaldi? I've been reading material that was known to be kept during Skyspear times."

The scroll was returned to her satchel, Ember speaking more on how she believed Artorian saw people. "You treasure them. Treasure time with them. To exist in the flow of their lives and experiences as they occur. You can also stop frowning, because you mumble when you think, and that humming fooled nobody. You've been fretting this entire time, and I speak fluent Artorian."

She then pressed her hand into her own sternum, shifting the subject to herself. "I do *not* treasure people as a whole. I treasure individuals. I treasure specific patterns in those specific people. I am far beyond any specific age, caring about age, or even caring what Age I am in. If I can get time with the specific people that I treasure, then I am content and satisfied. When I cannot, then it is because I have chosen that whatever I am doing needs to happen first."

Artorian nodded as he followed, receiving a head rub for his patience as she stated her point. "I choose my fate. I choose my battles. If you are in your seed core, and have no power to speak to me? That matters not. I will be seated next to that core until I am satisfied about the time I have chosen to spend. I do not miss out. There is nothing to miss out on. If I did not choose to spend time in a place, around people, who were doing... whatever they were doing, then that is the choice I live with, and feel neither urge to look back, nor flicker of guilt."

She slid from his lap, stretching as her bones popped. "I, even as Ember, and a mortal, refuse events that I do not actively choose to participate in. If I am making realms, then I chose to. If I am hanging around somewhere? It is because I chose to. This is why I get so up in arms about people butting into my time."

She motioned in the direction that the Dwarves had fled. "For all the power I have to choose my own hills, I cannot choose anyone else's, and currently cannot properly prevent them from infringing upon mine. I won't hide that Shaka didn't irk me, and it was clear that I am upset at the Nidavellir boys. Yet, never, and I mean never? Do I feel any regret that I was not part of someone's life? That I missed some battle."

She flashed him a wide grin, hands pressed to her hips. "That there are problematic things happening which I cannot control? Fine. That events are at times detrimental to me and my wishes? Fine. I will make time to attend to these problems as I can, but it will always be because I chose to."

Ember motioned sharply in the direction of a missing mountain that had been turned into a lake. "Unlike Odin, I despise the victim card. Life does not happen *to* me, as he feels like it does to him. Life is not a constant attack laying siege, where every ebb and flow is a woe to assail him, as he eschews responsibility."

Her breath was deep. "Life merely happens, and it is

entirely my choice and up to my agency to decide both where and how much I want to engage with it. Dependent on how able and energetic I am at that moment. No more. No less. Sometimes I am unable. Sometimes my head is not in the right place. This is part of life and is factored in my decisions as I need to make them. Are my choices perfect? No. Do I regret some things? Always. Do things happen that I would rather not have to deal with? Far too frequently."

Ember walked a few paces away, stretching her hand out towards him as an invitation to an evening stroll. "Marie's blunder? I will openly admit I felt things that no Incarnate should feel. Will it always be the case that I have the option to choose my fights? Of course not. However, when I engage those fights, it will be because I chose to. I do not waffle on decisions. I do not care about the gray. It may take me time to choose a side, but I will choose it, even if that means that I choose violence."

Artorian got up and grasped the offered hand. Instantly, he was tugged along on a walk as Ember continued providing perspective. "That I have made poor choices? That's called reality, and true for everyone. You, darling, teach the lesson that it is more important to get back up, when one falls down, than it is to worry about falling in the first place. Because everyone falls down. In every aspect. There is no perfection. There are no perfect people. No topic can be attended in full unless you are a Heavenly devoted to the concept, and even then, Shaka says there's things about **Fire** that he still doesn't know."

She paused to reflect on a quote she'd heard, reminiscing about the Demons turned Nephilim. Soni, Ludere, and Caro. "What is better? To be born good, or to overcome your evil nature through great effort?"

Ember set him straight and brushed the shoulders of his spirit clear of worrisome chips. "Do I ever feel like I have missed out? On life? On time with people? No. If you feel that way? Then, sugar, you feel that way, and that's a part of you that you can hold in your hands like a pebble from the ground. Ask what you can do about it. If you can do anything about it at all. Because if you can do nothing about it, then that is not a rock you should be carrying around in the first place. You are the king of questions. So why are you lamenting in the swamp muck? Do you worry about people? Talk to them. Are you concerned about some trees? Talk to them. Does the specific angle and velocity of the winds fill you with concern?"

Artorian was smiling and laughing now, nodding along as he matched pace. With a squeeze to her hand, he picked up what she was putting down. "Talk to them."

Ember beamed, gripped his chin, and proudly kissed his cheek. "That's my boy. Now don't fret too hard. We will find time to talk to every person you're worried about. As you can deduce from the Dwarves trying to cut in line, they're all chomping at the bit to see you."

She then firmly hooked her elbow in with his when he became a blushing wreck and marched onwards to stay focused. "Now let's go sneak into some places we are most definitely not supposed to be! Us Agents of Agency do things only at our own speed! Like I said before, here comes A and A! We ask ze questions! If we can rope Adam in, or anyone else whose name begins with an A, we'll be a scream of a good time! Abyss, bring Luopa the rock!"

Artorian momentarily forgot all his worries, in love with a good scheme as the smile on his face grew. "You are a wonderful pillar, Ember. You lift me up."

She pushed her chest out, proud once more as she affirmed that truth. "I always will."

CHAPTER TEN

Artorian could tell when they were reaching the edge of the current segment based on three distinctive features. One, the amount of palm trees and bushes sharply increased as they approached the border of what he'd termed the Cat's Meow. Two, a decorative stone arch had been built across the twenty-meter-wide walkway, adorned with Bashers of all kinds on the C'towl side. He could already tell that the arch was adorned with sculptures of C'towl on the Basher side. Three, the four main members of the A-team were lounging atop said arches.

Hannibal, the older C'towl enjoying a smoking stick of wood, looked down fondly, observing them as if their well-timed arrival had all been part of some elaborate plan that had nicely come together. Peck and Murdock waved their paws excitedly, while Baracus of the thousand golden chains harrumphed and pitied a fool.

No offense was taken. Mr. Baracus was known to be wise, each of those chains a gift, representing a physical piece of respect another had given him. He was right to call out fools as he saw them, for he saw a lot of them.

The squad of A-ranking C'towl let them pass without incident, as Hannibal tipped a metaphorical hat their way before resuming his most important appointment. The luxurious lounge on the best, tallest perch.

Crossing underneath the arch, Artorian felt a strange rush of spicy air roll across his skin. He instinctively took hold of Ember's hand, as something noticeable had shifted when they entered the Basher Plains. His inability to discern what stopped him cold, his head on a swivel as he tried to find what felt so different.

Behind him; palm trees, tall bushes, a civilization of cat nooks and scratch towers. Before him; a natural open plain with tall grass, the occasional tree, and openings to burrows lurking just out of sight. He snapped his fingers when it hit him. "No buildings! There's no buildings. Where is everything?"

Ember tugged him along the path that cut a clean, straight and narrow path through the rolling hills of the Basher Plains. A large section of Avalon land, devoted to its hoppity-poppity bunnies. "Underground. The point of the segments is so that the populace living here is catered to when it comes to living arrangements, rather than living arrangements being catered to visitors. There's not much for us to see here right now, but the Bashers are more active at night. And while the tall grass and rolling hills do a good job of preventing us from seeing them, they have already spotted us."

Ember motioned at a patch of tall grass as they passed through the plains under the illumination of moonlight, a Hopsecutioner stuck its head out, wiggling its little nose at them for a solid sniff. The advanced Basher seemed plenty placated, vanishing back into the tall grass with a rustle.

Artorian decided to have a sniff himself. The Basher plains smelled like a place with low precipitation and humidity, much wind, and sudden changes in temperature. He then sneezed hard as pollen tickled his nose, his eyes watering as Ember satchel-snatched cloth tissues into existence. Artorian blew his nose, thanked her, and chose not to ask when the tissues vanished. His sneeze had caused the entire surrounding area to rustle all at once, hundreds of unseen Bashers shooting away from them.

He wiped his eyes, seeing the aftershocks of the rustling. "That sounded like a lot of Bashers."

Ember nodded, turning her gaze to spot the same Hopsecutioner poking its head back onto the path. It sniffed left, then sniffed right, then quietly observed them as they cleverly chose to keep walking. Passing through the plains was not a problem. Causing a problem was always a problem, and Bashers loved bashing problems. The Hopsecutioner licked its own nose, scuttling away when Ember and Artorian crested the hill and escaped mundane sight, though never too far out of reach of them as it commenced stalking operations.

Ember didn't seem concerned, but Artorian was getting that distinct hair-raising sensation on the back of his neck, his gait subconsciously increasing until he was breathing loud and labored.

His hand was tugged, Ember soothing him. "Slow down, sugar. You're breathing hard."

Not having noticed he'd done so, Artorian dropped his gait back to normal, wiping sweat away from his forehead. "I…? Yes. Sorry, dear. I feel like there's something behind me, and the distinct knowledge that I can't do anything about it is driving some sense of mine up the wall."

"Fear, precious." Ember tugged him close, her arm squeezed about his middle. "That's fear. Nothing's out to get you. Do you know the amount of Abyss that would descend upon a rogue leaf that so much as brushed your cheek in a damaging way? That bunbun is just doing what buns do. Being protective. Sitting on its butt and stowing away with its ears up. Checking to make sure we're on our way."

He nodded but failed to shake the unease. He was silent for a few minutes before adding his commentary, not any more comfortable than he'd been. "Maybe a light run would help clear the head?"

He was prompted to take a large drink of water, Artorian

emptying the bamboo canister in one go. *"Ahhh.* Deliciously cold and fresh. I'm not even going to question how it was kept cold. That seems like a very non-mundane thing that just holds true. It's amazing how quickly you forget that the world is magical when you have none to wield yourself."

Ember swapped out his empty container for a full one, then tapped three extras from her satchel against his Silverwood bracelet, storing them within the item. Or assigning them to the storage location assigned to the item. The logistics were complicated, but it worked, so she didn't worry about it. "You feel them?"

Artorian was stuck on the specific words in her question. He eased his wrist up to look at the bracelet, gave it a shake, but didn't feel any different about it. "Is 'feeling' the correct operating sensation?"

"It is for me?" Ember raised a brow, lifting her own bracelet before shrugging as she checked how she operated her version. "Yes? Yes, 'feeling' is correct for me. I felt all the items it contained, for lack of a better word. They're meant to be intuitive. I specifically went with Silverwood because it tries to work *with* you."

Artorian had no such luck, staring at his version of the item. Another wrist shake accomplished nothing. A pensive stroke where a beard would be in many decades accomplished an equal amount of nothing. Upturning his hand, he thought of one of the bamboo containers, then fell forward as his balance shifted when the added weight appeared in his palm. "Whoa!"

He caught his own stumble, staring wide-eyed at the bamboo object. He then thought of the water container being stored, and *pop*, it was gone. "I figured it out! Mine is intent-based!"

Ember tapped her lips, holding her elbow. "Y'know, that makes a lot of sense… Can you intend your way into getting an answer for what all your bracelet contains?"

Artorian hadn't considered trying that and gave it a go. A list of objects slapped him like Unexpectus rocketing out from the depths to whack him across the cheek with an especially wet and vengeance-fueled limb. Ember caught him when he stumbled this time, ready for side effects. "Success?"

He groaned and held his head, working out his response with some difficulty. "Yup. Success. Lots of items in there. Also warm greetings from the Inkquisition. *Ow*, my face."

Ember smiled with a complicated expression. "Nobody is coming to beat up your storage bracelet for you, sugar."

When he found his footing, he held his head as the memory of the items quickly faded. "Good news. Idea works. Bad news. I retained none of the information. I have no idea what's in the bracelet, save for the three water canisters. I know there's more but could not tell you what."

"Upturn the contents in Eternium; most of its goodies are meant for there, anyway. The small armory of weapons tickets I hid in yours won't really do you any good here, nor will the equipment tickets. They *should* work in Cal, but those tickets do not work properly. Not yet. I know for a fact that we don't have the Rosetta Pylons back in play. Some objects work, some don't, and it's a case-by-case basis to find out. If you want equipment that isn't just normal clothes…"

She crossed her arms, staring at the star-filled sky to think. "So, complication. I was going to mention a segment as a reference for where we could pick up equipment, but I would be misleading you. We can find equipment in any section if we ask for it, but the kind and type is going to change depending on *which* segment we ask. This isn't important yet, but the segments we didn't ask will be jealous. Nothing to be done about that."

Artorian resumed his walk, Ember falling in tow as he passed her. He stuck a finger to the sky, adding an idea as he knew a thing or two about the politics he claimed to dislike. "What if we wanted a single piece from each segment? Shoes from the buns, pants from Dark Elves, or such?"

Ember's expression changed to suddenly realizing the obvious, sprinkled in with some confusion on why she hadn't thought of that. She grumbled loudly. "I don't like my non-cultivator mind. I miss far too much."

"Speaking of..." Artorian hooked his arm with hers on the stroll. "Cultivation wise? I've got nothing to work with. You mentioned something about rebuilding in Eternium? I can't even feel Essence right now."

"Yes, that's the plan." Ember squeezed the hook in closer, matching his walking pace. "There's a small problem, specifically for us new-body people, to cultivate in Cal. For you, it's that Mana **Loves** you. We can't see it, but I'm informed it hangs around you like the most worried litter of Fenrir wolves. The energy is trying awfully hard to 'go home,' but there is no home for it to re-enter, and while it's remaining calm for your sake because it can tell a Mana storm would erase you from existence, the Mana in your vicinity is barely holding back panic."

Artorian looked distraught. "Come again?"

Ember released him for the moment to speak with her hands. "As a visual, Tim explained it to me this way: Artorian went from the excited pup that this energy type loves the most, to a pup lifelessly lying on the side of the street that it no longer has a strong connection with, and it knows that directly helping Artorian means killing Artorian. So the Mana is pacing around him, making the most worried of whimpering calls, while it watches him get up and stumble forward, with Artorian completely unable to hear it."

Artorian became a statue, feeling rooted to the spot. He blinked at the horizon, his expression staunchly tight and filled with worry. His arms then shot to the air, the boy racing in circles as he tried to grab emptiness and hug it. "You poor baby, come here! It's going to be alright, you Fenrir sweetlings. I'm okay! I'll be okay!"

Petting empty air in the hopes it would accomplish literally anything, Artorian sighed when he just couldn't tell if he was making a fool out of himself, or if he was finding any kind of success. His arms dropped with a frown, looking around to see nothing different. "I now feel frustrated. I can't help something I have no awareness of."

He shot a pleading look at Ember, but she shook her head. "Don't ask me, I was working via informants, and we're still deep in the don't-bother-us time. We would have to walk up to an A-ranked Mage and ask for them to specifically look at the ambient Mana flows. This is the wrong segment."

Artorian squeezed his own hands, then relented and nodded, feeling like a disappointment. "Well, when I can ask someone, I will. What does this have to do with Cal cultivation problems?"

Her answer was blunt. "The Mana would attempt to enter you right away, the moment you developed a center that could draw in Essence."

Artorian rubbed a growing crease on his forehead before giving the act of air-petting another try, purely out of blind hope. "Would that make me explode?"

"Sure would." Ember retained her flat, blunt tone, hoping he would click the puzzle together. "Instantly."

CHAPTER ELEVEN

Artorian paused from his air-petting endeavors with a painfully slow wrenching motion. The implications dawned on him like his head being dunked in a bucket of ice water. The answer of the finished puzzle was sobering. "Me going kaboom... happened once already. Didn't it?"

"Might have!" Ember turned on her heel, speaking with a distinct sharpness in her voice. "Let's avoid that fate when you don't have a seed core, yes?"

"Yes!" Artorian dropped all his questioning and hustled to match pace, feeling the topic of his cultivation to be forcibly concluded. He would find out in Eternium what the deal was, not in the mood to check out of existence via that particular fashion of explosions. "Same problem for you?"

"Nope." Ember's laconic response felt like a flick to the back of the ear. Her tone spoke volumes, so Artorian dropped his words like a hot potato, thinking of another topic. This one was spent. A long descent awaited them as the hill went down from their current crest and appeared to keep going down for quite a while.

Ember beat him to a replacement. "Think a run would still be nice?"

"Very!" Artorian did not look the gift horse in the mouth, peering down the same straight path. "Is there supposed to be another arch at the end of this segment? I don't see one. Are the Basher Plains larger than the other segments?"

Ember nodded. "By a good bit, yes. The main road is still the quickest way through all of them, though I hear they're still building the bridge in the next segment. This road connects all the exterior segments"

She motioned ahead of them. "We're not going to be able to run for long, sugar. Non-cultivator bodies can't sustain what you're used to. I'm in good form because I've been cheating with a potion or two, but you are going to collapse if you overdo it."

A spicy breeze whisked across the scene, the rustling of the grass soothing as the density of energy in the air increased, adding a hint of more potent gravity.

"True." Artorian was already rubbing his hands together, excited. "I want to, though. I love a good run, regardless of my form. The act brings me joy and provides me a sense of... fulfill-ment. I liked it as a geezer, and I liked it when I was Merli. Even if I never did touch the sky. Mage-version running required—more? More oomph. More speed—to attain a similar kind of sensation. There was... a liberation? Yes, a liberation, to running. One I never properly reached in my younger days. I always felt that right before my fingertips, there was something to grasp. To hold. To catch."

A word appeared in his vision, and he spoke it aloud as if possessed while the gravity pressed down on his shoulders like an interested force. "The Canvas."

Ember released him when a static-like pressure was felt, a tiny burst of electricity crackling between her fingertips.

Something had changed in her boy. There was a vacant, yet piercing quality to his eyes, but he was focusing on nothing but a flat stone on the paved road. She knew something was off, even if she, as a mundane girl, couldn't directly sense the problem aside from being aware of the electric oddity that had already passed.

Ember, however, knew **Fire**. She knew the smell. The taste of ash. The feeling of heat sticking to the skin. A similar sensation clung to her now, regardless of that power being beyond her reach. There was a density in the air. A feeling of... expectation. An expectation that had to do with her boy, and him running.

Her hand pressed flat against his spine, knowing she would give chase as her Iridium eyes reflected moonlight, support, and conviction. "Go."

Artorian had no recollection of his walk turning into a jog, and his jog speeding up.

His feet took him and took him.

The path of stone went abandoned. He stumbled, hands pushing away the tall grass to keep moving. His heavy breathing betrayed his location, and the stalking Hopsecutioner found him right away. But the danger-bunny went ignored, even when it bounced to be right behind him for a takedown. Something unknown spooked the rabbit, the advanced Basher rolling sharply left and abandoning the chase when every strand of fur on its body looked to have simultaneously been straightened.

Artorian thought of a hand reaching for him. The image shattered when instead of grasping and reeling him in, the palm pressed to his back. A whisper in the voice of his father encouraged him onward. "Go."

He ran faster. His eyes filled with tears, his jaw grit as the stars swam in the sky. A painting of colors began to present itself, forming a lengthy evening aurora in his vision. A corona of lovely oranges, reds, and violets streaking the painting under which he ran.

He was struck with visions of stark, organized halls. Rules and dumb customs. Pills, and being sick. He abandoned these visions and raced past them. There was color ahead. Color splashed onto the canvas of the sky, unbridled and wild. Free.

Liberated. A canvas filled with nothing but choice, and possibility.

Existence broke around him, his senses failing to keep up as his mortal body, two hearts or no, began to fail in keeping up with his mad dash. He heaved in breath, his chest pounded, his sights swirled. He thought to jump, but broke though the impulse and planted his foot down instead, racing one after the other. He stopped seeing the grass, the ground, or the space in which he ran. He was on the canvas. He was *in* the canvas. He was one with color, and sound, and the *wild* of the pattern.

His heart pounded louder in his ears. His eyes noticeably wet. His cheeks stained. Flickering thoughts of being chased iced down his veins to grip his heart. His mind knew fear, but his spirit? His spirit was free.

A pang of pain told him collapse was imminent. Merli's vision had gone dark before collapsing onto the ground, the Vital Energy within him having forced him unconscious.

Artorian, wiser and less frail than when he'd been Merli, recognized the sensation of Vital Energy. Like an old friend long lost, his intent gripped it firm. Artorian's Vital Energy surged, spiked, and reached ahead where Merli's had made him fall.

Vital Energy was different from Essence, yet similar in mysterious ways. He realized he'd lost this delicate sensation on the long walk of his cultivation path. Here was the spark of his very existence, reaching out.

His eyes lost all color, the gray eating away all the blue. Merli's eyes had also gone gray when this had happened in his first life, glazing over. Reflecting the quiet tapestry of colors above, rather than the spirit that lived within.

Instead of the sky, Artorian's Vital Essence reflected the spirit within.

He was free in the bliss of the moment.

A point in his existence where existing, by itself, was enough. A lifetime of philosophy came to his rescue when, in that moment, he nearly lost himself. The flashing image of a bonfire, consumed by a silver tree, scurried across his thoughts. He knew the question before it was asked, and he knew the answer before it had to be given.

Time slowed for him, until nothing moved, and the world stood still.

Silence followed.

The click of a heel entered as an interlude to break that silence. Then another, and another, accompanied by the swish of a white cape. The canvas around Artorian drew in a breath and shaped itself into reality. Golden filigree adorned the cloth's flawless edges, the cape knitting out of the vacant space on the canvas. The hint and flicker of pale blue gems shimmered, like power gathered before a majestic entrance.

A feminine shape filled the confines of the large cape, black fluff blooming from the collar. A mixture of black on white clothes formed around the featureless being made of stars and possibility, the empty space on the canvas stepping forth to make a person.

Short blonde hair, pale blue eyes, black lips, and long, matching black nails added details to the shape as it gained recognizable form. Soft, flawless white skin replaced the starry vista while a large 'M' emblazoned itself on the shapely, motherly bust that the being decided was necessary.

A smile blossomed on her face as she approached the boy paused in time, touching the edge of her own ear to curl more golden filigree into place as a cuff.

Existence bent to make way for her, the grass awkwardly oblong as the very idea of what it meant to *be* moved for this being, rather than the contents it contained. She brushed Artorian's cheek, her expression proud. Her blacks lips spoke without word being uttered, but Artorian would hear the message regardless when the forces of the universe settled themselves.

Obediently, reality bent to her will.

Satisfied, the **Law** tapped his nose, made a swirling motion with her finger, and filled his irises with a bright, healthy, neon

78

pink sheen. She kept the gray, lifted it as if the color was to be judged, and dismissed it. The **Law** then clicked her heels past Artorian, placed her palm on the top of his head as an act of praise, and shunted his Vital Energy back where it should be. She tutted him like an amused mother, the behavior of the hellion well known to her.

People with centers should be far more careful when moving the adenosine triphosphate stored in their physical cells as a single, collective whole. Silly cultivation-capable people, they needed that energy to be where it was in order to live. **Order** would thank her later for this minor convenience.

Few were the number of mortals that met her strict conditions to see the divine. Being a non-cultivator was one of them. Of this treasure and gift, she held sole jurisdiction. The **Law** considered a whim, held the boy's chin, peered into his soul, then turned her head to ignore distance and terrain to see Scilla. The holder of this **Love** bound one's Liminal Force sitting and laughing with family at a bonfire, in the center of some cozy village.

Satisfied, she vanished as if she were never there when time resumed, all aspects of reality seamlessly restored. The retreating sound of slow clapping followed the boy's descent, Artorian crashing into the tall grass.

He tumbled head over feet, coming to a hard stop in a crumpled heap. His vision swam, his breaths unable to keep up with the amount of air he needed, and he couldn't hear a thing save for his hearts using his ears like one of Shaka's drums.

Ember was with him in no time. Between the flashing spots, the topsy-turvy world that spun regardless of his prone position on the ground, and his stomach becoming a hamster that had gotten itself stuck in a spinning wheel, Artorian was spent.

"Sugar, are you alright?" Ember did her best to hold him steady, which for the most part meant keeping his head in her lap while the rest of his body weakly flailed about without strength in his limbs. He'd run himself dry, and the rest of him wasn't faring any better. "Because if you are, I am going to *scold* you. What did we *just* talk about with the not cultivating business!"

Artorian covered his eyes. Seeing hurt. Seeing hurt a lot.

There was a pain in his legs, but they merely felt tight, and burned hot, pulsing with intervals of more pain. Nothing was broken, but he'd definitely done far too much with legs that hadn't been close to ready for that kind of activity. The feeling of having his Vital Energy shoved back into place was a boon, regardless of how sick it made him feel.

A weak, meek, helpless mewl broke out of him rather than any kind of coherent response, prompting Ember to bury him against her stomach and protectively curl around him. The scolding would wait. Her guess that a Heavenly had popped by gained merit, when she saw his eyes before they were hidden. "You're going to be okay, honey. Just stay with me. Breathe and stay with me."

Ember glanced over her shoulder to find the entire host of Hopsecutioners present, none of them appearing remotely happy with the situation of the duo having intruded deep into the warrens. One of them thumped at her, causing Ember's head to swivel, her eyes piercing it with a livid gaze. As calmly as she could, restraining herself, she spoke with measured heat. "You don't want this fight."

The Hopsecutioner thumped again, but a stone paw dropped from above and gripped the aggressor's head, encompassing the Basher's face in its entirety as Raile himself was awake, here, and handling this personally. The considerably more intelligent, armor-plated Basher looked at Ember, and deduced the entire story at a glance.

The trespass onto burrow lands had not been intentional, and some outside force had spooked the Administrator into fleeing for the hills. Since the hopsies were known to be doing a lot of spooking with their stalking lately to get back at the C'towl who thought they were being stealthy, Raile questioned nothing and took immediate action.

He proceeded to stand on his hind legs and hurl the threatening Hopsecutioner far into the distance. From the tall grass, signs with scores on them popped up. A seven, a nine, and a four. A four?! One harrumph later, and the rest of the Bashers scattered, their scoring signs abandoned.

The large floor boss from Cal's original dungeon then trudged forward and made a head motion to Ember to toss the Administrator onto his armored back. They were catching a ride to the edge of the Basher's territory, and that was both the beginning and end of the story.

Ember considered this a far better outcome than needing to open her cooking repertoire of all the ways one could flambee a hare, and both helped the half-passed-out Artorian onto Raile and sat herself behind the boy needing severe support. "Thank you, Raile."

Raile snorted in response, and without missing a beat, trundled back to the path and padded his merry way to the border. The Basher Colonel saw no need to humanize, as this was a clear cut and very dry problem. As soon as the Grand Saintess and Administrator were in the hands of Eminence Lucia, he could go to the Winchester, have a nice cold Dwarven pint, and wait for all of this to blow over. He had cards to play against Major Snowball, and he was going to win his favorite smoke stick back!

It was banana flavored!

CHAPTER TWELVE

At the border of the Basher Plains, both Sisters of the Paw and Godhand Clan Glitterflits awaited Raile in a clean, Ecclesiarchical formation. The orderly Bashers assumed a polite, human shape, with quite simple and unassuming robes. The humanization control of some was sparse, the ears above the cowl a dead giveaway. The control of those with higher rank was notably better, and the insignias on their sleeves matched that of their skill level. They all waited like sentinels dedicated to the concept of patience, while the Colonel took his sweet time trundling up to the border of the Faith Foundry.

Ahead of the welcoming committee, Leporiday Lagomorpha binkie-bounced about in her Basher form. Zipping left and right, she came to a stylish standstill in the middle of the road. Leporiday undid her reverse humanization with a sparkling, streamer-filled transformation, and returned to being a bunny-loving High Elf. Both of her hands held a flag with a bunny-face on it, cheerleading without a care in the world. Leporiday waved excitedly as Raile ambled into view across the hillcrest, having been the bearer of good news as she'd sped ahead of the Colonel to inform the Faith.

Ember recognized this individual as the F-ranking High Elf that had once perished in the depths of Cal's dungeon and spent a few centuries as golem. Ember had plenty of years to study up on Cal's entire 'embarrassing statue' collection. When Leporiday's mind had been recovered from the golem her memory core was stored in, returning her to the life stream of Caltopia had been a cinch! With a restored mind ready to decant, a new body had been a cakewalk. Ember was pleased to see the bunny-obsessed Elf living her best life.

The High Elf was as excited as could be about being a Basher.

Many Beasts wanted to humanize, but Leporiday had been an excellent case study for the reversal of that order. Sometimes, people were meant for a simpler existence.

Her task fulfilled, Leporiday danced her way into a spectacular magical girl transformation. Morphing into a Glitterflit, she engaged the zoomies to exit the scene with a rolling aerial-dodge binkie.

Ember nodded sagely. Truly, Leporiday was meant for that bunbun life.

She tapped her lips at the sight. They had humanization as a word for a Beast taking on a humanoid shape. What would be a good word for a humanoid taking on a beast shape?

She wasn't good at this. Clever names were more her boy's pot of soup. Still, she counted on her fingers. "Beastification? Not great. Animorphing? Eh. Animalization? That's rude. Therianthropy? That's... too complicated."

"Boopening." Artorian grunted while still collapsed in her lap, his hands protecting his head as it hadn't stopped swirling on the inside. "They all develop sniffers, meaning they all have such boop-able noses. Boop boop boop."

Ember held him as his boop noises devolved into obvious pain and discomfort. "Adorable, sugar. You keep yourself together, Glitterflits are in view. If you don't remember, they're the speedy gold ones focused on healing. We'll get you patched up."

"Potion?" The whine from the confines of her arms was truly pathetic.

"No, dear." Ember sullenly apologized, glad he couldn't see her face. "Potions won't fix this. Potions require something to fix. As the Dwarves say about heartbreak: don't make your liver handle what your heart can't. You'll just black out and be more miserable. Or in your case, your eyes. They also say don't break your arm patting yourself on the back, but that was an intrusive thought that I honestly have no way of making relevant."

Artorian made a set of whining noises. Ember replied as if he'd been coherent. "Yes, sugar. I know what's wrong with your eyes. The short of it is that nothing is wrong. They're just brand new, and you've never used them before. So they hurt. Much like the rest of you after you just about ran yourself to death? Foolish boy."

She flicked his ear to chide him, then let him cling, since he was injured plenty as is. "I know I supported you in this endeavor, but foolish boy!"

Once on site, Raile smoothly helped to deposit the Administrator into the hands of a Sister of the Paw. Ember was reluctant to release him, but she could recognize a veteran when she saw one. Even if it was a veteran in the healing arts, rather than the killing arts.

Most of the cloth-wearing people who did not swiftly step to the injured turned to Ember to bow. One of them, a Prioress or Canoness from the look of the sleeve markings, addressed her. "Grand Saintess, may we carry you to our Temple?"

When a Godhand Clan offered to carry her, she considered rebuking the humanized Glitterflit. One glance at Artorian changed her mind, deciding to raise her arms up. "You may."

Special white cloth with golden trim was unfurled and draped about the pint-sized Saintess, her mortal form lifted by a Rosarius Sister that stepped out from behind the Prioress as if arriving by a wave of light. Not being able to tell how the Rosarius-ranked Glitterflit had accomplished that feat irked Ember slightly, but only slightly. The cost of mortality was one she knew to be expensive, and her curiosity was just going to have to grow.

Raile saluted them with a stone paw before turning about with all the delicate swagger of a fat battleship, spinning in place as if he were a balled-up hedgehog obsessed with going fast. The Colonel then took off at his favorite speed back to the warrens with a nice zero to sixty *ka-bang*. Ramming speed!

Ember chuckled at watching the floor boss go, her attention turning to the segment they were supposed to be sneaking into. Instead, they were getting a procession. There was no arch separating the Faith Foundry from the warrens of the Basher Plains. An unavoidable landscape feature did all the heavy lifting to exemplify the change from one zone to another, the very same one that was responsible for adding the word foundry to the zone's name.

She had seen her share of caldera before. Calderas? They all looked like a meteor had slapped the planet in one way or another, or a volcano that had pitched a fit. This caldera fit that mold, except that both nature and civilization had cropped up within the walls of this one. Half to protect against the harsh winds that cut through this patch of Caltopia, as a lack of trees meant no windbreakers.

Half... due to the story of its actual creation. That tale was rather infamous.

The center of the caldera doubled as an impact crater for the very first Heavenly that had successfully managed to completely manifest in Cal's Soul Space, in full physical form. That she had done it in the sky and had completely forgotten gravity existed was a detail that mostly went unspoken. The very hard clap against the ground was a detail difficult to ignore. No matter how nicely you spun the explanation, a Heavenly pancaking spread-eagle into the ground while screeching like a distressed coyote was hilarious.

The meek 'ow' at the end had everyone in stitches.

Ember smirked as she thought of it, a glance at her boy stolen to check on him. He was fast asleep against the shoulder of a Sister of the Paw, a glowing barrier of light bound tight against his skin. She hoped that was there to abate the pain, rather than reverse what had happened to Artorian. That would bring the sky down upon them all.

She ignored the thuribles all the Sisters had brought to bear; the frankincense smell was rather pleasant as it poured out of the swinging censers. The choir song humming out of the group was equally pleasant and made people in their path make way. To Ember's quiet satisfaction, they paid adequate respect. Some clasped paws. Some bent at the midriff. Some placed a hand on their heart. Others drew in the air to mimic the shape of a solar symbol.

She rumbled from the throat, then decided it was fine to relax a bit. Placing her cheek solidly into the shoulder of the Rosarius-ranked Sister, she observed the world.

The Faith segment was the opposite of the Basher Plains. Busy, full of hummed songs, and tightly packed since living space was limited. The inner sides of the caldera were riddled with narrow walkways instead of wide-open plains.

Once inside the protective ring that the caldera provided, the wind stopped beating across her ears, and the winding paths along the sides brought one beneath the overhanging cliffs. Technically, the fastest path to the next segment was to jump straight down the cliff, land on the water, race across the lake, slap the gong in the middle of the Divine Pavilion on the way by, zip across the other half of the lake, scale the cliff, and dive headfirst into the Goblin Derelict like you were delving for precious metal in a scrapheap.

Plans for a bridge connecting the Basher Plains directly to the Goblin Derelict were in motion, but progress was being measured by the siesta, and the actual bridge was nowhere to be found. Some nubs and support struts were visible on opposing caldera edges, but that was it.

Blocking the sun with a hand, Ember squinted to see the sparkling blue lake that occupied the majority of the caldera's center space. Another good reason to carve deep into the cliff sides instead. The lake was covered in green lily pads, and a decent number of Goblins and Bashers were doing exactly what she thought when it came to rapid crossing. "Whose idea were the lily pads? Those are massive."

"Eminence Lucia, Your Grace." The Rosarius spoke with deep, respectful courtesy. "She has been attempting to cultivate beneath the light of stars, as per the stories. While seated on a lily pad. We should be approaching the time of deepest night that this begins, as we release the floating lanterns during the advent of the Serenity Bees."

"Serenity Bees?" Ember felt momentary suspicion. A bee was an odd creature to base the timing of your nightly events on, regardless of how much she liked them.

"Special fireflies are what I believe they are, Your Grace. Entomology is not my strong suit." The Rosarius motioned at the place where lake water connected to the caldera shore. It was a tiny shore that immediately gave way to personal cloisters hanging over the edge, but it was a shore.

The hives were given their own dock space, dedicated to honey production. "Serenity Bees are devoted to freedom. For you can take their love, and their stand, and all the places they could land. They do not care, for they are free, none can take the sky from thee. You may chase them out to the black, they will merely tell you that they will not be coming back. One may burn their hives and boil their breeze. None can take the sky from these bees. For there is no place that they cannot be, as in their hearts, they are born knowing serenity."

"I like them already." Ember enjoyed a massive grin as it spread across her face, her Iridium eyes darting about to look for them. She focused on her ears when her eyes gave her nothing, paying more attention to the surrounding banter and picking up some conversation.

Some Basher Sisters spoke from a personal cloister to the left. "And we're blending, and we're blending!"

A different cloister to the right. "If the men find out we can shapeshift, they are going to tell the church!"

A different voice replied in harsh exasperation. "Girl, we *are* the church!"

A third feminine voice cut into that banter as if the Basher had stuffed its head into both the room and the conversation. "Hey, did you know that all women are slightly psychic?"

To which the second voice tersely replied. "Well, that one is slightly dumb."

The first voice wasn't taking that lying down. "Says the Sister who kicks the cats out of the bed when too hot at night, sending them flying into the lake as they yowl for help, and now we have a diplomatic incident!"

The second voice hissed back at the first. "That was *one* time!"

"Yes!" The first snapped back with force. "*One* time that I told you would happen! I am a Seer! I am *very* psychic, and based on the position of the stars, moon, and your giant behind that should be considered its own orbital body, you—"

Ember rubbed her ears to stop listening when banter turned into beatings. That had not been what she was hoping for. Distracted by the choir song that reverberated through the background like pleasant static, she focused on that instead of trying to locate bees. The singing was far more pleasant. Finding it soothing, she closed her eyes for just a moment.

Ember never noticed she'd been close to falling asleep.

Potions were great, but their effects ran out.

The Rosarius Glitterflit could not contain her joy. "Bless my heart and the grace of her Eminence, the Saintess fell asleep on my shoulder. Someone steady me, because this is too precious and I'm gonna cry."

A Prioress restrained herself from grooming her face with her paws, as in the human shape, that was a faux pas. "Sister. You outrank us. Unless you actually say to support you, we have to politely let you weep your own sorrows."

The Rosarius contained herself. The Basher's golden eyes watered, her lower lip thick. With a shuddered breath, she too found her restraint. "Yes. You are right, Sister Prioress. It is in this trying time that I shall recite a holy verse, for my strength. Let us mentally turn to the book of Lucia, Steps on the Path of Virtue, chapter twelve, verse four."

The entire procession resumed moving as one, reciting the verse as a group, with the Prioress leading. "The hallmark of an open mind is not letting your ideas become your identity. If you define yourself by your opinions, questioning them is a threat to your integrity. If, instead, you see yourself as a curious person or a learner, changing your mind is a moment of growth. This is a step on the path to virtue."

As they each picked verses to test the memory of the others, the procession made its way to the center of the caldera. From the cliffside of the Basher Plains, they continued venturing south to cross the bridges and levies where water from the lake of the Holy See spilled into the actual sea. They detoured through an underground warren section of the Faith segment, passing the hot springs, to come back up at a bypass that connected to the main bridge leading to the Divine Pavilion.

The space beneath the caldera was much the same as the space above, with the odd exception that the holy sites below were kept as the ruins they'd become. The Sacred Temple of Verdant Green, lush with vegetation, was beautiful specifically because it was wild, consumed by nature. The Goblins loved it. Destruction, delicately allowed to simply be, and be respected for it, led many of them to develop an understanding of the concept of **Grace**.

CHAPTER THIRTEEN

When the doors of the Divine Pavilion opened, Eminence Lucia, who with many complaints about her desire to be outside and escape both prayer and paperwork, was dragged back into the pavilion by a small army of Goblin Protectors.

When the doors closed again behind the last fluffy tail in the procession, the Bees of Serenity chose their moment. The floating lanterns, thousands at a time, were released!

Unlike Lucia, who was still definitely biting into the handle of the front door to continue her attempts at escape. Regardless of the number of Goblins trying to 'protect' her and wrangle her away from those same doors. Even more bite marks were added to the already scarred mulberry wood, as Lucia was as fervent as she was stubborn.

She didn't need any protection! It was lantern time! She could handle herself!

People were only going to slightly mob her.

Anything to escape endless charting, and that loudmouth fond of his throne!

One Goblin, whose weary expression deepened as the archer sauntered up with her hands sunk in her pockets, understood that there was no way for the Goblin Protectors to win in the current situation. Lisette, hand of the Eminence, looked at the horde of green trying and failing to get Lucia's mouth off the door handle, but that would never work. Not like that. Attempting to be gentle and forceful at the same time was an artform, and the Protectors were only good at one of them.

She shook her head and cleared her throat. "Lucia? Those two youngsters that the procession just brought in? That's the Administrator, and the Grand Saintess."

A muffled fighting cry from an already occupied mouth made the archer's large green ear twitch. She translated the unimpressed grunting as: "What of it?"

Lisette considered that response. Lucia may not even have heard her right. She listened to the whispers of the Prioress that zipped over to inform her of the situation and played one of the cards that Lucia was never going to be able to ignore. "One of them is exhausted and has collapsed. Seemingly after an over-reliance on experimental potions. The other is 'injured' in bunny ear quotation marks and seems to have brand new eyes. With pink irises. They *need* you."

The mountain of wrestling at the front gate paused. Lucia drew a deep breath, thunked her forehead against the door like a Basher leveraging a complaint and released her mouth from the handle. "It doesn't matter to me who they are, Lisette. If you say they need *me*, then they need me, and I will be there. I just wanted to see the lanterns today. I miss my lanterns."

With her Eminence no longer trying to escape, which meant secretly going on a giant escape escapade to pet every single Serenity Bee in their segment, the Goblin Protectors picked themselves up and formed neat lines to let her pass back to the pavilion's interior. Lucia brushed herself off, and stomped her way to her right hand, the Goblin archer now beaming a smile as the short, gleeful troublemaker was already writing up a nursing chart.

Lucia grunted, relenting like a tired house doctor. "Tell me everything about my new patients."

———

Artorian had simple dreams of a simple life. He was an old man, wearing the robes of a collegiate lecturer. He was on the dais, waggling his finger with enthusiasm. "Authority should be derived from consent of the governed, not from threat of force."

Urtu, Heavenly of **Holy Fire**, removed his digits from Artorian's forehead. Skipping to the luxurious mulberry pillow-covered bed on the other side of the room, he snuck a peak at Ember's dream instead. The boy was an elder on the inside, which was comedic to Urtu, as Artorian was easily the youngest in the room, when referencing the age and experience carved on the Stele of his Soul.

The girl?

Urtu beamed, then frowned and held his own forehead as not one, but both of Lucia's visitors were spending their dreams educating someone else. The girl was just doing it while yelling, while the boy was mastering the art of the finger waggle.

Ember's dream was also simple. In the shape of Dawn, her first Incarnation, she was using both her hands to motion from her head to a bunch of creatures arranged in a circle.

Explaining a matter of import to another Incarnate wearing a plague doctor's attire. "No! A dragon is not the same as a drake. Which is not the same as a Long, which is not the same as a... Look. Just, look! Dragon; four legs, two wings. Drake; four legs, no wings. Hydra; four legs, no wings, many heads. Long; four legs, stretched like a noodle. Lindwurm; only two front legs, stretched like a noodle. Salamander; many legs, long noodle. Wyrm; no legs, *only* noodle. Sea Serpent; only noodle, fins! Quetzalcoatl; only noodle, feathers! Ampithere; noodle, no legs, two wings. Wyvern; two wings that are also the forelegs, with two normal back legs, no more noodle. Now we are back where we began."

Urtu pulled his fingers from Ember's forehead, his expression fouled. He looked over to the boy, then at the door, then back to the boy. Only Lucia could see him, and he had taken the form of an average piece of air, but Lucia could and would chase him if found.

Hovering back to Artorian, Urtu snuck a peak. Ah-ha! The old man was no longer on a dais. He was instead in some office, angry at a piece of paper. Urtu listened to Artorian's ranting. "They want three tons of rock, and a boulder of extra death, transported via... One moment, let me push my glasses up to make sure I am quoting this correctly. A five-foot spiral staircase, in a structure that has zero ramps? If this designer isn't in my office apologizing to me about this atrocity within the hour, I will inform the Dwarves that he pays only in vegetables and milk derived from soy. The one *without* the protein."

Urtu sputtered with giggles, his hand moved to where his mouth should have been as his sister, Hella of **Hel-Fire**, snuck in through the window when her brother had clearly found some good entertainment. The Heavenlies, schemers in arms and comrades in the ways of delicious gossip fire, swapped stories. Trying to one up the other with who had the better funny anecdote was a treasured pastime of theirs.

Urtu ended his peeking adventure, sitting with his sister on the balustrade edge of the open-air balcony, enjoying the atmosphere of this Divine Pavilion that they had both become so fond of. To the endless chagrin of the Eminence that they kept badgering with an equally endless supply of requests, demands, stories, and wants. Hella cleared her throat, taking form as a pale lady, donning malevolent shadow-green clothing that disobeyed the laws of lighting and colored itself whatever they pleased. She toyed with her knee-length raven black hair, her burning black-flame eyes filled with cadmium greens and infernal delight.

Hella's voice was sweet, like candy, as if to lure the unsuspecting into the spider's web. "Shall I go first, brother mine?"

Urtu took form, a perfect mass of male physique. He chose sun-kissed bronzed skin, edified muscle, simple, brightly colored shorts, and rings of metal that banded his muscle. His hair was wild, like a blonde lion's mane, while his eyes burned with white flame, an ever-wide smile plastered on his face as he looked to always be excited about everything. His eyes were perpetually wide, and full of life.

His voice resounded, full of energy, like a warrior who liked to shout and laugh at the same time. "I shall win this round, sister mine. You have the honor!"

Hella began with a zinger. "What is Atheism?"

Urtu did not answer, smiling as he crossed his massive arms for an answer.

Hella tried not to smirk at her stolen joke. "A non-prophet organization."

Urtu sputtered, erupting with deep, gut-fueled laughter. "A good one, sister! My turn!"

The Heavenly pointed his stubby finger at the frowning young girl balled up in the bed, Ember having rolled over and pulled a pillow over her head. "Mine is from that one. It is an introduction she once used when asked how she identifies, going through multiple forms. She said: I identify as a threat. My pronouns are: try, me!"

Hella did not laugh, but her cowl did bob. "Not bad, brother, not bad. However, I believe mine takes the victory."

Urtu pretended to have forgotten that component, his laughter stopping short. "Indeed, sister. The first round goes to you!"

Hella leaned over to flick his nose. "You always let me win the first one, brother."

Urtu grinned from ear to ear, shimmying in his seat. "You love it so, sister! The pleasure of first blood."

Hella procured a note from the inside of her tightly fitted attire, even if green shards of smoke and shadow did their best to make her retain a threatening aura. "The second shall be mine as well, brother. Observe! A pilfered list, obtained from one of the dungeons helping the **Order** one, as they attempt to cobble their adorable game together."

Urtu took the shadowy scroll, not minding that it dissolved

in his hands. He just had to be swift! "Suggested statistics for the characters assigned to people, referred to as players. Gumption. Chutzpah. Moxie. Childlike wonder. The cut of the gib, and a certain *Je ne sais quoi.*"

The scroll's remains fell from his fingers as the door to the room burst open.

Urtu turned his head in time to get thunked in the face with a hurled war-ladle, the soup spoon thrown with enough force to make him flail and fall right off the balcony's edge. He gripped the balustrade to dangle, with Lucia already advancing through the recovery room and marching out onto the balcony in her nightgown. "Be! Quiet! People are trying to sleep! It is too close to morning!"

Turning in place, the humanized Glitterflit pointed accusingly at a rogue patch of darkness against the wall. "Hella! I can see you, woman! I know you're to blame for this as well! I could hear the both of you from a full floor up. Urtu! Clamber your overly muscled behind back over that balcony and return my ladle! I snatched it from the kitchen on the way over here. What's the use of all those push-ups if you can't hoist yourself over a little wood?"

The ladle was flung over the balcony, clattering near Lucia's feet.

A half-asleep Goblin closed the door to the recovery room behind her, a nightcap with a fluffy ball at the end bobbing as she, with questionable coordination, snaked her way to the balcony where Lucia was going off. Lisette, the three-foot-tall archer, right hand of her Eminence, rubbed a balled fist against her eye. "The Protectors want to know if you're yelling at the invisible people again, Your Grace."

Lucia, using the full strength of both her arms, power-motioned to the two Heavenlies now once again sitting on the balcony. Both of them grinning wide. "Yes! Both of them! Did you not hear how loud they were? They're shouting their stolen jokes again!"

Lisette ran both her small hands under her nightcap, held

her head, and brought the full scope of her ears to bear. She listened in the directed area. Nothing. She then tried to see anything except Lucia in the directed area. Lisette shook her head. "There's nothing, Your Grace. I can neither see, nor hear them."

"Let me help." Artorian's tired, upset, irritated grumble bled out as he walked right past Lisette. With his eyes open by a bare sliver, he picked up the convenient war-ladle laying on the ground next to Lucia, sauntered right up to Urtu who'd freshly taken a seat, and began whacking the Heavenly repeatedly on the knee with it. "People are trying to sleep, you small-nosed constellation!"

Urtu laughed harder, as the ladle did nothing, and the youth was most amusing!

"Not like that, sugar." Ember cut in sharp and snide, as she too sauntered past Lisette, stole the ladle from Artorian's hand, and rolled her arm as if preparing for a particularly large swing. "Like this."

Her hand shot into the satchel she'd clasped back onto her hip, pulled free a cube that sort of looked like a memory core, and homerun struck that object with the ladle to point blank smash the Master Box right into the center mass of Urtu's forehead.

Deng!

Urtu once again fell off the balcony, cat-yowling the entire way down. The core struck the ground instead of Urtu, as the Heavenly was sucked into the cube-shaped stone, before it began to bounce on its sides while pulsing with a light on the front. The cube captured the Heavenly like a refined version of the item that had trapped Artorian during his initial Eternium foray.

Hella, ever the cunning woman, tactically remained quiet.

It appeared this was it for their days of leisurely ransacking other people's dreams, because when she turned to look at whose pies Urtu had been poking his fingers in, it was quite a sight. Lucia, she knew, the five-foot nothing pure-momma physique Basher stacked with curves. Gold Glitterflit fur turned bright blonde in the human shape, but those golden eyes always held that penetrating gaze that was ever so inescapable.

Particularly with that dangerous touch of *je ne sais quoi*.

Lucia could see her, and those who could see her could also hear her. Which made the case of the boy very curious, as the bright pink eyes dug into her like they were ready with a powdered back of the hand, laden with judgment, and a question. The question was easy. *Who didn't let me sleep?*

The young girl, on the other hand, had no recognizable means of seeing her, or being aware of her presence at all. Yet Ember was glaring the kind of fire at Hella that the Heavenly couldn't help but admire and appreciate. There was a kinship there. Iridium eyes were neat, but their special quality had nothing to do with seeing the Heavenlies. Then again… neither did Lucia's, and she'd never had a problem either.

Hella experienced a Nixie tube moment. Was this finally the answer she sought? Were **Aurum**, **Argent**, **Aeris**, and **Aereus** conspiring? The boy had the classic case. She knew who had granted those. Yet if copper and bronze eyes also gifted a version of Profound Sight along with gold and silver, then she would win the greater gossip game! Iridium counted as silver, surely? This hopefully wasn't a large hole in her plot already. Many golden-eyed Glitterflits couldn't see or hear her at all. No! Her plans had no such things as plot holes! Even when she failed, the results were spectacular. There was a reason that these three could see her, and by **Hel-Fire**, she would find out!

Hella folded her pale fingers, her smile becoming bright as moonlight while her expression mirrored the moon's dark side. "My apologies, oh esteemed guests of the pavilion. My brother is an… enthusiastic flame. Could you release him from——"

Hella looked down, noting Urtu was very much stuck in the Master Box. "No. Never mind. I have never known him to be so silent!"

There was no response from the upset trio that only wanted to go back to bed. The war-ladle made a trip through multiple hands, being handed back to her Eminence. They had done zero communicating with one another and appeared to have instinctively decided that they were all on the same team. Team *sleep*.

Hella fixed her posture, her expression that of a viper as she recognized a losing position when she was cornered to one. "I believe, as the mortals say, one should begin with introductions. I am Hella. That which is **Hel-Fire**. I wish to converse at length, but Hella respects the fire within you. I shall silence myself, and disturb your slumber no further, oh mighty who wield the power to inconvenience those of the *Tower*."

With a cackling laugh, she folded in on herself, vanishing from view.

Handing the ladle to the Goblin, Lisette took it from Lucia with one hand while the other remained outstretched at the maddening, nonsensical scene that had played out on the balcony. Not being able to see or hear who her Eminence and the guests were having a tiff with was very confusing. Her face scrunched in an attempt to understand, something that the Goblin abandoned with both hands in the air as she turned on her toes and waddled out of the recovery room. "Above my head, I'm out!"

Lucia tiredly watched Lisette go, then turned her attention to the two children who had risen with an energy that could make a corpse stand and looked to be on their way to collapsing about just as swiftly. The boy was covering his eyes, groaning in pain. The girl had already fallen asleep on her feet the moment the perceived threat had left. Her hand posed as if leaning on a spear that she didn't actually have.

Lucia, ever the mommy Basher regardless of her status as Eminence of the Faith, scooped both of the babies up like they were just two more kits under her care, and swept them both into the bed.

Pulling Artorian and Ember close against her chest and side, she tucked them in like a fussy mother, and protectively bundled them under the safety of multiple covers, an arm rolling around the head and back of each. Because if this happened again tonight, and her beauty sleep was disturbed a second time, Momma Lucia was going to tear someone's head off. The way only a very upset Glitterflit could.

At *ludicrous* speed.

CHAPTER FOURTEEN

Artorian woke mushed into the softest substance known to exist.
Chest.

Unmoving, he wondered at first if this combination of perfect warmth and coziness ought to be disturbed, in order to cease this unknowing impropriety. The difference in breath by itself gave him away, as a hand pressed to the back of his head and trapped him in place. The mother-tone combined with a clear demand ordering his action. "Sleep."

Not fighting the command, he had to excuse himself for having a follow up thought concerning a contender for the best substance to exist, or perhaps to rest one's head on.

Thighs.

This eternal debate now found a foothold in his head cavern, and Artorian immediately expected something or someone to barge in with a rolled-up newspaper to whack the thought right out of him. But no. Intrusive thoughts were the way of the mortal. The correct thing, when having them, was to live with them, not necessarily act on them. Right?

But which was *best*? Were there other contenders?

Butt. Hips. Thighs. Bust?

Curtailing those considerations, as he thought it poor form to dwell on them, he decided that having thoughts should not be punishable. One could not stop their own thoughts. The act that followed, on the other hand, was the key. To not dwell or act when the thought was poor was best. When the thought snapped back into place, he batted at it, instantly replacing the used space in his mind with another topic. Artorian then thought deeply of Roberts the Ruminating. For ruminating was the solvent and salve here.

Roberts taught many great concepts, including one that Artorian recited as a whisper. "You can't control the world around you. You can, however, control your reaction."

Opening his eyes to find them hurting somewhat less, his first proper sight was to see that Ember cared for none of this propriety business, having draped herself completely onto and into the most comfortable position between all of Lucia's curves. No restraint whatsoever to be found. Artorian gave up and surrendered to the call of the bonus nap.

The chirping of birds woke him once more.

Except that it was bright. Doors to the outside were open. While not on the balcony, Ember was in deep conversation with that new voice he hadn't properly placed yet, a floor or two down, and their voices were difficult to ignore. The Eminent Lucia? Emanci... something. Something with an E. A third voice joined the fray, but his mind connected that one to Hella, Heavenly of **Hel-Fire**. She of the three L's.

Grasping at the covers, he pulled them over himself, having the entire bed to claim. His eyes were still not doing too great, but now was not the moment to barge in downstairs. No, the bed was too comzy. Cozy. Comfortable. No, comzy was a pretty nice accidental word. Just mush two of them together, none shall be the wiser. Mostly because none would understand without some explanation.

The conversation downstairs was about... mulberry fabric.

The words qipao and cheongsam happened a few times. Some commentary on how the architecture didn't fit the climate, with Hella performing that table-slap maneuver. Her voice emphasized that Grecian environmental conditions did not clash with Chinese arches. Whatever those were. While he didn't properly recall the other Heavenly's name, Urtu's voice was suspiciously absent.

He'd had this dream about smacking a **Law** with a ladle. Surely that had just been a dream? Yeah! He wouldn't ladle a **Law**.

Distracting himself, he kept an open ear for more snippets of conversation. There was some kerfuffle about Immortality, and no escaping death or mistakes. People dealing with torn faith. Gods not being what cultivators thought they were. People lost and aimless because some of the **Laws** had personalities that didn't at all match what believers held true their entire lives. Some story about Lucia dragging a **Law** by the ear. How Urtu was far too obsessed with his fancy throne room.

"Fancy throne room?" Artorian peeked an eye open. The big religion and faith talk, he didn't particularly want to nose his way into. Sneaking into a fancy throne room? "Now that sounds fun."

First, a clothing check!

Artorian threw the blankets up. "Success!"

He was dressed in white shorts and a shirt, and both were soft, but a different kind of soft compared to what he was used to. He rubbed the hem between his fingers, remembered the word mulberry being thrown around, and shelved the thought for later.

He wiggled out of bed and ambled through the door while covering his eyes some, before he was caught as that door closed behind him. On the plus side, the hallway lighting was very dim, and he could pull his hand away from his vision. Candle illumination at most appeared to help prevent bright spots and dizziness.

"Going somewhere? If you sleepwalk your way to the bathroom again without anyone giving you instructions for the where or how, I'll be impressed. Or did you fever-sweat your way through another set of clothing?" Lisette the Goblin greeted him from her dark spot against the wall, the archer nursing a piece of honey-drenched bear flank that was still smoking with wafts of steam. Artorian's stomach made the most embarrassing sound in response to the archer's question, making Lisette chuckle before she pushed the flank into his hands. "Eat. Sit. Don't go down there."

"I had a fever? Wait. Why not?" Artorian's silly question earned him a tug on the flank he was being handed, Lisette already trying to take it back if he wasn't going to focus on the food. "Never mind! Food first!"

"You did. It's been about two days. The amount of water you can make vanish while half-asleep is incredible." The Goblin could agree with the food-first choice, then tapped the bench next to her, and crossed her arms while pressing her back against the wooden craftsmanship. "Good priorities. Very Goblin. Lisette like."

Artorian found his rear a solid seat and dug into the flank. He lost all track of time as he devoured it with a very attentive Goblin studying him. "Eats like a Goblin too. Lisette like."

The duo's attention was then pulled to the left, as a Feline Sister without chevrons on her sleeve hurried out of an adjacent recovery room. "Dr. Bun! Come quick!"

"Yes, Nurse Whiskers?" A gray-haired elder lapine leaned on a walking stick on her way into the adjacent room, not nearly as panicked as the young sister.

The fresh hand had good enthusiasm but lacked experience with the situation. "Our patient is still not feeling good, what should I do?"

The elderly Glitterflit moved one hand onto the other, going through the stages. "Did they finish their thirty-minute purr therapy?"

Enthusiastic nodding from the sister followed suit. "Yes, Doctor, I even added in an extra fifteen minutes like you said. Then I tried some head-bonks, and grooming the patient, but she just won't get out of bed!"

The elderly Sister, who was proving to have the patience of a minor saint, kept calm. "Ah, that is troubling. It'll be a long night once more, Nurse Whiskers. Hopefully we shall all get proper sleep this time, unless her Eminence sees fit to chase the divines through our blessed halls once more. At least the kitchen got their war-ladle back."

Artorian slapped his forehead.

He had ladled a **Law**.

"I'll call in some more staff for closer monitoring. Would you like to order a CAT scan?" The younger Feline Sister's question was shot with a severe side eye by her lapine elder.

The Doctor's eyes narrowed dangerously. "...Was that a pun, Nurse Whiskers? You know what we do to those who are sick with that most terrible affliction."

Sister Whiskers, intimidated, must have shrunk into herself. Her voice became tiny, and she made a distressed cat noise.

"Do you remember the sheep?" Dr. Bun sounded as if she was looming over the young nurse. "They got flocked."

Artorian forcibly pulled himself out of that conversation, turning to the Goblin that he about matched in size. He'd always been a late bloomer, especially in height. "Was that not just a pun?"

Lisette took the intact bone out of his hands, chowing down on the edge to get to the marrow. "That's Dr. Bun for you. She'll help you until you annoy her, and then that old Glitterflit will scare you witless. Still don't know why she's the one we have to call Dr. Bun; there's a dozen skilled Glitterflits roaming the pavilion. On the other end of the ransacking stick, she'll bop you with that walker of hers without remorse."

Artorian stole another glance at the door to the other recovery room, but the duo in there had devolved to more hushed whispers on actual patient treatment. He didn't know who was in there, but today was not the day to keep playing hooky. "Are you going to stop me from going down to see the rest of them? Miss... err."

"Call me Lisette." The Goblin pushed herself off the

bench, offering both a hand and an arm. "I'm Lucia's right hand, and in normal circumstances? Lisette is the chaotic one! Lisette, sadly, cannot be chaotic when her Eminence Lucia has to contend with the will of the unseen divines. Life can be difficult when your main motivation is the enjoyment of a good feast and rampage. Only to realize that you can't see what other people are fighting but have proof that what they are fighting is real, and you have no hope to join the fray."

Artorian shook the Goblin's four-fingered hand, accepted the arm for stability, and shuffled along as they got to walking down the dimly lit hallway. The lack of light made his eyes hurt less, and that was pleasant. Maybe he and Ember should travel at night?

He'd mention it. "That sounds like a heavier topic than you're giving away, Lisette. Pleasant to meet you, but a fight against that which one cannot see, that torments you daily, is one I believe I would be proud to see you stand tall from. Regardless of it never going away, or it haunting you in ways others could barely comprehend. Victory against such endless assaults is derived from survival. Not all illnesses can be defeated, as not all people can be. Those Tower munchkins have both a lot to answer for, and a lot to make up for. So if you are content in helping Lucia as much as you are able, then is there really more one can ask?"

Lisette squinted her eyes at him while moving her head away, perplexed and confused until she stole some silver from his metaphorical pouch to inspect the quality. "You're not actually a child, are you? I was told you're the Administrator, but everyone has some fancy title around here. The Saintess coming had everyone in a tizzy, but supposedly the Administrator is an Ancient Elder, who is everyone's wholesome grandpa. So, when I saw you, I thought you were mimicking or an imposter. It's actually you, isn't it? Like the Saintess down there is actually… the World Serpent Skybreaker? She has a Goblin's population worth in titles."

"Does Lucia?" Artorian cut the topic away from him and

Ember, more interested in who he was about to walk into a room with. Hella he was starting to remember, but there was nothing about a Heavenly that one could really prepare for. "I'm sure there's a story or two."

Lisette grinned, showing her sharp teeth in the friendly but concerning way only Goblins managed. That careful mixture of enthralled and intimidating. "Before she was the Eminence? Lucia sauntered down streets like Death himself owed her money, and she aimed to collect. You could always tell when she was coming, because Lucia wove all her gold and silver coins she had into a decorative belt. One of those noisy ones that clinked and jangled with each wiggle of those big hips. She likes to be trouble, to drink often, and party hard! Why else would Goblins love her so? That her vocation led her to the healing arts? Well, our own fault for getting hurt all the time and getting used to Lucia picking up the slack. I'm sure I'll never get that paw-shaped imprint out of the back of my skull from how often she bopped me for my behavior. Or lack thereof."

Lisette rubbed at a crease in her forehead, trying to remember a quote. "What was it she said? That was a long night, with lots of running, and even more empty tankards. A thousand cups of wine between bosom friends is never enough, but a word between unalike minds is too much."

Artorian rubbed at his beardless chin, lamenting the lack of one as he listened. He didn't get much of a chance for more questions when Lisette pushed open a massive door that he hadn't noticed, needing to shield his eyes as the light stabbed in. Turned out, he'd found the throne room after all, and the whole thing was painfully Urtu-themed.

Spacious architecture. Massive pillars. Multiple stairs all leading to the same raised area. Red and gold colors spilling over bombastic themes as far as the eyes could see. Ceiling to floor flags and drapery. White stone that was engraved by the square inch, and statues, statues, statues. Also a single potted plant. He supposed every indoor space should have a potted plant.

Between the flashes and spots of brightness, and the scant detail that slipped between his fingers as Lisette helped him inside more than he walked of his own volition, Artorian made out the shape of Lucia having made herself comfortable on some hefty golden throne. A cube was angrily bouncing in a bowl on a pedestal, but his attention was stolen away from that movement when he saw Ember nested deep and cozy into both Lucia's chest and lap.

When his ears caught up, she was talking, and the mood had shifted to one of giggles and laughter, because they were swapping jokes. Hella appeared to have just slapped them both with a zinger, and Ember had difficulty not stepping up to a good fight. "Why should you never fight a priest in a church that specializes in ranged combat?"

"Why?" Hella smirked while lounging in her own seat, a shadowy version of the throne that had been mimicked with a frankly absurd attention to detail.

"Because they have a lot of pews to throw your way!" Ember was already grinning from her own funny comment while Lucia snickered, and Hella bobbed in her cowl. The Heavenly, unfortunately, did not laugh.

"I thought it was funny." Artorian ambled up the stairs with Lisette, the Goblin currently the only reason that he was making any headway, because the room was starting to spin, and everything and its statue counterpart was too bright. He then suddenly felt himself get smashed into Lisette, who he was sandwiched against when Ember leapt from her cozy cuddle spot like a wild C'towl having spotted her favorite piece of rogue fluff. She slammed herself into him without care, then cat-purred loud as she ground her cheek up along the side of his face. She smelled suspiciously of mulberry.

Fermented mulberry. Lots of it.

Artorian held her while poor Lisette held them both, not at all bothered by the weight, or sudden antics. She was used to the antics. Her exhale was deep, already blaming Lucia for the wine. "Just another day at the pavilion."

CHAPTER FIFTEEN

When Ember returned to being mushed deep into all of Lucia's curves, the wine had severely gotten to her. Her face was flushed. Speech slurred. Everything was unbelievably soft, and she couldn't not comment on anything that made it into her hands. Then, for the life of her, she refused to release the Pillow Bun. Snuggliest of wugglies. That Lucia was in her most comfortable white- and gold-colored qipao had something to do with that, but most of the comfort was still won by Basher plumpness.

Ember kneaded Lucia like a kitten in need of comfort.

The mortal Incarnate then immediately got slammed by a wave of unstoppable emotions and started crying. Weeping out words that roughly translated to her having no idea how she was going to make this schedule work. How they were supposed to see everyone while she still got her Artorian time. How they were going to sort the entire mess in Eternium while doing all of that, and when she was going to find the time to go fight!

Lisette's solution was to pull her weapons off her back and slide into an absurd pose. For she had heard one of her favorite, chaotic, trouble-making words. "Fight!"

Lucia's solution involved instant activation of the mommy mode, holding the stressed child to her chest, and kneading the kit to relax Ember while working those divine Glitterflit paws over her back. Grooming the fussy baby's hair. Babies got tired and whiny and loud when overwhelmed, and more was worse. That was just how babies do.

Ember's mini tantrum demanded that she get to hold Artorian, so he ended up in Lucia's lap as well. That there was plenty of lap space, based on the power contained purely by Lucia's thighs, went unsaid.

The mortal version of Ammy was still someone that Artorian was getting used to. However, this was fine. While people changed, and changed all the time, their patterns remained consistent. Just because Ember was having a tough time now, did not mean that under all those top-layer reactions, she wasn't still exactly who he knew she was. Regardless of how she draped herself over him like the most demanding cat, wanted all the attention, and kept making distressed sounds until both his arms were snug around her back. At which point, she was satisfied. Her face pressed into the crook of his neck as she made lip-smacking miam-miam noises, mumbling about food.

"Well, so much for Pillow Bun." Lucia smirked, teasing them both like a teacher working on a shipping project between two students in the classroom. Poking fun and oozing out delight at doing so, because the boy's cheeks turned the most precious shade of pink, and his ears were so red! "All that fuss over adoring Glitterflit warmth and look at her now. Clinging to her favorite. *Adorable.*"

Artorian grit his jaw, eyes flicking to Hella, who was beaming and soaking it all in. He had to fight at least some smugness. "Out of curiosity, Hella. You should be able to waltz all over us like the fat lady singing is the only part that ever plays. Why the politeness?"

"Heavenlies are here by invitation, Ascended of **Love**." Hella's sudden, sharp, and cold attitude shift to being serious took Artorian by complete surprise. "Should we lose that invitation, we will also be rebuked from this place at that same moment. This is not something any of us desire, as life and liveliness are prized treats. Regardless of how poorly it bodes that we manifest at all."

The Heavenly of **Hel-Fire** slid one of her legs over the other. "Regardless of capacity, if we are hit by a ladle? We shall fall. We have unanimously decided as a whole that while our output is not something we can diminish, we can choose to act accordingly for the setting we find ourselves in. To play the mortal guise, with mortal standards. For the pleasure of being here is equal measure fun and games, as it is a weary exercise in restraint. Those we can interact with is a number that remains as low as the Abyss is bright. The act of manifesting to where *anyone* can see us is a costly, time-consuming endeavor."

Her face wreathed itself in black and green flame, her form no longer quite human, yet indescribably familiar, nonetheless. "I am made of unfathomable power, boy. Every day that goes by where I do not twist an impolite soul into pâté sausage is a day where I ought to deserve a medal. My energy may bend me to extremes, but it is I who delight in the cruelty. That I refrain from these desires is a show of strength and force of will on my behalf. My show of goodwill, to the host of the realm."

Hella turned ever more monstrous and viper-like as the heatless flames around her grew to consume her mimicked throne. "We choose to follow the rules of the realm, Ascended. Cal may be beneath us in overall power, but here, in this time and place? Cal is lord and master, and that is the hard truth."

"Did I... offend you, Lady Hella?" Artorian pressed himself back into protective Glitterflit arms, suffering from a severe anxiety spike as he watched the Heavenly increase in intimidation factor.

Hella sustained her gaze and cold expression for a moment more, then let the entire facade melt away. She compressed her monstrous appearance back down to the simple, long-haired human. A smile returned to her features as she spoke with allure once more, her black-flame eyes locked to his wide pink pair.

"No, Ascended. It was to make the point. We *choose*. Just as powers above us choose, and we continue to play the game. What surprises me, if anything, from reading the record on the Stele of your Soul, is that you have not yet asked anyone here about your eyes. The carvings of your curiosity run deep."

Artorian felt validated, and far less panicked when the answer was laid on the table. He exhaled a held breath and leaned into the hand rubbing over his head. The stress would not leave his small body so easily. "I think, in part, because even without looking in a mirror? I know what it means. I know of the old Church poems. I know the rumors. I know what was whispered to my ears, for my mind only, when I came to my senses. I know that my eyes are new, and if 'reading the Stele of my Soul' means what I think it does? Then you know that this isn't the first time that I have experienced having new eyes."

He held his own hands, frowning with concern as his gaze dropped. When he picked it back up to look at Hella, his voice was filled with doubt. "What I don't know is a name. I don't know who. Or really… Why? Yet I feel the sensation of that Heavenly crawling through my bones, like the very thought, if it pleased her, could erase me from ever having existed at all."

He swallowed. "Who did I offend, Lady Hella?"

Hella studied him with care. Her vision studied his Stele as well, but there was no treachery here. **Hel-Fire** found no foothold in Artorian's pattern, save on a particular pedestal where it would be presented for study, in the halls of a happy old man, delighted to lecture. When she copied a mannerism from his Stele and laced her fingers to lounge and lean back on her throne, she mulled over the response. Half to make the Ascended in mortal form squirm, half because he was owed a serious answer, and it would reflect poorly on her to misguide him.

Hella drew a deep breath and took a page out of the book of her brother. Honesty was the best policy, Urtu frequently said. "You did not offend, child. You…"

Hella tapped her fingers together, trying to word this

correctly, as there would be no second chances. "The **Law** of **Existence**? Her name is Dasein. She is the arbiter and judge of all that is allowed to exist. If she chooses that a concept is to be removed, then at her will, it is removed, as if it never existed in the first place. While she chooses to be unapproachable and unseen, she exists on your Tower Tier. For all of Dasein's brutal, raw, direct power to influence reality? She is..."

Hella couldn't stop her own smile. "Smooth. She is charismatic, and patient. She will wait anytime she is unsure, allowing events to play. She is the slowest **Law** to act in the entire Tower, and her areas of interest lie heavily in that and those which have the ability to surprise her."

The **Hel-Fire** Heavenly adjusted her posture, feeling that she was being observed by the dungeon after having piqued his interest. As if Cal had quickly fetched a notepad and added someone to the 'do not anger' list. "Dasein's confidence, on the other constellation, is a literal legend. If she acts? Then you are, at best, in her way. At worst? Pâté. The stories of Dasein being... interesting? Are many. She loves... well. This is perhaps a topic that you will understand well, boy."

Her smirk turned wide, and telltale. "She *loves* mortals. She loves the cycle of their lives. She loves watching them as they find a reason to exist. To find meaning in existence. To exist with meaning. To question her concept and come up baffled. She loves to sprinkle in conditions to see what one would do differently, when the same cycle has played out too often without change. Yet she despises any and all that would force the perpetuation of a cycle that she finds displeasing."

Hella directly motioned at his eyes. "Your optics are one such meddling act that she takes enjoyment in facilitating. Too often is it the case that a Heavenly will... sneak off? We are truly not supposed to. Our mere presence could devastate your entire world by the mere act of us *showing up*. There are unpleasant side effects that ripple and end up making waves. An Incarnate, as you know them, is already pushing the hard limit of that boundary. Their Spiritual Force, and thus their being, is instead shunted to the other layers to protect your own. You may have seen this as a complete shutdown effect in grayscale? There are many manners in which that emission resolves. Most are catastrophic."

She returned to the topic. "Your eyes, as they are, allow a mere non-Essence-affected mortal to see the ebbs and flows of Quintessence, and other higher energies. You may know it as Profound Essence, instead? There are many names for your sight. Profound Sight is a common nomenclature, but there are others."

The Heavenly curtailed an unspoken question. "The lower forms of basic Essences, Mana, and Spirit? Those will remain a stranger to you, until cultivation allows your touch to reach them. Yet, all that which is Heavenly? That shall be revealed. Such was Dasein's amusing, clever ploy. To let the mortals themselves rat us out. She can't stop smirking about it to this day. Copycat methods exist, but only hers can reach the state of the omnipotent. Only Dasein is the arbiter of the true Profound Sight."

Artorian remained quiet as that information filtered in. Hella of **Hel-fire** went quiet to shoot an intrusive glare at both Ember and Lucia, since they both possessed some variant of the copycat version. A dilemma that the Heavenly was burning to uncover. Why was Dasein allowing this? Why was *she* even here?

Hella ran a finger down and across the cube which trapped Urtu, a vicious smile crossing her face. She then controlled herself, stealing her own hand back before the impulses could find root. "I shall give you one more boon, child of **Love**. The world of Cal is bright, while the world of Tim has no functioning sun. For the health of your new eyes, find your way to the **Order** dungeon. Sooner is better."

Artorian suddenly had a terrible question strike his brain, and unlike Hella who was showing excellent control, the words fell out of his mouth. "Why are you being so nice to me?"

Hella exploded in laughter. Finally, something she hadn't expected, or saw coming. "*Aaah*, it is rare that I am bested in this arena. A shame, now I must give you more respect than I have been. Shall I provide you the respect to use your intended name, and a lesson? Yes, that seems adequate as a reward."

Hella smiled deep, genuine warmth momentarily leaking from her expression. "Anger and mistakes. That is, getting angry at people for making mistakes? That doesn't teach them not to make mistakes. It teaches them to hide their mistakes. I have made many mistakes in the course of my existence, Artorian. Being dishonest with an Ascended of **Love**, favored of Cal, and touched of Dasein? There are worse ways to make enemies, but I currently do not know them, and I am not keen to discover them. I do not make it a secret that my inclinations and wants lead to less-than-optimal outcomes for the lives of many people. I equally do not make it a secret that I go out of my way to not act on such things, when I know that I should not. Please do not confuse me for being a pariah of honesty and a scion of ethics. Self-preservation flies its own flag, and while I could wax poetic with you on philosophy, I will tell you only that while I exist in Cal, you shall find neither an enemy in me, nor an opponent. 'Nice' has nothing to do with it."

She tapped a chaotic-looking Master Emerald in the middle of her chest, a detail that had been hidden from Artorian's eyes before Hella had pointed the object out. "That which I am, and that which I stand for, do not necessarily walk the same road. **Hel-Fire** can be a force for good, and Infernal Essence only wants to help you see to the pinnacle of your goals. There is no malice in either, save for the malice one invests. While I cannot offer my power to you conveniently, I do intend to offer it to your companion. As does Urtu, regardless of his voice making the sweetest music to my ears at this moment. True forgiveness sounds ever so sweet."

"What... sound would that be?" Artorian could have stopped his curiosity, but it was too late not to indulge. He believed Hella, after all. That was a lot of words to say 'I will not stab you in the back, but I do want to.'

Hella smirked, pleased at the expected question. "Screaming, and then silence."

CHAPTER SIXTEEN

Artorian treasured the simple meal later that day, surrounded by Basher Sisters of multiple Orders, and Protector Goblins in the commons hall. He had been provided a white blindfold made from a fabric that they used for hospital blankets, as his eyes could not keep up with the rising brightness as the day tracked forward. He could live with the blurry painting aesthetic of moving shapes if it meant he didn't suffer terrible headaches and pitchforks applied directly to the skull.

Ember became his eyes instead, as the embarrassing stories that circulated of her wine-infused antics had sent her straight onto a self-imposed penance track. Something that the Sisters wholeheartedly appreciated and supported. It turned out that, outside of the private meetings, Lucia was in fact an eminent figure, and treated as such. Her public appearance had been far less... mommy attack-bun. Instead, Lucia presented herself as a regal, stoic, smiling, forward Faithful. Complete with hymns and lyrical words. All that chutzpah made the other Bashers fawn all over her while she floated across the pavilion in the attire of a Cardinal.

Or so he was told.

The downside of the protective cloth over his eyes, was, of course, that he couldn't see celestial feces. So Artorian was certain that it was all very pretty, and inspiring religious awe. Probably. He'd just eat his vegetable stew and didn't at all keep poking at the bowl's contents with the wooden spoon, silently wishing for more of that bear flank. Where had Lisette procured that from? Was there a secret underground black-market thing going on? What was the currency? What was of value to Goblins these days?

His questions whisked to the ether when Ember's hand pressed to his back, the creak of the bench telling him she'd sat down next to him. "Don't like the local soup?"

"This is soup?" Artorian was genuinely confused at the descriptor. "I thought this was stew. I could shove the spoon in and expect it to stick straight up."

Artorian's ears picked up that some switcheroo was at play. His bowl scraped across the table, being replaced with another. Ember played it off like nothing was wrong. "Looks like soup. Try it again."

He did so after a moment of his hands searching for the correct smear in his nonexistent vision that represented the bowl. He gave the meal a try and found this version to be far more palatable. Bonus that it was actual soup, even if still only made of vegetables. "Thank you, dear. I appreciate the soup, but I think I'd appreciate a plan more. I am sorry for hampering the Avalon tour."

"No plan survives contact with the enemy." Ember stated the tactic like she'd learned it yesterday. "The enemy, in this case, is anyone that could possibly derail my time with you. So that gives me a lot of enemies."

Artorian put the bowl down, holding onto it with both hands. "That advice from Hella to skip town sounded rather good. Accidental boon with the Eternium sun problem, perchance? There was also something about you wanting to push the sleeves up and throw your knuckles into something. Caltopia isn't going to give us that."

His answer contained an error because Ember growled. "*Avalon* isn't going to give us that. I know plenty of nuisances on Caltopia that I'd like to throw through a few walls. Not everyone is reasonable or holds to the kind of reason you can agree with. There will always be someone upset with anything you do, regardless of what it is. There are people who despise that others find success. My hunt for them persists."

Ember wrapped an arm around his neck, her side mushed to his. "I have *concerns* after talking to Lady Heck-fwoosh. I don't know whether that was because she was making a dangerous amount of sense, or if I simply can't trust the woman, yet feel considerably inclined to. I think we should skip town, yes. Though, my reasoning has to do a lot more with diminishing your suffering. The moment we pop into Eternium, Tot and Turnip are going to think we're there for work."

"Would that be so bad?" Artorian leaned heavily into her, not seeing the downside, as they were going to find no peace whatsoever in Caltopia anyway. "Work there, work here. There's not really a difference. People are giving us space and time, but I know that eventually the grabby hands will commence. Why don't we take the day off, go pet some bees, watch some lanterns, have a nice dinner and sleep, and pop to it in the morning? I don't know how the back and forth works without a gazebo, but if we get injured in Tim-topia, and need to flee? Plopping back into a pavilion full of Glitterflit healers sounds like a pretty sweet deal to me."

Ember poked at the bottom of her soup bowl with her wooden spoon, scraping it back and forth in thought. "The bracelets allow us anytime transfer, but a bind point would be a convenience. I suppose we could go see Turnip. Saunter about the Eternium beta world as they try to pull it all together. Tot got through the ice with Yuki's guidance, so we have a proper way in for non-Incarnates now. Still wouldn't suggest it. Not until we sort out a few major problems. Without an Incarnate to ferry you, or a bracelet as a link, there's no crossing the frozen fjord."

"Why do you need *me* in there, dear?"

Ember likely made a complicated face, but Artorian couldn't see it. He did catch her deep breath, and stressful exhale. "Combination of tiny details. Can we do it without you? Yes. If we're willing to take on twelve times the work. Or we can make the way and get you in there, and leisurely walk through a whole host of problems as you turn the sun back on, saving us a mountain of work. All it will cost you is a title that you weren't using anyway. Don't expect to get them all back on re-entry. That's all."

Artorian thought it best not to press. "Sounds like an Eternium trip is the plan. I like this plan. I'm sure there will be problems, but when are there not? I do like your bunny bouncing idea. Some time in Eternium, some time in Cal, Tim, Cal, Tim, good cycle."

Ember was quiet for a moment, then slapped his back and got up. "You stay put. I'm going to talk to some people. I think I know of a Mage in the vicinity that is a connoisseur of bees. Apiculteur? Yes. The Hive Mage should be at his apiary. I think I can get a messenger out to Eri's Emporium that way as well? Bee Cavalry is speedy. There's a few tickets I need from the Armo-Eri. Plus some pollen for T.C. will be nice; he's still working on those tulips in Eternium."

Artorian listened to her mumble ever more complicated battle plans to herself as she wandered her way out of the commons hall and began enacting ideas.

This left him to his own devices.

That never went poorly.

Artorian held his own hands, laced his fingers, and copied the local Basher custom of slightly tilting one's head to keep an ear out. He didn't have full on bunbun wigglers, but his ears weren't broken. The eerie silence, cessation of voices and activity, and the lack of so much as a pin dropping was not in the expected playbook of fun things to overhear.

A hand reached toward his vision, and like the rest of the Sisters in attendance, Artorian didn't move a muscle. The hand then corrected his blindfold, sliding some cloth layers around. The strip was adjusted and re-adjusted in silence, Artorian keeping nice and still. The distinct sensation of being paused in time struck him, with the equally distinct sensation that it was running just fine both for him, and whoever was nitpicking the details of his ocular protection.

When the hand was satisfied with his admittedly much more comfortable wrap, young Artorian felt the palm brush up his cheek before fingers rustled his hair, and black nails ran across his scalp. Feeling them brush back and forth over his head, Artorian started to find his courage. "I faintly recall something about the lower-tiered **Laws** manifesting first. Can't say I understand the reason beyond knowing that detail, and as much as I appreciate the tender love and care, would a hello be alright? Are greetings acceptable? Are there social rules on floor seven-twenty that I'm simply too small of a boy to be privy to?"

"Precious boy." The breathy voice of Dasein was smooth as silk, and sweet as Hella's allure. Pleasantly, the words lacked the venomous edge that the latter's voice hid like a dagger. There was **Love** in Dasein's tone, and it sent warm shivers all across Artorian's skin. There was no judgment here. There was the feeling of an aunt visiting. The one that doted on you, happy to drop by purely to see you, because her day was all the better for it. Yes. That was the sensation crawling up Artorian's spine. Exactly that.

For all her dangerous, extreme, raw power to bend the universe and everything in it? **Existence** wanted things and people to exist, otherwise, the current conditions of the universe could not be true. She held his cheek, her thumb brushing. "Better, soon."

Artorian could only nod, his ability to speak lost somewhere in his stomach as the warm ripples kept brushing over his skin. How pleasant the feeling was. A soothing, wholesome bliss. The feeling didn't reinvigorate, but it did mend some wear that Artorian didn't recognize as tear. Was he forgetting some upkeep requirements of mortality? He must have, if he felt so much better now. Was he not eating enough? Maybe the sleep had been too disturbed.

He did feel awfully sleepy, and his head was now laying on his folded arms. Which rested on some table that was probably there. He should likely get up shortly and begin causing trouble! Havoc! Fun social schemes! Goblin black market ploys!

He was asleep with Dasein still petting his head moments after.

She was satisfied to see that there were no terrible side-effects from adding Profound Sight to the boy. His Stele was a mess, but it was deliciously interesting. Many minds were going to extreme lengths to keep this particular soul up and running. And while the body that had been crafted for him was accept-able, it lacked… Dasein liked the term 'a certain *je ne sais quoi.*' A light alteration for his proper health was in order, after her chat with **Order**. That Heavenly's tardy replacement was meddling with what might as well be called old magic, and the old ways, with some of the Madness they were using to stay afloat in this realm of Cal.

Dasein enjoyed the old ways. They were wrought of mystery.

Her hand stayed on the head of the boy as she once more read over his Stele, intrigued at the mixtures of patterns. He had been mortal. Cultivator. Mageous. Two distinct Beasts. Then… Something *new*. Reaching out, her fingers traced the carvings. "Nascent. Being."

What had they done? What was this prized, fresh, intrigue-filled puzzle of a new creature? She craved to know, and instantly knew that there was nobody to ask. No answer existed for that question. The truth of that event riled her up, a rush of excitement bringing a sincere and enthused smile to Dasein's black lips.

The bone scripting was a cute, if crude, solution to adhering to a critical pattern inscribed on the Stele. Without that pattern in place, the boy could not exist. The piece was required for his pattern, even if he had barely an inkling of knowledge of how to use that gift properly. Luckily, there was leeway for what the script was supposed to do. Perhaps the **Order** dungeon should be slipped a whisper or two?

She moved on. His eyes had seen multiple iterative states of being. That was good. He would take to the Profound Sight easier than most. The dormant Beast core? That was questionable at best. The existence of both Long and Liger carvings were cause for concern. Too many mixtures on a soul, and even a Stele could be damaged.

Luck lived in the boy, but then again, luck lived in all those who **Love** reached for. She had a knack and preference for that trait. It was the defining factor of why she chose some over others. Why luck? **Love** had never told her. **Love** just blessed **Existence** with that heart-melting smile of hers and kept her secrets. Like she knew that the secret was what kept Dasein interested.

How cruel **Love** could be. The witch was correct, too.

Dasein continued inspecting the Stele but felt some investment after looking over this particular one so often. She had many that she liked. Many she returned to. A soft motion brushed her hand down the side of this Stele. It held, for now, but the boy was going to have to choose. Too many paths lived on this record. To deepen them all would crack that record. That would not do. She could not choose for him. Even then, she staunchly refused. There was only merit when the boy made the choices.

Still, this would not do.

Too many flaws and issues that had never been considered resided in the mortal's body. Too many irrelevant contingencies accounted for. The creators had clearly poured effort into the attempt, but crucial components were lacking. A Mageous could handle all the details on the Stele being reflected upon their form. A mortal, unfortunately, would not do as well when the soul began to carve itself back upon the body and mind. Not with so much **Discord**.

Dasein frowned at that note as it played in her head.

Holding the Stele, influences of **Chaos**, and **Entropy** bled into her digits. There had been too much meddling on this Stele already. Too many fingers secretly trying to adjust the pie recipe.

That too, would not do.

Her touch brushed across the deep carving of **Love** at the top of the Stele. There was only one who was allowed any say here. It was the one who the boy had reached out to. Who the boy had chosen. The concept he wished to devote to. **Love** could be a picky piece of Abyss, but she picked them well.

With a motion, she struck the clinging, external influences from the ledger of Artorian's soul. The guilty would all certainly feel it. There would be commotion when she returned to the Tower. To finish up, she read up on recent events. Urtu and Hella? Hella appeared to have cleverly decided not to stand on the wrong side of the fence. Good.

Shifting her perspective as she left the Stele, Dasein observed a sleeping Artorian in mortal boy format once more. One last pet to the head, and time resumed without a fuss as she left. None being the wiser as to when Artorian had put his head down and fallen asleep. He would wake just in time for dinner, and then feel tired all over again after cramming a small feast into his stomach from ravenous hunger. He would not think to complain about the vegetables this time.

Dasein had mended some minor details for the mortal's health, but those details required nutrition. The nutrition would come, the sleep would follow, and water would be plentiful. When he woke tomorrow evening, having slept a whole day away, it would all get very interesting very quickly.

Dasein couldn't wait for the show to exist.

CHAPTER SEVENTEEN

"We gotta go!" Artorian woke in shock when Ember shook him, falling out of the bed as he rolled and was spurred to sudden action. The sun must have just gone down based on the colors outside of the open balcony doors, but Ember was in a complete tizzy, holding a large, wriggling bag in both her hands. "We gotta go, right now!"

Stumbling and not in the land of the fully cognizant yet, Artorian tripped his way to the open center of the recovery room. Ember pulled an object out of her Silverwood bracelet with her teeth and threw it on the ground. Having no hands free when Artorian hustled like a foal up next to her, she bit into the shoulder section of his shirt to tug and turn him, then hurriedly dinged their bracelets together as it was getting very shouty in the pavilion suddenly.

Vwoop.

The transfer from Cal to Tim was smooth and instant.

Artorian's feet left Caltopia ground, and immediately found purchase on bounce-house bedding when they touched down on the moon in Eternium. One small step for man. One giant step for all those who hadn't woken up properly and were still not fully awake yet.

Falling on his rear, Artorian harmlessly bounced on the floor. He rubbed his eyes, blinked, rubbed them again, still had no idea what he was looking at, and closed them. He swallowed to wet his mouth, then cocked his head without taking in the scene. The scene didn't make a lot of sense. "Ember?"

"One second!" The shouting was close by, and the rustling of a large bag culminated with a victorious, "Aha!"

One loud ripping sound later, and the voice of Lucia stretched across the bounce-house playhouse plains as if rising from long captivity in a heavy puff of mushu smoke. "I liiiiive!"

Artorian covered his left eye with a hand, slitted his fingers apart slightly, then peeked in the direction of the noise so he wouldn't need to process too much in one go. The lack of brightness wasn't the problem. The problem was the amount of sense that was going to need to be made of where he was, and why his surroundings looked the way they did.

He hadn't really left Eternia in such a devastated state, right?

Surely not.

Surely, he hadn't broken *gravity*.

"Freedom!" Lucia howled to the perpetual night sky, pumped her fists, then twisted and morphed into the form of a large golden Glitterflit to enjoy a wild case of the zoomies. The living lamp sped back and forth around the child-proofed playhouse that stretched as far as the eyes could see. The moon's playhouse design was speckled in all sorts of stacked blocks made of solid colors. Though, the region appeared very muted from the constant blue sheen that pervaded Eternia like some kind of persistent nautical twilight. The effect was almost in the hue of astronomical twilight, a sliver of a difference classifying the non-light as its nautical counterpart.

The twilight sheen had no discernable source. Nothing had a shadow, and reality felt like it played second fiddle to brand new Pylons 'just making the place work.' At least no plants were clipping through any walls. That didn't make Eternia feel any less bizarre.

Artorian kept his eye on Lucia, the shiny Glitterflit a source of brightness and luminance that did cast shadows as she passed by corners and turned bends. He repeated himself, but this time added his concern. "Ember. Did you *steal* her Eminence out of the pavilion?"

Ember's voice shone as a beacon of burning pride. "I did not steal her. I smuggled her! This is a rescue, and we discussed it beforehand. For about fifteen seconds. Which was all the time we had before we were overheard, and events needed to proceed quickly from that point in order to escape the clutches of the Mother Superior. You would not believe the face she made when she turned the corner to hear us, nor the sound that escaped her throat when I snatched Lucia."

Lucia zoomed up to them, twisting back into her human form, her large golden ears standing straight up as her humanization didn't fully complete. Her Eminence honestly looked better this way. "It was a great heist! Ember said you two would be leaving shortly! I mentioned that I was so sad I could not go with you, I was feeling so stifled being the Eminence. Then she got that twinkle in her eye, and a smile on her face that lit flames in my chest."

Ember giggled, and Artorian could hear the smirk. One shouldn't be able to hear smirks. Why did it keep happening? Ember picked up the thread. "So I asked her, doooo you want to come with me? I couldn't find bedrolls, and do not have a suitable alternative… yet."

Lucia thumped her foot and shoved a fist into the sky with an *oo-rah!* "I said sign me up! Then Ember pulls this cloth out of her satchel, looks at me with scheming madness, and says—"

Ember took over, the laughter heavy in her voice. "Get in the bag!"

Artorian rubbed his forehead. "Which sounds to be about the same point that the Mother Superior caught the foul wind of your antics, and fled to tell the Protectors, while you fled to the recovery room with a Basher in your bag. I take it Lucia can alter her size some?"

"Sure can!" The Eminence posed with her hands on her hips, suddenly growing to a full eight feet in height, though the effort immediately began to deflate like a leaky balloon. She would return to the standard five-foot-tall humanization, but larger and smaller were temporary allowances. "Just had to be quick. Going smaller is a lot harder than going bigger. I don't know how Ember knew that already, but I could tell."

Ember performed the sage nod. "Went through it myself. Larger is easier. Shortstack Ammy and Smol Ammy are both forms that were more difficult in upkeep than Oni Ammy or the full Amaterasu definition of elegance. I never did manage to decide on a favorite shape, but I'm sure it'll come to me. I did decide that a bronzed skin tone is my favorite when it comes to my own. I played around with different tones for a while, but I like this one the best. Makes the supernova eyes pop, which I am very excited to get back to! Not that I am complaining about Iridium. They're very nostalgic, and the perks are nice. Es-illian-Yaran was such a long time ago, and now every time I look in the mirror, I can't help but feel that this is what should have been correct all along."

Artorian closed his eye, pressed his palms together, and asked a dumb question when Ember finished her trip down memory lane and cleared her throat, indicating that she wanted to break from her own reflecting. "Why did you feel a need to mention the bedrolls?"

The silence that hung in the air didn't feel like it was fore-boding. Artorian worried regardless, until Lucia broke the silence with a gasp as she understood. "Oh my Heavens above. He's *precious*."

"Isn't he just!" Ember gleefully added to the commentary as they both rushed to pet and rub the top of his head, the boy clueless as Lucia devolved from a Glitterflit into a giggle fit.

Ember took pity. "Sugar, I don't want to sleep on the cold ground if we need to camp. I want soft bedding! The heat situation in Eternia isn't great either. Outside of the moon, the realms are frozen, iced over, and barely hanging in there. Snowstorms are rampant, the Underground is the only real way to get around, and before you ask, yes, this is a brand-new moon. I don't know if you remember slapping a Ragna Rock into Hel, but you indirectly broke the second one. Planetary billiards is one catastrophe of a show. This is moon number three. Possibly haunted."

She paused to look at the horizon, and the literal rogue planetary chunks floating in the sky. "Okay, so gravity isn't cooperating, and they'll hang around until we fix it, but no sun means no heat! It's cold! Most of what I've been doing here as an Incarnate, when not oil-deep in repairs and beating Pylons with my wrench, is being a space heater."

Artorian didn't budge. Something just wasn't clicking. It seemed... so obvious. He was missing something. They were hinting at their hidden meaning so hard, and it just wasn't connecting for him. A Nixie tube lit up when he thought he got it. "Ah! Lucia is swift! So you wanted to have her aid in brightness and ease of travel, without hurting your butt! Bashers are fluffy and soft, and Glitterflits are both extremely fast, and potent healers. I got it! You were making a strategy against both the cold and the lack of *wheee!*"

When the girls both shrieked with laughter, the finger he'd shot to the air at his revelation slowly lowered itself. Had that not been it? Surely that was it. There was no alternative. How were they ever going to get horses or the like in here, with all the traveling they had to do? Worse still if the realms were frozen. What did they need, ice bears? "I am very confused."

"No, precious." Lucia appeared at his side, curling her arms around his head. "You did very well. That was darling and wholesome and very sweet. You keep being you and don't let anybody change you."

Ember leapt into his stomach, which he did not see coming with his eyes closed, slamming him to the ground with a *duff*. "Yeah! What she said!"

The pain expected from Ember bashing him was diminished because all the soft padding absorbed so much of the force. There was still some pain? Enough to register that hurt had happened, but not remotely what he thought such a slam should have felt like.

A worry crossed Artorian's thoughts, his voice sad. "Are you making fun of me? It's really not a good time. I already didn't feel too good, and now I'm being left out."

"Nooooo!" Ember sat up and pulled him up with her, squeezing her arms around him to knead at his back while Lucia re-joined to hold him from the other side, mushing the concerned emotional youngster between the girls for warmth and comfort as they doted on him, so his mortal mind would stop sliding down the ramp into a land of ever-increasing worries.

"You're actually precious, sweet boy." Lucia kneaded him with bunny paws while getting the affirmation in. "That was a very good answer to Ember's very crass and grandmotherly joke. The comment jumped over your head like an excited kit doing a binky, but the answer you came to was so sweet and wholesome that we both appreciated you all the more for it. You did nothing wrong. You're very dear. Ember is lucky to have you. No foolishness on your behalf occurred."

"No, no, I can be pretty foolish." Artorian felt much better about the effort they were pouring into the attempt to soothe him, rather than the awkward methods that he wasn't going to fight. He still hadn't grasped the bedroll comment, but he let it lie and might figure it out later. For now, he gave them both an appreciative hug. They put such care into the consideration of his well-being, and he did like that. There was a comfort in it.

Artorian then flailed in a strong desire to get up. "Alright, enough of the sap, I'm well! Lemme up! I have a status board thing to check. I forgot the name."

Ember scratched the top of her head, getting up and walking a few paces away. She hopped onto a colored block, taking on the role of presenter. "Speaking of names, I should introduce the place properly. This iteration is part of the last one that you recall, because we no longer have full-reset capacity. Time has not stood still."

With a wide swing of her arm, she motioned at all of Eternia. This mess of a beta version. "Welcome... to *The Pale*."

CHAPTER EIGHTEEN

Artorian rubbed his forehead. No longer able to delay his problem until later, he opened his eyes as slow as he could to see Ember's ridiculous pose. The less he saw, the less he'd have to contend with. He felt like the warmth and giggly happiness that had come before entering Eternium was going to play an important role in keeping him on his feet, because the state of Eternia was currently anything but.

Dreary, melancholy, cold, miserable. A horror show. Pale.

Those were his starting qualifiers.

Recollecting what happened the last time he was here, Artorian recapped to himself that several continents had been slapped together. Entire Pylon banks had turned into Pylon no thanks. The distinct memory of Tim appearing as he escaped an exploding Niflheim came to mind. He supposed that explained the web of cheese connecting multiple orbital bodies as if it were a very creepy galaxy-consuming organism. The whole feel of the sight creeped him out, because while he knew it was cheese, the visual was too… fleshy. Pulsating.

He didn't like it. "The Pale? Painfully accurate."

Artorian then sighed and picked at some broad details.

"Well, I can tell which chunks of fragmented orbital debris are Niflheim. They are all DeBrie! By which I mean, obviously yellow, full of holes, and terribly sticky in appearance. A very cheesy situation."

One orbital chunk covered in metroplex buildings threatened to crash and bump into the moon, but a soft shield of hexagons flared to life and gently thumped the country-sized rock chunk into a new orbit. "That's definitely a Vanaheim piece. Nice touch with the shield. I almost experienced negative comfort and a need to exclusively wear brown pants."

He held his head, trying to remember the names of the other continents. Realms? They'd had a name for all the floating planet pieces. He made a loose hand motion at the sky, feeling that conveyed his problem well enough. "Emby, do you have a list concerning the state of...?"

"All that? Yes." Ember dug into her satchel, pulled out several pieces of paper and vellum, then stuffed back all but one. "Here you go."

"Oooh, paper." Artorian's small fingers rubbed over the material, intrigued. "Why is it paper this time, but was vellum last time?"

Ember thought that to be simple. "Work with what ya got, not with what ya don't. Be happy that papyrus was a phase and the press worked as intended. Read me the list, I need a refresher as well. Or rather, Lucia, can you read the list? I like your talky talk, and sugar needs to save his voice for the thousand questions that are about to come."

Artorian didn't mind and handed the list over.

Once Lucia got the piece of paper in her paws, she whistled at the damage report. "Well, there's sure a lot less compared to the last time I was here."

Artorian quirked a brow, surprised. "You've been here before?"

"Oh, yes! You're going to have a hard time finding anyone who hasn't. Only Heavenlies and the people from the last big decanting haven't experienced Eternia yet, but most should know of it by now, the place being available or not. Lots of folks have been getting antsy to come back. There's not a lot of opportunities on Caltopia to release steam unless you want to get embroiled in big diplomatic incidents." Lucia's bunny ears wiggled like antennae, adjusting as if to be on the correct frequency while she was recollecting memories. She adjusted her qipao and recounted her experiences. "I wasn't in the last big Eternia event that took place. I, at best, have stories about what happened. Before that, I was the candidate to test the Overhealer Specialization, though my strength lies in shields. Better to mitigate damage than to patch it!"

She cleared her throat. "Let me narrate this list."

Alfheim – Boom.

Asgard – Boom.

Hel – Boom.

Jotunheim – Boom.

Midgard – Present.

Muspelheim – Present.

Niflheim – Boom.

Svartalfheim – Present.

Vanaheim – Boom.

Lucia then neatly folded the piece of paper up and returned it to Ember for safekeeping. "There you go, baby bun. You let Momma Lucia know if you need something. I'll be figuring out why none of my anything seems to work, and why I can't pull up my panels or Status Screen."

Ember kneaded her fingers into her temples. "I was getting to that, and it's part of my boy's thousand questions. First item on the docket was wrapping up Artorian puzzling out which pieces of landmass belonged to what realm, or I'll never get his entire attention span back."

"True." Artorian hummed the word with his nose pointed to the sky, doing exactly that. A piece of floating, over-polished marble with inlaid metals was easy. Artorian tagged that one while tapping his lips. "Asgard."

Chunks of black ash, compressed coal, and other dark

material were the remains of Hel. Artorian squinted at some questionable formations. "Is that... corn?"

"Whole wheat grains and cracked corn." Ember confirmed with a nod, though the detail didn't add any clarity until she continued. "Wagner's favorite treats. From the early days where Cal was still trying to lure that Goose into Eternia. Admittedly, Tim can be very corny. It may not have been Cal who had the idea. The other three are here as well. Beethoven, Mozart, and Weird Al Goosevitch are all present and accounted for. Wagner is off exploring Incursus, last I heard. The place where 'everything is on fire!' Which happens often in Incursus. That dungeon builds forts well, but the endless ordinance tests in there make that skill a laugh."

"Huh." Artorian moved on. The icebergs in space with frozen dinosaur dioramas were Jotunheim. Pieces of soul-draining gray office and cubicles? That was haunted moon number one. While the giant construction yards in playset design and foam detailing were likely the shards of moon number two.

Then there was the eldritch horror of Niflheim. The place of Phosgen, intelligent fungus, and cheese. He could swear some of it was looking at him, giving him terrible thoughts of another Cheese Overmind. All... "*Ghugh...*"

He pressed his hands to his knees and bent over as his stomach did somersaults. "That is mighty unpleasant. With the muted colors, and that sensation of creeping cold, and knowing I'm likely going to end up there for one reason or another, I'm not doing too hot, and clinging to thoughts of tipping frozen cows."

He looked around to find the still intact realms, but Alfheim was a wasteland of frozen tree chunks and very much a victim of galactic pinball. Svartalfheim appeared intact but was a frigid rock, Midgard was likely somewhere in all this mess, but he hadn't found it yet, and Muspelheim looked like a gnomish bomb that badly wanted to go off. The glow of heat was breaking out from within through cracks of volcano-scarred crust, all its deserts now shiny glassed ballrooms that twinkled with rainbow light. "Well I think I figured out where people might still live."

Ember joked in full deadpan. "Would it be the only place that looks like it has its own heat?"

"Oh, y'think?" Artorian swiveled his head, quipping back. "I was going to say the first moon. On account of it being haunted and whatnot."

Lucia interrupted to get the confusion off her chest. Like the other two with her, she was feeling off after freshly entering The Pale. The place had an unpleasantness to it that made her skin crawl. "Ghosts are people?"

"Momma bun—" Artorian dared a deep breath but prevented himself from falling into a lecture. It was not the place or time. "I know *rocks* that are people. Animals are people. Trees are people. At this point, if it has a mind, meets some kind of vague sentience and sapience barrier that I mostly venture on by feeling, and has the capacity to self-reflect and learn from mistakes? That's a person. So, unless ghosts or other creatures of the haunt can't meet that rather loose standards? Yes. I would consider ghosts people. I used to have some measurement for a capacity to feel pain being important, but as I am perfectly capable of feeling pain on the behalf of some-thing else, I threw that out. I have also, at complete random, named a quill and carried it around like it was alive, and did so for months without thinking anything of it. Which is nothing to say of my opinion on treating energy as if it were living, because I have done that always."

He rubbed his hands over his head. He hadn't meant to do that. That had been rude. "Here I *just* told myself I wasn't going to lecture. I'm sorry, momma bun."

Lucia appeared next to him, the Glitterflit's fingers sinking into his hair to add to the rubs and scratches like a Basher teaching a kit how to groom properly. "You're precious, and a good boy. That was a good vent. Venting is good. You heard something that bothered you and you got vocal. That's how people find out and we all get better. Are you feeling a skin crawl perhaps? It's been growing and now it's rather noticeable, and I'm getting irritable for no reason."

Artorian and Ember both blinked, checked themselves, and found that to be the case. They both nodded at her quickly in tandem. Lucia purred as she reached for the both of them, surprising Ember and Artorian as they discovered that was an actual sound in the bunny lexicon. Unlike a cat, who made the sound from the throat, Lucia's was softer. Akin to rubbing teeth together? A happy noise, in any event. One they only noticed from having their cheeks mushed to hers.

Lucia didn't mind the attention, though the stares did make her ramble. "Humans are known to pack-bond and do so with anything. *Anything*. You leave a human alone long enough, and they *will* find something to love. Usually something large, dangerous, and perfectly capable of killing anyone else the human shows it to. While at the same time calling the murder-beast something intensely innocuous. To the stressful discovery of all those involved."

Ember placed her own hand on Lucia's head. "Bun? Are you okay? That sounded like personal experience."

Lucia cleared her throat, snapped her hands back against her chest, and straightened up. "*Mmm*, yes. I'm fine. I'll be fine. I'll be fine sooner if I can get some shields in place. Honestly, whose bright idea was it to call a leopard that can live and hide in steam Snowflake?"

Ember scrunched her face. "The... Major? No, no, that's Snowball."

"It's Snowball's *son*." Lucia hissed at empty air. "I helped deliver that litter, and there was not one in the bunch named by a human, that didn't grow up... different."

"That's a loaded word." Artorian felt unpleasant about that linguistic choice, adding his own grumbles. "At least give us something now that we're this deep into the segue."

Lucia ran her tongue over her teeth, her face trying and failing to compose to a socially appropriate form as the irritation ran through her. "I have to deal with a lot of nonsense from beings that are so far above my head that saying no isn't actually an option. While doing so to whatever tune they are singing as they themselves are trying not to get their invitation revoked."

The momma bun slapped her hands together, rubbing at her nose. "So every interaction, until comfort is found, is this awkward game of cat and mouse. There are several of them that are here—and I mean in Caltopia, not here-here—who all follow humans around like they are the single most entertaining thing to exist in the universe. At complete random, a human will do something innocuous, and an entity with power will get... I'm going to call it a 'genius idea.' Suddenly, a normal leopard offspring has very out of the ordinary affinity channels from the get-go, and since the channels were strong, they also strongly affected that leopard's personality, before the personality could really comprehend that it could or should say no. Now we have a leopard who trails snowflakes everywhere he goes, is obsessed with pushing objects from high ledges, and can't differentiate that people aren't objects."

Lucia wrung her hands, her form having trouble keeping the humanization in place as she was getting very fluffy. "So please just let me use the word 'different,' yes?"

Ember squeezed her lips together, nodded, and dropped it. One glance at Artorian, and he jumped into her boat with a salute. They then looked up at Lucia, thought of how to help, and shared some cleverly whispered ideas. In agreement with the solution, Artorian moved both his arms into the air. "Okay, momma bun."

Lucia instinctively picked him up, carried him on her hip, and fussed to herself while pacing in a circle. Bobbing the child while her mind was elsewhere, her free hand still trying to make the status screens come up.

Ember looked at the sky, then at Artorian. "I have one comment before I consider it my turn and unpack the big ticket items so we can get started."

Artorian, currently acting as teddy bear, turned his head to give his attention. Ember snickered and added her piece. "There is an Enclave in Midgard where a bunch of humans are successfully weathering out the endless storm. Duchess, the daughter of Katarina, is holding down the fort and playing life's most dangerous game of frostpunk. The Solar Gate ruin creates heat when provided mana. I take it we're sticking a tack in that and adding a trip marker into our to-do list? I'm going to warn you beforehand that there's not a lot left of what you remember."

Artorian's eyes sharpened, the pleasantry in his face turning into burning determination. "Yes, dear. That is now on the schedule. Thank you for telling me this early. Katarina deserves that of me."

CHAPTER NINETEEN

Ember exhaled a heated wave. "The big ticket items."

She stretched her arms above her head, shoulders and back popping. "I have more bad news than I have words for, and only a few pieces of good news. One of these bits of bad news is that the squiggly Niffleroids up there are in fact a living organism and have cheesed the system. We're going to need to blow up Mr. Dead Space and his Markers, but we can't do that unless the sun is on. So, until then, a few of our fights will include bonus inconveniences of the sticky variety."

She stretched, bending her left arm across her head to lean over. "When the scarabs un-thaw, we can return to having bugs in the system, rather than cheese stuck in the Pylons. I know that's one of those 'lesser evil' situations, but the insect swarms we can handle."

Artorian felt poorly about his bad feeling being true, then put his hand in the air. "About scarabs, I remember those being the Pylon-eating 'bugs in the system,' but where did they come from? That's such a random event."

"Remember that one scarab you sent me in the prototype item box, ages ago?" Ember grunted, and stretched the other way, the other two starting to copy her like she was leading a class. "That dastardly thing ate its way out of the prototype, skittered into the Pylon holds, and praised the heavens for the sight. Disbelieving its beady little eyes as the most scrumptious buffet laid before it. We then had many more, many quickly."

"Many quickly?" Artorian snickered during stretches, pushing away the thought that there was barely any difference in tactile feeling between Caltopia and Eternia. Shouldn't he be sick and throwing up? No, best not think of that. Nor the daggers being sent his way for pointing out Ember's flub. "Many quickly is fantastic grammar, dear. Any other bug threats? My fireball senses are tingling."

Fireballs were a topic that Ember could whole-heartedly agree with. "The flambérge mosquito swarms will wake up alongside the scarabs. That will be a stinging adventure, but one that stays contained while The Pale is frozen over. Bugmageddon plays second fiddle to the Cheese Penguins obsessed with unification. I swear, the first time I hear them chant 'the time is due, all shall be fondue'? I am ripping a splitting maul out of their sticky hands and going on a rampage. Fins? Flippers? Whatever Penguins have. The lesser variants hold cheese knives, but in our current situation, they're more dangerous to us."

She motioned right up at the exact mass of connected orbital bodies that Artorian had so badly hoped not to need to deal with. "The Cheese Overmind is going to be our main problem. Brother Moon, specifically. It took me years to figure out that it was not saying 'make us whole' and was instead saying 'make us holes.' Then hissed the word 'Swiss' for hours on end. I spent I don't know how long thinking we had leaky pipes. ElCazorro has been handling it with his buddy Isaac. The last time I checked in, all I got back was static, and 'cut the limbs!' I figure they had it handled?"

Artorian made a noise of sincere discomfort, so the topic was changed.

Ember's arms dropped into a roll as they fell. "Basic Eternia functions are all being rebuilt. After Cal was with us again, he and Tim managed to hash out the Pylon problem. Cal had the plans for synthetic Pylons but couldn't figure out how to make them with any kind of speed. Tim knew how to make Pylons quickly, but not what kept blowing them up all the time. Which... surprised everyone else when we found out, because based on how a lot of people see Cal and Eternium, people thought that scenario would be flipped."

Ember then shot Lucia a conciliatory smile, one of the bun's ears droopy in confusion while the other remained straight. "Screens will become available when either Tot or Turnip finds us and realizes they can get the ball rolling, or I pull a particularly rusty trumpet from my satchel to get their attention. It's the one thing a Gjallarhorn is good for, because celestial feces, that *pwaamp*-tube sounds terrible."

Lucia smiled back, but with an expression on her face that plainly conveyed that she had no idea who any of these people were.

Pressing her hands to her hips, Ember stared at the sky. "We've got a few big problems to tackle before we can request backup: Barry left Abyss behind, the sun needs igniting, cheese has gone stale, and we have a pending swarmy situation. For flavor, vampiric versions of critters are rampant and as unfriendly as you can imagine them. Those, of course, have developed a preference for the flavor of people with healing abilities. I wonder why."

After shooting Artorian a look, she hung her head and addressed her least favorite component. "As *pièce de résistance*? Somewhere in this entire mess, space station thirteen misplaced their clown. If we're lucky, it's still just *one* clown."

She ran a bronze hand through her red hair as the other two ogled her, the concern living deep in their wide eyes even as they had trouble following. "You can thank Invictus for the mosquito swarm and accompanying alteration. That rat of a Wisp! We had mosquitos well packed away, never to see the light of day. I was wondering what the scheming play was going to be after he'd been lurking about. I bet he was expecting his cleverly hidden bundle to not be found between all the asteroids, but Wo'ah has been having a field day cataloging every last object in orbit. Invictus will be meeting the back of my hand for that stunt, and then he will divulge every last detail to me on how he got it in here under all of our noses. I am going to cube that little—"

Steam purged from Ember, her body hot, hissing like a Majin teapot.

Artorian continued his morning workout routine, flat on the ground as he was bending over a crossed leg. "That's a buffet of a to-do list. Here I was still stuck on how we're even getting off this lunar bounce house. The kind of mobility we need to traverse this terrain and get from point A to Z is too far of a hop for even a Glitterflit. Or are you extra magical, Lucia?"

"No, precious boy." Lucia mulled over the problem; her ears flat against her head at how dreary this all sounded. The Pale was a far cry from the game world she had enjoyed. "You give me steady gravity and stable ground, and I'm game. This gravity-broken perpetual-frost chunks-of-realms deal? I got nuthin'. I can make lanterns, light, shields, and a roof. I can also zippity-bop-da-dum-doo-dap outta there. Unless I see charts, because then I choose violence. I hate charting. I don't wanna do it."

"The monster, or the paperwork that nurses do?" Ember pulled a black box out of her satchel. The same kind that had trapped Urtu-mon. The end of his name had been tacked on with the suffix, 'mon.' Short for 'monster'. She forgot why she pulled the box free for a moment, then it came to her. "I did mention I was going to talk to a Wood Elf about some bees."

Lucia's ears shot ramrod straight in concern. Had she the power, her paws would have caught golden flame, ready to throw down. "There's a *monster* version?"

Ember rubbed her forehead, trying to recall how this version of the box worked. "*Uhu.* Floating scroll, covered in eyes, yells 'Be afraid' at people. As if it needed help. Weak to fire of all kinds. Destroying one gets you the buff: *a nurse's sigh of relief.*"

Lucia felt determined. Her answer would be violence.

Artorian couldn't look away from the box. "Sugar? Tell me there's not a person in there?"

"I can't do that, dear." Ember remembered how the device worked, then tossed the black cube at the ground, forcing it to spill forth all contents. "I brought both Apiculteur the Hive Mage, and an entire hive of Serenity Bees. Hello again, Api! Let's continue our prior conversation! What were you saying?"

A person covered head to toe in the simple cloth garb of a beekeeper appeared, visually indistinct from any other in that full attire. The outfit came complete with a circular face covering built into the hood, constructed from wire and reeds.

His silence was telling.

Apiculteur, a Peach Tree Wood Elf, had a particular fondness for the time when Wood Elven civilization had been condensed to a few groves. Specifically, the sensation of being part of a collective whole. The more intense that feeling, the happier Api was. To that end, bonding to a hive of variant honeybees was a way to rapidly expand that pleasant feeling. The number of individuals contributing to a single being was far higher than a Grove Tree could provide, and the sensation of being one with many was perfect for Api.

The Hive Mage had performed trades before but had grown ever more picky after the constant stories of Tarrean's misadventures kept assaulting his ears. That Tarrean and Wux's T and W brand mead was a competitor in the Fifth Annual Honey Expo? That had nothing to do with it. Yes. Nothing. Maybe they wouldn't win thanks to *his* bees this time.

When he spoke, control was considered first. Api had a deep voice with a flat tone, but highly expressive from a little buzz that accompanied how he spoke. As if several people were speaking in sync, and some of those people were definitely bees. As requested, he picked up right where the conversation with Ember had been paused.

"My desires revolve around gardening, brewing mead, and creating small gifts for others. My aspirational goals in Eternia's resurgence would include becoming a Sage of brewing and throwing a party bigger than Oak can grow. Tools and apparatuses necessary for brewing, especially glass, are paramount. I would gladly trade a hive of bees for shaped glass, and bottles for storing honey wine. Alternatively, the secret recipe to Oak's special hookah blend."

The Hive Mage was obviously grinning ear to ear under his beekeeping suit. "Smoke in general affects bees the same way that smoke affects Wood Elves; it dampens the communication between the swarm and increases the level of individuality. Tobacco and alcohol are both substances bees and other insects consume in controlled amounts for recreational purposes. It's hard for us researchers to divine why insects knowingly consume these substances when they lack the pleasure centers for addictive behaviors, but I am driven to discover this secret."

Api rubbed his gloved hands together. "Have you any of these components?"

Ember was already writing out a formula on a piece of vellum. Or rather, a cobalt quill was searing letters into the leather. Rolling up the completed product, she tossed the writ at him. "One secret formula."

The Hive Mage pocketed the vellum without a glance, instantly veering off towards the hive of Serenity Bees that were all very confused about their current situation. The creatures were swarming over the nest, alarmed and protective. Api calmed them with his sheer honey-scented presence, petting a few of them before his gloved hand phased through the hive to reach deep within. "What is their purpose?"

Ember kept it short. "Mobility."

Api considered this direction and lectured as he began the shaping of some of the hive's newest bees. "It wouldn't be wrong to say bees are biologically designed for their role and function in the hive. An egg is essentially a blank slate; fertilized eggs will always be female and unfertilized eggs will always be male. A queen will consume mostly royal jelly until she reaches full maturity while regular females will only consume a small amount during the first stage of growth. The *exact* balance of nutrients at this stage will decide if they grow into a scout, forager, food processor, or guard. Any bee that grows too old or has a birth defect will automatically become a nursery bee, raising the next generation."

He paused to glance at the three others in the... strange environment that he wasn't going to ask about. Size was deemed a matter of import. "If you want the bees the same size as a horse, it's important to note that a Queen Bee is roughly twice the size as any other. Bees can't navigate without light, so adding bioluminescence like a firefly would allow them to fly day and night, as well as communicate with each other over greater distances. This makes the Serenity variant particularly capable."

When the Hive Mage pulled his gloved hand back, the cloth utterly untarnished, it opened to show three glowing orange globs. "They are ready but require sustenance that I cannot give them in this realm. Without a character sheet, or a player profile, or whatever it might be that I need here now? I cannot provide them with the Mana necessary. Nor the mana that is spelled without the capital M. Will this suffice?"

Ember approached, offered an open hand, and was provided the orange globs with a delicate touch. She nodded after a short inspection. "They will suffice. I shall send you back to your apiary."

The Hive Mage motioned at the hive next to him, followed by pointing at his extended finger. "May I?"

"Do so." Ember approved the action, her fingers trailing over her Silverwood bracelet as Apiculteur stored the hive in his hidden ring. "Ready?"

Artorian put his hand up before they could proceed. "Ember? Why did you have a Mage trapped in one of those cubes?"

The impending handshake between the Mage and tiny

Saintess paused. Ember flashed her teeth in the facsimile of a smile, her eyes hungry. "Yes, an excellent question! Api, do you want to tell him how you ended up in that cube?"

Discomfort and unseen sweat poured from the Mage, the cloth doing nothing to hide the obvious spike in body language discomfort. After a beat of silence, Api chose the most diplomatic, non-confrontational answer that came to mind. "Honey Aura."

"Is that what we're going with?" Ember beat her lashes at the person twice her size, her smile devoid of friendliness, regardless of its presence on her face. "How about you take my hand, and this wraps up?"

Api wasted no time doing exactly that and vanished with a pop.

Ember exhaled hot, promptly stored the sequence of the unborn bees into her Silverwood bracelet and turned to face the other two as her smile evolved from forced to genuine. "Much better! That's transport sorted as soon as we can get someone with clearance to flip some levers. I don't have my statistics and permissions right now either. Wrong body."

She then cocked her head at a ticking noise that had turned both of Lucia's swiveling ears. "Speaking of someone with clearance, I think we have incoming."

CHAPTER TWENTY

T.C. folded into space with the ticking of a clock, then looked around and clapped his hands together. The Incarnate of **Time** was glad to see he'd arrived exactly on the dot, his Irish accent instantly present. "*A-ha*! Thought so! Good to see ya! Got meh fancy pollen cakes? Meh tulips are in need of love."

Ember's head snapped to the large man like it was on a swivel, a fire roaring in her gaze for half a second as if they were searching for the source of a threat, before she calmed at seeing who it was. With hair even more fiery and red than hers, the scruff of forgotten days covering his face, and his hands brown from being elbow-deep in dirt? That was T.C. alright. The rest of him sported a healthy tan, and those green 'ever-clean' overalls could be spotted from a full league away. She chose to say nothing about the smell of potatoes. It made her crave the soup. "Teagan Conaghan! Good to see you, gardener. I notice you're in your apron! No more Temporal Adjudication work?"

The large Incarnate took a knee, easing the path for Ember to stroll up and press their cheeks together, making a mutual 'mwah' noise before T.C. resumed talking, happily accepting

Ember's not so secret delivery of pollen cakes. The package vanished into a pocket of his overalls like ill-gotten gains. "Aye! What's the craic?"

"The news?" Ember questioned the word and clarified the meaning she knew at the same time. A nod from T.C. was enough confirmation. "Well, I brought my boy, so the Antelucan Age is about to get clapped into a sudden end. I'm sick of dealing with The Pale, and its entire iteration. It's cold, clammy, dark, and all the things that remind me of walking through a ceaseless wave of gray fog. My Blade of War days are long behind me, but that does not mean I want reminders."

T.C. understood implicitly, then nodded at Artorian and Lucia when Ember was done growling like a volcano. "Top o' the morning, so to say! Can't wait for this place to have mornin's again. Good to see you, long beard! Don't much care that ya haven't got it right now, I can see you age before my eyes and just like that it's there again. Majere isn't the only one who can toy with that gimmick! The tales of Hickman and Weiss are magical in their own way. Krynn was a cornerstone for me."

T.C. crossed his arms, his face pointed to the stars. "Or, well. Majere had the hourglass curse version. I have the ability. Somewhat unfair of a comparison."

The Incarnate then whisked himself from his musings and clapped his hands together a second time. "Back to it! Clock's ticking. Ember, is it?"

The Saintess nodded a single time, as that was what she was going with for now. "Until I figure out what to call the new Eternia profile, Ember is the current designation for this particular mortal form, and period of experiences. I'm constantly surprised the rest of you don't do this. I'm feeling like the only one comfortable with the changeovers."

T.C. dropped his hand to dismiss the conjecture. "*Bhah*! Ya became an Incarnate while in a very transitional time in yer life. I've been happy with who and what I am for eons and am content. Ya have the opportunity to find and shape yerself in the way that ya were denied the first time. We all understand, lass. Some of us have found ourselves, and generally, by the time ya become an Incarnate, you don't want to change much anymore. People are set in stone by then, stuck in their specific ways of thinking and being. That's just how it goes after a few hundred years of life, much less a few thousand. The longer you keep ticking, the more set the course of your river becomes! Ya learn what ya like, what ya dislike, what hills ya stand on, what hills ya die on, and once you've got all the answers for who and what ye are as a person? What's left? Why be inclined to add a new bend to the river? That only works for those who wanted to keep it flexible in the first place, and you'll find a mere handful of strange souls with that kind of outlook."

He shrugged and walked away a few paces to emplace a glowing sigil onto the ground, ending the lecture that he was uniquely capable of grasping. "I've always understood, lass. I am the foremost expert here when it comes to the workings, functions, and effects of **Time**. Until **Time** shows up and I pass that baton. Though that event is... unlikely. That's just not who **Time** is. Now chin up! I'm glad you're back! The place is too much of a boys club without you, and the moment you arrive in the garden and Tot sees that you're in, he's going to fall over himself to get out and run to Chandra. He's been talking about her every day for the last... Oh, I lost track. Come! Step into my circle."

Ember joined the circle purely to give T.C. a massive hug. "Thank you for understanding, Adjudicator."

"*Phah!*" The Incarnate flushed red, tried to play the act off like it didn't affect him, but hugged the small girl back like an over worried parent. "I'm off the clock, Ember. Ya can drop the title. An' really, 'course I unnestan'. Yer using your naming convention as a way to mark periods in yer life, aye? An yer usin' Ember a second time to overwrite what ye remember from the first time. Because the first time is very drab and painful, and this second time is the rare chance at what it coulda been? There's lots of folks that'd wish for a chance like that. To do it all again, without losing what ya stood for, or who ya stood with."

He nose-motioned at Artorian when the boy, accompanied by Lucia, joined them on the glowing sigil. "Same story for the Merl who is in! Merli became Tsu. Tsu became Elder. Elder became the fabled Art Historian, Artorian. Artorian branches off into Sunny, and Love, but they are side streets to the main thoroughfare he represents. Your path is made up of only thoroughfare. A highway that represents who you are. So if you want to come up, or have Sunny help you, with a name for your time in Eternia version beta point insert that ridiculous string of numbers Tim is so fond of? Then do it. It can only help you."

T.C. got up, pulling the metaphorical lever.

With the ticking churn of a grandfather clock's small finger moving a single second, the lot of them were translocated seamlessly from the surface of the bounce-house moon to a place that made Artorian cover his eyes, screech, and curl up into a ball.

"Welcome to Demeter's Dream, in the Fields of Elysium two point oh." Eternium spoke loud and proud, his Rhys Dwarven accent bleeding through, until petering off at Artorian's yelp and losing all of his introductory thunder. He took one long glance at the shivering, curled ball of a boy before understanding what was wrong.

Tim cursed under his breath and slapped at the air like he was in a fight with the wind in order to quickly turn the entire location overcast. The light in the whole zone dimmed significantly as the torches and fires picked up the slack, sputtering to life throughout the whole acropolis to create non-eye-murdering brightness.

Tim was dressed in a fantastically comfortable Grecian chiton, having expected that he would get to make a fancy introduction to a place that was meant to be a present. The older dungeon instead knelt next to Artorian, broadly rubbing over his back. "It'll fade, it'll get better."

Artorian frog-croaked but didn't move.

Eternium instead felt panic brush over his skin and looked up at Ember. "I didn't do it! It wasn't me! I swear the eyes weren't me!"

Ember crossed her arms, inhaled deep, sighed slowly, and dropped a hand towards the dungeon to chastise him. "Turnip. I know that you don't know that you didn't do it. Because unless you did what we asked and spent more time with people? Checking your messages instead of working all the time? You would have gotten to my missive where I told you about this, and you would have known already. I was also expecting the game lever to get kicked over the moment we were in here, and not for the whole place to remain static, to where T.C. is who came to get us. I was expecting you or Tot."

She looked around, taking a perception check. "Where *is* Tot?"

Tim picked up a Tiny-torian to bundle him into an over-sized towel pulled from hammer space. The dungeon carried the lad and shielded his eyes by pressing the boy's face into his shoulder. He swirled towards the direction of granite stairs, lit them up from within to dictate the walking path like a guidepost beneath their feet, and talked as he walked. "Zipped off the moment we felt you come in through Yuki's borehole. As to the Pylons? I did throw the lever, and nothing happened. Not so much as a squeaky wheel or a light popped on. Tulip, can you go check the holds? Deverash ran out of breath minutes ago but he's still trying to scream, as much as an eight-sided crystalline die can do either of those things."

T.C. saluted with two fingers and vanished with a clock chime.

Lucia filled the newly vacant space, bounding behind the rest of the group. She followed Ember as they marched off behind the large, rotund, beefy man of muscle and might with the kind of stride that said he knew exactly where he was going.

Captivating as that might have been, her eyes were busy trying to take in the sights. Just as the bounce-house moon had been a first, Demeter's Dream was a new experience. The pavilion was great, but Fields of Elysium two point oh was a carved-out piece of paradise.

The place was idyllic. Gorgeous. A Mediterranean climate. A pleasant soft breeze. A gentle flowery scent. Peach blossom trees bearing shining golden apples were growing out of limestone mesas at incredibly defiant locations. As if nature had appraised an aesthetically pleasing cliff face, ignored the need for topsoil, and declared 'I'mma grow there.' Regardless of the Dream's very haphazard allowance to let nature be where nature pleased, there was an uncanny, unavoidable order to the design of it all.

The stairs were all precise. Their steps were even, identical, and leveled flawlessly. The detail and carvings in both the floor and surroundings didn't have one millimeter of mistake to them. Each embossing was a perfect copy of the one next to it, repeating a consistent pattern of delicate imagery.

In contrast, the mesas in the distance were wild. All the greenery of their current location grew as if by teamwork between trees and stone. Each peach blossom had branches as they pleased, but not one of them was taller than another, and each was intelligently placed so as to provide consistent shade on a sunny day.

Lucia inspected the stone that she was walking on, trying to suss out what material it was. It wasn't limestone like the mesas in the distance. Marble? No. She was on a material of a bold texture that came primarily in a white, cream, or light gray. Patagonia? Yes.

The whole complex that she strode forth on was carved out of a single, massive block of Patagonia granite. Including the ionic columns that seemed to sprout from the ground like impossibly intricate, natural formations. Specifically, in exactly the places where they were needed most. Like the Patagonia had chosen to push up its sleeves and grunt like a patron of Osha's tavern, deciding that 'more support goes here and that's final.'

The U-shaped structure she climbed stood in the center of

the Elysian Fields, likely positioned on its own mesa based on the view distance available. Demeter's Dream, which she believed to be the name of the complex, was divided by tiered segments, each with its own set of wedged in stairs that connected to the center square one level lower. T.C. had brought them into the largest square at the very bottom, with the most open space. As they climbed up the tiers in a straight line, the public squares became smaller.

Able to see some of the smaller structures better from above, the homes built into both sides of the complex all had the same imbrex and tegula tiles. The details tied the location's theme together nicely, though Lucia did get distracted by some particularly pretty interior courtyards, fabric overhangs, and a strangely large number of balconies.

She had to tear her vision away from those small details when a particularly large balcony served as a connection point to one of the far-out mesas. Specifically looking for that detail once spotted, she noticed that from each level, bridges led out to the separate mesas based on equivalent height.

On the edge of her vision, and what must be the edge of the Elysian Fields, waterfalls poured in from every horizon. This seemed true regardless of where she turned her head, reminding Lucia of the caldera she called home. Interesting how this place wasn't flooding. There was water below them when she snuck a peek off the edge of the complex, but its state was calm. The waterfalls must not connect to the main basin.

Overall, she thought this entire area was a place in which Urtu would happily live. Demeter's Dream had that feeling of grandiose openness to it, except that when she looked up, Lucia could definitely see that the ceiling was a fake sky. Magnificently done, but a mimicry nonetheless. Her guess shifted to being on the inside of a hollowed out, gargantuan stone ball. Given she'd seen many colossal orbital bodies floating about space not too long ago, this was likely one of those. Hiding a piece of paradise like a needle in a haystack was one way to keep hidden, she supposed.

When her head caught up to her eyes, Lucia's mouth shot questions while adding hops to her jog in order to keep up. She was ogling the scenery too much. "Who is Tulip?"

"Teagan is Tulip." The groan accompanying Artorian's pained voice sounded very forced, and equal measures unpleasant. He had easily put two and two together. "I would put money on Ember having a name that begins with an T as well, but everyone is too worried about the fist of god that would descend if anyone mentioned it without her consent."

The sudden, intense silence that followed only proved Artorian right.

He chuckled with his face buried in Tim's large shoulder. "Sorry about my eyes, Tim. Recent development. If I drop the name Dasein, will that help?"

Eternium choked on air and stumbled over absolutely nothing in the topmost agora. Wheezing, he paused in place and needed to press his spare hand down on a knee. "It just doesn't stop with you, does it?!"

Artorian didn't have a reply ready for that, growing more confused than anything else. "That was... a bit much for a response? You alright, Tim?"

"Yes. Give me a minute." The triple-S ranked dungeon, an existence older than Cal, most potent of creators, movers, and shakers, hymned a short prayer to the empty air above him. He made a holy motion over his own being to request a blessing of forgiveness, then turned to Ember. "*What?!*"

Ember pushed her hands into her pockets like a tomboy who couldn't be bothered. She kicked a rock she pretended was there and smacked her lips. "Aw, shucks. Y'know? Shaka gave me the full rundown on the pink irises deal. So I know who is who, and you seem to know who is who as well. So how about we skip the blame portion of the test and move right back on to why I can't pull up my character sheet?"

Tim snapped his mouth shut. He stared into the distance, then returned to marching through the agora, entering into one of the four temples on the topmost tier. The structure was adorned with blue and white themes, ice sculptures, tassels, and tales of heroic deeds sewn with platinum thread into hanging heraldry. "Fantastic idea. Explains why we can't even try flipping Artorian's lever. We had it all keyed to his existing pattern, but the pattern he has is not the pattern I have. Like remembering to add the olive trees to dreamland, we'll fix it before Yuki knows anything went wrong!"

"Too late." Yuki's ice queen voice cut through the chatter like a cold front slicing up a hot summer day. Unlike Tim's flagrant robe, she was comfortably dressed in one of Zelia's prized kimonos. Complete with a platinum-bladed fan in her right hand, thin sheets of ice connecting the segments. Her entrance was eye-catching. Her kimono scintillated in the reflected light with a delightful blue gradient scheme, and frost pattern snowflake details!

The pale as snow **Kenopsia** cultivator moved with the silent grace of a comet's coma, her brilliantly pure hime-cut white hair not needing even a touch of adjustment as she slid towards them. Moving her icy blue nails away from her equally icy blue lips, she reached out with an open hand, icy blue eyes completing the set of three as they cut towards Eternium. "You enter Demeter's Temple and think I will not hear you? Give him to me."

Tim obeyed without question, handing the boy over. "Yes, ma'am."

Lucia felt very confused. The man clearly wasn't Heavenly, and she hadn't understood the hierarchy yet, but he was built like the foundation that an entire world could stand on. So what gave this cold lady such clout? A slight look left brought her golden eyes in line with the statue of permafrost, standing front and center against the arctic temple's back wall. The statue was a massive, true-to-life copy of the frosty lady who had just taken Tiny-torian into her arms. The frozen throne of ocean depth stalagmites at its base told Lucia plenty. "*Ah.*"

Satisfied that Tim was doing such a marvelous job listening to his lady, she approved immediately and trudged along with a far greater allotment of respect for the newly met individual. They'd be great friends! Surely, some mischief could be—

A sensation of ice in her veins killed that thought dead.

Yuki shot one glance over her shoulder at Lucia, as if she knew. This single icicle of a look froze the bun in place. Yuki *hmphed*. "I know all about you, Lucia the Luminant. Pray to remember your politeness, or I'll parlay the story of what made you *penitent*."

Yuki got an instant salute from the bun, like a spring trap snapping into place. "Ma'am, yes ma'am!"

CHAPTER TWENTY-ONE

Artorian heard the rumble of an engine kick to life. He returned to his senses in a cozy bed. The room was pleasantly cool, smelled nice, and best of all? Was very quiet. No, that was not the best part. The dark room and emperor-sized blanket were the best part! He contemplated rolling over and conceding more time to slumber, but a growl from his stomach reminded him of that darn mortal need for food and constant maintenance.

Kicking off the covers without actually wanting to get up, he laid on his back and groaned at the ceiling. Like him needing to get up was somehow the ceiling's fault. The blame was quickly shifted to an obnoxiously happy chime erupting from his right, where a tiny screen blinked into existence, flashing in pulses with equally unwelcome brightness.

How rude!

Without leaving the bed, Artorian swat at the screen with his hand, but came up short. He then indignantly shifted to reach it with his leg instead, pointlessly determined not to get up. The sole of his foot smacked into the screen, upon which the chiming ceased. Indulgent in this minor, but clearly massive victory, he remained as pudding upon the bed a moment longer. For his efforts, he was rewarded with a stomach that complained some more.

Grabbing a piece of blanket, he ground the cloth against his face to clear his eyes, then grumbled and threw up a hand with an upset mumble. "Status."

To the Pylons' credit, a screen did pop up.

The contents... the contents left much to be desired. While a statistics screen did appear, every value showed a flat ten, and every field not a value was blank. He didn't even have a registered name. "I completely forgot that information was tied to the body you entered the game with."

The door to his room peeped at the hinge, parting just enough to let Lucia through. She closed the wooden door with her foot and ambled over with a scrumptious pot of seafood on one hand, and some rolls packed in silvery foil on the other. Her ears picked up his words. "The game works, and that's what's important. Hungry? I'm here to check on my patient. Just because you left the pavilion does not mean you left my care."

Artorian's head churned slowly, his mind catching up as an order of questions began to form. "Ember?"

"At the table with the Incarnates, as I learned them to be. They're in some heated discussion a few doors down. We're in one of those small homes we passed on the long trek up." Lucia plopped her big butt on the bed next to Artorian, patting the edge so he would get up and scoot. "I'm sure it's all very important and very over my head, but I did catch pieces of conversation I was definitely not supposed to hear."

She unfurled a piece of thick cloth over his lap when Artorian moved to sit where instructed, placing the rolls in silver foil down first. "Do you like gossip?"

Artorian's hand shot to his chest. "Do *I* like gossip? Do birds live to fly?"

Lucia pleasantly snickered. "Healthy curiosity? Good. I hope it comes with a healthy appetite. Here are tacos from Ulysses' Taco Stand, with a Mangonada. Or what's left of the

Mangonada. I sort of attacked the drink when I realized there was chili in it. In the cauldron, we have garlic butter boiled crab. Be careful about the powdery one, that one is coated in cayenne and paprika. The crab needs lots of fidgety peel and puzzle work, so have the tacos first. After kicking my door down, one of the Heavenlies asked for them immediately upon manifesting, then dropped to his knees when we told him that we didn't know what those were."

She patted his head so he needn't worry. "Ulysses explained the components, got them together, set up shop as a taco stand, and—"

Lucia needed a moment. "I have never seen a Heavenly just be... happy? He was happy to be making tacos. The warmth radiating from him when he could feed people was a delight."

She smirked right after, recalling Ulysses's banter. "He dramatically cried again when we also told him that we had no idea what churros were. Then he said: 'Hold my tapatio and valentinas,' and began assembling an oil fryer out of whatever the Goblins could get him that sounded accurate enough to his needs. That man was determined to feed the world."

Artorian already had one of these mysterious tacos half-buried in his mouth by the time Lucia had moved on to the churros. The entire taco had been inhaled by the time her sentence was done. He had questions and responses, but his hands were entirely preoccupied with opening these silver-wrapped presents so he could keep scarfing breakfast down. Goblin priorities! The ones with egg and potato were particularly to his taste.

The motherly bun continued to pet his head as he ate, clearly pleased about his appetite. She was firmly resisting the urge to groom that messy mop of hair, settling for making a bigger mess of it instead. "Good kit."

When Artorian vanished his third taco, he looked up with that sparkle in his eyes for more of this promised gossip, not at all bothered by the mothering. Yvessa had made the care coming his way feel like a natural part of life. He caused problems, and those more responsible dragged him by the ear back to safety. This was true regardless of age.

He momentarily wondered what Yvessa the Caretaker, now Titania the Wisp, was up to. He felt like she would leap at the opportunity to come sit on his head through the Eternia beta foray. Thinking of it, he hadn't seen a single one so far.

Artorian stopped wondering anything when Lucia used words that made him choke on shredded chicken. "The big man said you can't take any healing abilities."

Hitting his own chest and working through the cough, Artorian looked up at her as if she just flubbed the worst joke. "*W-what?*"

The momma bun nodded with a solemn apology. "The argument was loud, and I didn't have to snoop for my ears to pick it up. Ember was not allowed to tell you, appears to have kept that promise, and included that in her grand strategy. As due to sheer coincidence, a primary healer class was whisked along with the two of you to partake in this grand adventure."

Lucia not so subtly motioned to herself.

Artorian swallowed, maintaining eye contact as understanding settled, and the scheme became clear. The smile took time to form on his face, as any wicked scheme of Ember's was a plan he'd eagerly jump into the boat of. She had planned around Tim's plans! He loved it when that happened. "Ah. I see. What a… *happy* coincidence. So lucky!"

Lucia sputtered out laughter, her paw slapping her knee until she got a hold of herself and returned to having proper human hands. "You two are such a treat! I'm not even mad. I already wanted to escape the pavilion and have for a while. Urtu is ear-breakingly loud and Hella plots like a discount villain. To find out a grand adventure awaits, and that I get to play the game in the way I want? While following people around who can benefit from my specific bag of tricks? I'm happy, precious. Very happy. It may not be petting bees, but Lucia the Luminant is simmering to shine."

"Speaking of." Artorian stuck a finger up, pausing his attack on taco number five. "What's the right thing to call you? If you told me, it slipped my mind, and I keep remembering the word Eminence."

"Eminence is for people who don't know me, or official business. Emmi, for short but professional." The motherly bun leaned down and pressed her cheek into the top of his head, grinding side to side with the bottom of her chin. "You and Ember go with Lucia. Momma bun, momma, or anything of the like that you need to yell to get my attention, works as well. I have many kits, but a special fondness for the runts in a litter, and those always manage to be the loudest. I miss the years where my busiest day involved a lung-full outcry of '*Maaaaaaaaaaaaaaa.*'"

Artorian covered his ears and considered writing to the complaints department but shrugged and took the Basher's care. He did qualify. "Nice to properly meet you, Lucia the momma bun, most eminent luminance of penitence."

He got a swat to the back of his head for his cheeky comment. Artorian grinned, the damage on his ears vindicated. The harmless clap was well-earned as Lucia stole away his last two tacos and shoved the heavy cauldron onto his lap instead. He recoiled with an *oof* as Lucia played coy. "Heard that, did you?"

"I did!" The glee was unavoidable, Artorian moving right along to breaking open arm-sized crab legs. "I'm very curious about anything that Yuki threatens people with. There's rarely anything more potent than the stories she can leverage or bring to bear. Whole Asgardian mead halls will snap to behaving if she deems it necessary."

Lucia laced her hands, safeguarding the stolen tacos from counter-theft. "You know the Lady of Ice and Frost? I've heard of a cold shoulder before, but she can make a room arctic faster than I can down a drink, and I was a member of Flasks Before Tasks!"

"*Mhm.*" The youth nodded with a disappointingly tiny hunk of crab meat in his mouth, having forgotten to properly tug when Yuki was mentioned and leaving the majority of the food stuck inside the shell. That or he was breaking the leg down wrong. The pointy bit came off first, right? Then work your way up to the big leg, so when you pull out the piece before it, those non-bones keeping the big chunk trapped couldn't bother you when you broke the main prize open. Only eating more crab would bring him this answer.

Time to brave that powdered one.

He finished that chunk of spicy treat, coughed as his eyes began to water and the heat crawled up and got into his nose, then forgot entirely what he was going to say when the suffering struck. Delicious suffering but suffering all the same.

"Cleanse." A hand movement from Lucia that waved over his head made the tingling and burning pressure in his eyes and nose fade. Unfortunately, all the flavor in his mouth went with it, and Artorian wasn't sure if that was a worthwhile trade. The layer of garlic butter on his hands getting cleaned up, he had to admit, was always a trick he'd like.

One he missed immediately.

Artorian thought it best to be polite. He was a youth again. Lucia either had no clue of his background, didn't care, or couldn't stop herself from being momma when there was a smol that needed care. Better to lean into it, and surprise her later.

That would create juicy gossip!

"Thank you, momma bun." Wondering how appreciation worked for Bashers, he copied behavior and slammed his forehead into her side. A motion that was well received as the Glitterflit went '*d'awwww*' and curled her arms around his head to love on him. A small number zero appeared above Lucia's head, the digit trailing upward before vanishing outright.

"Good kit. You're welcome, and try not to get it down the wrong hole this time. Or up. Both are terrible." Lucia flopped her ears down the sides of her head, struck by terrible flashbacks of the Basher Plain residents trying to plant cayenne fields. "Sniff not the spicy death."

"Sniff not the spicy death." Artorian mimicked her words of worldly advice. This reminded him of a similar idiom: don't eat the glowing moss. He then leaned against the Glitterflit and looked at the pot in his hands. "I think I'm full."

Lucia reclaimed all the food and rubbed his head. "Wrap yourself in the blanket and come join the huddle outside. There's a few people here to see you? All equally insistent that titles get nudged under the carpet. I haven't fully figured out who you are, kit, but either you know a dangerous number of high-rollers, or a dangerous amount of high-rollers know you. My gambling days are behind me, but there's a story here, and I want it."

Artorian chuckled. "I'm sure there's about twelve books before this one about me by now? Thirteen's in the process, and about to start the portion where I'm going to need a reminder on how damage numbers work."

Lucia threw the blanket over him with a click of the tongue and left him to wrestle with the covers. She finished her check-up with complicated, glowing hand sigils. Her incantation, on the other hand, was kept bare bones simple. The words conveyed exactly what they were meant to before she left. "Bless this mess."

By the time Artorian was out the door and wrapped up in enough soft fluff that could protect the boy from an elephant's tackle, he learned that his improvised shell was actually an insufficient amount of padding for the tackle coming his way.

Halcyon smashed into him and forced Young-torian into a serious rolling tumble. The giant Orca woman had lost none of her enthusiasm, regardless of Cy looking like she could bench press the average mountain. The ten-foot-tall humanized Orca dressed in sportswear, bound to the **Law** of **Aurum**, sounded as sweet and jovial as always. "My Dreamer!"

"Hal—!" Artorian got halfway through his mid-tackle greeting before he was gripped by the scruff of the neck and deposited next to a fire as if he'd never been tackled by Halcyon at all. He had, but Zelia the Argent cared for none of that and had teleported him to exactly where he needed to be. She was already adjusting his clothing, utterly disappointed by it.

Zelia's considerably more upright standing and self-control came with a glance to the seat under his butt, before her silver iris on black sclera eyes locked gazes to quietly ask why he was standing. Artorian had the sudden thought to sit, did so, and was greeted by a large smile as Zelia found this far more suitable. Careful not to shift her horrendously expensive-looking black and red kimono beyond a minor movement, and keep her paper umbrella away from the fire, she pressed one of her six arms to her midriff, bowing gently. "My Dreamer."

Starting to choke up at the reunion, a cold hand of ice pressed to his shoulder. He glanced up to find Yuki honest to the celestials above beaming at him. Like for once in her life she was glad to see him. A calm, cold, calculated nod from the snow lady followed before Yuki claimed the seat next to him. "My Dreamer."

Before Artorian could unchoke himself and find the words, his fourth Chosen realized he was present. Voltekka the Teslasaur slammed head-first into the youth's chest, bit into the clothing that Zelia had just got done adjusting and stole him away with arcs of copper lightning trailing behind the speedy dinosaur's path.

"Tekka! Get back here!" Halcyon boomed after Voltekka, engaging in a high-speed pursuit. "I knew you were going to do this!"

Artorian had many things to say but dropped them all and crossed his arms. For now? For now he was along for the ride. When this was over, he would sit down, ask about the game, and fill those fields in. The topic was bothering him, and it was time. A feeling that certainly had nothing at all to do with the unwelcome recollection of creatures known as cheese penguins, and a 'Brother Moon.' How does one blow up a planet again? Or a loose collection of landmass chunks connected by intelligent fondue? There had to be a better way than asking Tim for an oversized grater.

A moment of genius struck him as Halcyon tackled Tekka to the ground, sending him skyborne. Zelia caught him with seamless grace, and his butt was back on the seat in front of the fire mere moments later. Artorian felt the queasiness but was otherwise unbothered by the flow of events that had Lucia's jaw on the floor at the insanity she'd just witnessed. She saw him turn green and spoke her spell as a question rather than a statement. "Cleanse?"

"Lightning has struck my brain." Artorian stuck a single digit to the air, his complexion turning glittery before normalizing. "I've just had an apostrophe."

Yuki smirked wide, sipping hot herbal tea as she had never left the seat next to him. "That must have hurt."

CHAPTER TWENTY-TWO

Artorian did the requisite rounds of sitting in different laps as he went through the motions of reacquainting himself with Tim's version of Cal's game. He played the part of plushy as needed but kept his focus on the new screens he kept gaining access to, and saved his apostrophe for when Ember or Tim were available.

He had meant to say epiphany, but now it was a joke that stuck, and he was on the hook for his flub. Hopefully people would forget, and it would all pan out.

His cadre of Chosen had already informed him that they were not here to join him, only to sneak in momentarily and grant some technical help or offer advice. They each had to get back to tackling problems of scope. Except Voltekka. Tekka was never going to grow up, humanize, or be anything other than a clever dinosaur at heart.

Which was why Halcyon was sitting on him as he thrashed about, trying to get free.

Artorian looked over from his screens, the majority asking for input that he didn't know how to start on. "Say, Cy. Why not use that absolute Beast Authority thing? I don't actually know how it works, but he knows he'd never beat you in a fight, right? You mentioned something about always knowing for sure. Why isn't Tekka behaving?"

He then waffled on his statement. "I mean, I also had a run in with some boars where it didn't work, but with the mortal mind, I'm far too fuzzy on the why or why not."

Cy looked back and cocked her head in confusion. "That Beast-rule is absolute? That's about Beasts in the same Clan or Sept not taking action until the leader does."

Artorian shook his head. "The bit where you always know you'd win?"

The statement then hit her like a ton of bricks when it clocked in her head. "Oh! That is only under very specific circumstances! If I said that as a general statement, that is very wrong. Apologies, my Dreamer. All Beasts know the ebb and flow of how much in their favor something could go, but nothing is actually preventing us from acting against that feeling. Normally, I mean. My problem with Odin was a special case and serves as the foremost example of when it's a major problem. Because with Odin, I knew for certain that I would lose, thus had trouble getting into a headspace where I could fight him properly. Or see myself win. That's why we developed Speedball. Otherwise? A C-ranked Beast will fight an A-ranked one… because. Pick a reason out of a hat and nine out of ten times, it'll be good enough."

Artorian was still confused. "But… Blanket?"

Halcyon rolled her head from shoulder to shoulder, grumbling. "My Dreamer, this is not so much something to explain, as it is something to experience. You're asking about a very complex set of feelings, reactions, and senses all going off based on very sudden, acute, and hair-trigger changes. If you want this answer, you're going to have to experience it directly. There are going to be times where you can stare a Beast down, and it will just know, and concede. There will be equally identical times where that same Beast will hit you with a glare and just don't care, and I hope you were planning to bustle because now you have to tussle. Primal instinct is how Beasts do."

Halcyon tapped the side of her head. "The higher thought stuff? A Beast is more likely to use it to improve the thing that it was already good at. Why be merely scary, when you can be extra scary? Beasts really don't care about broadening their horizons that much, only to be better in their specific niche. Additional modifiers don't mean that a Beast is going to surprise you with an entirely new theme to its skillset. They are going to look at those modifiers and bend them to improve the one thing they were already focusing on. The same is true for a majority of monsters in Eternia. The real monsters are the people you meet along the way that don't do that, and can... What did you call it, Zelia?"

The silver-eyed Arachnid looked up from her blueprints and number napkins. "Diversifying their portfolio. There is nothing scarier than facing a player with an unknown number of tricks in their bag, when it is very likely that they are good at all of them. This is one of the three reasons why trying to focus players into Specializations and Law-type concepts is so important. The support dungeons can't plan for everything, and Tim has to be focused on content that will suffice for everyone. So in addition to bolstering people's *raison d'être*; the Administrators, Dungeons, Game Masters, and Quest Adjudicators suffer less headache. Because while our issue isn't going to be the broad numbers, it is most certainly going to be those few individuals who strive ahead, aim at the sky, and go *wheeeee*."

Zelia folded her napkin covered in numbers after shooting her hand up to the stars. "I don't know how big of an influx of people we're expecting to save when the doors open, and we're likely going to have a good clean millennium of the game actually running before they do, but even my napkin math has the number of starting souls we should expect begin with a B. Eternia can't handle more than ten players right now. H is doable when the sun is sorted, and K can come in when The Pale has been debugged, but we have no hope of getting to M while Barry's bunches of Abyss are lying around. Especially if we don't at least have nine floating continents back in place."

She cleared her throat, pushing the conversation back to Halcyon. "I got off topic. Please return to your point about Beast niches, Cy."

"That." Halcyon pressed her hand into her chest. "My niche is being an Orca Matriarch. I excel and focus on being in charge of a pod of otherwise problematic children composed entirely of top-shelf food-chain predators. Taking non-top-shelf Beasts under my fin isn't out of the way for me. It's part of making a good social structure that allows the entire whole—which the non-Orcas are now a part of—to grow, thrive, play in the sod, lead even better lives, and build up the pod."

Proud of her own rhyme, she shot a sharp-toothed grin to Yuki, who chuckled and wrote it down for her on a sheet of ice paper. Halcyon then gave Artorian a much shorter answer. "On Tekka? None of it will work. It doesn't matter how much ferocity I exert. He will fight me. The entire postal code's worth of my behind, on the other tailfin, works tremendously well."

Artorian dropped his question and put his hands up.

He leaned back on Lucia's lap since it appeared to be her turn for the Torian-Teddy Bear and returned to studying the screens. "Different question. Rank and rarity currently do... nothing?"

"Those Pylons are dormant." Zelia cut to the chase, her six hands now full of fabric that she was working into a starter set for her Dreamer, having picked out which blueprint she was going to use. "That's going to be a common theme. I hear Eternium is working on brand new banks, but if he turns functions on for you, they also turn on for everyone else. Currently, your opponents would get far more use out of this."

"Joy." Artorian's tone fell as flat as his mood. "So, I'm really only looking at effects, interactions of those effects, and how well they scale or play nice with the numbers in my character sheet?"

Yuki replied but didn't look up from her scribbling after handing Zelia a brand new frost needle for more sewing. "That is correct. Items, in particular, are vague. The name will show up, and if you're lucky, something about the item you're holding. The full breakdown of material, rarity, damage, special quality, and such? Forget it. Those will begin populating on new items as the Pylons become available. Expect to be hit by a slow trickle of ever fancier functions. Tim is trying hard to get the groundwork stable and steady. Once things work as intended, we can describe them as intended. The only items you'll find with full descriptions are older ones. They do exist, but for the most part, they live in someone's inventory. For now, if you pick something up that doesn't do what you think it should do…"

Artorian rubbed a growing crease on his forehead. "This is Cal's adventure in Liminal items all over again."

Yuki had no good words of comfort for him. The situation, as her stories had it, was fairly similar. Artorian leaned over to pat the top of her hand as a 'don't worry about it,' then returned to his screen and finally found a section that appeared to be interactive. "That looks promising."

One tap later, and the values on his statistic wobbled in place. Progress! "*Aha*! That made the values move. In place. Made them move in place. On second thought, that did nothing. I have no idea why they are wobbling."

He tapped his strength rating, and a prompt came up. "Never mind! Activity is afoot!"

Finally excited that things were happening, he pulled the prompt close like a physical panel that could freely be moved in space and gave it a read. "Rolling your statistics. To roll your strength attribute, push the prompt button that says 'roll.' To take the average of your strength attribute roll instead of rolling, push the button that says, 'average.' To quit, press… yeah, yeah."

He knew what the first button might do but didn't understand the second one. Of course, he pressed it. Ten points added themselves to his strength score, though Artorian felt not one iota different. He shrugged and copied that action for all the values. Twenties were better than tens, and he was still looking for something more interesting to delve into when it was all said and done.

Now that his numbers were settled, he tapped the empty space where a name should be. He didn't expect it to work, but an empty prompt box did come up. "*Hmmm*. This one might be broken."

"What's broken?" Ember's voice cut through his lull, though Artorian gladly made a hand motion to the screen that he was looking at. She was leading the pack of Incarnates, but aside from a polite smile and head nod, the rest of them vanished to their separate ways.

Tim hustled over to scoop Yuki up. "Be right back!"

Yuki made an absolutely incredibly cute noise to Artorian's extreme delight and massive grin. She fussed at Tim and slapped his shoulder but was clearly not resisting when he stole her away.

A spark of pink light pulsed near him, and Artorian high-fived the color without thinking about why. T'was just the right thing to do. Something about glorious success in the pursuits of **Love**. When nobody reacted to him interacting with empty air, his attention turned to Zelia when she mouth-clicked for him, as if attempting to do so with mandibles that she did not have.

She had goodies!

"This set is designed to provide Endurance Bolstering, Cold Resistance, Frost Resistance, and a feature I call Extra Fluff. You don't need it, but it will make you happy. Three sets done, only the Glitterflit gave me sizing difficulties, as she's the only one who needed her clothing to morph with her during shape changes." Zelia folded up his new clothes on the spot Yuki had occupied, and politely performed her midriff bow.

"This is all the time I have, my Dreamer. Call me if you need me." Zelia teleported herself out. Artorian thought she may have Slipstreamed, but he had no hope of sussing the difference out in his current state.

Reminding himself that he'd be a Mage again one day, and could ask then, he picked Zelia's latest gift up and started working to get it on. The Yuki-themed attire already looked pretty before he had it equipped. The white, blue, and silver outfit was insulated, very fluffy around the neck and wrists, and outright comfortable. As all of Zelia's crafts are always were. He put his finger to his mouth and kissed them away. "Chef's kiss, Zelia. Chef's kiss."

With people returning to their work, this left Artorian, Ember, Lucia, and Halcyon to enjoy the crackling fire with significantly more peace, as Voltekka had finally managed to escape due to Halcyon's kindness, scrabbling away in a crack of copper lightning.

Artorian turned his screen towards Ember, thinking it was a good time. "I'm making slow headway; this doesn't seem correct. Good meeting?"

"Busy meeting." Ember walked right up to Lucia, motioned with her hand for Artorian to scoot, and claimed herself a spot in the Basher's lap. "Tell you when it's time. Need company now. Small disagreements with Tim."

"Is it the bit about me not getting to take healing abilities?" Artorian rattled off the first thought in his head, but the squeeze that Ember applied to Lucia's thigh, and accompanying yelp from the Basher, made him snap his mouth shut. "I said nothing."

"You said what you said, sugar, and you're right." Ember threw the topic coal onto the fire. When the door to the tavern got kicked down, you addressed it. "There's a massive problem with any new Pylons related to healing. They have a scent that we can't work out of the crystalline structure yet, and that scent causes unwelcome attention. We've got some older Pylons already set up that don't have this problem, but because we had to take a bunch of banks off the grid that allowed those functioning Pylons to form connections to new people, it's one abyss of a wiring mess down there."

Artorian motioned up at Lucia, believing the smuggled-in Glitterflit's earlier gossip. "Ergo, the reason why her toys will work fine, but the ones that I would want to pick up, don't?"

Ember sighed and nodded. "Healers, and healing-related abilities are going to be picked on when we get them to work. Until that scent is gone, people will invent reasons to go after healers, and we already have a whole sub-category of monsters that specifically think people with health-restoring tricks are extra tasty. Heal-Aggro is a very real and pervasive problem, and we just aren't going to turn that around anytime soon. Neither from monsters being of the opinion that a healer is a bigger threat than a damage dealer, nor because they taste twice as good."

Artorian took that information in stride as best he could. "What you are telling me is that there are Pylons with complete abilities, and Pylons with incomplete abilities. That I do not get to play with the former and am locked to the latter. While many of the problems I am likely to encounter has that scenario flipped? Unable to acquire new abilities, but in possession of functional, complete toys?"

Ember pulled a stick from her spatial bag, shoved on some marshmallows she'd acquired from Adam, and handed them out so they could all roast the treats and enjoy a sweet snack. "That's the quick and dirty, yes."

She half-glanced at his prompt, seeing the issue right away. "These Pylons aren't as flexible as our previous batch. Not yet. You have to start by filling in a name and work your way down. I actually have no idea how you managed to change your core statistics without going down the line. Did you mess with it to the point that the Pylons were shivering in their boots?"

Artorian chuckled. "I did get the numbers to wobble!"

Ember rubbed the bridge of her nose, tore into her roasted marshmallow, then leaned over to press their heads together. Lucia saw this as an excellent opportunity to hold them both for added support, and neither of the small children in her care appeared to mind.

Ember swallowed her sugary confection and had found the words to turn this around. She innocently waggled her stick at the fire. "So tell me about this apostrophe."

CHAPTER TWENTY-THREE

"Epiphany!" Artorian shot upright from Lucia's lap and threw his brand new bright blue beanie down. He snatched it up right away to brush it free from leaves, then shoved it right over his ears in case Zelia decided to take that exact moment to pop back.

Artorian instinctively jumped when he heard the *pop*.

"Back!" Tim's timing was impeccable, popping back into the exedra, and quickly finding a seat on the semicircular Grecian stone bench. He brushed some leaves and petals from the spot next to him, expecting Yuki to come back on her own terms. He noted a flaw and adjusted the apsidal podium. "Is he about to tell us about his apostrophe?"

"Epiphany!" Artorian turned in place, walked two paces back to Lucia, and buried his face into her stomach, letting free the groaning yell noise of great childish grievance.

Lucia proceeded to bite her tongue and pet the kit's head. This was all far too funny, and she was still far too busy puzzling the hierarchy together. The only thing that was easy to deduce was that Halcyon fiercely triggered her need to throw shields around like candy, and that you listened to Yuki, with an 'or else' attached. The conversation earlier had been very revealing, and after seeing the massive Orca woman cuddle the kit she was adopting, she felt much better about life. That such a massive powerhouse could be so tender, openly warm and sappy, and gush about how nice it was to see him again, definitely warmed her heart.

Little Artorian had lots of people who loved him.

The Arachnid lady in human form acted far more formal when it came to showing her fondness, but Lucia swiftly puzzled out that Zelia worked with different love languages than Halcyon. Cy, the Daimyo in charge by default unless she deferred, was all about physical touch. Zelia, seamstress and eternally diligent XO, was one for gift giving with a strong second in acts of service. Yuki, the frostiest of snowflakes and wielder of all the knowledge you did not want her to have, was a hoarder of quality time. Voltekka was... not going to qualify. Tekka was one of those 'no take, only throw' boys. So Lucia didn't continue the thread.

Lucia herself was firmly in the camp of words of affirmation, while she figured that Ember was deeply invested in acts of service, with a growing fondness for physical touch. If Ember learned of something she could do that would make her boy's life less burdensome, she had plans for it. Or plans for those plans. Or plans for *those* plans. Likely with the direct help of the six-armed, kimono-wearing spider, who knew everything.

Ember had thrown up her own character sheet and clicked her tongue. "Still stuck."

This opportunity made Artorian push up from Lucia, roll right over to mush his cheek against hers, and take in the information that Ember was fighting. To assist, of course. Not at all to avoid talking about the apostrophe. "Can I help?"

"Maybe." Ember bit her thumb, then moved between the character screens with far greater proficiency than Artorian had managed. She stopped on the main design for the Character Sheet, showing the compact list that they would be using as the default state. Artorian recognized the organization as the

same detailed entries from his first foray, and watched Ember
tap the name entry. A prompt came up, and she tapped it
several times, uncertain and without answers. "I need an
Eternia character name. The reason you know. Anything that
comes to mind?"

"Yes." Artorian whisked himself from Lucia's lap while
holding his hands behind his back, pacing around the center
circle in the middle of the exedra with an immediate mumble to
his words. He paused in place to face her and ask some key
questions. There was more to a name than was visible on the
surface. "Not a suggestion, but a question. How are you with
War?"

"I *am* War." Ember straightened up, her body language
fierce, strict, and direct. "That will never leave me. The body
doesn't do much to change that. Not something I'd want as a
game name."

Artorian nodded, then faltered in his step when he felt a
hand on his shoulder. Not again. Now who was it? He didn't
fight the influence when he glanced to see the armored, scarred,
bloody gauntlet. The perks of pink eyes was to see the Heavenly
intruding, rather than merely have the awareness. Something
about reality changed when one was about. A feature that some
of them seemed aware of, and able to suppress.

Artorian heard the gravely hush when his mouth began to
part, and thoughts of different questions formed. He instinctively felt that it would be taken poorly if he looked behind him.
So he did not. The gauntlet patted him with appreciation, the
edge of a Corinthian helmet dipping into view as words were
whispered for his ears only.

An opportunity for growth presented itself, but it would
require him to make a painful choice. Artorian nodded not to
himself, but to the hidden entity doing its best to remain as
such. He agreed with the whispers that brushed past his ears, so
he wet his lips, and asked Ember another question, as currently
nobody but him had noticed the additional company. "How are
you with **Love**?"

Ember's expression broke into a myriad of blush colors. "Sugar!"

Artorian grinned like a cheeky boy, then let the expression fade as images played across his vision. His eyes stopped seeing what was in front of him, and instead saw a reel that played like a fantasy. "I'm sorry, dear. That was to distract you. We have company."

That detail snapped everyone to silent attention.

Artorian gathered grit and narrated what he was being shown. "I'm being gifted... I don't think they are memories. The perspective is wrong. Emby, they're of you? I see Grandma Ember, the Ancient Elf, in heaviest armor. Her Iridium eyes burn as they see the future, but not as hot as the silvered flame wreathing her weapons. She strides across torched fields, and into the fray."

He wet his mouth, starting to hear sound. "An enemy called out: 'You are surrounded!' To which you lit the wrath of your blades and replied with coldest heat: 'All I am surrounded by is fear, and dead men.' A blur of death haunts your wake."

Artorian flexed his hands, trying to keep up. "I see fields of broken bodies. Scores of dead men. In her approach to a tent, giants in equally heavy armor take a knee in unison at your passing, their spears aglow with Mana-fueled might. Shoulder to shoulder, they form the path on which you tread.

"Someone attempts to address you in a tent, but you crush his skull in your hand, and stride through to the other side. Standing on the edge of a cliff, you oversee an ongoing battle. One that you have just now realized you have lost. In that moment, on seeing the last flag of your birthplace be inciner-ated on what may as well be a pyre, there is a light that leaves your eyes. The burning torch in your sight fizzles. You see a path that, much like the cliff you stand at, has no further way to go."

He swallowed, trying not to frown as he still couldn't see the people in front of him. Only the reel. "The giants behind you expect you to charge. The glorious last hurrah. You walk past them, telling them to do as they please. A hundred years pass until you are back at that cliff's edge. The giants are gone, but their weapons and armor have been placed in the locations where they took a knee. Hollow, scorched, and vacant of the souls that you knew. The sight over the cliff is desolate. Glassed into obscurity. There was never any going back."

The reel ended.

Reality filtered back into his pink eyes to see Ember gritting her jaw, wet lines running down her face. "You took Ember as a name twice, to overwrite what I can only assume to be visions that someone is feeding me. There's a message with the reel, and I don't particularly want to play messenger here, but I am a firm believer in people having more information to work with being the better option."

He shook his head, disliking the particular sensation of violence inherent in the sensation on his shoulder. He squirmed in place but relayed what was requested. "They seem to know you well, and there's some confusion about a question you may at one point have asked. They say: You know better than us that no amount of trying to be someone else changes who we once were. The best we can do is work to be better than who we were yesterday. If we even want to be who we were yesterday. To compare the progress of oneself, only to oneself. Being Ember again for the purpose of replacing who you were is only going to lead to heartache. Accepting who you were and working through the last vestiges of those painful memories, is the unfortunate truth that will lead to the actual growth that you want to accomplish. So when it comes to a name, dearest love of ours, then we think that during this game that allows you to do exactly that? You should be the God of War, and accept that you are one with violence, as much as **Violence** is one with you."

Ember, Tim, Cy, and Lucia remained deathly silent.

Halcyon was on the brink of jumping up and fighting a threat she could not see. Lucia's hands were glowing with a spell that was half a millimeter away from finishing. Ember had shot up from Lucia's lap and was gripping the new arctic clothing over her own sternum with fear in her eyes. Tim had gone pale as he looked not at Artorian, but the vague outline of what was behind the child-sized philosopher. He couldn't see the Heavenly, but two particularly pointed **Law**-emphasized words gave him a lot to work with, and a lot to be worried about.

Lucia and Cy felt the tension bristle cross over their hide and fur, but only Lucia and Ember had both the clear line of sight, and the clarity of sight, to the two imposing beings hovering behind Artorian. Ember knew exactly who was intervening and showing her boy things she never wanted him to see, and that was causing her more dread than any fight she might be in.

Unfortunately, neither was **Love**. Though she believed the duo on their statement that they loved her, for she had spilled many offerings at both of their altars.

Tim, with far more insight and power in the situation, made no threatening moves. The Dungeon hadn't noticed that he'd gotten on his feet, but he was using dungeon senses to try to figure out which Heavenly or Heavenlies had just intruded on what was meant to be a pleasant number-crunching session. The outright ominous feeling he was getting also did not bode well.

Not all Heavenlies were kind and talkative.

Artorian felt the squeeze on his shoulder as the sign of a job well done. The intent of the squeeze hit harder than the actual pressure, but he nodded regardless, saying nothing about the figure as it left. The harsh, ominous presences of pure danger vanished with it, and Artorian tried to smile as he looked at Ember. "I have a name, dear. Are you sure you want it? The source isn't entirely mine."

The Incarnate in mortal form frowned, deeply conflicted. She opened and closed her fists as Tim exhaled hard and fell down to sit on the exedra bench. Halcyon looked around in confusion as she had been completely preoccupied with locating a threat, knowing that it came and went before her social functions returned. Both of the Beasts calmed, but their hard-beating hearts would take time to slow.

"Goddess of War?" Ember had to wet her own mouth before repeating the qualifier. Her thoughts raced as there was a lot more to that. That had been an old nickname of hers, one that she wasn't too particularly proud of these days. The Blade of War phase of her life was fraught with events she didn't want to remember, but it appeared that Artorian wasn't the only one who was being forced to face some regrets. "I need... I need a minute."

Artorian said nothing, nodded, and waited for her. He wanted her to have agency, not having expected to be the sudden bearer of Heavenly news. He noted that Tim had fallen on his rear, and momentarily wondered why he wasn't having the same problem. Everyone else had gotten hit by a presence wave that made their warnings flare and hair stand up, but he appeared to be decently alright in comparison.

One empowered inhale later, Ember dropped into the mode of a stoic and tackled the opening as she did best. Directly. She pulled the naming prompt close, gritting her teeth. A name from her boy would have been ideal. A tribulation from a **Law**? She would not be found wanting. She looked at Artorian with meaning, expecting an entry. "In the end, it will always be my choice. No matter what life throws at me, nor how curved the ball. It's not the answer I was hoping for, but it is the answer I will take. Give me my name, sugar. It does not matter what the Heavenlies think they are doing. I will make it mine, and the meanings attached shall be how I mold them."

That strength of character comforted Artorian. He felt relief, nodded, and drew breath. Power gathered in the vicinity of his mouth. Not one, but two Heavenlies finding this chess move in the universe particularly important. Tim's dark choir leaned onto the scene as Artorian began to speak, his voice slowly subsumed by greater powers as the mechanical organ music grew to swell. "She who is Violence, and War."

Three voices spoke instead of one from Artorian's frame,

with his own completely drowned out beneath the deeper, darker, more throaty depths of the other two. A wave of pressure pulsated away from his location, his own being unharmed as gravity in the area trembled upon the spoken existence of the word.

"Astarte."

CHAPTER TWENTY-FOUR

Ember added the name to the prompt without looking at it, her Iridium eyes burning into the space behind her boy as she challenged the interlopers who dared interfere. Heavenlies or not, there would come a day where she would confront those two about this. That day, **Laws** would come to know the new description of strife, and a location known as Geneva would need to have a convention. **Violence** and **War** would both relearn why one must respectfully cast their gaze away when confronted by the glare of the **Sun**.

She finalized the entry with a confirmation.

"I am Astarte. Goddess of War."

A twinkle joined Ember's expression when the voices behind Artorian fled, the rumble of music vanishing with them. Their disappearance came accompanied by a small victorious smile, as her character sheet also filled in her class. "Plus a little bit of love. Just because I am accepting a tribulation does not mean I don't also get to throw a wrench in the plan."

She then moved her arms to ask for a hug, which her boy responded to by squeezing her tight. Her voice was full of worry after she calmed from her anger, her hands kneading his back.

"Do you think of me differently? I don't know how much you saw, but I will not hide that I did not want you to see."

"See what, dear?" Artorian pulled away gently, purely so he could press their foreheads together. "See what I already knew? Knowing more about your past isn't going to change anything at this point, Dawny. I'm only concerned about the way forward. If you're happy to walk with me, and work with me when things come up, that's all I can ask. In fact, I'm the one who is glad you are not upset. I was not expecting a hand on the shoulder."

Ember chuckled but didn't alter the proximity or the pose. "I know the Heavenly drill. I've spoken to my fair share of them. They're all from different times. Different eras. Cultures. Belief systems. All stuck in the repeating cycle of existence that they each try to chip at and improve. They flock to me as if *I'm* the safe one to talk to. Between myself as the Precursor of the new **Law** of **Sun**, and Tatum the Progenitor—the less said about his **Law** the better—we're unpleasantly popular. Which makes me all the more thankful to have Lucia around."

She raised two fingers to add clarity. "Lexicon of the Heavenlies: Precursor? The node comes first, and the guide second. Progenitor? The guide exists first, and they lead to the creation of their conceptual node. Bringing it into existence."

Ember buried her face into his neck. "Really though. Not mad? I killed a lot of people, sugar. An incalculable amount of people. Many not in a gentle fashion. I earned my reputation. There is a reason that people act with deference, regardless of my status, position, or cultivation rank. I was once a fairly accurate description of evil. You would not have... approved."

"Are you that person now?" Artorian shifted to pull her head against his shoulder, allowing him to knead over her back in turn. He found her surprisingly compliant, but this was not a detriment. "I don't believe you are. I believe you've put in a lot of effort to figure out where the lines are, and you've been open and accepting of both comments and critique. Don't think I don't know about that conversation you had with Henry. I don't recall if it was before, after, or during the act of me making the whistling mountains by shooting a hole through them with your Damocles bow? But I am aware that when he came to you with concerns, you gave some very open-minded responses. I was immensely proud of you. That has not changed."

He pecked her temple and pressed his cheek to her head after. "So what if who you were is not someone of who I would have approved? Look at you now. Striving for the better. I know that in The Pale we're going to need to get our hands dirty. That didn't particularly bother me. That we were rushed? That does. Are you happy with the name, dear? I admit I have no idea what it means."

Ember pulled away, looking conflicted. She had an apostrophe of her own when she recalled her earlier words. "It will mean what I want it to mean. Some Heavenly may want me to get over something, but it's my name, and my life, and I will decide what happens to it."

She took him by the hand and tugged him back to the edge of the exedra so they could sit. She spared a glance at Tim, who had stepped away to pull up a few hundred screens and scan through them. The man looked a combination of baffled, and drowning in confusion as to how a Heavenly, possibly two, could have slipped by him. This was *his* Soul Space!

Lucia and Halcyon had retreated to their own corner, having given the rest of the group some privacy while chattering up a storm about their own feelings on the matter, complete with the both of them throwing around Artorian-quality hand motions. As Beasts, they had experienced far more visceral reactions to the event. With each of them knowing a part of the story concerning Heavenlies that the other did not, they had plenty to chitter about.

"I think it's fine." Ember decided as she moved one leg over the other. "It's a game name. I'll roll with it. I'll roll with the base class that decided to assign itself as well. Goddess of War is intense as a base class, and really should be a specialization, but it's fine. We still need to connect the Soul Forge and make certain that cultivation and game progress are properly connected. That's more important to me right now. Having more ideas to add to the great work, than the capacity to implement them, isn't anything new. We have time."

Ember was sated with her choices. "Astarte is fine, sugar. What about yours? The game name can be anything, but I'd prefer if we didn't have another emotional intervention? One scare like that is enough for me. I was devoured by the thought you'd think differently of me at seeing any chunk of my history. Though, I did like the Onslaught variant of my Iridium armor that you likely saw. The version you knew me in was the Deep-Sea version. We can get into why an A-ranked Fire Mage needed armor meant for the bottom of the ocean another time, okay?"

Artorian's apostrophes just kept coming, conjuring genius ideas. He clapped his hands together, drew a symbol and a number three in the air. "Where there is war, there must also be love. So you may call me: Less than Three."

"Okay, Three." Ember grinned, her chin leaning on her palm. She was okay, her boy didn't feel any different, the name she would overcome, and no important pillars had been shaken. She was good, and her heart settled. That meant she could get right back to being a pain in his butt. "Time for that epiphany."

"Ember!" Artorian moved away in mock shock, a hand pressed to his brand new fluffy white and blue winter attire. "You wound me! After I was so supportive? You... Wait. You said epiphany. Why did I think that you said apostrophe?"

Tim loudly sat himself down next to them with an old man's grunt, having thrown all his screens into the bin when he'd clearly not found any positive results. "Yes! Tell me the apostrophe! I'd like to get started with your numbers and whatnot, there's an entire fondue of sticky problems that I'd like to have removed from my hair as soon as possible."

Artorian felt neither mirth nor enjoyment. He wanted a nice, smooth, easy conversation at this point. "You know I was going to have fun and make a big deal out of this, but now I'm spent. So I'm just going to tell you flat and monotone. Have the bugs eat the moon brother. There. That's my apostrophe. Make cheese a healing type Pylon. Then we can have what's left as a combination of trophy, currency, food, and potion replacement. I also don't remember where I cobbled these thoughts together from, but if the bugs are Vampiric, and Vampiric was one of those tags or qualifiers that caused injury when afflicted by healing? That's a big discount in an expensive store."

He motioned at the ceiling, knowing the sky was fake. "We ignite the sun, Bugmageddon eats the cheese. We then deal with Bugmageddon because bugs can be swatted. The cheese moon and connected asteroids up there give me the creeps, and I have no idea how to handle an opponent that is obscenely colossal unless you've got some more Ragna Rocks lying around, fully charged. Even then, I no longer have Accelerator, and cannot get the glorious explosion damage to the location it needs to be. I do not want to deal with being cheesed, or fondued, or any of these penguin things."

He motioned at himself, and then in a general 'out there' direction. "There are problems that I can handle, and problems I cannot. The swarm of bugs? Bug Zappers are in my wheelhouse. Moon-sized cheese overminds obsessed with adding holes to people, who I really hope doesn't judge threat level and likability like the last Niflheim Pontiff did, based on how you've treated cows? No thank you. Not with all the crackers in the universe. There is neither a Wallace nor Gromit who can convince me to go visit."

He then motioned at a completely different part of the ceiling, purely to make the point that he was changing focus. "I am here to remove whatever annoyance Barry left behind. My cultivation being restored while I go through those motions is a delightful double whammy. Anything else? That's just in the way and needs a strikethrough on the to-do list. I have zero interest in being fair, playing fair, or really doing anything other than what the cheese has already done to the place. I want all the tools and toys that will let me rig the fight. I would like to trivialize this combat as much as possible. Preferably without a single pun ever being flung my way."

Tim tapped his fingers together, considering the outburst with calculating finesse. "I did have Flash Runes from the Elves that I'm to teach you. How do you feel about those?"

Artorian slapped the bench and couldn't believe it. "Those are *done*? I told Brianna yesterday!"

Ember cleared her throat, leaning over to him. "Been a bit more than a few days, sugar."

Tim boisterously laughed when Artorian slapped himself on the forehead, having completely slipped up on that fact. "As soon as Brianna got me the initial plans and schematics from Gomei, I knew what you were trying to do. Your fingerprints were all over that pie, no matter how hard Gomei tried to take credit. Flash Runes are an excellent idea! A nice filler for a gap in the repertoire of external cultivators. It'll be Flash Incantations or the like for C-rankers, but the whole gist of performing the trick with your Aura instead of your body is magnificent. I saw it. I liked it. I built it properly. Gomei's version had a strangely large number of little quirks that would prove fatal to any humans that used it. *Tsk tsk*."

"You found time to do that?" Artorian raised a brow while turning to look at Tim, Ember tugging him in so she could lay her arm over his shoulders.

Tim raised a hand to deny that assumption. "I *made* time. There is a difference. There is an order of operations to problems getting solved in my Soul Space. There are people who are optimal for that solution. There are toys which are optimal for those people to pick up in order to accomplish that goal. Henry and Marie, as example, wanted to help, but one glance at their history had Yuki put them on ice. After a very lengthy, angry, ice-cold lecture, she shoved both of them into memory cores as a punishment. She had her own version of an angry response to what Marie did to you."

Tim momentarily stared out into space. "Best if you don't ask what Zelia did. That is one *scary* dungeon Lady."

CHAPTER TWENTY-FIVE

Artorian's gaze landed on Lucia and Halcyon when Tim turned introspective. The Beast ladies had moved even farther away to show off their game abilities to the other, completely absorbed by the excitement as a series of tail slams and martial arts maneuvers exploded against a bewildering array of luminous shields. Their forms darting into the distance and sparkling along the sky as bright, shimmering lights of back-and-forth action. Lucia's movement line remained recognizable as a mixture of white and gold, whereas Halcyon's line stood out more as an ocean blue, mingled with white and black. He wondered if the lights would be colored differently if their attire or equipment changed. Would Halcyon's super heavy Daimyo armor make her darker and imposing?

Artorian nodded and let that be. "Cy didn't do anything?"

Tim made a face where he physically contained himself, preventing the laughter coming out of his nose. "Cy was ready to turn people into pretzels but arrived during Zelia's turn. Cy put her weapons away and apologized every step of her tactical retreat back out of the door. Like I said, Zelia is a very scary dungeon. Currently Henry and Marie are being returned to

Cal. Quietly, mind you. To live out some life in a remote patch of land until my Midgard is ready for their brand of activity. They made quite the stir, and while I look forward to the two of them getting a round of kingdom building going in Eternia, there's going to be a lot of fighting to do when they get their chance. I know there's a lot of questions buried in that information, but let it go for now."

Artorian accepted, then waited as Tim's introspective mumbling sounded like it was about his idea of getting rid of the moon brother. He felt as if other problems were a larger concern, but this one was so in his face that he couldn't let it go.

Tim sat back and laced his thick fingers on his lap as he considered the apostrophe. A moment of silence lapsed before he grunted, satisfied. "Healing cheese as a trap. I like it. The bugs are going to be a pain, but they'll be enemies that are more reasonable. Brother Moon is… Admittedly, I should have actually intervened and not let that get out of hand, but I soft-promised my Wisps to have a rather severe non-intervention policy. Which is also why help is so prized. My attention needs to be on the very functions of the game that one can build mechanics on, and it really does need all my work time. Yuki has thankfully convinced them that it should not take all of my free time as well, and Oberon had a very difficult time facing the combined front of Titania and Yuki on the matter. So I have time to myself that I can use for my endless extra projects, but it did let me get Flash Runes underway."

He clapped his hands together, clearing his own mental buffer. "Enough of that. Let's talk about character sheets. We've got some limitations and need to fill that ledger in from the top down. I see you picked a… name? Artorian, how did you get symbols into the prompt field? What is Less than Three?"

Artorian beamed, motioning at himself. "It's me!"

"Very funny. You realize that's stuck now?" Tim glared at him as if he was a librarian quietly judging a book being returned late over the rim of his spectacles. He then whisked

Artorian's new character sheet to the forefront so everyone could see it. "At least now I can fix this."

One tap on Artorian's race later, the words Nascent Being filled themselves in. Tim decided to save himself some headache, and more distractions. "Don't ask. Find out."

The dungeon then tapped his class entry, leaning forward to rest his elbows on his knees while holding his own hands. "Generalist is not available. A lot is not available. I also won't be giving you any hints or suggestions. I can only shoot ideas down."

Artorian rubbed his chin. Given what he was here to do… "Janitor."

Tim moved his hand to the prompt, expecting a rejection. When the field filled in with the class without problems, he looked perplexed and flustered. "*Uhhhh*. I don't think that was supposed to work."

He tapped the prompt again, but it denied him with an upset beep. The field had been filled. "That's there then. Hope you're not making terrible jokes. Profession?"

Artorian leaned into Ember, who was stifling her own laughter at her boy being a doofus. "Dream Weaver still on the table? I know I went hard on bows last time, but I think I need to freshen it up. Knowing that I can actually enter and exit at any point this time around frees me up on the coping front."

Tim made a comical error sound. "Dream Weaver doesn't seem to be free. Well, available. Assigning doesn't cost you anything. Dream Weaver would not work well without the accompanying title either. You do have multiple slots if your profession idea does not pan out, those are easy to open."

Artorian scratched his head, not wanting to duplicate his last go around. "Professions were meant for the purposes of finances, I think? Never really used them like that."

Ember waggled her hand. "As an option. Professions were mostly used by happy-go-lucky crafters who wanted to make all their own things."

Artorian didn't feel like that helped, flipping through his

mental rolodex for options. "Something concerning Flash Runes would be excellent, or while I have the intrusive thought, Bonescripting. I know I have them, but I never really understood what any of it was about. Could be a nice time to turn that around. I don't know how Artifacting factors in these days. No... that wasn't a profession."

"Bonescripting works very well, and you are correct. I will add Artifacting as a backup but expect someone to change the wording. I think that I can make it work." Tim worked diligently, adding the entry and resolving a few errors when they appeared. "Flash Runes are going to be Abilities bolstered by Skills, and I mean the capital A and capital S versions. When referring to abilities and skills in *my* prompts that you do not see capitalized, those are the mundane variants which describe what you can do, and how well you can do it. If you see them with capital letters, those refer to the versions that cost special energy and stamina."

Artorian crossed his arms and leaned his head back. "I never did get the difference explained to me by Yvessa. Is there a particular difference between the four aside from the capital letters, and that some use limited game resources?"

Tim rubbed a growing crease on his forehead. "By ability, I mean something that you are able to do. To jump is an ability. Breathing is an ability. Photosynthesis is an ability. The possession of the means or skill to do something. The very basic and broad 'can do this thing at all' is what I mean by a non-capital A ability. By a skill, no capital letter, I am talking about how well you are able to do that particular thing. Also called proficiency or expertise. If an ability refers to a lever switch of 'can you do this,' yes or no? Then a skill refers to the grade, and difference between photosynthesizing poorly, and photosynthesizing well."

The dungeon made visible two different dungeon master charts. "You may remember from last time that your Skills and Abilities were separated in two distinct lists, the version with the capital letter. I said before that Abilities cost mana and Skills cost stamina, but that gets mired and proven incorrect rather quickly. There are nine energy types, of which mana and stamina are two, with dozens upon dozens of different names for those nine types. Some Abilities use stamina, and some Skills use mana. Some tricks use health! Some spells cost experience. There's even toys that eat up your attributes or skill points as fuel per use. So perhaps it's easier to categorize the difference as one subset belongs to a game, those with the capital letters; and one subset belongs to reality, those without the capital letters. Expect prompts not to... be as consistent as I might want."

Tim then pulled the other two charts in so all four were at the forefront. "While we're still in part using the mundane descriptions when we speak about the gamified versions, because a capital A Ability *is* gamified; breaking that entry down by rank, level, and measurable instances in difference is necessary. There is a difference between you being able to jump, as that act being something you are simply able to do, and to Jump with a capital J. Using the gamified version, we are now adding an energy cost, and significantly increasing the output of that particular act. A C-ranker normally cannot jump up to the clouds and bounce on them like platforms, but as a mortal with a gamified body, C-ranker or not; to Jump and Bounce with Abilities and Skills ought to be feasible. This wouldn't be much of a game if it wasn't fun, and you couldn't grow through your intended path of difficulties."

Artorian squeezed his eyes closed, conflicted on a detail. "Aren't we doing the opposite with Mana? Mana with the capital letter is the real stuff, while mana without the capital letter is the game variant that isn't remotely the same?"

"Correct." Tim agreed, then paused as he realized that order was flipped from the rest of the script. He slapped his hand over his face and slumped into a groan. "We are past a point where we're able to change that. How did I miss this?"

Artorian chuckled, apologizing by reaching over to pat him. "I'll drop it. Send me a prompt later when it's all sorted. Can you tell me more about why you slotted Bone Scripting as a profession over Flash Runes? It's even two words."

Eternium pushed himself back up from his slump. "There's no current profession related to Flash Runes. That's all there was to it. Fame and Infamy currently do not work, either. The reputation system is experimental, and I've left that bank dormant."

He moved Artorian's character sheet down, tapping the next entry. "The last section is Deity. You can't pick yourself, and I'm sorry to tell you that Lunella's children have been trying to copy you. Making *incredible* messes. Do you remember Ra? She went hard on the route of your sun Deity concept. That character of hers is named Ra-torian, but she has *none* of your finesse. She got to the minor Deity stage in one of the other dungeon worlds, and then got stuck."

Artorian wheezed, slapping his knee as he found that hilarious. "Let her keep it! That's going to confuse so many people if her version is imported into Eternia! I love it! Let her be happy."

He wiped the back of his hand under his eyes, removing undeveloped tears that had merely made them wet. "Ah, that made me feel pleasant. I think the real question is, do you need me to test that feature again, or can I actually select someone else?"

Tim scratched the top of his head. "Ideally, we'd want as many people as we can trust in the Deity positions to begin with, because they can mess with far too much in the game world, regardless of how expensive I make D.E. rewards. You managed to get serious use out of that mechanic, but you also had ninety percent of the populace under your wing. In my conflicted opinion: You both got nothing, and far too much done. Setting every follower to level ten was such a nightmare on my end that I scheduled time with Astrea for a consultation. She's good with that concept. I expect **Nightmare** to be her **Law** when she gets there, or she may adopt the **Sleep** position you unknowingly vacated."

Artorian conceded with a light shrug, leaning into Ember's adjustments to his winter clothing. He had messed up an entire row of buttons and not noticed. "Then sign me up for another Deity run, just don't slap me with as big of a headache. Last run, we had so many options that I didn't have time to delve into most of those features past some cursory attention. In fact, if you need some kind of Overdeity that specifically can't do anything unless the celestial feces rises and hits the oscillation? That would be ideal, because I want to retain my health regeneration bonus effect. So I might as well hold onto the role, both so nobody steals it, and so that if it ever becomes important, it's still mine. I went through a lot of work with Cal to set that up, I don't want to lose it."

"Easy enough. You won't be able to be chosen as an option by any players, but I doubt that bothers you. There's currently no benefit to Deity forms aside from being Astral in nature. You're more a lightshow than you are a living, breathing thing, and the duration is limited." Tim made several other screens appear that only he could work on, adding that detail in no time at all. "You won't get the kind of bonuses you did for being a... I don't remember if it was Minor Deity or Major Deity, but you know what I mean. Lastly, we get to your statistics. I see you've nosed your way into making Pylons work that shouldn't have worked already. Can't say I'm surprised. Adding your old cultivator statistics is a title, and I have to leave to work on those. Next for you is choosing some of the toys and components you want to play with, and we work on the numbers after. Halcyon will have options for you. I need to go make sure you have ground under your feet."

Tim stood, gave them a poor man's salute, and popped out since it was clear that Yuki was not coming back. Zelia had also not returned, so Artorian surmised that people were busy. He squeezed Ember's hand, rubbing a thumb over her knuckles. "Well, that wasn't so bad."

Ember had to agree, watching all of Tim's screens wink out one at a time now that he was gone. "Pull up your own sheet, let's make sure it says what we think it says."

"Good idea." Artorian did so, and for the first time in a

while, saw a filled in, shiny new character sheet. "*Aw*, Tim changed my name to all letters. The snoot."

———

Name: Less than Three
Character Level: 0
Race: Nascent Being
Class: Janitor
Specialization: None
Profession: Bone Scripting
Profession: Artifacting
Characteristics:
Strength: 20
Dexterity: 20
Constitution: 20
Intelligence: 20
Wisdom: 20
Charisma: 20
Perception: 20
Luck: 20
Karmic Luck: 0

CHAPTER TWENTY-SIX

"Why is my level nil?" Artorian zeroed in on his concern. "That value should be a one, right? Not a zero?"

"The Soul Forge needs to be operational, sugar." Ember pulled some tickets from her bracelet, each stamped with a red-ink seal from Eri's Emporium, before she rifled through them. The enchanted white tickets all had the same circular symbol on them: Eri's personal insignia nested between a horned Oni mask and camellia blossoms. "There's a sequence we spent a lot of time planning out, and while the people who we built it for will not be getting the important chunks of that sequence in order, we built it with their safeguards in mind, and have to engage the levers in a very set pattern."

She tugged free the ticket she was looking for, holding it out for Cy when she and Lucia returned from their practice bout. "Halcy? This is a tonfa replacement, though I still have not figured out why the damage is one to one. They can do a lot more at the rarity you have. Why is the baseline set so low?"

Halcyon leaned over to accept the ticket. "Is Eternia's weapon damage priority still calculated in the same order?"

Ember scrunched her face while digging for that obscure detail. "I believe so? Plusses first, then multipliers. Except for the end-tallies like Ki Arrows that don't get multipliers on them."

She tallied her fingers while she was mentally entrenched in the topic. "Base Weapon Damage. Bonus Weapon Damage. Flat Damage Bonus. Flat Minimum and Maximum Damage Bonus. Percentage Enhanced Damage. Percentage Enhanced Maximum Damage. Percentage Damage Bonus Versus Specific Target Range. Critical Hit Chance. Flat Non-Physical Damage Bonus. Percentage Skill Damage. Conversion of Physical Attack Damage. Source Penalties. Unit Modifiers."

Halcyon grinned, showing off a set of non-human jaws. "Not identical. Percentage Skill Damage in its new order kind of hurts, but that's good enough! If C.H.C. is unchanged, then critical hits are still in large part determined by base weapon values, and the highest crit chance is best achieved with the conditional of lowest base damage. I will be remaking my crit-fisher build, new and improved!"

Artorian had several questions. "Sugar? Soul Forge doesn't tell me why my level isn't a one, I have no idea what people you're referring to, and please don't leave me out of a conversation that includes the big, delicious damage numbers. I like the big, delicious damage numbers!"

He slapped the stone seat next to him for effect, and while a zero did come up from the exedra bench, a small explosion in the background boded ill as one of the mesas erased itself from existence. Especially when his floaty zero vanished mid-rise instead of slowly phasing out.

Tim popped back covered in soot, his mustache the victim of a close-range explosion. He was holding a pose that spoke volumes on him not having expected a calculation Pylon to go critical with him nose-deep in the inner workings. When he opened his mouth, he coughed out a blackened cloud, lifted a finger, and pointed at Artorian. "No."

Tim then popped out, leaving a very dirty spot behind as the shed soot obeyed gravity and fell to the mosaic floor.

Artorian turned to look at Ember, but she had her face in her hands. When he turned to Halcyon, she was very quietly hiding the weapon ticket in an inner pocket. Cy paused like a deer in bright light when she was caught, and rambled. "I think you're in need of personal damage calculation Pylons, My Dreamer. Shall I go find some volunteers?"

He barely had a response, not wanting more explosions or responsibility when he had no clue how he was causing them. "Please? Maybe some from the **Nuts** and **Bolts** line. I believe Kronk might be cooperative. I'd rather have good numbers than a racer I can't roll around on. Can you tell me about critical hits and give me this list that was mentioned before you go?"

Halcyon adored the direction, as that gave her something to do other than quietly cringe from Eternia breaking and seeking escape. "Ratatoskr of **Bolts** and Kronk of **Nuts**? I know them, but they're very peculiar with how they do things."

"If you already know individuals who would be willing to come help, that's a big win that I'm thankful for. In fact, if Kronk used to be the calculation Pylon that I remember, tell him that I am willing to have all my formulas calculated as nuts." Artorian sat on his hands so he didn't blow something else up. "Critical hits?"

Halcyon blinked, sorted the information, and resolved to get both of those squirrels to be cooperative. "Critical hits? Ah! Yes, my crit-fisher build. So, critical hits are often misunderstood. Anytime they come up, the Beasts I speak with have this notion in their head that all which happens is 'more damage,' but that is not the case. A critical hit allows a critical effect to happen, and more damage is one of the entries on that table. What I actually specialized in was getting to choose what effect on the table occurred, and then building my kit to have access to an endless stream of critical tallies."

Fishing the crumpled item ticket free, she ripped the object in the hopes that delivery would work, then squealed in delight when a replica of her lost tonfas hovered in a soap-bubble before her. "There used to be this mechanic that I hope is still around. The mechanic massively increased your chances of landing a critical hit the lower your base damage output was, relative to the quality or rank of the thing you were attacking with."

Halcyon inspected the bubble first. "Like most other game values, those are generally hidden unless your Class or Specialization specifically lets you see them. Some mechanics aren't even generated unless someone becomes able to play with them. In the Incursus Dungeon, someone figured out how to tactically attack from above by using their mini-map as a targeting point. Until they did that, there was no such mechanism, or need for the values."

Taking the replicas in hand when she reached into the gravity-defying bubble, both items dropped to the ground with a metal dull thunk when said bubble popped. "*Ack!* Forgot I deactivated my statistics. I can't pick these up. That was... not smart."

She tapped them with the bottom of her foot, making a familiar screen appear.

Name: Ten Ton Tonfa
  Renamed: Halcyon Days
  Material: Gravity Iridium
  Rarity: Special
  Damage: 1 – 1
  Special Quality: Graviton
  A weapon from Jotunheim. Used by the most powerful Daimyo in the realm's history, Halcyon. These tonfas have a strength requirement of 500 each. Not meeting this strength threshold makes a person entirely unable to

lift a single tonfa. A strength of 1000 is required to wield both tonfas. If wielded as a set, their Special Quality activates.

Gravity Iridium is a variant of the base metal that quintuples in weight when they strike an opponent. The tonfas may seem deceptively light if you meet the strength requirement. That is because to the wielder they feel five times as light regardless of being at rest or in motion. This comprises the basic function of the special quality: Graviton.

A Graviton weapon does not cost stamina to swing. Repeated attacks will still incur the normal stamina strain penalties. On Impact, a weapon with this quality doubles the base damage resulting from the strike. While their base damage is negligible, this calculation includes the strength bonus that is added to the weapon's raw damage.

Notice: Tonfas are considered a monk weapon. Martial arts maneuvers can be used in conjunction with this weapon.

———

Halcyon beamed with pride. "I love having these back! As a big bonus, they shed a lot of insight on what does, and does not, affect critical hits. As you can tell from the entry, while the base damage is negligible, the item effect is beefy. Item effects aren't calculated into critical hit formulas, and those old Pylons only looked at damage for the starting chart. A one-to-one output gets you the brackets holding the best charts. My Dreamer, can you hold these for now?"

"Of course, Cy." Artorian momentarily moved to *tink* his bracelet against them, then returned to his prior spot when both tonfa had been stored.

Cy then shot a pleading look at Ember, who smiled with a light roll of the eyes from her fist-to-cheek resting position. "Sure."

Ember summoned a secretive black screen that was furled up like a piece of vellum, looked around conspicuously, then slid the document into Artorian's hands. "Don't let anyone see that. Public charts currently don't go past eight or nine entries."

Most intrigued, Artorian half-unfurled the blacklight vellum to sneak a peek at what appeared to be a rarity chart with quality entries that he'd never seen before.

———

Quality
   Trash
   Damaged
   Common
   Uncommon
   Rare
   Special
   Unique
   Artifact
   Legendary
   Mythical
   Cal
   Dani
   Note: Sub modifier list related to Quality not included. For entries relating to: Synthetic, Mirrored, Temporary, Artificial, Grand, Greater, Lesser, Least, Boosted, or other SQAS: Second Tier Affixes or Suffixes. Please contact the relevant library for Affix or Suffix strains.

———

Quietly furling that list up, he snuck it back into Ember's hand as if never having been the wiser. "How helpful. I take it each rarity provides a different chance of a critical hit occurring, or associated chart? I know how difficult it was to reach higher rarities and have received a stern talking to when some of my Artifacts became accidental Legendaries. System confiscation is not something that I'm going to forget, and anything above Unique seems impossible to attain through standard acquisition."

Halcyon bubbled with enthusiasm. "Several, and yes! The formula I remember is the numerical value of the rarity, divided by the averaged base damage, rounded down. A special quality weapon doing one to one damage normally has a six percent chance of landing a critical hit."

She counted on her fingers just to be sure. "Rarity rank six, divided by one. To compare, a Unique Quality weapon doing four-hundred average damage, means you divide seven by four hundred, which ends up as a zero point zero one seven five chance of your hit being a crit."

Halcyon turned gleeful, her hands clapping together as she had all but forgotten her need to fetch the squirrels in lieu of getting to gush about one of her favorite game activities. "Chart types were determined by…"

Cy thought for a moment. "You count from Common as the standard measurement and then adjust up or down. Trash and Damaged Rarities mostly have chart entries where the weapon is destroyed on a critical hit, and some where an additional negative effect happens when it breaks, like being stabbed in the foot by what's left of your sword."

Halcyon's tone rose in chipperness as she got to the fun part. "Uncommon and Rare give improved lists and better critical options, but the Special quality is where a threshold gets crossed. Critical chance triples when you hold any Class or Specialization related to critical effects, and there's two particularly desirable critical effect charts that are added at that rarity. The same is true for Abilities and Skills, but unless you're specifically branching into maximizing critical hit chances, you won't actually see an uptick in how often they happen. If it's not your specialty, the game tries its hardest to keep you at baseline. Since Crit-Fisher is specifically about critical hits, the chance is quintupled instead of tripled. So my baseline critical chance per hit, before skills were added to the mix, sat at a very comfortable thirty percent."

She grinned again, her teeth on display. "Then we enjoy the first skill that Crit-Fisher grants you, which increases the number of times a critical hit chance is rolled per attack."

Artorian whistled, impressed. "I like that mechanic. But Cy? Breathe."

His remaining response was cut off when Ember quiet-nudged three more of those unassuming blacklight scrolls in his ribs. He quietly took them while Halcyon took a moment, giving each a glance before returning to the topic. The first one had hand-written bonus commentary!

———

Ranks

Novice - I have no idea what I'm doing!

Beginner - Oh, that's how that works.

Apprentice - I think I'm getting the hang of this!

Student - I most certainly did not have the hang of anything and see where I went wrong.

Journeyman - I know what I'm doing.

Expert - I see the flaws, I know the reasons.

Master - I can teach this, for I know the details, and speak them simply.

Grandmaster - Intricacies lost, have surfaced under my touch.

Sage - This entity holds no secrets from me.

Deity - I made this.

Cal - No, I made this.

Dani - I don't care who made it, it will do what I want!

Note: Sub modifier list related to ranks not included. For other SQAS: Second Tier Affixes or Suffixes. Please contact the relevant library for Affix or Suffix strains.

———

Artorian was mighty curious about Affix and Suffix tiers, wondering just how deep that rabbit hole went. The topic was shelved for now. He could only focus on so much. Finding a refresher on the ranks helpful, he slid that scroll back to Ember and peeked at the other. She'd likely slipped him this one because of his Ragna the Rock question.

Core

   Memory - Can store: One.
   Flawed - Can store: Ten.
   Weak - Can store: One hundred.
   Standard - Can store: One thousand.
   Strong - Can store: Ten thousand.
   Beastly - Can store: One hundred thousand.
   Immaculate - Can store: One million.
   Luminous - Can store: Ten million.
   Radiant - Can store: One hundred million.
   Dungeon - Can store: One billion.
   Silverwood - Can store: Ten billion.
   Eternium - Can store: One hundred billion.
   Note: Sub modifier list related to Cores not included. For other SQAS: Second Tier Affixes or Suffixes. Please contact the relevant library for Affix or Suffix strains.

"I'm a little concerned that this doesn't say *what* Cores can store." Out of sheer curiosity, Artorian counted them all out to find twelve entries in each of the lists he'd just read. A thought struck that there might also have been around twelve Avalon segments? He might be off by one or two, but had to push that thought away or he was going to find himself horribly off topic again. The second scroll was slid back, and his mind snapped to Halcyon's Crit-Fisher build. "Any chance I can learn those tricks, Cy? I would like something that actually works to be in my hands, because if I slap another bench and the calculators explode because some background feature wasn't ready? That's counterproductive."

Halcyon squeed. "It's a Specialization track! If you hit the requisite level and open one up, come tell me instead of selecting anything, and I can push a Specialization Trainer prompt."

Artorian nodded, consuming the information on the third scroll. "I'd like that, Cy. While I'm not-so-secretly going over charts, can I have the one you were holding?"

———

Connection

Lineage Hunter - Reputation: Minus 7000.

Vendetta - Reputation: Minus 6000, and special events.

Blood Feud - Reputation: Minus 5000.

Loathed - Reputation: Minus 4000.

Hated - Reputation: Minus 3000.

Hostile - Reputation: Minus 2000.

Cautious - Reputation: Minus 1000.

Neutral - Reputation: Zero.

Reluctantly Friendly - Reputation: Plus 1000.

Friendly - Reputation: Plus 2000.

Friend - Reputation: Plus 3000.

Ally - Reputation: Plus 4000.

Extended Family - Reputation: Plus 5000.

Family - Reputation: Plus 6000, and special events.

Kin - Reputation: Plus 7000.

Note: Sub modifier list related to Connections not included. For other SQAS: Second Tier Affixes or Suffixes. Please contact the relevant library for Affix or Suffix strains.

———

Ember accepted the third scroll, disappearing the item into her bracelet as Halcyon opened a physical bag and procured a physical scroll without the use of spatial trickery. Her version of an inventory did not have bells and whistles. She preferred it that way. "Here you go! I also just remembered I was supposed to go squirrel wrangling! So I'm going to swim my way down to the bottom square so I can be ferried out. Get a hold of me however you can when you need!"

Artorian slid free to give her a hug. Cy got down on a knee to accept it and nuzzled the life out of his hair before giving him a good-boy pat and leaving the way she arrived.

Via screaming Incarnate Goat boat.

CHAPTER TWENTY-SEVEN

"So why level zero?" Artorian turned back to Ember while opening yet another scroll. He frowned at the contents, finding them damaged from Halcyon's bout with Lucia. "I didn't follow the Soul Forging mention."

Artorian was also going to need time to puzzle this chart out. Was this list what he had to work with? He needed some context. Seeing Critical Hits present in the list was nice, but still. Context! Very few of these words meant anything to him, and half of them were illegible. He partially turned it to show Ember, but she was already trying to hand him the blacklight version. An object when he gratefully took, to read over the more legible list.

———

List of available tools:
  Bomb
  Bounce
  Bubble
  Cast on Self

Cast on Target
Charge
Concentrated
Conditional Allspell
Cone
Critical Hits
Cylinder
Domino
Double
Explode on Hit
Gatling
Grenade
Homing
Laser
Line
Mine
MirrorSpell
Penetrating
Pierce
Proliferation
Quad
Quin
Spread
Synchro Casting
Tornado
Triple
Weapon Ignition
Weapon Modes

———

Lucia poked her nose in from the side of the abnormally long black lit scroll, looking the writ up and down before her ears drooped. "I'm going to be blessing a lot of messes."

Ember held her own head, still trying to think on how to explain the Soul Forging issue with clarity. She'd been convinced her initial attempt would have been enough, but when reality proved not to line up with assumption, something had to give. As was always the correct call, the assumption was hurled from the window. "That list of available tools exists to give you an idea of what kind of special effects can be cobbled together. If it's not on that list, then there's no guarantee that the Abilities you make will work. You and I both have an Adaptive Pylon bank ready for inscription, but it can't be inscribed with functions or tricks that we don't have."

Her feelings waffled on that objective slap of a statement. There was always flexibility in Eternia. "You can technically do it? You can technically also blow up a mesa every time you take the risk of employing it."

Ember's comfort increased by shifting her position to be pressed against her boy more, curling a full arm around one of his. "After making sure that 'I hit it with a stick' worked, we thought it best to start a limited run of special effects. That list is them. There's of course an exception, as Conditional Allspell is a nested entry that by itself gives you access to more options. You should take that one when we have to divvy the list up between us. I have to use the same list, and we don't have enough Pylons to support duplications. All of Lucia's existing tools work fine, but they're only going to work for her unless one of us has MirrorSpell or Synchro Casting."

She inspected his reaction, then shifted her explanation. "If you're having trouble imagining how that list interacts with concepts, think of a fireball, and how those listed words might change how that fireball works. Pick something as a base. Slap the specials on after. Play with the order. The more specials you add, the more expensive the trick. Expect the number of specials you can add to be limited by your experience level with the toy you made."

Artorian took the moment to chew on those details, perfectly happy with dividing this list in half. There was too much to choose from, and Ember likely knew what was going to be more useful for her. "No complaints here, dear. It slipped by me that a new body for you also meant leaving your old host of tools behind. Thank you for mentioning it."

Ember flushed, secretly happy at the praise.

A Nixie tube popped to life above her head. "Soul Forging's intended purpose is not actually meant *for us*. I think you've had this line of thoughts before, or at minimum heard someone talk about it? I'll explain in stages."

Artorian handed the list to Lucia so she could inspect it, to have something to do as she was tuning out these esoteric explanations. The direction of her ears was a dead giveaway.

Lucia didn't see her shields on the list. That was cause for concern, but a flick of the wrist and a successful Basalt Bubble Barrier later, that worry left. If she grasped the conundrum, then she had everything in her old kit, but couldn't add new toys to the kit that didn't originate from this list.

Artorian leaned his right shoulder against the stone wall of the exedra, curious why Soul Forging was a long explanation and what that had to do with his level. "You have my ear, dearest."

Ember nodded, speaking slow and steady for her own clarity with her hand raised and fingers squeezed together. "When Moonfall happened, and everyone had the big retreat into Cal, there were no planet-side survivors after that event. Every person, dungeon, creature, and anything else that could perish, did. This leaves the local sphere to refine Essence on a planetary scale with wild abandon. Without Dungeons in those key breakthrough points to act as Curator? The planet should be seeing the continuous bombardment of confused, undirected, messy Essence. With nothing and nobody to stop it as the energy dedicated to changing things, goes about to do just that."

Artorian pinched the bridge of his nose, his head a rumbling cloud. "Didn't that not happen? I feel like there's a reason that didn't happen."

"Correct." Ember reached over to slide her nails over his head, getting rid of the thundercloud in his thoughts so he could listen and not overthink from the get-go. "Cal, before all that, had a... ritual? In motion? It's not called a ritual. His laying lines? Ley Lines. A network of energy absorbing lines that, as a broad idea, function like a jetstream or an ocean's thermohaline circulation. The lines gather and trap the energy, keep it moving, and feed all of it into Cal. This particular trick of his could proliferate itself and grew to successfully cover the planet. Now, what does this do to the local sphere?"

"Ice Age." Artorian rattled off that answer with Jotunheim flashbacks waving in the background. "Cal got all the Essence, so no chance for the breakthrough points to spit out Essence and kickstart changes to foster the kind of life that could live in such conditions. I'm suddenly having very invasive thoughts on prior conversations concerning there 'being something to return to.' That's a tough cracker. What's next?"

Ember poked her own chest. "Centers. Centers are next. Because creatures are dependent in large part on the conditions of their surroundings to guide growth and evolution. That means that for us to have centers, we developed in an environment where all the checkboxes for a center to exist were ticked. While a body can house a mind purely by virtue of biology, it is very much the case that a center is responsible for acting as a glue that latches a soul to that mixture and provides the mind the option to exist outside of that body."

Her hand did the side-to-side waggle. "Given the right kinds of energy. C-rankers and below are still meat-people, the mind and the body are one, and you die if your brain leaves your body. Mages are energy-people. The mind is still there, but no longer constrained by a component that you kind of no longer have. Having been a B, and A-ranker, you're very aware that as a Mage, you're entirely made from energy. That means no brain meat for your brain-thoughts, but you are obviously still having brain-thoughts, and you didn't forget what happened to you in life, so you didn't lose your memory either."

Artorian was firmly and fully on board. He had given this lecture! "Yes, I am following very well on this part. Do go on."

Ember felt comfort in knowing he was on the track with her.

"The point circles back around to the conditions a creature grows in. If our local sphere becomes capable of hosting the kind of human life we recognize, there will be no Essence in circulation for them to adapt to, because *Cal is still taking it all*. Since it is impossible for us to conveniently poke our noses out to check if there's life on the planet, that means we have to throw a dart into the cosmos and hope we get our stopping point right. Which is why Cal is slowing his time scale down, so that when we need to flow concurrently with time outside, we can."

Artorian kept a hand on his chin, reminiscing. "I'm still following. This leads to the new humans, whatever form that might take, developing on a mundane local sphere. No Essence to have them develop centers means they will evolve up as a species not just without one, but without a place for one prepared, should Essence come back. Say, when Cal flips a lever and shuts the Ley Lines off, and all that Essence once again gets chucked out all over the local sphere."

He swallowed loudly. "Everything Essence touches will undergo forceful change, because that's what Essence does. Since neither creatures, nor structures, nor really anything on the local sphere will have any kind of defense—or mechanism to even interact with the stuff—it's going to be global chaos, and likely a quick extinction."

Ember agreed, her hands making a switcheroo motion. "*Mhm*! So, since we badly need people, and also can't exist on a local sphere that has no Essence—as we are the kind of creature that cannot live without Essence, given we have centers, and their removal is guaranteed death—we're planning a swap."

She uncoiled herself for a quick stretch. "Cal, Tim, and a few other Dungeons can host people without Essence, because they have fine enough control over their Soul Spaces to not let rogue energy interact with a creature that would die from being exposed to it. Cal explained this to the group by showing me what happens when Mana enters the body of a C-ranker, even accidentally."

The bronze girl paled, Artorian not far behind. "Gruesome."

Ember shuddered, brushing the thought and feeling away. "Mutation Rampancy is a term you might hear the Incarnates throw around, and that's what we're referring to if you overhear it. That which does not die from Essence contact and exposure is getting the 'forceful change into the kind of creature that can survive in the new environment' treatment. Meaning we're going to have a lot of insane, mad, hungry, power-frenzied *things* to contend with as we disembark from Cal. Ranging from G-rank, all the way to Incarnate class. There is no way of telling what unleashing long-held energy types onto an unprepared sphere will do. Aside from the guaranteed catastrophe that it will inevitably cause. Returning to the local sphere, and turning the Essence back on, unequivocally makes us the villains to whoever or whatever is currently living on it."

She then made the switcheroo motion again. "From Cal: People, cultivators, and whoever is not ready to disembark will act as townspeople, friendly faces, welcomers, shop keeps, quest givers, and such in the main game world of Eternium. Beasts especially will have this problem, as we currently don't think a humanization effect can be upheld outside of Cal. We're going to send out information and requests for volunteers. Particularly for area bosses and mob populations so they can acclimate as a 'just in case.' With the knowledge that it might be the case."

Lucia's ears snapped to attention and swiveled to Ember; her face contorted in horror. "I like my person-form! I like it a lot! I don't get to keep it?"

Ember apologized breathily. "I want to be proven wrong, momma bun, but it's not looking good right now. Cal and Tim both make doing certain things much easier than they should be. I don't even know who can and cannot leave Cal's dungeon influence, when he can re-exert it. The concept of a Dungeon Born, or what qualifies as a Dungeon Outbreak, has become muddled."

She stuck a finger up, turning to look at Artorian so this

gossip was delivered properly. "While I'm certain that he's going to support everyone trying to leave and make their own way, one Dale that could talk to him at any time was already too much. He's been very vocal about paring down the mental connections he has to uphold once people are out. He was even talking about condensing his Dungeon Core down to the size of a Beast Core, shoving it in a body double of Kota the scholar, and existing as a person instead of a dungeon so he could go on vacation."

CHAPTER TWENTY-EIGHT

Lucia had to sit and hold onto something.

Ember returned to her prior explanation as she gave the Glitterflit coping time. "The non-center will be entering people directly into Eternia. They will not be going into Cal. Cal is... clearly still demanding his privacy back. Cal also cannot properly poke his nose into Eternium while Tim is playing passenger inside of the main Soul Space. You already know what happens during recursion. Like when Cal tried to go into your Soul Space? I'm a little foggy on the story, but I sure remember you exploding."

Artorian hastily nodded with trepidation. "Say no more."

Ember dropped the hot potato. "Cal has secondary means of meddling in Eternia, but directly, he cannot properly go. Dale is a good example since he is disconnected enough for it to be safe, as sharing a bit of soul or not, Dale is a different entity from Cal. He has his own Soul Space unless Cal recoups him entirely. Never tell Dale that he was the test case, and we could have all been dead if that had gone wrong."

She took a breath, relaxed, and continued. "That's why we made the first version of the game world in Cal's space. I have the distinct sensation that Cal is going to want to play in his world, rather than be an eternal developer. That aside, back to topic."

Artorian copied her switcheroo motion with a smile. "Non-center people in the game world?"

"Need a center." Ember confirmed as she flicked his ear. "Like us, they're going to want to go home. I doubt we're going to have any willing survivors from the future local sphere, so we're going to need to keep game features adaptive depending on the society that we pull people from. We might get very unlucky."

She tried to keep the reasons simple. "Someone who has never seen a building before is going to react very poorly to a town. Same with any and every piece of technology. We have to keep Eternia mundane and simple enough so that someone can wake up there and have a reasonable chance of figuring out how they can fit. That said, some people aren't going to want to fit, and we can make out roads for them. None of that, sadly, solves the problem that no matter their achievements in Cal's game world, they cannot go home. Because..."

Artorian understood. "Because to leave means to be exposed to the aberrant forces of what, to us, is very friendly, helpful, empowering energy; and to them is a horrible, slow, freakish death by rampant mutation."

"Take 'slow' out of that sentence." Ember grimaced painfully.

"Well, that's unpleasant." Artorian matched her expression, cringing with his hands pulled close to his chest. His fingers rooted into the jacket's fluff to have a tactile sensation to hold and play with.

"Soul Forging." Ember wrenched the better topic back to the forefront. "Is the process, hidden by a lot of gamified means; to give, develop, or build a center into a person or thing without one. There are specific qualifiers in place for what gets a person the prompt, as we will never have the resources to apply SF to any kind of population at scale. Those outliers?

The people who were going to say no and forge their own path up and out? They get priority. They are the most likely kind of person and personality to be able to cope with what they see when they leave the game."

She motioned at the outer shell of Demeter's Dream. "That includes specifically putting some nonsense into their way that rocks their worldviews. It is also why, when we pull the floating continents back together, it will be done haphazardly. To guarantee the randomness of, say, a forest that connects right next to an open plain, when all reason says it shouldn't. Uncanny division lines of terrain and headscratchers are positive outcomes."

Artorian's concern was instant, but Ember had a strong lead on why. "Their weapons, tools, and abilities can't leave the game with them unless those skills reach the Master rank. Because at that point, they can develop the skill, lower case S, from scratch. They will have the ability. Anything less and you're still relying on the game for details, and we're not having anyone blowing themselves up because they tried to apply half-knowledge with their entire energy pool. The knowledge will be stripped from them if they can't prove to grasp every step and building block."

Artorian paused her with a begging hand. "Energy pool? Why would they get to keep their energy pool from a game?"

Ember laced her own hands. "We can give the new humans, or elves, or whatever ends up developing the center they need to survive. Far ahead of the time when they qualify for exodus. Not everyone will want to leave, and may find their new living circumstances favorable, but those are easy to account for. As a big bonus, we may be able to artificially boost the trailblazers up to be cultivators. Or creatures *like* cultivators. Zelia expects that we might need the firepower, as she termed it."

"Slow. Stop. Back up." Artorian wildly waved his arms. "One madness at a time."

Ember tried for a joke. "So don't start talking about worlds that communicate in songs or smells instead of words and sentences?"

No laughter was returned, and she got a flat stare for her troubles. Artorian answered with monotone words. "Ha. Ha."

She grinned, leaning her chin on her hand. "Did it clear your mental buffer?"

"Yes." Artorian grumbled. "While I am curious about the artificial cultivator thing, wrap up the Soul Forge talk. I still don't know why I'm level zero."

Ember made a swirly motion at her chest. "Soul Forging has a few uses. Pylon recycling. Getting rid of toys that don't work so well or didn't work as intended. Allowing developers to hand out new toys, which are mostly ideas that we need tested. Or a place to sweep certain creations under the rug. We can't always use the desert."

She winked, amused as that had become her own favorite place to hide mistakes. "There are, of course, set outcomes depending on combined additions, but it's one of those places where we can really meddle. To make custom tools and toys for whoever we end up playing favorites with. We want them to succeed, have fun, and climb up in power to where they can join us, after all. The trailblazers are going to be easy to keep an eye on, and since those people are who we would need adaptable inscription Pylon banks for anyway, that works out."

She reached to hold his hand. "To anyone who doesn't understand the calculation of how the entries you drop in the Soul Forging cauldron are combined, the results spit out may seem random or like a dangerous gamble. There are plenty of methods to the madness, but we've learned that explaining too much to people both removes the magic and diminishes their sense of adventure and exploration. Soul Forging will remain a mystery, as one of the many game features for people to bash their heads into. I am always astounded to see how much people enjoy the reward after a struggle to attain it."

Ember then poked his chest. "For people *with* a center, like us, Soul Forging is a necessary Pylon bank because it is also linked to what allows us to gain cultivation, or in the case of your question, experience. No SF? No experience gained. No level one. The chart may say you need a thousand experience, but for us, that number being a 'one' means half of our calculation Pylons suddenly work."

She motioned between them. "Our level, both yours and mine, are going to chime and *ding* to a one when it's done, and that will be our level. We do not get to increase our level yet, as we don't have the means. This also means that the level of everything else you'll meet is static, and that you'll be very dependent on non-level-based improvements."

Artorian squeezed her hand back, settling in to listen as she waved a tiny booklet of weapon and armor tickets. "There are a lot of Abilities and Skills tied to a person's overall level, and those will all be terrible for us. Different toys look at different sources for their calculations, and we've intentionally mixed it up that way, should someone want to do something strange or spectacular with an idea they have. This is just as meaningful for us, who will have to mix and match the details of our Skills and Abilities until we eventually arrive at an entry that works."

The tickets were stored after she made her point. "Because these toys are gamified, the very flavor text we enter to our prompts will change what our entries do. You might not get a power boost, but if you write into the prompt that the effect looks blue, then that matters."

She conjured an example from recent memory. "If a person has high Dexterity, but suddenly discovers that what they really loved about their class wasn't blades, but the bloody poisons, then the system has a way of offering them a method of growth towards this goal. Yes, Dexterity as a core calculation stat for poisons is very strange, but people are very clever when in pursuit of a goal."

Ember looked proud, a smirk curling into the corner of her mouth. "Which, in great part, is a big enjoyment for us. In testing, we've also found that almost everyone has strayed from their initial plans, after they were made. Someone wanted to make an Intelligence build based around water magic but kept making strength-oriented choices because that made them happy. So while they ended up with their water magic, they were using it to make themselves look perpetually glossy, so that when they flexed before dropping a people's elbow, there was more show to it. We're constantly flabbergasted at what people discover about themselves, and how it rarely lines up with what they initially thought they wanted."

She then cleared her throat. "Statistics don't necessarily line up with how someone thinks, feels, or acts. The gamification of it all does its best to substitute how that person believes the statistics should reflect their... say... physical form. Some people with a hundred strength will be beanpoles, because the meaning of strength, to them, does not translate to a larger physical stature, or bigger muscles. As you've likely seen with real Mages these days, people like to adapt into forms that give them comfort or happiness, which is how we end up with a lot of physically incredible specimens to ogle and drool at."

The Saintess spoke from experience. "When you can choose how you want to look, people will generally not hold back on the details. When you then remember that in the Old World you only got a single chance at that, since it was unlikely to be a point of focus when entering Magehood, that transition carried a world's worth of weight. Cal's conveniences are... appreciated."

Artorian pondered aloud, daydreaming on returning to his appearance as a high-powered, long-bearded Grandpa. Complete with cozy robes, hiding very functional muscles underneath for the day he needed to toss those robes and make a statement. "Convenient."

Ember agreed, motioning at herself as she was still working out the kind of form she permanently wanted to host. "That was the idea. The short version of turning non-center people into artificial cultivators, or whatever end result we're able to attain, is currently measured by how deep into a Specialization tree they can get. Much like choosing a **Law** in the Tower, since it's all about focus and what you want to dedicate yourself to."

She conjured a list to show some numerical examples. "This

gets combined with a certain requirement in the amount of unmodified base stats. We only look at the lowest common denominators when considering how much of a cultivator or Mage someone might be from the game world, and currently that matches up with the cultivator title that you should be getting soon. We're considering a third or fourth requirement, but that's outside my purview right now."

The teacher of ways instead motioned to the screen. "A person with the correct amount of Specialization depth, and the minimum matching Attribute values across the board, will be considered a cultivator of equal rank. Pretend there's a person with one-hundred twenty as Attributes in all values, and whatever the right amount of Specialization depth it ends up being? That's a B-ranker if they leave Cal, it just might not be a B-ranker as you currently know or understand them. They will have no concept of how true cultivation works. They might not even need it due to some of the Beast core unification projects. They're entering the game with an energy body from Tim, not their own. Their own body won't make it in."

She rubbed the bridge of her nose. "One of the many reasons being due to needing to reach an Oath agreement with Cal, like we did on entry. The Memory Core project has come a long way. We are already able to retain everything important before they are ever imported to the game. So we're not even going to try preserving the original body, and we're merely copying the existing virtues and flaws it has onto a blank body template. Then go from there."

Ember rubbed some sweat off her forehead with the back of her hand. That had been a mouthful. "Please don't ask me about what an exit might look like. Body wise or otherwise. I have no idea. That's dungeon work. Last I heard, the number one-fifty was being thrown around and I have no idea what the dungeons were talking about with their mortal-limit yelling match. All I understood was that some people were going to be plain unable to cross it. Again, no idea why. I did not want to be in that room."

Lucia held the list up, pointing at the entries. The part where she had begun listening again was roughly where the topic had returned to the scroll in her paws. The bit about centers, spheres, and weird things happening to weird people had been tastefully tuned out. "These can be connected to any statistic? *What?* I want to play with this! That's so much freedom!"

Ember cackled, slapping her knee while glad for the complete topic change. "I know! When Cal got hold of the list, the first thing he did was make a Blue Bubble Gatling. Grace screeched from the far side of the workroom and broke sound barriers to chase them while Cal howled like a Gnomish inventor and let rip. The bubbles were all fun and games until Grace succeeded at popping them faster than Cal could make them. Then he was all 'no, wait, I should be winning.' To retake the lead, he slapped a proliferation effect on, in addition to what was already there. Then we had to flee the area because now the bubbles were coming *for us.*"

She smiled, sighed, and press her cheek against Artorian's forehead to whisper. "Don't go to the workshop for a while. They still haven't cleaned it all up."

Artorian laughed hard. "Don't go to work… Ha! Sugar! I'm *mortal!*"

"Oh, right." Ember slapped her forehead, that detail having slipped. "Still. We have enough moon problems. One moon at a time! Want to put some Abilities together? We can start dividing the list up. There's only one of each, and I do have a preference or two."

Lucia smiled at them both with childish happiness, her golden eyes gleaming with sparkles. "Can I make one too?"

"Of course you can." Ember made grabby hands for Lucia's head, hugging the Basher when that long-eared face was pressed into her stomach. "We're in this together. Until the Heavenlies show up all impatient with their own player characters. Then I am going to need a lot of mess-blesses to keep my patience."

CHAPTER TWENTY-NINE

Artorian made a pained noise. "We're expecting Heavenlies? I don't need any preamble to understand that activity is going to come with a lot of problems."

Ember shrugged. "Would you rather they meddle in Cal, with real people? Or be given a crack at Eternia, and all the system problems, they're going to stick their nose in somewhere. We can't actually stop them. We can, at most, slow them down."

Lucia sat next to Ember, making hand motions as she needed a blessing herself at that revelation. A strong one. "Prohibit the taking of omens and do away with superstitious doubts. Then, until death itself comes, no calamity need be feared."

Ember waffled on that blessing, trying one of her own. "A knight finds virtue in balance: too heavily armored and he won't be able to get to the enemy. Too little and he also won't be."

They then both expectantly looked at Artorian, whose eyes were digging into the scroll with all the options on it. He blinked at the silence, looking up as the gears in his head slowly moved into place. "Oh! Uhh... Sorry, dear, I was thinking about attacks, and how I wasn't so much interested in duelist skills as I was toys that erase terrain features that may or may not have bad guys on them. Unlike what has become my normal toolkit, swarms and satellite bodies aren't going to care about my ability to one versus one them."

Ember ruffled his hair. "Well, don't sunburn your soul shedding light on the idea. Add to the teamwork so we can make the dream work. Blessing?"

Artorian blew air from pursed lips as he sat back. This was not his forte. He drew in a big breath and put effort into energetic dramatics. "Punch projectiles. Soak in style points. Heal in the blood of your enemies. Then rampage to the sun! For work or not. Games are meant for fun!"

Lucia and Ember both respectfully soft-clapped at his attempt. Lucia then handed him the full list of options so he could stop craning his neck to lean over and take in the scroll. "That was more of a war cry in my opinion?"

Artorian mumbled about nothing in reply to his blessing not being very good. He was of the wrong persuasion for those. Instead, he tapped Conditional Allspell. "Sugar, I take this one?"

"Yes! I'll show you how. You don't have to say it out loud, but examples help." Ember clapped her hands together, speaking commands words. "New Prompt."

A blank canvas of a screen hummed, glowing into existence in front of her. She then poked it, and a dot flashed on and off in the top left corner. She motioned at Lucia and Artorian to speak the same command. "When you touch the screen and speak, it will record what you say, then someone will try to put the information you added into a sensical enough order for the Pylons to understand. Depending on if you want measurements for your toys in Imperial freedom fractions or metric zero, specify that detail. You can guide the prompt collector to be more likely to send your entry to either a Gnome or Wisp that way."

Artorian copied her, a fresh blank prompt ready for him as well. "Which is which?"

Ember blinked. "That... is a fantastic question. I forgot."

He snorted, hiding his face to stifle the laugh. "I'll figure it out the hard way."

Lucia leaned over to point at two items on the list, curious about something. "Can I have Tornado, and Mine?"

Ember laughed, nodding. "Sure, that will bring the rest of the division out to a clean fifteen for Less than Three, and fifteen for Astarte. As you have an entire bevy of existing abilities, Lucia? Just those two, please."

Lucia gladly finished her list, quickly and easily. "Mine Tornadoes! Tornado Mines! That's going to be so much fun when I specialize in shields and can stand there to revel in the destruction!"

The other two looked at the rabbit with concern.

Ember scratched her own cheek. "You're supposed to be our healer, girl."

"A healer can still contribute to the DPS!" Lucia was so excited to play with her new toys after having been static for so long with her existing ones. "I attended the lectures of Roberts the Ruminating when he puddled about them."

"What is DPS?" Artorian felt like the dumb mook in the room, not knowing these terms, and still being lost on most of the meanings of the listed entries. "I added the Allspell to my note prompt. Can we skip to the list, or are these terms critical?"

"Damage per second." Ember explained rough and quick. "Different dungeons have developed different methods of damage calculation. Lucia was saddled with the version that calculated damage in ticks, and a tick happened every second. DPS also refers to the rough aggregate of damage you are doing, numerically, in that frame of time, when it comes to talking with other dungeons. For the most part, you're not going to need to worry about it. Tim calculates damage in a setting much faster than real time. Just because Cal is slowing the global timeframe does not mean Tim suddenly forgot the value of having more time to react to dumbassery."

She counted on her fingers. "I think… Tim was using ten times frame? One second, this is going to bother me."

Pulling in a fresh prompt, she wrote out math with her fingers, and Artorian did his best to follow her formulas as she narrated them. "Tim uses this 'sixty frames in a second' function. So each real time second for us is actually sixty moments in time where something can happen, tabulate, and finalize. This also means that the maximum number of hits an entity can take per second is capped at sixty, since the Pylons can't tabulate more than one instance of damage per tick, even if the tick can be complex in the event venom is involved and needs to proc during that frame. *Hmm…* so, if I want to flurry blades, I'm stuck at sixty hits per second? That's too slow for me."

Ember drew a new line. "Tim can intervene and allocate additional resources if an event gets particularly complex, increasing the allotment to his time frame, which would be six-hundred frames since he has ten times the leeway, last I knew. Only when that happens would my available hits per second increase to six hundred as well, but I can't constantly keep Tim's attention like that."

She paused, her face complicated. "Why am I calculating this? He can buffer and skyrocket up to seven-hundred and twenty times the existing frame rate, if he wanted to. What I would need to know is which Dungeon gets assigned to oversee our math and frames, and that I don't know."

She dismissed the prompt and erased the contents by throwing it away. "Never mind! Tangent finished. What were we doing?"

Artorian pointed at the scroll. "Which ones do you want?"

She leaned over and scanned the options over. "Well, with you and Lucia both already being casters, I should take both Synchro Casting, so I can cast one of your spells while you do, and Mirrorspell. So I can punch your magical projectiles, as you elegantly termed it, sugar."

Artorian chuckled. "My turn? Suggest me some must-haves."

Ember tapped the Cast modifiers, and Critical Hits. "You are definitely taking these, otherwise you can't designate targets correctly at the moment. Sorry, precious. I know that fills up slots."

Artorian pressed his temple to hers, remaining for a moment to say he did not mind. "I will add them to my list. Currently, I am worried about Proliferation, and the differences between Pierce and Penetrate."

Ember made a loose hand motion to his list. "Add Proliferation to yours, then pick ten more words that you happen to like. Don't worry about what entries do. We can get into that after. I will say that I definitely want all the shapes and projectile multipliers, if you wanted to ignore a few. Including the first three entries on the list, and Grenade."

Artorian copied her loose hand motion at her own list. "Add them to yours right away, then I can mentally cross them out. Pick and choose doesn't normally work well for me."

She did so, having a quick count. "I'm almost topped off already? Do I get to pick Concentrated?"

Her boy laughed, happy that this was being made terribly easy for him! "Ha! Honey, I would rather you choose what you already know you are going to have fun playing with. I don't even know what they all do, but I know that it's the opposite story for you. So pick up Concentrated and nick your fifteenth entry based on what you would have fun with. My choices would have been random, and this is a much more loving solution to my eyes. You know how I feel about those."

She flushed and held his chin to peck his cheek. Leaning against him to pick up the list and look for her last choice, which would conveniently auto-select Artorian's fifteen options. "*Hmmm.* Oh, bother! I completely forgot about the weapon ones!"

She groaned and writhed about like she'd done something stupid but bit her thumb and continued scanning her eyes over the remaining options. "They're no good without each other. If you pick one, you should have the other. Moving on."

Starting from the bottom, she angry-mumbled. "Don't want Spread when I have Concentrated. I want to bundle my effects together, not go fishing with explosives."

Ember reached back to pat at his jacket fluff, thinking of a theme. "If you're going to offer mountain-removal services, I'm going to aim for the duelist kit that you don't want to do. Don't worry about changing your mind later, we might have more Pylons by then. Anything particularly big or single target threatening? I should be handling that anyway. I will have Incarnate class statistics bonuses. My job is to keep the problem off of you, and buy you time, while Lucia's is keeping everyone up and running. If she heals and shields, then I am the armor and war cry. You blow stuff up."

Artorian and Lucia sharply nodded, not arguing with the superior tactician. Artorian might have a bead on being better at local theater strategy, and grand strategy, but Ember was the queen of any close quarters combat that they might encounter, and she had the most functional knowledge on the game. Her word was how they'd do it, that needed no discussion.

Ember had difficulties choosing regardless. "Pierce or Penetrate could be useful… They do the same thing, but to different kinds of defenses. So it's having them both, or having neither. Skip. Sugar? You did ask earlier: Pierce physical armor. Penetrate esoteric magic. Although you can Pierce magic barriers, and Penetrate physical protections, those keywords won't work as well for those purposes compared to using them in the correct word order."

Artorian tapped her shoulder to confirm his understanding, letting her continue uninterrupted. This was helpful! "Lasers are fun… but not for me. Soni burned me out with the Crystal Beamer project. Since we might have to use those in the future when we have to shut whole banks down for safety updates, I'm not touching that option."

She paused, reaching back to hold Artorian's hand on her shoulder. "Speaking of. There's going to come a day when we will not have access to any of the toys we are about to make. Where all we have is lowercase skills and abilities, so do not skimp on developing those. We're going to be reliant purely on gear when that needs to happen. It won't be soon, but it *will* happen. Pre-plan for the long term."

"Of course, dear." Artorian purred out the words, quietly falling in love with how she thought, did things, prepared, and looked out for him as she thought through situations and events, making sure to loop him in.

Lucia noticed how Young-torian dreamily looked at her, even if Ember didn't. Lucia's smirk was quiet as she soaked in the sappy scene. She wasn't interrupting this for the best carrot in the entire crop. Romance was one of her favorite themes, right up there with gossip. She was going to milk this and let the meal simmer on a low boil in a crock pot until the flavor was ready. This delicate love was to be savored, and Lucia wanted to indulge.

Ember was all focus. "Homing would be fantastic, but I recall it's one of those tricks you asked for in the Alpha run and did not get. So you take that one. Gatling... I love Gatling. The daka-daka-daka-daka is music to my ears, but no. I have done a lot with Gatling and you should get to enjoy it! I did hear the story of you Gatling-punching Marie, by the way! Loved it. Show me more of that sometime."

Artorian made an affirming noise, so she continued at pace. "Explode on Hit is my baby. I'm so sad, and so sorry, that I am responsible for breaking the Explode Pylon. The wholesale all-in-one version. So, you get this one too. Which leaves Domino, which is not particularly to my liking, and Charge. I suppose I could up or overcharge quad-quinned grenades? Concentrate them in a cylinder and laugh. Yeah, that gives me the option to skip fuses and timers and detonate my Ability effects at will.

That's a lot better than merely raining craters. I'll take Charge, sugar. With all the multipliers, if I can afford them, that's... two, times three, which gets me six. Times four, which gets me twenty-four. Times five... One hundred and twenty bouncing bomb grenades per activation? That sounds fun. Not very duelist, but fun!"

"Is *that* how this works?" Artorian was trembling with excitement. You could combine these keywords into multi-stacked messes? With effects that changed depending on which order you wrote the effects in? "This is going to be a lot more fun than I thought."

Lucia's list was tiny, but she made it visible to set the precedent. She didn't mind only having two picks, in possession of well over fifty other tips and tricks in comparison to what her current teammates had to work with.

She then felt guilty. "Astarte, let me know when you want these two back. They sound fun, but if you need them for your kit, I can do without."

———

Lucia's Allotment:
Mine
Tornado

———

Ember cackled, showing her finished list as well. "I'll let you know, bun. For now, you play with those. I would love to have Tornado, but I have already done exactly what I said people normally did and deviated from my plan. I really don't have any duelist toys."

———

Astarte's Allotment:

Bomb
Bounce
Bubble
Charge
Concentrated
Cone
Cylinder
Double
Grenade
Line
MirrorSpell
Quad
Quin
Synchro Casting
Triple

"Just make people eat those grenades! That's plenty personal! Can you set them to multiply after you shove a bomb down some oversized critter's throat? That's *still* personal." Artorian beamed, looking over his shoulder at Lucia as he showed them both his own list. "We are going to need so many blessings."

Less than Three's Allotment:
Cast on Self
Cast on Target
Conditional Allspell
Critical Hits
Domino
Explode on Hit
Gatling
Homing
Laser

Penetrating
Pierce
Proliferation
Spread
Weapon Ignition
Weapon Modes

CHAPTER THIRTY

Lucia not responding to the good jest made them both look.

Artorian reached out. "Momma bun?"

The Basher shook her head in clear discomfort. "I can cast the group clean, that's not the problem. It's that I had the small thought to give the entries back, and that has very suddenly and very quickly spiraled into a big pit in my stomach, causing me discomfort. It sounds fun, but I already have so much in comparison, and now the guilt is creeping in, and…"

She shook her head, unhappy.

Ember rubbed over the Basher's head. "No, that's fine, momma bun. Give them to me. We will get you a copy of Mine and Tornado when we get spares, so you can feel better right now, and still get to play with the ideas later. Though that will make me feel a little guilty in turn, so I will be giving Artorian the Bounce entry."

Lucia, conflicted, shoved her prompt into Ember's hands. When the prompt was deleted and two new entries popped up in Ember's list, her ears sagged in relief. "That makes me feel better. I'm sorry, kit, that was a very sudden discomfort and it got to eating me right away. I shouldn't be taking enjoyment away from my babies."

"You're not, momma bun." Artorian joined the head-rubbing activity. Lucia's features had shifted to far more Glitter-flit-oriented shapes, so her current head was that of a Basher, giving both Ember and Artorian plenty of extremely soft fur to brush. "You let us know what you wanted to do with it. We will give it a try, and then when you get your copies, you can plat-form right up to the current version. Since you will already have some information on what didn't work, this is fine. We don't mind. We're happier that you told us. This happens."

Artorian accepted the prompt to acquire Bounce when it appeared but paid the screen minimal attention in favor of helping Lucia through the sudden discomfort spike. "You're going to be alright. Give us a good hug."

A full-sized Glitterflit ended up curling around them both as the massive mommy-bun snuggled into a protective coil, burying them in plushy, warm rabbit fluff. Ember hissed out a most joyous reaction. "Yesssssss. This pleases meeeee."

Lucia released a chittering sound that Artorian interpreted as amusement. He patted the oversized golden rabbit and was broadly licked across the forehead for his trouble. "*Ack*! Bun! My face is clean! I'm already cl—*Ack*!"

Ember lost to the onset of weak giggling, her whole face hidden and buried, as the smallest glance at Artorian fruitlessly pushing a big nose away devolved her laughter to shrieking fits. She then choked on that laughter when it suddenly became her turn, fighting the rabbit nose away herself with an indignant, but powerless: "Noooooo!"

"Ha! Serves you right!" Artorian sniped, pulling a towel from his bracelet to wipe his face clean. He had to stop to look at the towel, having no recollection of adding one to the storage item, and at most holding a vague sense that a towel had been there at all. He then shrugged and didn't look the gift horse in the mouth.

He chose to say nothing about the number printed front

and center on the item that matched the exact spot in the Tower where **Hitchhiking** had put up shop. If the Heavenlies were going to use Lucia, Ember, and himself as a source of amusement, he might as well accept the whole gamut. Wouldn't that mean that they were being watched at all times? Like some kind of reality play? Tim had appeared oblivious to Heavenly influences poking their noses in. How unlikely was it that there were a group of those fine folks seated in plush comforters, watching his little group's adventures in The Pale on some large screen?

Gears turned, and the image of a wrench being shoved into turning spokes made him smile. This was a silly thought, but he could test it. While safe in the protective fluff of momma bun, he tapped his fingers together in a pyramid, then moved the universe with some words. "Say, Emby, why don't we invite a Heavenly to our little merry group of three? If they're going to come meddle anyway, we might as well ask if one of them wants to come along. They're game-numbers bound like the rest of us at that point, if I understand right? Could be fun."

Lucia stopped licking Ember's face like she was a bratty kit to be taken care of, the Glitterflit distressed as her ears and head sprung right up. The mother bun's gaze dropped to look at her boy kit like he had just said that going for a swim in acid might relieve itching. "Can I pretend I didn't just hear you say that?"

Artorian shrugged, knowing the damage was done. It was probably already too late. As a small convenience, he should know how that little gamble paid off in about three... two...

Pop.

Shaka appeared in a whirl of flame, holding onto a singed broomstick with all its bristles missing. His crown-style kufis hat sat crooked on his head, and his dashiki looked as if it had been subject to a riot from how ill it fitted against his shoulders. His voice was accent heavy and hurried. "*What did you do?* Suddenly there was a fight!"

"*What* caused a fight?" Shaka looked distinctly disheveled as Artorian took in his appearance, and that broom had some dents around the places you'd reasonably hit someone with it. Artorian knew what he'd done, but that was no reason to let Shaka think he'd done it on purpose! Not yet. First, the enjoyment. "Shaka, take a seat, you look like you got into a rumble with a clothing tumbler and lost."

"I do not have the drums or the time!" Shaka clung to his broom, adjusting his outfit since it was mentioned. "I must hurry! If there is an open slot on the expedition team, then I wish to—*Glrk!*"

An arm broke through a sudden rent in empty space, grabbed Shaka by the throat, and dragged him whole through the opening. The event happened with the kind of comedy of errors in physics that had physics pull its hands against its own chest and resolve to not touch that rent with a ten foot pole until it resolved itself.

The singed broom clattered to the floor.

Shaka was gone a moment after, the attention of the three Eternia players glued on the rip in space that someone else reached through and closed with a zipper. Afterwards, the rip looked like it had never been never there in the first place.

"Maybe you shouldn't a' did that?" Lucia drawled out, shifting back to her dressed human form. Once more with the ears still present. "I would like to stay far away from Heavenlies, please and thank you. I have my paws full normally, and would like to keep my happy escape, both happy, and an escape."

"Eh, better this way." Artorian shrugged. He then got up and brushed himself off. Pulling his character sheet to the forefront, he sighed as he noted nothing had changed. "Still no statistics, titles, or level increase. Are we supposed to just sit here and muddle with tools until the lever gets tugged?"

Ember looked from the point of empty space, back to Artorian. "Tim was planning to give us Demeter's Dream as a staging area, given how it has stable gravity, light, water, and food. The works. There was always a chance we would show up before The Pale was ready for our siege, and I think we showed up on the cusp of Tim being ready, but not just yet. I think he's doing what he always does and is rushing through the holds to activate the bare essentials of what we need. Then as we need new things, he will prioritize activating or building those. Don't be too concerned about Tim, he's doing it with a giant smile on his face. Better this half-ready endeavor where so much could go wrong than a perfect, quiet, solitary order in a world where he is the lonely god."

She rolled her shoulders, working through some thoughts as that commentary earned her an odd look. Noticing, Ember tried to explain her mystery segue. "The downside of being able to adjust your frames to where the rest of time seems to stand still is that you trade this complete freedom for complete loneliness. This is why Tim's rarely been dipping down below ten times the existing rate of time. Life is better with people in it, even as a dungeon, who are most certainly not people. They do their best to play the mimic, but many Dungeon Cores in the Silverwood had a very difficult time coping with the concept of the world, and everything in it, *not being made of food.*"

Ember then stood, pressing her hands to her hips as the confused look from her party wasn't going away. "Tim is exemplary in that regard, sugar. After your run through in the alpha, he couldn't ignore the love that many were trying to give him. You sped through his world and put a crack in that armor of stoic, cold, logical order."

She beamed at him with a massive smile. "When he looked up at what used to be a colorless sky, he couldn't tear his eyes away from the spark your interference had left behind. The color on the canvas smeared messy and blue. The question of how an insignificant speck could leave such life behind, when he had made actual life. Many of his creations didn't carry so much as a sliver of that splendor of a smear."

Artorian thought this talk was going to be about game mechanics, but he quietly slid the topic cup further onto the table. Was she maybe responding to Lucia in a roundabout way? Ember was going somewhere with this.

"Do you know how difficult it is to make a dungeon cry?"

She chuckled, pulling a towel out of her own bracelet to clean her hair. "I see you do these… small, seemingly mundane things. These words whispered to the ether. You moved a Dungeon who was previously perfectly sated, and while I don't know how much you had to do with placing Yuki in his path, Tim is different now."

She motioned at Lucia, copying her argument the first time this had come up. "A very *good* kind of different. You then say something innocuous, and Heavenlies shift their attention from meddling in Soul Spaces, to having what I surmise to be a massive argument with each other instead. Keeping them not just out of Cal's hair, but Tim's."

Her jaw moved around like she was chewing on some jerky. "I don't know how much of this you plan, and how much of this is off the cuff silliness that you play off like you planned, but never stop, sugar. Never stop."

Ember then looked at Lucia. "You don't feel unpleasant anymore either, do you?"

Lucia reshuffled her position, sitting with her arms crossed, her eyes squinted as tiny gears spun behind them. She had also come to the same conclusion, as Heavenlies keeping each other occupied meant that they weren't going to keep her occupied.

Having seen that they could, very much at will, break into the game world, Lucia no longer felt like the separation between spaces was worth as much as the distraction her adopted kit had slapped onto the proverbial table. "I feel much better. Though I'm approaching the point where I would rather not think about it."

Artorian quietly moved the topic cup back in place and motioned both of his hands to his character screen. "Game?"

Lucia looked at the screen and motioned to dismiss it. She was then confused when it didn't and clicked her tongue. "Right. I forget. Those are yours and you control them. I am so used to the times where only healer classes could pull up anyone's information at all. I still have the spell that lets people see their own health and energy bar too. I haven't used that one for other people in... gosh..."

Artorian motioned at his character sheet. "That information is all fairly visible?"

Lucia frowned and paused, then pointed at empty space to her top left. "You don't see that?"

Ember and Artorian both looked, but saw her point at empty space, and really not much else. He scratched his hair, mostly confused. "See... what? Bun, there's nothing there."

The healer of the group squinted, thought of something, and threw both her hands up. "Do you see these?"

As there was nothing for Artorian and Ember to see, they exchanged glances before shaking their heads to the negative.

Lucia reached out to grab empty space, then a screen appeared as she turned it towards them. "How about now?"

"Eyyy!" Artorian and Ember both shot their arms up, cheering as Artorian returned commentary. "There's a character sheet there now! Though... Is that your character sheet? That doesn't look like the one from earlier. Wasn't Overhealer your Specialization? How did it end up in the Class field?"

Lucia smirked, placing a finger over her lips.

———

Name: Lucia, the Luminant
Character Level: 120
Race: Glitterflit - Humanized
Class: Overhealer
Specialization: Heartfire Shielder
Profession: Medic
Beast Core Rating: Beastly
Core Pool: 100,000.

———

Characteristics:

240

Strength: 815
Dexterity: 1,140
Constitution: 771
Intelligence: 780
Wisdom: 800
Charisma: 1,140
Perception: 1,140
Luck: 772
Karmic Luck: 0

CHAPTER THIRTY-ONE

Ding!

"Eyyy!" Artorian and Ember both shot their arms up again, cheering as they both got the update to become level one, and their character sheets came alive with new information. Soul Forging was but one entry in a horde of prompts, which all arrived like a happy whirlwind of cheer named Vash the Stampede! The whirling prompts far too happy to see a player as they piled on Artorian like a horde of cats all aiming to be on the highest perch.

Ember held her hand up. "Hold that smirk, momma bun. I'm going to want to see the extra screens you have access to in a bit, but we have to accept these prompts immediately. Sugar? Sift through the twelve dozen screens trying to drown you, find the title prompt that has to do with your cultivation rank, and accept it. That step has to be next. The Soul Forging prompt is only going to be a confirmation one."

"You got it!" Artorian did just that, digging himself free and neatly sticking the screens up in the air in a neatly arranged checkerboard pattern. Ember, on the other hand, whistled a shrill tone. Her screens all jumped to attention and organized themselves in neat, militant rows. Artorian could swear that her screens were all saluting her, even if they didn't have the limbs to do so. The prompts just gave him that feeling. "You definitely got it."

He tapped the prompt giving him the title he was looking for, then laughed when it gave him the cookie cutter copy of the exact same one he'd gotten the first time. "Ha! Someone has a good sense of humor."

—————

Title: 'Cultivator'. Cal assigned. Cannot Combine. Gain ATB based on personal Cultivation Rank. F-rank: 1. E-rank: 2. D-rank: 6. C-rank: 24. B-rank: 120. A-rank: 720. S-rank: 5040.

Note: Dani, remind me to settle on ATB or ATTB. I've been using both and that acronym just means 'attributes.' I'm going to confuse people at this rate. That being myself. I know for sure, because it just happened. Thanks, love!

—————

Ember was waiting for his numbers to roll over, while hers fell into her character sheet like the wheels of a slot machine having a conniption fit. She nodded when his attributes tallied, then pulled up the next screen to excitedly point at it. "This one next! You're who put this piece together."

Artorian glanced, felt his eyebrows shoot up, and quickly turned to find the relevant matching tile on his checkerboard. "Growth and Flat bonuses!"

Ember copied Halcyon, flashing a smile of shark teeth. "Your complicated, adorable mess. We currently don't have a good grasp on if Classes need to have stats linked to nothing, Flat bonuses, or Growth bonuses. Or both. There's already too many Classes, and we'd have to go over each one individually if we're going to assign it that way, so we're probably not doing that at all. Currently all classes are set to 'none' when it comes to these bonuses. We need an adaptive way to tell the Pylons when to assign a Flat bonus connection to an attribute, and when to use the Growth type. If we're to apply one at all. That wasn't in your notes."

Artorian held his chin. "Would it be such a terrible idea to allow people a choice?"

Ember chuckled. "Everyone and their grandmother would pick Growth type increases if…"

She frowned, looking at the floor and pressing her hands to her hips. "No… in the case of a caster with poor Con, the Flat Con bonuses would be so much better… There is no point in adding a multiplier to a stat that isn't worth giving percentage increases."

Artorian pondered and needed a fresh opinion. He looked to Lucia, who had one of her ears turned his way. "Momma bun? Question."

He tugged the screen close as additional text rolled in, updating with better entries in real time. He motioned at the math he'd put together a long time ago, keeping his eyes on the updates. Ember had just mentioned the assignment difficulties, and Tim appeared to have heard her. "Thoughts? I currently want to try the 'choice' route, though based on how the entry is now worded, I have the definitive understanding that the choice is permanent to your Class once chosen. If you choose Flat bonuses for a statistic, then you're stuck on Pattern A for that statistic, and can never benefit from the Pattern B bonus. I mean, Attributes? You know what I meant."

Lucia padded up, pressed her hands to her knees since the screen was rather low, and gave the entry a read. Her eyes then shot wide. "Are these… *base formulas*? These are one of the most impossible to unearth secrets! You just *have them*? I could understand that you had connections and knew people in the loop, but this? This is *impossible* to get."

Default Ranges:
  Base Health: 50.
  Health scaling: Remove 10 points from Con, then apply multiplier 10.
  Base Mana Pool: 0.
  Mana Pool scaling: Total Intelligence, then apply multiplier 10.
  Base Mana Regeneration: 0.
  Mana Regeneration scaling: 25% of Wisdom.
  Base Stamina: 50.
  Stamina scaling: Dual source addition.
  Remove 10 points from Con, then apply multiplier 5.
  Remove 10 points from Strength, then apply multiplier 5.
  Base Stamina Regeneration: 0.
  Stamina Regeneration scaling: 25% of Con, plus 25% of Strength.
  Base Languages: 1.
  Language Scaling: Realism limited.
  Language Scaling alternative: Dependent on Improvement Pattern A.
  Base View Distance: 2 miles or 3 kilometers.
  View Distance scaling: Dependent on Improvement Pattern A.
  Base Currency Gain: 5% of base, impacted by relation to source.
  Currency Gain scaling: Dependent on Improvement Pattern A.
  Base Shop Prices: 150%
  Shop Prices scaling: Speech Skill
  Shop Prices scaling alternative: Dependent on Improvement Pattern B.
  Base Notice Obscure: 0%
  Notice Obscure scaling: Dependent on Improvement Pattern B.
  Base Fun Item Find: 0%
  Fun Item Find Scaling: Dependent on Improvement Pattern B.

Improvement Pattern A: Flat Increase - Values are additive.
  Stamina Pool Bonus: Threshold calculated per 50 points in Strength.
  Pattern: Increase Base Flat Bonus by 50, per Threshold, starting at Strength 50.

Pattern: Each earned bonus will stack. Pattern Confirmation-
Increase Base Flat Bonus by 100, at Threshold 100.
Increase Base Flat Bonus by 150, at Threshold 150.
Stamina Regen Bonus: Threshold calculated per 50 points in
Dexterity.
Pattern: Increase Base Flat Bonus by 5, per Threshold, starting at
Dexterity 50.
Pattern: Each earned bonus will stack. Pattern Confirmation-
Increase Base Flat Bonus by 10, at Threshold 100.
Increase Base Flat Bonus by 15, at Threshold 150.
HP Modifier: Threshold calculated per 50 points in Constitution.
Pattern: Increase Base Flat Bonus by 50, per Threshold, starting at
Constitution 50.
Pattern: Each earned bonus will stack. Pattern Confirmation-
Increase Base Flat Bonus by 100, at Threshold 100.
Increase Base Flat Bonus by 150, at Threshold 150.
Mana Pool Bonus: Threshold calculated per 50 points in Intelligence.
Pattern: Increase Base Flat Bonus by 50, per Threshold, starting at
Intelligence 50.
Pattern: Each earned bonus will stack. Pattern Confirmation-
Increase Base Flat Bonus by 100, at Threshold 100.
Increase Base Flat Bonus by 150, at Threshold 150.
Mana Regeneration Bonus: Threshold calculated per 50 points in
Wisdom.
Pattern: Increase Base Flat Bonus by 5, per Threshold, starting at
Wisdom 50.
Pattern: Each earned bonus will stack. Pattern Confirmation-
Increase Base Flat Bonus by 10, at Threshold 100.
Increase Base Flat Bonus by 15, at Threshold 150.
Language Bonus: Threshold calculated per 50 points in Charisma.
Pattern: Increase Base Flat Bonus by 1, per Threshold, starting at
Charisma 50.
View Distance Bonus: Threshold calculated per 50 points in
Perception.
Pattern: Increase Base Flat Bonus by 1km, per Threshold, starting at
Perception 50.

Currency Gain Bonus: Threshold calculated per 50 points in Luck
Pattern: Increase Base Flat Bonus by 5%, per Threshold, starting at Luck 50.

Improvement Pattern B: Growth Increase - Values replace existing multipliers.
Stamina Pool Modifier: Threshold calculated per 50 points in Strength.
Pattern: Increase Multiplier by 0.1%, per Threshold, starting at Strength 50.
Stamina Regeneration Modifier: Threshold calculated per 50 points in Dexterity.
Pattern: Increase Multiplier by 1%, per Threshold, starting at Dexterity 50.
HP Modifier: Threshold calculated per 50 points in Constitution.
Pattern: Increase Multiplier by 1, per Threshold, starting at Constitution 50.
Mana Pool Modifier: Threshold calculated per 50 points in Intelligence.
Pattern: Increase Multiplier by 2.5, per Threshold, starting at Intelligence 50.
Mana Regeneration Modifier: Threshold calculated per 50 points in Wisdom.
Pattern: Increase Multiplier by 1%, per Threshold, starting at Wisdom 50.
Shop Prices: Threshold calculated per 50 points in Charisma.
Pattern: Decrease Cost by 1%, per Threshold, starting at Charisma 50.
Notice Obscure: Threshold calculated per 50 points in Perception.
Pattern: Increase Chance by 1%, per Threshold, starting at Perception 50.
Fun Item Find: Threshold calculated per 50 points in Luck.
Pattern: Increase Chance by 1%, per Threshold, starting at Luck 50.

Lucia blinked, looking up at the both of them. "Who *are* you people?"

Artorian looked at Ember in deep confusion. "Did we fail to introduce ourselves properly? I vaguely remember some ploy I had in mind, but I have forgotten what it was. The imperfect storage device strikes again."

Ember scratched her red hair. "We might have? I honestly don't remember, and I'm so used to people outright knowing us, that it never occurred to me."

She turned her full attention to Lucia. "Momma bun, are you playing a joke? Or do you seriously have no idea who we are?"

Lucia made a humming noise as she squinted and bit her lower lip. "I think… Lisette might have yelled something while I was trying to escape the pavilion, but I didn't register the words. I have heard some titles being flung around, but with you two being kits, I didn't put weight to them. That said, you clearly know some… frightening people."

Lucia stole their accounting system, using her digits to count. "You can interact with Heavenlies like I do, if not better. You have rapport with people who are clearly potent dungeons, and equally potent cultivators. You have seemingly free access to information that is so secret, Heavenlies don't have it, and I know that for sure because the entire lot of them are blabber-mouths and cannot shut up when they realize there is an opportunity to gab."

She restarted her count. "Yuki is a person I met once and immediately learned to fear. Halcyon is the single most fantastic Beast I have ever met, but she could bend me into a pretzel if she wanted to. Then given that you know Shaka on a first name basis? I'm starting to feel very much out of my depth here. Zelia and Tim were clearly Dungeons, based on their smell, but Tim visibly has run of the place, like this *is* his place. Which is an assumption I'm leaning into a frightful amount. Zelia is…"

Lucia didn't even know what to say. "You're not Heavenlies,

you're not dungeons, you're not cultivators, you gave off no power signatures whatsoever, and yet the statistics on your character sheets tell me an entirely different story. You have equipment so advanced that I've not even heard stories of the bracelets you're wearing and are being given very public affection by all of the people I just mentioned."

She ran her hands down her ears, admitting defeat. "I am wholly confused by most of the things you talk about. I adore you two as kits that I have already adopted, but it is becoming harder and harder to keep seeing you both as kits. You two *look* like children. Neither of you *act* like children. I am *lost*."

Artorian barely held his smirk. "I am heavily tempted not to explain anything."

Ember giggled. "Yeah, but that wouldn't be very loving, would it?"

Artorian pouted, his lower lip curling. "You just had to bring that up right away?"

Ember snickered, casually walking up next to Lucia and extending a hand. "Your kit needs her hand held. How much do you want to know?"

Lucia tensed, feeling the danger inherent in the question as she cautiously took Ember's hand. Wanting answers was great, but she knew all too well the burden of knowing too much and knowing the wrong things in abundance. "What... is the safe amount that I can be told, without getting into trouble, but also without me having to live with this headache?"

Artorian considered the question, and Ember waited for him to reply since he stared off into space. "Well... You're on the team, but if you believe you're the one who adopted us, we have some laughing to do. I suppose I only have one real concern. Emby, what's our timeline looking like?"

Ember checked the prompts still waiting on them. "We need a few more prompts than this before we can actually go do anything, so we have time. Snuggle puddle and fireside chat?"

Artorian nodded in agreement. "Snuggle puddle and fireside chat. Lucia? Please sit and make yourself cozy. We will get on your lap and tell you the tales of a long-bearded grandfather, and an ashen blade of war."

CHAPTER THIRTY-TWO

Lucia held each of their hands, starry-eyed after a whole day of story time. Many boring screens, information to read, explainers, and other administrative and tutorial prompts had come and gone in the meanwhile. Lucia went to sleep afterwards, needing a nap.

Ember and Artorian huddled together next to the fire, poking and prodding at screens, swapping thoughts and ideas as they occasionally checked on their momma bun. Lucia had taken their history well enough and had at many points felt like she'd missed the obvious.

In the end, the momma bun had all the apostrophes hit her at once. A sight that had amused them both greatly when Lucia finally understood where to place everyone. She had curled up into a ball and held her ears to her face, quietly screaming.

In bun's experience, there should have been at least five to eight steps of being stopped by other people before interacting with the kind of caliber and rank she'd encountered.

Lucia had Sisters that would stop visitors at the door, if they even managed to make it to the door. Those visitors would then have to get past her Goblin guards. If her Protectors approved, then it was good luck with the Mother Superior. If a visitor got past that, Lisette would normally be the final stopping point before anything or anyone not a Heavenly made it to her directly.

Ember had whispered to her boy to let the bun cope, so Artorian had nodded and done just that. They were both going over the Growth and Flat attribute increase tables again, with Artorian holding his head at the maddening number of options in which a single attribute could change. "So there are Radiant versions of an Attribute, Dark versions of an Attribute, and Elemental versions of Attributes. They can have colors, alignments, allegiances, energy types, concept themes, and *moods*? That's just one column of options out of…"

He counted with a quickness. "Fourteen!"

Ember stealthily moved one of his screens to shift his attention. Artorian's eyes snapped to the other prompt, his mouth not having taken a speaking break other than to breathe. "Then, depending on this other list that's so complicated that I can tell a Gnome put it together, Attributes can have neither Flat nor Growth bonuses. Attributes can qualify for one or the other. Or Attributes that might qualify for both under what I can only call ridiculous conditions. Then as a cherry on top of the pie, that Attribute change and advancement is not necessarily related to the main Attributes that a Class is going to focus on? This is a cluster cluck even with all the information at my fingers. Is there a Wisp version instead?"

Ding!

Artorian looked up, annoyed at yet another bevy of prompt mail. "Oh, now what? This is endless. At some point, I would actually like to play this game instead of tackling all these screens! I'm getting so bogged down with new information that I'm losing out on using any of it, and I'm starting to lose the thread of what was supposed to go where. This is seriously too much. Especially all at once."

He then motioned at the formulas screen they'd been taking

apart. "Do we have to do this now, dear? I'd really like to make some damage numbers appear that aren't zero."

Ember agreed, equally eager to play with fire. "We do not, but while we can leave our Attributes unaffected, we should pick a few options to test this. I know that I desperately want Notice Obscure, or Fun Item Find. Those Pylons aren't available without a player having the correct track active and won't trigger at all if they can avoid doing the work. Charisma, Perception, and Luck don't affect the numbers most people will be looking at most often, but to me they are more valuable."

Her tone soured. "I am still very unhappy that there are penalties for deviating one Attribute score too much from another. I understand *why* it is that way, and why the game tries to simulate what it's like for a cultivator to have their senses and drives be out of whack, but I don't agree from a gamification standpoint. There should be no reason to get slapped by those awful punny penalties just to play the game. I currently don't get to enjoy having double the strength than I do any other attribute, if that's what I wanted to focus on."

Ember then spoke to the sky with a hopeful note. "Turnip? If you're keeping an ear out, I want a title that gets around that!"

"Have them!" Artorian was certainly not going to deny her mechanics that Emby knew she wanted. He nodded in understanding of her balancing concern, as both perspectives made enough sense for him to sit on the same fence. If the purpose of high Attributes was to simulate being a high-powered cultivator, then knowing what being unbalanced felt like without having to suffer the more serious effects was a boon. On the other hand, if this was meant to be something done for fun, the penalties associated for not keeping your attributes clustered within the same ranges were... very annoying. "Since there are eight Attributes, how about testing four Growth types, and four Flat types?"

The question pulled Ember out of her distaste for the unresolved problem. "I like that. I'll pick four as well."

Artorian pulled up purely the Attributes portion of his character sheet, then drummed fingers together. He glanced back and forth between the effects listed, and what he could apply them to. As Ember had said, the bottom three entries connected differently. He wasn't going to fuddle with Radiant or Dark versions of his Attributes if he could help it, or any of those other fiddly choices.

For a system that was light on core functions, the existing functions had so many added options that the rabbit hole felt far too deep. He then recalled that Earth dungeons had a thing for focusing on a singular problem, rather than branching out. The thought made him nod to himself, as Tim did seem to be the kind of person who would dig these sorts of rabbit holes.

―――――

Characteristics:
Strength: 740
Dexterity: 740
Constitution: 740
Intelligence: 740
Wisdom: 740
Charisma: 740
Perception: 740
Luck: 740

―――――

"Any suggestions, before I play pick and choose?" Artorian hummed the words with an offhand mention, but Ember pushed directly into his field of view and poked his Constitution attribute.

"You shove Growth on this. The difference is minor, but the more health you have, the more chances Lucia has to get you back on your feet." When Ember leaned out, he tapped the Constitution entry, and selected the Growth type advancement out of the multiple-choice drop-down list. He didn't know what many of the other options were, so he ignored those for now. There was too much to keep track of as it was, and he really did want to start small. Being flooded with too much information at once would likely see him take a path of exile out of the game, never to return due to obnoxious, poorly explained complexity. He wanted bite-sized introductions!

"Growth on Con it is." Artorian confirmed the entry, then tapped a few others that he'd already decided on. "Luck was my happy place last time; I expect that to hold true. I'm joining your Fun Item Find bandwagon and slotting Growth as well."

He looked over to see where Ember was slotting her options. "If you are putting Growth on Charisma and Perception, then I will slot in Flat on my end."

At seeing her apply Growth to both Strength and Dexterity, he went ahead and did the opposite. This immediately filled up his personal-choice limitation of four Flat-type choices. Which made it equally easy to slap Growth into the other options, and not need to think about it twice.

––––––

Characteristics: Improvement Choice.
Strength: Pattern A: Flat
Dexterity: Pattern A: Flat
Constitution: Pattern B: Growth
Intelligence: Pattern B: Growth
Wisdom: Pattern B: Growth
Charisma: Pattern A: Flat
Perception: Pattern A: Flat
Luck: Pattern B: Growth

––––––

Characteristics: Threshold 700, Total Bonus:
Strength: 5,250 Base Stamina Pool.

Dexterity: 525 Stamina Regeneration.
Constitution: Multiplier of 10, replaced by Multiplier of 24.
Intelligence: Multiplier of 10, replaced by Multiplier of 45.
Wisdom: Value of 25%, replaced by Value of 39%.
Charisma: Bonus Language slots: Plus 14.
Perception: View distance clarity: Plus 14 Kilometers, or 9 Miles, rounded up.
Luck: FIF chance, Plus 14%.

Artorian then realized that, regardless of his update, he wasn't seeing his health, mana, or stamina, anywhere. The entries were all blank. He poked at the vacant slot, forcing it to make an unhappy error sound. "Emby, am I missing something here?"

She perked up to look. "Ah, remember that bit about us needing a few more prompts before we could begin? That's one of the blocked features."

She held up a blue private message screen. "I did just get a missive? You're getting new Pylons added to your personal bank. Neither Kronk nor Ratatoskr gave Cy any lip or trouble when she fell from the sky to kindly ask for their cooperation. Who knew that a thundering orbital drop, followed by a slow and smoky rise, only for a several ton, ten-foot-tall Orca lady in heavy armor to point at you while making angry growling noises, could be a convincing argument all by itself."

She slapped her hand to her chest with a wistful sigh. "*Ahh*, I shall learn from her example."

Artorian squinted at her. "You say that, but didn't she pick that move up from you in the first place?"

Ember smirked wide. "I can neither confirm nor deny this accusation."

Artorian chuckled, pushing confirmation prompts on his choices. They could be good choices. They could be bad choices. That currently wasn't very important to him. Others, he expected, might be screeching in the peanut gallery about optimizations or how one choice would be better than another, but to Artorian that was moot. He wanted to have all his ducks in a row to get going, and if a convincing argument came his way later for a change, that bridge could be crossed then. Or burned, depending.

He knew that Deverash, his system-loving Gnomish friend, would love to spend days talking his ear off about the minute differences between the numbers and why they mattered, but Artorian wanted none of it.

Ding!

Artorian closed his eyes. He didn't want to look at the next flood of new messages and prompts. He hadn't even addressed the last chunk sent his way yet. "That needs to stop."

"There's only one, sugar." Ember clarified to be helpful. "You can press accept, it's the **Nuts** and **Bolts** you requested. My message says that Kronk and Ratatoskr were both appreciative of your thought to have them do things by the nut. They would have done the work as instructed, but they are both thankful for the creative liberty, and have requested to change the names of some of your core features. Such as renaming your energy bar. There's a note in here that this change will allow them to use... the Nuttelator? I don't want to know."

Ember pointed at the single new prompt when her boy peeked an eye open. "That's their yes or no query."

Artorian slapped accept. "Let the good times roll. If it will make them happier to be working with me, then I will be happy to have them. The Pale is enough of a downer, and if I can get to know the Pylons I'm working with on a personal level, that would honestly bring me joy."

Ember held her response, feeling awkward with the red screen she was holding. "*Uhhh...* well, they heard you just now, because I opened up a communication block with them. So, consider that successful? They're sending me written messages, because as Pylons they don't have a voice, but they're saying that they really appreciate that you feel that way, and that they'd be delighted to have you, should you find the time to go see them. They say that the Nuttelator will be up and running shortly, and that as soon as your health bar shows up, you will be a functional player character as far as the system is concerned. Plus, that your damage calculations will become available as well, as they are doing the math. They do warn that all your damage might be referred to as a value in nuts."

Artorian beamed. "That's fine. Hello boys! Glad to hear you're both happy! I had concerns when I heard how Cy picked you up, but I am ecstatic to have you both here, and thank you so much for agreeing to help. I know that, in the end, you could have declined. I don't know what life as a Pylon is like, but do let me know if something is amiss, or otherwise missing? The last time I was in a Pylon Hold for a long time, I made it a party."

He then bopped and bobbed his head thinking of it. "Speaking of, now I miss sunglasses, music, and the dance moves."

Ember considered that, then had a devious idea. "I think... that would be a lot more fun to have! Let me send out a few messages. There is no reason we can't make the work we have to do a lot more fun as we're doing it. We're as strong as Bosses here! We need Boss Music!"

Ding!

Artorian looked at the prompt instead of the flurry of Ember's gleeful, devious-minded activity. "Oh, hey, my stats!"

He then frowned at seeing some worrisome differences, and that he might have just made a terrible mistake by not asking his more math-inclined friends some questions. "I see that this could have gone better."

Update: Current values.
  Hit Points: 17,570.
  Mana Pool: 33,300.
  Mana Regen: 288 / second.

Stamina Pool: 12,600.
Stamina Regen: 710 / second.
Note: The path not taken.
Hit Points, Pattern A: 12,600.
Mana Pool, Pattern A: 12,650.
Mana Regen, Pattern A: 710 / second.
Stamina Pool, Pattern B: 9,394.
Stamina Regen, Pattern B: 577 / second
Other:
Language slots: 15.
Vision Range: 17 Kilometers.
Fun Item Find: 14%.

Artorian grumbled, kneading his forehead. "Well, that's my hubris costing me for wanting to rush. I should have gone for Pattern A on the Mana Regeneration, given I'm going to be spell-flinging. Ah well."

Ding!

Update:
*Your Mana Pool has been renamed to: **Nuts**.*
*Your Stamina Pool has been renamed to: **Bolts**.*
Note:
Rules concerning capitalization were discovered, and ignored.
In addition: Hlmlrmrmmllmrl!

Artorian jerked, a slight rush of electricity coursing under his skin and between his fingers as the update took effect. "*Whoof!* Tingly!"

He then pressed two fingers together, not certain why

copper lightning was consistently appearing and without fail managing to manifest like that. "Ember? I am confused."

"I'm not!" She shouted her revelation, turning the communication screen that connected her to the Squirrels toward him. "Voltekka found your new friends! They're both screaming and hiding at the top of the proverbial tree because a large copper-lightning dinosaur is tail wagging at them. Your Stamina turned **Bolts** is joined by a possibly non-thematic lightning effect. I suggest getting used to it. Tekka is not going to leave them alone anytime soon, and they apologize for any issues this might cause with calculations. They say the Nuttelator is never wrong, but that their calculator is dependent on them being able to add all the numbers in before Tekka can catch them."

Artorian held his face. *"Wonderful."*

CHAPTER THIRTY-THREE

One extraordinary good sleep later, Artorian woke in a delightful bed by his lonesome. He had wanted the quiet time after the events of the day before had become too much. He pressed two fingers together and said nothing until a spark of copper lightning connected his digits as they separated. "Tekka... You..."

He didn't finish his sentence. Voltekka was part of the family, but family could be frustrating. He had no idea how the dino had gotten to wherever his personal Pylon bank was hosted, nor how he was accosting Pylons, but he had no trouble believing it. The finger-crackling alone was proof enough, and in lieu of that, Voltekka was one of *his*. If that dino had gotten even a glimpse of the memories that his other Chosen had become privy to for their growth, Voltekka was possibly the most clever, dangerous dinosaur of his kind.

He imagined Tekka sneaking in somewhere, to the shock and screaming detriment of whoever was present when they came face to face with a carnivore's dinosaur mouth. "Clever girl."

He then wondered about Tekka's gender for half a second but shrugged and let it go.

Artorian spent some hours wandering about the place since he was the only one awake and found all the facilities necessary for a mortal to keep healthy and untroubled. Once fresh, washed, and in possession of a snack, he fought with his own legs as they carried him back to where a horde of screens still waited on him. He didn't know how to feel about them all hovering in the same places he'd left them, half-hoping they might have winked out of existence.

He sighed, sat, and made a 'come here' motion. "Alright, let's crack on with it. These biscuits won't eat themselves."

The broom that Shaka had dropped was the only item to actually respond, the cleaning stick hovering up and next to him. Artorian chuckled, storing the broom in his bracelet for now.

His ears picked up faint music, but it was too faint to place. He discarded the sensory information and got to administrative work. Some prompts were updates, little messages, things to press accept on and let go. He liked those. He also received an unexpected prompt from Halcyon, who had somehow figured out a way to offer him the Crit-Fisher specialization early. There was some bubbling around the brook concerning Specializations otherwise not unlocking until the tenth level, and he currently didn't have a method of leveling up at all. Some scribbling about necessary exceptions to make the game work.

He accepted the offer for convenience and was surprised there was no information pop-up like there had been with his prior Specializations. He took it in stride. That prompt could wait, as the most important information on those was how many Attributes increased, when, and where. Plus what the Spec actually did, which he had a decent idea of.

He was humming to himself when the music was getting noticeably louder, but he remembered that Ember had been devious yesterday, so this was likely one of those surprises that was going to get sprung on him. He might as well let them have their fun and ignored the music a second time.

When the sound of a building being kicked to pieces overrode that music, he thought it best to stand and look at what was going on. Ember had, in a blur of heat and fire, whisked her way around a large statue and now stood on the top of that effigy's head. Her stance was… combat ready? What?

She looked around, seeing him make the 'what is going on' gesture. Ember boomed down at him. "Do you hear that music as well?"

Lucia whined out from the house now little more than rock and rubble, wiping dust from her ears as she sauntered free. "That's not all I heard; my ears are still ringing from you kicking the entire wall out! Also, yes, the music is coming from over there."

The healer pointed, partially at the ceiling, mostly in the direction of one of the mesas. "What is that instrument? It does sound nice."

Ember was not of the same opinion, and Artorian recognized the tension in her stance as it shifted from caution to warmode. He instantly dismissed all his screens and ran for the statue. "Lucia! Form up! Now!"

Lucia's instincts kicked like a mule, her form flittering into that of a full-sized Glitterflit as a golden smear slashed across the landscape. Their healer arrived at the base of the statue before Artorian was halfway there.

Mid-run, Artorian looked again to the place Lucia had pointed, and had no idea what he was looking at. A smallish creature was slowly rising, head first, above one of the hip-height walls next to one of the empty homes. The black and white colorations reminded him of Halcyon, but the orange beak made him think of a goose. He wasn't worried until the creature rose high enough for one of the flippers to become visible, as at the end of one of its flippers, there was a knife. A knife made entirely of cheese. A knife that was part of that creature's flipper.

"Is that Lacrimosa, by Mozart?" Ember yelled her question, but neither of her teammates had an answer for her. "If that Goose is— Aw, Abyss. It's the *Cheese Penguins.*"

Artorian made it to the base of the statue and was instantly bopped by a golden paw. A thin shield bubbled around him before changing shape to cling skintight against his being, before fading out of sight. He could still feel it exist, but it wasn't in his way in any form.

He then heard one of his new, least favorite sounds as the Penguin did something strange with its eyes. Like tiny pinpricks of red light slowly increased in intensity, as it made a sharp, high-pitched call.

"Noot noot!"

Ember cursed violently, then shifted her focus. "Three! Don't use anything other than game names around these things! Do you have attacks ready?"

Artorian took that order like it was a command to live by. "Understood, and negative! I'll put one together!"

Ember exploded from the statue head, turning it into molten slag as her form shot like a burning arrow toward the Cheese Penguin. "I'll buy you time! More are coming, and I will bet my favorite left sock that—"

The rumble from something larger, more cosmic, and far more intense in lung-capacity cut Ember's words off at the same moment that it solidified her worry. The ceiling to Demeter's Dream cracked wide open as giant tendrils of string cheese peeled it apart. The fake sky failed to continue being present, bringing the party face to an asteroid-sized not-face. Brother Moon, whose horrific mouth was far too octopi-like for anyone's liking, coiled it open wide and hungry as an innumerable number of sharp, cheddar tentacles descended upon them from the sky. The sound it made was that of the Penguin's but originating from a location so deep from the back of an ocean-sized throat that Artorian didn't think he could possibly replicate it.

"Noooooooooot nooooooooooot!"

"I do not like The Pale!" Artorian howled back, full-body shivers wrecking his senses. He could see Brother Moon eating the torn off chunks of Demeter's Dream as its cheesy knife-arm-things pulled away whole wall sections, far faster than he was comfortable with. "Astarte! Do you still have those Serenity Bees? This is not a good battleground! We gotta go!"

One explosive Penguin-punt later, and Astarte had turned in place with enough force to crack an entire chunk of Patagonia granite out of the foundation, everything built on it going down with it as the chunk tumbled from the mesa. "On it! Stay put! I'm coming to you! Bun, I can only do two bees, grab Three!"

Artorian took that information and shifted to pulling up the prompt that would let him slap an attack together. He hurriedly adjoined it with his sixteen custom build options and didn't fight Lucia one bit when she picked him up and jumped onto a horse-sized Serenity Bee. He hadn't seen Ember fuel the globs Api had given her and pull them into existence, but he had other priorities!

With Artorian fully invested in trying to make something useful for the situation, they zipped through the cheesy infestation, darted between teeming tendrils, and dodged goopy nets of fondue. They broke free from Demeter's Dream's confines by the sheer incredible skill of the Serenity Bees who were determined to burst out into the black. As if this paltry, sticky blockade was an affront to their freedom with its very attempt to hold and confine them.

The sky was theirs.

Seconds of being alive or not, the bees entered existence, understood implicitly who the queen was and what she needed, then engaged their engines and asked no questions before pushing to full throttle. Their butts burned with a bright orange glow, and like a bat out of the Abyss, blew on through the cheesy blockade like they were smuggling illicit honey.

Ember's focus was entirely on piloting, while Lucia threw out static shields that bought enough fractions of a second for an incoming attack to hit something other than both of their bees. When through the worst of the DeBrie field, Ember snapped out a need for direction. Artorian heard her voice come out of a small spider insignia that he hadn't noticed on his inner collar fluff before. He most certainly couldn't hear her say anything from her actual position. "Where are we going?"

Artorian felt like this was his area. His mind snapped to an answer to avoid paying attention to the cessation of the pleasant conditions that Demeter's Dream had provided. Outside of its protections, empty space proved to be a cruel mistress that he didn't miss one iota. Especially not without a full set of Iridium armor between him and the void.

The cold hit first, joined by the eerie quiet. The buzzing of bee wings turned from prevalent, to missing outright, the moment they crossed over the Dream's protective shell. He couldn't focus on that emptiness right now.

The answer provided was one of simple instructions. One should begin at the beginning, and if a certain portation platform remnant was still using the same chunk of Artifact? Then perhaps Solar Gate still had that one option to become exorbitantly hot. How much access to the system did he currently have with his prompts anyway? Had they been set to Administrator level by default? A stone's throw into oblivion returned an unexpected prompt, but one that made the youngster grin from ear to ear.

Activity Log:

Teleportation Beacon 14

Magical wreckage, titled: 'Solar Gate'

Location: Midgard

Status: Active

Claimed: Artorian

Effect: Absorbs loose and directed mana to power latent functions.

Function: Uncertain, original function unknown. Appears to cause a 'create heat' effect, as the byproduct of what was intended. Wreckage open for alteration to remove the unknown latent function.

———

Activity Log:
   Magical wreckage, titled: 'Solar Gate.'
   Alteration option one: Replace current effects with an ability of the claimant. A Core is required to power this effect.
   Alteration option two: Shift the absorption runes to power the connected beacon instead, amplifying the beacon's power and teleportation range.
   Alteration option three: Shift the beacon runes to power the magical wreckage, activating latent functions by forcibly revealing them. Warning, it might get hot.

———

Activity Log:
   Selection: Alteration option two.

———

Activity Log:
   Pylon damage, entries lost.

———

Activity Log:
   Forceful Deactivation, critical Pylon failure.
   Alteration option two, non-functional.
   Forceful Decoupling, critical Pylon failure.
   Claimant: Entry blanked.
   Forceful Desynchronization, critical Pylon failure.
   Portation network: Disabled.

Activity Log:
 Access attempt: Teleportation Beacon 14.
 Legacy Quest Invoked.
 Quest: To be the best there ever was.
 Rule right, rather than with might.
 Requirements: As both a person and a ruler, strive to be the best you can be. Act in the best interest of your people and see them flourish and be merry.
 Access: Granted.
 Current Assignee: Duchess of Katarina.

Activity Log:
 Teleportation Beacon 14
 Magical wreckage, titled: 'The Generator.'
 Location: Midgard
 Status: Active
 Claimed: Duchess of Katarina.
 Selection: Alteration option three.

Artorian had his direction. "Midgard! Find Duchess! We can deal with this on the way."

Lucia thought that was a carrot too big to take a bite out of, but if her kit was convinced that he had something that could take out or slow down the horrific thing eating their prior safe haven? She was all ears.

From her understanding, Three was the boy with the crazy, quick plans that tended to work out, and Astarte was their resident powerhouse. So if Three said Midgard, then Midgard it was! Frozen over Abyss-hole or not. She couldn't see how that location was going to be of any help, but one look over her shoulder made her very glad not to be the one needing to make any of those decisions. "Brother Moon is leaving the Dream alone, instead of munching on it, and is turning toward us!"

She then paled uncomfortably. "That is a *lot* of hit points…"

CHAPTER THIRTY-FOUR

Artorian furiously fought the system, slapping away error messages to force bits and bobs together. When one of the prompts outright shattered after flashing a few sickly variations of red, he pulled his hands to his chest. "That did not work. Astarte! I need a lead!"

Her voice returned with outstanding clarity from the miniature spider insignia. "Start with the basic idea, then the shape if it needs one, then the details, then add special effects!"

"On it!" Artorian threw up a fresh prompt, pulled a cobalt quill from his bracelet without thinking about it, and began to write on the screen as if it were any old piece of paper. Would this work? He would find out!

The other method was failing. He became too stressed to do it Tim's way, too unused to the process. Tim's method was orderly, but slow, laborious, and fine on the details. Well-ordered prompts required time that he didn't have, given the attention span available. When nothing occurred, he swiftly inspected the quill, discovering it was out of ink, and had no well to draw from.

A stroke of genius thundered through his mind, and Artorian dictated his thoughts to the waiting prompt. He didn't want to dictate his abilities at all if he could help it, expecting Brother Moon to be able to hear him just fine in the void. Even if Brother Moon could not, it was in general a poor idea to telegraph your repertoire in detail, for all to hear. The current circumstance shouldn't change that pattern. "Ratatoskr! Ink to Bolts, Bolts to Ink! I need a way to work these prompts under duress. My inner scribe howls! Let me write!"

The prompt whisked away. To Artorian, it took but a moment for good news to arrive as some space was allocated to the Ability in his personal Adaptive Pylon bank. A notice bundle popped up along with his good news.

Ding!

———

Notice!
72 out of 1703 Adaptive Pylons used.

———

Notice!
You have gained the Profession: Scribe
You are a record keeper, jurist, and vessel of bound knowledge. Through your carved and painted words, eternity is cataloged, and remembered.

———

Ability Gained: Ink to Bolts, Bolts to Ink!
Where you write, your words remain forever.
Effect: You may use your Bolts meter to write using any valid scribing implement, including in system prompts. Your Ink has the properties of copper, cobalt, and lightning.

———

Notice!
Message from Ratatoskr: Bolts for the win!
Message from Kronk: The Nuttelator hungers for Big Deeps!
Message from Eternium: I'm terribly sorry, I now can't stop them from messaging you. You did this to yourself. Call up your New Game Plus prompt anytime to import a selection of features from your last playthrough but be careful! They will take up adaptive Pylons, and you only have so many. Good luck, bud. We're all ready for your lasers! You can use other base forms, but if you stick to the list that I know you were snuck, then it won't use up allotment on your personal bank. Try the command HitScan when building the base format! I just finished it!

Artorian could feel the electricity at his fingertips find purchase within the cobalt quill. Wasting no time, he barreled onwards as his eyes ate up the messages before dismissing them with a thought. "New prompt!"

The fresh screen flickered to life. It was grabbed by the edge and pulled in to double as a table as Artorian pressed his quill tip to the glowing panel. Focus filled his senses. The world and its nonsensical death race to dodge hurled cheesteroids muting further and further into the background. Leaving Ember to chuck multiplying miniature suns behind them as a minefield, and Lucia to play whack a mole with any sneaky beaky threats that danced and wove through that tapestry of *boom*. She improvised with her shields, using one like a slipper to whack the unruly! Batting away the dangers that Artorian was blind to.

Ember and Lucia had him covered. It was his job to bring the big damage, or as Kronk had enlightened him with terminology: The Big Deeps.

What was his basic idea? He needed a tool, or an attack, that let him damage or otherwise inconvenience a country-sized creature. Coming to the swift conclusion that such a feat was likely not feasible, he scribbled his next best idea into the prompt, added Tim's suggestion even though he had no idea what the word meant, and sent it off! "Let's see what that gets us!"

Ding!

―――――

Ability Gained: HitScan Laser - Nuttelator Edition.
Notice!
Ability Requires Renaming.
Notice!

HitScan: A hitscan effect is where the Pylon system determines where the origin of an attack is pointing, casts out a ray in that direction when activated, and sees if that ray comes in contact with any object in the line of fire. Unlike the physics calculation of projectiles, when an attack functions in this manner, there is no travel time between the attack's activation, and delivery receipt. Because the attacks have no travel time, merely designating the target is sufficient to register a hit, making them more forgiving for aiming at greater distances than projectile weapons. HitScan functionality prevents the need to lead your shots but requires a clear line of sight to the point of intended impact.

Note: A hidden benefit has been applied due to synergy with Perception Pylon: Advancement Pattern A.

Laser: A narrow beam of light that deals thermal damage via continuous-wave operation. Continuous-wave operation allows the laser to keep dealing damage so long as energy is fed into the effect.

Damage: HitScan Laser at the Novice rank deals damage per second proportional to the energy invested. Investing a drain of 100 Nuts or Bolts per second will cause the laser to deal 100 damage per second.

Note: Connecting this ability with a source of knowledge will improve this entry.

Note: Each rank increase allows an improvement to the entry.

―――――

Artorian had only one thought after scanning over the entry, scribbling in the new name and sending it back for an immediate update. For good measure, and because he expected it, Artorian also added some improvement ideas when the rank increased. It wouldn't eat into this Adaptive Pylon bank that he hadn't figured out the value of yet, so might as well! "This one's for you, Decorum."

He smiled like an Orca when the update was returned to him, until he frowned at the last line. Why would Domino and Gatling be unavailable?

Ding!

Update!

Ability: Shining Ray.

Special Qualities: HitScan, C-Laser, Perception Range Bonus.

Affinity: Liger Prime.

Rank: Student.

Novice: Deal thermal damage per second proportional to the energy invested. Investing a drain of 100 Nuts or Bolts per second will cause the laser to deal 100 damage per second.

Beginner: Critical Hits - Shining Ray can now benefit from this effect.

Apprentice: Request not compatible, update required.

Student: Request not compatible, update required.

He grumbled that even this was giving him trouble and accepted that it was time for help. He figured he might as well also use the complicated terms, as Ember likely knew them. "Astarte? The effects I'm trying to apply to a HitScan laser Ability aren't taking. Domino and Gatling both said no."

Her response arrived without a break in her Kessel-run stride. She was updating her own attacks as she used them, slotting her upgrades one at a time rather than the all-at-once debacle that Artorian was attempting. "You can't put a pulsing multi-shot effect on a constant beam. It's already going to deal single-target damage as fast as it can. Domino takes all the damage you overkilled the first enemy with, and puts it on the second enemy, which also doesn't work with constant damage beams. What did you successfully slot in?"

"Critical Hits!" Artorian glanced at his prompt for a quick check to be sure that what was on the screen was actually what he thought was on the screen. "Yes, Crits. Cy gave me the Crit-Fisher spec, even if it's not active yet."

"Helpful!" Ember's chipper tone lightened his heavy mood, as his inability to contribute was gnawing at him. "Great choice of base ability, hon! That's so smart of you, given the energy regen pools you have! Tell Tim about the spec and send your beam in for Weapon Ignition and Weapon Modes! I don't think it will work, but plop on the armor breakers as a substitute. Maybe we will get lucky! If that interaction works the way I hope it does, that's going to give you a surprise tool that will be helpful right the Abyss now!"

"Thank, and, you!" His quill shot across the prompt right away, penning the updates and sending it in, before pulling down a new prompt and throwing that one at Tim so he could have his tools! When the Ability prompt came back, Artorian laughed hard. A Wisp had clearly taken over the work from a Gnome, because the formatting was cleaner, and the explanations were far more lackluster.

Ding!

———

Update!
  Ability: Shining Ray.
  Rank: Student.
  Special Qualities: HitScan, C-Laser, Ranging, Critical, W-Ignition, W-Modes, Liger Affinity.
  Output: Deal thermal damage per second proportional to the energy invested.

Notice!
98 out of 1703 Adaptive Pylons used.

"What!" Artorian became unreasonably upset at the bonus notice. "Why did that use Adaptive Pylons! I thought using the list specifically avoided that?"

Ember snapped her head towards him while playing dodge the hungry space-mountain that was still giving chase. Artorian heard her clear as crystal through Zelia's brooch. "*Huh?* That's not right. How many did it take?"

"Twenty-six?" He rattled off a quick count, not sure if that was a big number, or a small number, when he had less than two thousand of the things to work with. "Is that bad?"

Ember shared his unpleasantry, her words upset. "That's dangerously efficient for Pylons, but it shouldn't have taken *any* Pylons. Is there any entry in any field that didn't come from your list, or didn't come with the base?"

Artorian shoved his finger on the Affinity that had turned into a Special Quality when a different developer had taken over. "There was a notice about connecting knowledge? I named the beam Shining Ray, which I developed during my time with Gomez. Then it added Liger Prime Affinity the first time around. That's now in the Qualities entry."

Ember clicked her tongue. "That'll unfortunately do it. You should have gotten several ranks out of that upgrade, but now the attack is customized based on your experiences, which the base function Pylons can't sustain. Careful with those, sugar! You're okay for now, and it was a cheap investment to learn that lesson. Fire it off! I wanna see it!"

Artorian wholeheartedly agreed and collapsed his screens. For the first time since being snatched up by Lucia and pressed into the sitting position in front of her, he saw the most unpleasant view of what was behind him. He wasn't sure he wanted to think too hard about a planetoid-sized mouth being aimed towards him while he barreled between asteroid littered space, pieces of old realms, and building chunks while on the back of a Serenity Bee that was putting in one Abyss of a performance.

"That's a nope from me! Eat laser, Moony!" He pointed his finger right at the center opening of the cheese moon's mouth, which was impossible to miss, and let rip. "Shining Ray!"

A ball of condensed energy collected in front of Artorian's finger, and while the void of space muted all sound, and Lucia's shield kept him well protected from any residual damage that letting loose a continuous-wave operation caused. The tree-trunk sized blast of radiantly white energy that Artorian mentally shoved his entire stamina Bolt recovery count into cut through space. The brilliant precursor to the wave motion cannon gave off enough dangerous luminance and heat signals to make it very clear that seven-hundred and ten thermal nuts per second was, in fact, Big Deeps.

The impact *stuttered* Brother Moon down to a crawl, slowing the creature's advance as Shining Ray made a stream of numbers appear and rise above the planetoid's center mass. A wall of seven-tens streaming from the creature as it lashed towards them with more sharpened string cheese.

Shining Ray would have been impressive if it wasn't punching into a health bar the size of a city. A health bar that didn't budge, as Lucia checked Three's damage efficacy. She hissed in a pained breath, wincing. "That's not doing anything noticeable! Brother Moon has a coughing bar so big, that you would need to do that for days to chunk off a tenth of it."

She then tried to be supportive when Artorian stuck out his bottom lip at her. "Good effort?"

"Suuuuu-gar?" Ember's call pulled his eyes away from Lucia and towards her. Her grin was telltale, Ember clearly not fussed about the lack of impact his still active laser beam was having on the cheeseball. "I didn't hear anything about the backups being implemented. Did you get both Modes and Ignition?"

"Yes?" Artorian kept his danger pointer on target, but with uncertainty. He had gotten those effects, yes, but how was that going to help?

"Ha-ha! Win!" Ember cackled and punched upward with a fist. "Sugar, think about the Ability you're using, and say: Ignition."

Artorian looked to Lucia, but she shrugged and made the 'listen to the lady' hand movement before her paw was needed to chancla clap one of the string cheese tentacle grabbers away like sticky fingers trying to sneak into the cookie jar. Ember's minefields were adding blazing holes to the arm, but that slowed the graspers down rather than stopping any.

"Abyss it, why not." Artorian focused on Shining Ray, and said the keyword, not particularly expecting very much. "Ignition!"

The radiantly white beam turned hot rod red, and Brother Moon caught fire.

All of Brother Moon caught fire.

Like a comedic scene where one holds a match for too long, followed by complete, full body, spontaneous combustion. *Whoosh*!

Brother Moon appeared to not fully understand what just happened either.

The planetoid stopped moving, giving up the chase as something smelled funny. It performed the equivalent of a confused blink, then screamed into the void and wildly flailed its cheesy tentacles around when realizing that every last external piece of it was on fire. The immolation shouldn't have been reasonably possible, but that played second fiddle to the now-panicking cheese monstrosity who had to deal with it.

Brother Moon cried out like a wicked witch who had just been splashed by a bucket of water, because it was melting in all the wrong ways, and had not brought its safety pot today.

Holes were being filled, mass was being lost, and the fire

wasn't going away due to a lack of oxygen. Abandoning the chase, Brother Moon lashed out at any and all available chunks of landmass, tugging them in to smother or douse the flames. Vanaheim chunks were the most prevalent in this section of space, but it wasn't going to be picky right now. It was too busy suffering from the Ignite status effect, and that needed to not be there more than it wanted tasty morsels and treats.

The improbability of that event playing out as it did would likely have occurred to any of the three players, had they been able to stop laughing at the comedic panic-flailing as an entire moon developed a sudden fondness for hugging ice cubes like plushies, while building itself a house out of Vanaheim pieces in an effort to become an Ecumenopolis.

You didn't see that every day.

CHAPTER THIRTY-FIVE

While paying half attention to his beam didn't seem to have stopped it, a rogue chunk of landmass completely blocking his line of sight to Brother Moon killed Artorian's emanation by default. Some Vanaheim buildings gained artistically seared lines, but that added to their aesthetic. Interestingly, the buildings did not catch on fire.

Artorian waited for another clean shot but snapped his head to Ember when the light trails pouring out from the back of their bees died and snuffed out. They were running dark. She was looking at him when he did, having expected a reaction. A finger in front of her lips shushed him before pointing sharply to a different block of Vanaheim landmass that Brother Moon hadn't gone after yet. Though with Brother Moon being the new main light source—due to being on fire—the scenery looked vastly different. Amazing what a little bit of light could do.

Her voice came through the brooch as a whisper. "We just lost aggro. Let's not recapture it or remind that thing what direction we're in. Space is big, and easy to get lost in when it's cluttered to the high celestials with feces. I've dismissed all my mines, but we need to sneak out while barbeque cheese over there has no idea where we are, on account of being preoccupied with the fun side effects of Spaghetti Code."

"I know what that is!" Artorian clapped his hands, remembering from before. "We had that at the cat cafe."

"You're adorable." Ember stifled a laugh, chuckling with a smile. "Spaghetti Code is an unavoidable problem when all pieces of a system are supposed to be able to interact with all other parts of that system."

She led her silent-running mount through abandoned buildings in the Vanaheim chunk, pointing at an old piece of Jotunheim and making 'don't go anywhere near that' signals to her bees. "Weapon Ignition is designed to bring out a weapon's hidden attributes. Think of your old Astra form, but for a sword that you're holding. Problem is, when you're putting Pylons together, especially the synthetic ones? You have to use a lot of go-to commands and other tags in case something eventually goes wrong and the incoming activity needs to be rerouted."

A few stiff stop and go commands from Ember's hand had them tactically clearing and moving through main streets. "When a Pylon isn't sure what to do or where to send what it's holding, it will try to improvise a solution based on the information it has. Rarely is it a good solution. Sometimes, though. Sometimes you get those hilarious catastrophes, and this is one of them."

Safe to proceed to another landmass chunk, they abandoned the Vanaheim flotsam toward the direction of Alfheim, using Asgard pieces as cover. "We have a status effect called Ignite, where the target catches fire, regardless of the circumstances. Ignite was initially meant to help kindling along. Get cooking fires going. Light smoke sticks. Small stuff. Ignite by itself has a bunch of safeguards on it to prevent catching things on fire that it shouldn't."

Ember paused somewhat long before braving a main causeway, waiting for the landmass chunk to tilt more. When they were out of the light, she went for it. "Ignition doesn't look like it would cause any problems, but since the same Pylon also holds the Ignite Runes, it decides to go: Well, this likely does what Ignite is supposed to do! Then the Pylon goes ahead and does it. Except that it's not using the Ignite Runes to trigger that effect. It's using the Ignition Runes, and the Ignition Runes do not have the careful safeguards that Ignite does."

Artorian could already see where this was going but didn't dare interrupt as Ember had a massive grin on her face while she explained. She never got to gush about this part of her tasks. "Now the Pylon is applying Ignite's effect but is trying to pull from the Ignition targeting ruleset. Since Ignition is tacked onto items that are actually creatures, so they can have morphic effects, the Pylon then goes: I got it! I'm supposed to set a creature on fire. Caaaaaan do, boss!"

She pushed her hands together, creating a poof motion with her hands. "Whoof! Up goes the bonfire. Or in this case, one surprise tool that helps us right this second. I'll fix it later, but I saw the option and knew I hadn't fixed it yet. Bugs can be features! I think the Pylon looked at the attack, realized it was supposed to add something, got confused on what, and slapped on what it had. Et voilà! One fried cheese ball that's going to remain preoccupied for the entirety of the near future. Won't kill the thing, but I will take more time wherever I can carve it out."

Artorian felt the urge to hold his fluffy collar when responding. "Is there the option to ask them why they're doing that? Or do only the versions like Kronk have minds in them that are able to work with you?"

The exasperated grunt through the brooch answered enough. "It's so hard with Synthetic Pylons because you *can't* ask them. The only time you know something has gone wrong or strange is when the after-effects are making a big enough problem to be noticed. There's entire hordes of issues that are completely invisible because we just don't know if something is awry until it's too late. You put out fires where you can, but there have been times where we fixed one problem and suddenly had eleven more. There is a reason that Pylon has a dedicated **Law** spot in the Tower! You'd need to be dedicated to living and breathing that code in order to handle it correctly. Drives me up the *wall*."

The deep, calming breaths through the communication system put Artorian at ease. Before long, they were once more sneaking their way between the shadows of fragmented orbital bodies anytime that they wouldn't fall into Brother Moon's direct line of sight. Artorian chose not to think about how the moon's sight functioned. Darn thing didn't have eyes.

He'd been working on panels and prompts in the meanwhile, but it was all administrative and learning material that he'd been working through. Weapon Ignition turned out to have other things it could do. Weapon Modes, if it either worked correctly or worked with Spaghetti Code, would also stir the pot. Liger Affinity didn't appear to have any mechanical effects and was instead linked to Factions and Reputation. Neither functionality worked. Ranging, on the other hand, had been critically important.

Artorian wheezed when reading the entry, as this view range metric was coded to also determine the maximum range of some weapon shapes and damage types. Without the improvement that increased his clarity of sight to seventeen kilometers, HitScan attacks would have stopped dead after three. He wasn't sure if he was more uncomfortable knowing just how close Brother Moon's main body had actually gotten to them, or that Tim had thought this would be fine had Shining Ray not connected after there being no indication that it would do so in the description. "Tell me about details like this, Tim!"

Ding!

"Speak of the demon and it will appear." Artorian mumbled to himself as new prompts came in. He threw them open with a wave of the hand while Lucia was refreshing everyone's shields and monitoring their vitals for issues as she was trying to combat the many problems that came with being out in a vacuum. Protective fields did a lot as a first measure.

Ember was still busy playing local area tactician so they could make it to Midgard, even if that meant detours on detours.

He had time to work on his screens. Possibly to figure out a better attack as well. Would Shining Ray have worked well against that cheese penguin? What about the swarms they...? Oh. *Oh no.* If his beam only damaged one entity at a time, a swarm made from uncountable miniature entities would wreck him, since his ray currently neither pierced nor penetrated. A swarm could advance on him no problem with the rules of the world as they currently were. "Whoops!"

Lucia glanced down, but when the kit was furiously busy with screens, she got back to her own focus. He'd sort it, though she did peek at some of the entries.

————

Class Gained: Janitor

"Bless the cleaner and his broom. Bless the coming and going of him. May his passing cleanse the world. May he keep the world for his people." - *Shai-Hulud, first of the Allsand.*

————

"No level up bonuses?" Artorian's question took the words out of Lucia's mouth, as she too had never seen a class entry that small. Worst of all, it didn't *do* anything. No bonus skills. No bonus skill points. No attributes on level up. No associated free abilities. No title. Nothing.

————

Notice!

Message from Task Manager: Brother Moon will remember this.

————

Some notices had the uncanny ability to steal all of one's attention away. Artorian read the words, blinked, read them again, then felt the horrible realization running like cold water down his spine that one of the negative Reputation effects was that the enemy faction would be able to pinpoint you at all times. That feature *was* broken, right? He read more prompts as a palate cleanser.

———

Title Gained!
Administrator
Note: Nonfunctional. This is a placeholder.

———

Title Gained!
Overdeity
Note: Nonfunctional. This is a placeholder.

———

Title Updated!
Cultivator
Note: Personal Pylon bank now tallies calculation formulas in the correct order.

———

Profession Removed!
Bone Scripting
Note: If you used this, and it didn't work, the requisite Pylon bank went up in smoke. Only a reference Pylon was still present to allow the profession to be slotted. This does nothing, so consider your personal bone-scription to be an additional slot for a toy or option to import from your New Game Plus file. You're going to keep this when you leave the game, so don't

make it harmful to yourself. This is altering the actual Runes in your script, and you only get the one. Your game body is not separate from your current real body. Try not to die.

––––––

Profession Removed!
Artifacting
Note: Same problem, different reason. Turns out this does need to be an ability, can't give you a freebie for losing this one.

––––––

Artorian voiced his grumbles. "I feel like I'm losing more than I'm gaining and I don't like this. Hopefully by the time Eternia is out of the beta version, people will have options that work. Because I don't see a large amount of people doing the entries all nitty gritty like this. This requires a lot of mastering system knowledge. If there's ever going to be some kind of rarity update for Skills and Abilities, then please, for the love of my sanity, make the highly customizable ones more rare."

He huffed, complaining further. "These are so difficult to handle. Next to you all, I thought I knew what I was doing from having worked with this before. This is rough. Start me off with static, simple, small, and unchangeable Skills next time. I know I like complexity, but even I am needing baby steps here, and this lake I've been thrown in is awfully deep. The more versatility or flexibility a toy has, the higher the rarity should be counted. So people who aren't inclined to think like me won't scream from merely getting started."

A confirmation chime without discernible origin made Artorian feel better. He pretended it was from Tim and read the next prompt.

––––––

Specialization Gained!
  Crit-Fisher.

  A Crit-Fisher refers to a person who fishes for critical hits, attempting to create as many instances of the effects as they can, in favor of other ancillary effects.

  While any class that has to do with incurring a special effect under set conditions has their base Critical Hit chance tripled at the end of the formula, because Crit-Fisher specifically focuses on the concept of critical hits, your critical hit chance is multiplied by five instead. Also called quintupling.

  While increasing the number of times a critical effect happens is the main focus of this specialization, Crit-Fisher also opens the door for modifying what happens when one occurs. Additional Damage is the most common critical effect, but it is far from the only option.

  Critical chance is determined by taking the numerical value of the rarity, dividing by the averaged base damage, and rounding down. A one-hundred-sided die is then rolled. If the roll is lower than your threshold, you achieve a critical hit.

  Note: Due to limitations, if your critical hit chance reaches a zero, it will be rounded to a zero rather than be calculated down to multiple decimal points. No roll will occur, regardless of multiplier bonuses from this specialization.

  Note: Due to missing Pylons, many functions have been simplified until the bank can be redeveloped. All critical hit effects now exist on the same chart, because we only had one left when we went looking. The rarity and rank of your attack will impact which of the chart's choices are available to choose from, but it is recommended to set or slot a default effect. If you are at all able to slot one from the approved effects list, you will be awarded a bonus for not making my life more difficult.

————

Skill Gained!
  Critical Luck.
  Rank: Novice.
  When rolling the event of a critical chance, roll the die multiple times.

If any of the resulting rolls result in a successful critical event, then the critical hit occurs.

At each rank of this skill, one die is added to the pool, starting at the Novice rank. At Novice Critical Luck, your pool consists of two dice.

Artorian had hoped there would be more of an explanation on average base damage, as he wasn't sure how that worked with his only current attack being a constant stream of nutty numbers. "Well, that's unfortunate. If I pour one measly digit of power into the beam, it's going to do one measly damage as well. This does not satisfy my explosive numbers craving."

He then cocked his head to the side, considering the request in the prompt. That made for a current tally of a single, permanent boost for his bonescript. Since he'd actually know what it did by choosing it, he wasn't going to fuss. Plus a selection from the allotment list as a staple critical hit effect. "What all was in my list of approved tools again?"

He pulled up a copy to refresh his knowledge.

Less than Three's Allotment:
  Bounce
  Cast on Self
  Cast on Target
  Conditional Allspell
  Critical Hits
  Domino
  Explode on Hit
  Gatling
  Homing
  Laser
  Penetrating
  Pierce

Proliferation
Spread
Weapon Ignition
Weapon Modes

———

Artorian's sudden slow rise to evil laughter had his teammates wonder what blend of Oak's smoke had gotten in under Lucia's shield. When Ember made a 'what are you doing?' hand movement at him, Artorian couldn't contain his mirth. "Blessings to Torgue! I bring explosions, for all! Shai-Hulud was on to something. *Haaaaaa ha, haaa!*"

CHAPTER THIRTY-SIX

When the Serenity Bees landed on Midgard soil, ignoring that it was covered in a few hundred meters of ice and hardened snow in some places, Artorian had gotten a lot of work done! So much, that he enjoyed the deep breath of frosty air before his attempted dismount failed spectacularly as the visible cloud of exhale fumed from his mouth. He ended up face first in the ground with a mouthful of snow, after tumbling with the most ungraceful of non-balance from his seat. How he'd missed catching himself about seven times was going to need to remain a mystery.

What he also wished had stayed a mystery was the flavor of the icy blue and white snow. Luckily, no yellow was anywhere to be seen. Artorian spat the frozen water out, his face puckering. "Why is it mint flavored?"

He leaned over, stuck his finger in some snow coated in an emerald-green glaze instead, and tried it. "*Ooooh*, pistachio flavored!"

He then looked to where his other party members were inspecting a sign but couldn't lean left or right far enough to see what it said. His curiosity demanded answers. "Whatcha find?"

Lucia stepped out of the way, narrating the sign's contents as it became visible. "It says: Roberts was here. The hole is my fault. Pistachio is my favorite flavor. The Puddle thanks you!"

Artorian squinted, uncertain about the validity of the sign, even if he could spot the hole being referenced after getting up and walking a few steps. "That's a big hole. Wait, Roberts the Ruminating?"

Lucia chuckled, amused at his guess. "That's who I was going to suggest. I did tell you that I attended his lectures? The great puddle is who I learned all my game terms from. The puddle is most wise. The puddle knows."

Artorian was intrigued. "Any lessons you remember?"

Lucia paced as the lecturers of old, waggling a finger in the air as she copied what she remembered, with bonus sass. "Thou shalt respect the roles of thine healer and tank and accept that the DPS is there too. For DPS. Rule number one: A dead DPS does no DPS. Rule number two: If you spank it, then you tank it. If you attack the area boss before the tank does, congratulations, you are the tank now. Good luck."

Having walked a circle shaped divot into the snow, Lucia trudged right on and paced the same circle. "For tanks. Rule number one: Be the first person to die. Rule number two: Don't die."

She hadn't finished pacing half the circle before getting through those points, having saved the best for last. Her own role! "For healers. Rule number one: If the healer dies, it's the tank's fault. If the tank dies, it's the healer's fault, and if the DPS dies then it's their own celestial fault. Rule number two: Healer needs to keep the tank alive, DPS are secondary concerns."

She stopped her pacing in exactly the place she began. "So goes the lesson on roles."

Artorian huffed and made a 'mom is picking on me' face before crossing his arms and turning away. Ember sputtered with giggles as her boy had been assigned the DPS role, his indignant response pouring off of him as he mumbled something about fairness.

Lucia smirked, then considered a different scholar. "My favorite lecturer is the Dwarven scholar, Connolly. He says, with a very convincing argument: Life is a waste of time. Time is a waste of life. Get wasted all the time, and you'll have the time of your life!"

That got smiles out of everyone.

"Alright, very funny." Artorian paid more attention to his surroundings. Though winter wonderland was a nicety for a description. Combine pervasive darkness kept artificially illuminated, insidious cold, and just enough wind for it to cut and be unpleasant? That was Midgard right now, and Artorian suspected it was as nice as the weather was going to get. There was a storm on the horizon, and he got the strange feeling that the kyanite lightning he could see dealt a triple whammy of Cold, Frost, and Ice damage.

He then bounced on the snow, found it to have decent give, and flexed his hands. "How effective would Shining Ray be on some snow?"

Ember rounded on him and hurried to grab both of his hands before her boy had the terrible idea to try it. "No. You will blast straight through Midgard and give away our position."

"But Embyyyy...." Artorian whined like the child he looked like. "It's my only attaaaack."

"So make another one!" She released his wrists to flick his ear. "Fussy baby!"

Lucia wondered if that had been cause for a fight but given that the boy kit was grinning like a complete brat that had definitely done that on purpose, she shrugged it off as part of their romantic dynamic.

"Living Bonfire." Ember's sudden wave of heat was a surprise to the group, but definitely not unwelcome as the cold had built up and unpleasant status effects started to populate. Her aura of heat took those away, but it did make Artorian hop to be within ten feet of her, as the radius of the effect was tiny. The snow they were standing on was also not immune to the heat she was packing, so when Ember started to march after petting both of the bees and storing them in her bracelet, Artorian and Lucia hurried to follow. "We're on Midgard, sugar. Next part of the plan?"

"Find Duchess." Artorian had this part sussed out, at the ready with stage two. "She's currently in charge of whatever's left of Solar Gate, which may be a whole lot of nothing. The tag for that teleportation beacon that used to be in the middle of the coliseum is now called 'The Generator.' Which gives me hope for the group's survival, though I am doubtful about growth. We need access to that platform. Either to hop around properly if I can get the teleporter up and running, or to overcharge the snot out of it and see if we can't make a sun out of that wreckage yet. Gotta plan contingencies. We need to start the sun, but if I can get inside of it, that'd be a convenience! If none of that works? I've got a debt to Katarina. So her daughter will be receiving alms from the poor."

Ding!

Artorian grumbled as prompts slapped him upside the head, causing him to stumble. "*Ack*! Now's not a good time! I got walking to do. I don't want to prompt at the same time! That's begging to fall down a hole in the world, or off some obvious cliff."

Ember had a quick look but couldn't afford to pause her stride. "Looks important, sugar."

Lucia cleared her throat. "Kits, darlings, sweethearts; you remember that I'm a giant soft bunny you can both catch a ride on? Yes? There is ground and gravity here. Even if I had a different fur color, I am golden. We are set. I can cast all my spells while in my proper Beast form without detriment. Humanization is for being social."

She motioned at herself. "This shape is for politeness, but if I can zippity zap zoom and go nyoom? Then you better give me a direction, because I will move far quicker than Astarte's heat effect can melt our flooring away, and I have an ovoid shield specifically for going fast while carrying a group."

Artorian liked that idea but had to admit that he couldn't navigate Midgard. Ember must have been reading his mind because she looked around, made a hand movement as if rolling a die, then spun in place and pointed at a horizon. "Found it. A Fun Item is that-a-way, and since I doubt there's much on Midgard that can satisfy F.I.F. right now, that's likely our Generator. I can keep the frosty debuffs that our clothing can't handle off us, but it'll be all I'm doing with my Energy bar. Living Bonfire was very Adaptive Pylon expensive. Unless you can hop closer so I can hit something with my sword, I can't fuel anything else while Living Bonfire is up and running."

She then pointed to the brewing, rolling and roiling, thundery Jotun-clouds on the horizon, which stretched across the entire horizon. That spelled Trouble with a capital T. "I've got nothing against that storm right now. Barotrauma will wreck me. We need to *not* be in that, and my current idea is passing under since we can't pass through."

"The storm I likely have covered, but I'm on the same running track. If I keep my good shield up, that's all I'm doing save for basic movement and paw baps. The upside: It won't matter if we're plowing through snowbanks, a small glacier, deadwood, or a lightning storm that looks like it's abusing the ground. You give me a way to go straight, and I'll go straight. Point me at the target. Snowpiercer Glitterflit is on the job. I see just fine in dim light."

Ember and Lucia clapped hands together, then looked at Artorian to see if he grasped his part. He returned a thumbs up. "That leaves me with the job of making new attacks, and the time to eat these prompts."

Lucia rolled her shoulders. "Sounds like a plan, prepare a running start and hop on."

Artorian hustled and bounded towards Lucia as she went Beast Mode. The very large golden Glitterflit had plenty of room for both passengers, and he already knew the seating order. Artorian got snug in front of Ember so she could keep him steady if he got too distracted with prompts, or more likely, for him to not go flying when the Basher took off and turned into a luminant, brightstar smear crossing the landscape.

Which Lucia did with glee to show off just how speedy a Glitterflit could really be. For good measure, she even included a roadrunner's comedic '*meep*' before blasting away from her prior position. Breaking Mach one, two, and three, like Astrea dropping a musical bass beat like a decree. The ovoid shield hummed to life around them, made from a pattern of interlocked hexagons that pulsed outwards with a repulsion effect. The thumping smooth and steady as Artorian began to bob his head to the beat. The ovoid shape reminded Artorian of an eggshell. Eggshell was a nice shield shape! He'd take the eggshell and got going on his prompts.

Ember curled her left arm around his stomach, her right reaching out to open space as her bracelet flashed with glowing crimson power. "Arise."

Red electricity and a crackle of intense heat burned the weapon into being as she enclosed her grip. The weapon that appeared in her hand convinced Artorian that it was always best to be on his dearest's side. He remembered sword-spears from the olden days, but this thing that Astarte was one-handing was easily one Halcyon in height. She was also holding it from the wrong end? The T-shaped flat part was at the business end of the weapon rather than protecting her hand. He was fairly sure that those tended to be crossguards.

He had a prompt in hand, but he craved knowing. "Sugar? What *is* that?"

Ember leaned forward to peck a kiss on the top of his head. "Not a what, sweetheart. A who. There are workarounds to bringing friends with you. Isn't that right, *Surtur*?"

The sword-spear did turn out to be a sword-spear, but not in the way Artorian had thought, the full weapon being two Halcyons worth in size rather than one! The crossguard on the end of what turned out to be a ten-foot handle caught Dalamadur Flame, as Surtur's energetic effigy burned out from the crossguard to stretch, roar, and then snap into the shape of a glowing, Rune-coated buster blade. The searing hot, tri-colored carmine, vermillion, and orange energy blade crackled with doom-slaying might before it was swung with a hewing fall in front of Lucia. The swing released a blazing roar of fire that condensed into a fine weapon slash, cutting several kilometers of straight and narrow pathway directly through the permafrost.

Flames billowed from the energetic slashes as they traveled and carved.

Artorian blinked, and in that time, Astarte had cut at least four more times as the luminous golden Glitterflit burst onwards on the freshly laid track. Whether overland, through a drill-bored tunnel, a flattened chunk of blur that moved by so fast it couldn't be identified, or possibly a monstrous Ice Behemoth that hadn't realized it was due for a cavity check today before falling over dead, Lucia trucked onwards.

Now holding to a very comfortable Mach four.

The air displacement of their passing did a number on the landscape, but the landscape must have liked it after all this time with the Jotun thundercloud, because it looked to take on merely another flavor of devastation before settling behind them. Which was the moment that Artorian realized that Ember belted out a song in tandem to her crazy swift weapon swings. To the tune of landing a thousand punches into an immovable enemy. "Standing here, I re-a-lize that you were just like me, trying to make his-to-ry!"

A symphony of slashes illuminated and cleared their path, Artorian busy snapping his head back and forth between all the action to take it in and ogle at the lightshow. Anyone watching would be able to see them from an entire horizon away given the native illumination being so pale and blue, but that would require anyone to be watching, and they were long out of Brother Moon's reach. The new Vanaheim Ecumenopolis in the sky that burned internally like Muspelheim's ticking bomb was cause for concern, but it was a concern for later.

The weapon slashes also didn't create nearly the kind of lighthouse beacon that Shining Ray did, which made him snap to attention. He was supposed to be making more attacks of his own right now! First, scribbling an idea. Then, all these prompts. Maybe there was a useful one here yet, and his motivation to make something flashy enough to outdo the current spectacle lit a flame in his heart.

He let the fire guide his hands to the prompts and tried not to cackle like last time. Praising Shai-Hulud, he didn't notice Ember grin wide as she gripped him tight. Ember felt fierce pride when seeing the reflection of the flame in his pink eyes, displayed clear as day on the prompt when she glanced to look. Her grin only widened when she saw the details of the attack he was working on and purred out the name of what was going to be a beautifully catastrophic fireball. "To whom it may concern."

CHAPTER THIRTY-SEVEN

Ding!

Specialization Updated!
    Slotted Critical Effect: Explode on Hit.
    Note: Is the next age going to be called the Age of the Rule of Cool? If you lot keep bringing the heat like this, I'm going to be glad for this Ice Age. I said I'd award a bonus for using an item from the pre-approved list, so here you go.
    Bonus: You may mentally auto-toggle your critical hit effect between doubled damage, and E.o.H. without consulting a Critical Effects chart.

Artorian nodded, accepting the bonus! Tim clearly grasped the value of time and attention span in combat. He then pulled up the new Ability prompt, and continued nodding. "Excellent. Both are very nice. Astarte, you were right, having Cast on Target was important. I tried making this without that quality

but was welcomed by prompts trying to explain how spells functioned with physics, and the moment I saw the words 'likely to
miss,' I wanted nothing to do with needing to treat spells like
dumbfire projectiles. I want smart, or no projectiles, which gives
me this cookie!"

———

Ability Gained:
  To whom it may concern.
  Rank: Novice.
  Special Qualities: Explode on Hit, Cast on Target.
  Description: This Ability causes a designated target to explode, possibly
destroying it.
  Output: A designated target will explode, taking Explosion damage in a
five-foot diameter equal to one-fourth the energy invested.

———

Artorian sifted through his prompts for a moment, finding
nothing that said this had cost him any Adaptive Pylons. Good!
He liked not having to use limited resources. He noted some of
the upcoming prompts might be changing some of his statistics,
so he scratched at the base of one of the Basher's flattened ears.
"Oh luminant one, could I please see those bars you were
talking about?"

An amused chitter preceded the spellcast. "Acuity."

A small set of vertical bars appeared in the corner of Artorian's vision. When he moved his head, they moved to stay right
on his peripheral. He tried to reach out and grab them, but to
no avail. His hand went right through them. When he stopped
to take control of the information, he saw that a number was
imposed below a brighter percentage value. The percentages all
said one hundred, and that appeared to correlate to all the bars
being full. The number underneath was a slightly darker color
to what the bar was made of... Oh hey! Those were his health

and mana values! The Nut symbol next to his mana bar, and the Bolt symbol next to his stamina bar, was rather amusing. He pulled up his character sheet just to check, because the yellow bar with the shield icon was a new one.

Hit Points: 17,570.
Mana Pool: 33,300.
Mana Regen: 288 / second.
Stamina Pool: 12,600.
Stamina Regen: 710 / second.

"That all still looks the same?" Artorian felt puzzled. "Momma bun, I see the bars, but I have one that doesn't show up on my character sheet. A shield value? It's the only one that doesn't have a number tucked away underneath the percentage."

The Basher made a sound of affirmation, as that was correct. "Sanctity isn't a health shield. It's a condition-protection shield. It breaks the first time you take damage, but until you do, you gain outright immunity to a lot of annoying debuffs and demerits. You don't currently have it, but I can layer Lenity over Sanctity. That's a temporary damage absorption shell, the most useful feature of which is that taking damage won't interrupt your spellcasting. Lenity functions as a second health bar that always eats damage up first."

Lucia dodged though a small mountain as Ember's attacks dislodged granite in neat cubes. "Due to my build, you are going to see Prosperity pop up in your status effects when you take damage. It's a heal over time that affects you first, and Lenity second, but it triggers if Lenity takes damage. Since Acuity lets you see all your own status effects at a glance—on the left, under the bars, if you're looking for it—that can be helpful."

She paused speaking for a moment, focusing on steadying her speed before adding one more detail. "Lifesense is so far not giving me a lot to work with. Ice Behemoths have been it and did not tag as biological. Midgard is barren. I have no idea how anything can live here."

"Thank you, momma bun." That information was satisfactory, though he felt bad about agreeing with her on the barren state of the place. Fimbulwinter was no joke. Artorian let the bars hang and returned to prompts. An important looking one had a message covering the information, so that one was first.

———

Message from Eternium: Bud, this baffled me for a while, but I've found why we couldn't hit the ground running when you entered. A Heavenly patched you up, and that large number of tiny changes made the Task Manager block the process. The discrepancies made you look like a Pylon Scarab taking nibbles. Positive side: that old Nascent Being skill we had? Merged it seamlessly into the racial entry! I had a choice between providing percentage attribute modifiers like the Dragon race, or this. Given our predicament, I went with the merger. Have a look:

———

Base Race Update!
    Race: Nascent Being.

    As a Nascent Being, you gain Electrosense and Echolocation as new empirical senses on a base level, alongside sight, hearing, taste, smell, and touch.

    As a Nascent Being, you are always considered Well Fed and Well Hydrated. You can breathe in any environment and are immune to the effects of: depth crushing, thin atmosphere, vacuum, harmful gasses, inhaled venoms or poisons, and cloud or vapor-based attacks.

    A Nascent Being is never lost, and always has a vague idea of where to go. Regardless of what it is currently looking for.

———

Artorian felt like he suddenly had a headache straight from the Abyss. Both new senses popped like his ears had changed elevation too fast, as both Electrosense and Echolocation flooded him with sensory data.

Eyes screwed shut or not, he could hear and see Astarte's attacks as they cleared the landscape. Each of Lucia's pawfalls made a white on black sonar ping emanate from their location, and the terrain gained grayscale detailing as the soundwave came back. Blurry grayscale since they were moving too fast for any kind of clarity, but it was there.

Lucia's hexagon-patterned egg shield contained his Electrosense to a large degree, but there was still plenty of awareness to be found anytime his dearest swung that mountain cleaver of hers and launched another cutting energy blade ahead of the Lucia train.

He took deep breaths and felt the comfort of the Well Fed and Well Hydrated bonuses roll in like a hot summer breeze.

"Kit?" Lucia's alarmed tone brought him back to reality. "All your vitals just dipped, changed, and spiked up to a new average. I'm aware you just gained positive status effects, but as the medic, I'd really like to know the what and why. The vacuum and pressure protections from my high-level Sanctity just got superseded?"

Artorian quickly filled her in about his current race and the modifiers it provided, chattering about some of the background that had built up to him having it as a Skill in the alpha version of the game. Lucia thought the explanation satisfactory but did have a request. "Please let me know if you're about to work through a prompt that changes you internally, precious. I would rather pop a Prosperity on you and have that running before you need it."

That was amenable, and Artorian read off some of the headings on his remaining prompts. "Can do. I've got New Game Plus importing, Bonescripting slot use, Equipment Stats,

Flash Rune Freebie, Orbital Strikes, and one note called: Trans Am. Does any of that sound like it ought to take priority?"

"He finished Trans Am? Turnip, you Beast of a Dungeon!" Ember's fast retort and big smile made Artorian immediately interested in what this goodie could be. A squeeze around his stomach distracted him from reaching for the prompt. "Do that one last. Definitely last. Trans Am is a big one. You read them off in a good order, NGP is a big read. We're still far from the Gennie. Do it now if you're inclined, hon. Not sure if we'll have time later."

"New Game Plus importing it is." Artorian changed the direction of his arm, grasping that prompt instead. He bopped the activation section as his headache receded. As the information was populating in new prompts, he wondered why his headache was going away so fast, then noted 'Veracity' active in his positive buffs, and the counter on 'Headache' sharply dropped as they lightly pulsed at the same time. Interactions? Neat! "Bun? What's Veracity?"

Lucia kept it short. "Veracity is the effect-over-time version of Cleanse, a hard dispel. Instead of slapping a Cleanse on you and making your head take another shock, Veracity takes you down smoothly by chipping away at the demerit, debuff, or negative status that you're being afflicted by. It's targeted, so it only works on one of them. I have it to where I can fight disease with it, rather than Veracity functioning indiscriminately."

Artorian made a happy sound. He loved no headache!

He was then glad Veracity was present and already fighting the headache debuff, because even with it running, the number slowed its drop to a crawl, then began to climb back up. Both his hands slid into his hair, because the world in front of him was made of screens. Screens on screens of multi-stacked, several layer deep screens. "*What?*"

Ember gave a calming response, the hand around him pushing up to knead at his chest and provide comfort. "That's every Skill, Ability, and Feature from your prior Eternia body. We've only got the reference Pylons, but that's enough to rebuild from. You should have a smaller prompt that tells you how many you can import to this new body, but it won't be many. You've got a plus one from your Bonescripting option, but I'm sorry you had to lose the profession, hon. I would have been happy watching you spend a few decades figuring that craft out."

He leaned back to press against her, taking another eye break to indulge the few seconds in her hold. "It's alright, dear. It doesn't need to be something I get back from the game. There's always after. The useful things right now are enough. Then, when we're done, maybe we go install ourselves onto a pleasant farm in the middle of nowhere? Or on some tropical beach? Seems to have done wonders for everyone else."

"Time with you is how I want to spend my time, sugar." Ember pressed her bronze cheek into his forehead. "Farm, no farm. Game, no game. Caltopia, no Caltopia. The where is decoration. The who and when is easy. The why, you know. Only the 'what' matters to me, the how."

He nodded, gave her a squeeze, and got back to the library of prompts after her motivational words. "We're going to figure out the what and how, dearest. Luckily, we have time! Game for now, see where we go?"

She purred the words back at him, supportive and adoring. "Game for now, then see where we go."

CHAPTER THIRTY-EIGHT

Ding!

Welcome to New Game Plus!

Placeholder Primer: You have transferred to a new Dungeon! While you cannot import your entire character to this new game, you may select 3 prior entries from your existing character sheet. These functions will be imported as best as the new Dungeon is able. Your results may not be identical to your choices, with a lowered chance for ill-matching thematics. Example: Attempting to import crossbow-related Abilities into a Dungeon world that does not have crossbows will go poorly.

All selectable entries shall be listed en-masse. Please select 3 to highlight as your intended choices. Selection is final and complete upon confirmation of the third entry.

"Emmi, I need a blessing. I have encountered a messing." Artorian attempted to stay lighthearted, his words turning to

Ember. "Plus, is there a reason I should not pick the three biggest hitters? Celerity? Mass Driver?"

He received a head pat for his attempt, but no blessing. Ember then cupped her hand to his ear, whispering. "Read the warning again. Avoid complicated choices if you can. They won't be the same. Remember there's Pylon trouble."

Artorian rubbed his forehead, nodded, and got to reading. He wasn't sure how much time passed for him to narrow his options to five, but he did narrow them down to five. "I'm looking at Freedom of Movement, Freedom of Mind, Diffusion, Truesight, Supreme Weapon Mastery, and Adaptive Style."

Never mind. Six. He'd narrowed his options to six. He swore he could count and was glad to not have said that part out loud.

"I'm thinking Freedom of Movement for the bonus Bone-scripting slot? I'm fond of my movement tricks." He sighed wistfully, eyes lingering on his favorite entry. "I want Astral Celerity, but that begs for problems. So many problems."

Ember leaned her chin on his head. "Diffusion? To attack an entire zone? Good thought, likely problematic. Did Adaptive Style work last time? I don't remember seeing any logs where that has ever worked. Rest sounds good. I'm surprised you didn't choose Artifacting?"

He waffled his hand noncommittally. "Losing the Professions made me feel sour. Yes, I want that toy, but I don't know. Doesn't sit right. Feel like it'd be nothing but trouble to pick it up now when The Pale is still in pieces. Later, hopefully, I can pick Artifacting up out of a loot chest, hold it over my head, and go Goblin *Reeeeeeee*. I need tools that are useful right now, that don't look like they'd blow up a Pylon bank because I slapped a bench. That was my argument against myself with Rail Palm, because that had an option linked to the Mass Driver spec, and as Mass Driver was the fourth layer on the old progression cake, my trust is low. I remember what happened with Spirit Ballista. That didn't end well."

Ember squeezed him as he agonized over these choices. The

fear of missing out or finding out he chose the wrong one for the circumstance later, was awful. "Talk to me, sugar. Think of something random, get back to this after."

Her boy leaned back, giving his eyes a break from the screens to take in the audible swishes of Surtur chopping up the landscape, and thundering paws falls of Lucia between the thuds of her shield. A thought came to mind as he remembered her making a die rolling hand motion. "Did you use Fun Item Find actively? I thought it was passive only."

"I did, but then again I know all the secret ins and outs." Ember indulged him gladly. "Just like how every action in physics has an equal, opposite reaction, every passive effect has an opposite, active effect. The whole system is built on intent, and what you want to do with it."

She broke that down for him. "Memories help. Drives and motivations help. *Raison d'être* is powerful beyond belief, and even acts stemming from love get special attention. Whether it's by action, reaction, willful intent, or accidental growth and discovery? The system is meant to give you game toys equivalent to the growth you are undergoing. For those of us who make and maintain those methods, it also means that we know how to manufacture them. Artificially and otherwise. I know what to think, believe, and act like in order to get a very specific system result back, as it's very much the same method of how Essence channels choose a person. They don't align to you; you align to them."

She moved her arm around his chest out, flexing as an example. "In addition to the sheer madness of the system's inherent flexibility, there are secondary, tertiary, and more uses to everything."

Astarte made a fist and squeezed it, popping her knuckles as bright heat built within. "Let me use Strength as an attribute example. When I hit someone, and don't think about it? The Strength attribute is considered in the calculation of what my damage is going to be. However, I can hit using my Strength score, or I can hit *with* my Strength score, and those are two wildly different formulas. Most people do not think about the components of their inherent state. If one's mana recovery is two hundred? Then it's two hundred. System says so, and for most, that's the end of the thought. Yet, when either desperate, or intentional and focusing? That number can go higher, even if your core attributes remain unchanged."

She clarified with a more down to Cal example. "Think of a mother saving a child from disaster, and exemplifying a momentary, otherwise impossible feat of strength. Yes, she injured herself in doing so, but she clearly went above and beyond what everyone else thought her core attributes were able to accomplish."

Ember shook her hand out, releasing the tension. "Fun Item Find is a passive effect that doesn't pop very often, triggering when you brush your eyes over an item of interest for the first time. If you didn't succeed on the check the first time, then it won't ping that item any other time either. Knowing that's how the formula works, I intended and desired to make an active form of the check, and then poured mana into the attempt. Using resources forces the system to pay attention, so when it realized what I was trying to do, it offered me Novice Fun Item Find as a skill, allowing me two chances at a passive check finding success, and one attempt to force it and roll manually. I got lucky with locating the Gennie, but that's the process."

Artorian nodded, enraptured by these secrets. Since she had his attention, she indulged him a little more. "When it comes to secondary uses, there's an associated cost. Tertiary uses are mostly the do or die mechanics. A good Old-World example is… techniques that used corruption, and burned or purged some out of you when unleashed with that pattern. On the surface, this seemed like a fantastic idea! Release a strong attack, it's slightly better due to some corruption, and you lose corruption. Sounds great on paper. So why did we see barely anyone use it like that?"

Artorian puzzled, crossing his arms. "Does… it have anything to do with… patterns?"

"Mhm! Correct!" Ember praised him with a soft squeeze to the chest, needing to make sure her other arm remained free to carve the path. "The big downside to that method is two or threefold. The first is that you normalize using that particular attack pattern, and your attacks always cost something other than your Essence. You can say it eats corruption on use, but that's not what techniques are actually doing."

She pressed two fingers into his sternum. "The second big problem is that it requires you to keep corruption in your system, because there is going to be a point where you run out. The big, hidden downside? This leaves you at the precipice where your most used skill is no longer viable, because you don't have the correct fuel. If you use it anyway, and don't have corruption in you, the technique will still go off. It will also find a corruption substitute, and usually that's the cultivator who was foolish enough to try it, because *they're* the non-malleable 'stuff' that the pattern finds to eat, in order to accomplish its effect."

Artorian grimaced. "That's a pretty bad downside... I forget that it was difficult to get your hands on techniques in the olden days. Once you had so much as one, that was your big trump card. Like Gomei teaching Dale his... Sword Aura? Blade Aura? I forgot what it would have been."

Ember hummed in agreement. "Did that help clear your mind, sugar? Some of those distractions that you like so much."

"Yes." Artorian pulled his screens back towards him, feeling mentally refreshed from the distraction, even if it had been heavy news. "I'll take Freedom of Movement on the ol' bones, then my three choices are: Freedom of Mind, Truesight from the dragon evolutions, and Supreme Weapon Mastery. I will have to learn a new fighting style, but I bet you're eager to toss me around an entire desert again."

Ember grinned with glee. "A little."

Chuckling, he highlighted all three selection panels. There was no confirmation prompt, and his prior character sheet and all related entries winked out.

Ding!

———

Message from Eternium: Good choices, bud. I appreciate the lack of headache you are causing me with your choices. I am well aware you had options that were difficult not to choose. I'll process these and get back to you shortly. Shortly for you, I mean. A second for you is currently a month on my end, but that will ease back out. Cal got back to me with an updated Pylon design, and the ball on hardware is finally rolling again. There's a good chance your current Growth and Flat advancement Pylons will be incompatible by the time the beta rolls out of production, but we can update them back in after. Expect prompts shortly, and I may have a treat for you concerning your Bonescripting entry. Your current script is more advanced than the entry you asked for, and I can't remove existing script, only repurpose it. So, bonuses are coming. Expect to pass out.

———

"Expect to pass out?" Artorian wasn't sure he read that right. He did not have a chance to read the message twice.

CHAPTER THIRTY-NINE

Ding!

Artorian woke to the sound of more prompts, another helping of Veracity, and a very strong Prosperity heal-over-time patching him up.

Lucia was not amused. "Kit? Good job on the heads up. Maybe next time give more than half a second worth of heads up?"

Artorian was terribly groggy. "Sorry, momma bun. You learned it when I learned it."

He rubbed the back of his neck, trying to stretch out without impeding the land clearing onslaught. "I'm surprised we're not there yet. How long was I out?"

"Seconds." Ember remained laconic, upset at Tim. "Read your prompts, sugar. I need to send a strongly worded letter."

With a flash of heat and motion, she cut the letter T into the air and sent it flying ahead of Lucia to carve an extra upset and wide passage in the bottom of a crevasse they were zipping through. "Done."

Artorian cleverly chose not to ask and did as told. The prompts even came in a colored stack, with ribbons!

———

Congratulations!
New Game Plus importing complete.

———

Bonescripting gained!
Advanced Freedom of Movement.
Freedom of Movement provides full acuity of movement in any environ-ment, included but not limited to: Land, water, underwater, air, high atmosphere, and vacuum. Your feet will always find purchase, surface or no. As a side effect, due to the inherent features of the platform applying to every step, tumble, or hand movement, you will no longer destroy landscape or buildings when launching from, or traversing over, these floor types.

Elevation is a matter of choice but can only be sustained so long as movement is constant. Standing still in the middle of the air will allow gravity to take hold.

Advanced Freedom of Movement provides flight. As this feature will remain with you on leaving Eternia, the most potent Spell-quality Runes were applied. You are able to freely combine basic and advanced Freedom of Movement and can now choose to not allow gravity to take hold. Your top speed is limited by what you can withstand, and the energy cost per second is currently unknown due to excess variables.

———

Notice!
248 out of 1703 Adaptive Pylons used.
Advanced Freedom of Movement requires 176 Adaptive Pylons.

———

Artorian felt uncomfortable about the Pylon cost. On the other hand, he felt very comfortable with the bonus! Flight was a big deal! Flight on top of his already bounce-house-happy skillset when it came to movement? He kissed his fingers and blew them out. That he would get to keep this as a non-Mage cultivator should he need it? "Chef's kiss."

Sensory advancement gained!
    Truesight.
    See all as it actually is, ignoring all forms of obfuscation, guise, and illusion.

Notice!
    266 out of 1703 Adaptive Pylons used.
    Truesight requires 18 Adaptive Pylons.

"Ooooh, that one came cheap! A surprise! But a welcome one!" He blinked on purpose, trying to notice a difference. "*Hm.* I was expecting my eyes to hurt?"

Ember took his cheek for a moment, turning his head to look in his eyes and check. "There's some celestine or cyan mixed in with the pink in your irises, but that's all."

Artorian beamed in delight when his cheek was released. "This is a continued and pleasant turn of events. I don't notice anything different. Let's check the next one."

Skill gained!
    Freedom of Mind.
    Freedom of Mind provides full immunity to possession, mind altering states you do not allow, and grants a powerful boost to any speech-related activity. This does not provide a numerical change and will instead put you

on equal footing with any who use oration of a superior skill level. Regardless of your respective skill level.

———

Notice!
327 out of 1703 Adaptive Pylons used.
Freedom of Mind requires 61 Adaptive Pylons.

———

He nodded and made a happy noise at yet another pleasant addition to his comfort zone. "If this stops my headaches as well? Then I am one happy camper. Being possession proof also gives me a protective blanket of comfort over a wound I didn't realize I had. So glad I got that back before it ever had a chance to come up. Last one's up! Let's see if Tim noticed my master plan!"

Ember bumped him with her chin. "Master plan?"

Artorian grinned like Somnus of **Sleep**. "If the one, tiny, specific line I was hoping for is still there? Oh, you'll know, dear. You'll know and you'll cackle. Let me read this one out loud for you!"

———

Skill gained!
Supreme Weapon Mastery.
This skill gives a significant boost to the use of all weapons in combat. By obtaining this skill, the user is immediately proficient in all weaponry, of all types. When using any weapon, including one's own body, the user may act as if they were Sage-ranked in the equivalent weapon field.

Instead of variable damage, all damage rolls are considered maximized. In addition, each rank of this skill will improve raw damage dealt by +25%.

When using weapons of any type that impose a cooldown or 'attacks per round' limitation, that limitation is ignored.

Attacks made with weapons or the body no longer cost stamina.

Skills applied on top of this will still incur a stamina cost.

You are now Immune to the following conditions: Accuracy penalties, Range penalties, Moving while attacking penalties.

The maximum range of any ranged ammunition is increased by a category.

If you score a critical strike, your opponent dies.

———

Notice!
486 out of 1703 Adaptive Pylons used.
Supreme Weapon Mastery requires 159 Adaptive Pylons.

———

Ember instantly began to howl, laughing madly as she picked up what her boy was putting down. "Oh no you didn't! He let you get away with that? Did he even read the last line? Did he forget what you're trying to do?"

High pitched giggling broke out of Artorian, his hands clapping together like a wee child, excited about some small, silly thing. "It's there and that's all that matters!"

Ding!

"That's probably him now! With his hands in his hair, having just read the line." Artorian couldn't stop laughing, and tapped the message when it came in. Not noticing that it was fat, trembling with pressure, and green. The moment the seal was released, Yvessa's voice boomed at him. *"Artoriaaaaaaan!"*

The upset caretaker made him scrabble for a handhold as Yvessa, like a few other mighty figures in his life, had that uncanny ability to make him drop what he was doing and flee for the hills, as he was absolutely responsible for whatever he was being yelled at.

"Not the spoon!" He yelped, hiding in Ember's jacket fluff, fearful of Yvessa's whacking implement. With his luck, it would be a ladle and everything. Or worse, a war-ladle. "I didn't do it! Khajiit is innocent of this crime! Though I did enjoy committing it."

Ding!

Artorian kept his hands far away from the sudden prompt. "*Nu-uh*. I'm not doing it."

Ember reached in and tapped it regardless, making Artorian squelch his squeal as she read it out for him.

Message from Eternium: You ever slap your own forehead so hard that every Wisp in the room stopped what it was doing, and turned to look at you in concern? Oberon is still laughing. Titania is being restrained and prevented from sending you more messages under the Yvessa name. Dev doesn't understand how I missed this, and Cal is cackling and wishing me the best of luck. I for some reason thought that the line about condition immunities was the last entry, and that everything after were the listed conditions. That is a 'big oops' on my end, and I have to let you play with it. I'm lucky that it's limited to weapons. I need a nap.

"Is it safe?" Artorian peeked around Ember when she finished, daring to exist in a space that was not her protective fluffy attire. "I didn't get whacked by a spoon."

She ran her fingers through his hair. "Your evil master plan saw success. Focus on that. Read the next prompt. Tim might be taking a break after this set of messages. He's been trying to rely on other dungeons to pick up the slack, so don't be surprised if prompts look different. We should still be waiting on Equipment information, something about Orbital Strikes, a Flash Rune freebie, and the Trans Am system. I want to get to that last one."

Artorian squeezed her with a hug, felt it safe enough to get back to it, and brought up more prompts.

Item Set: Autarchy's Warmth.
Pieces: Boots, Pants, Shirt, Mittens, Parka, Scarf, Beanie.
Rarity: Special.
Set Effect: Extra Fluff - You are loved by the Floof, your comfort level is always one category higher in adverse cold conditions.

Item: Boots.
Name: Snowsteps.
Material: Spider Wool.
Rarity: Special.
Effect: The user does not sink through snow.

Item: Pants.
Name: Everwhite.
Material: Spider Wool.
Rarity: Special.
Effect: Cold Resistance - Ignore the first 100 points of Cold typed damage, then a flat 20% of remaining Cold typed damage.

Item: Shirt.
Name: Less than Three.
Material: Spider Wool.
Rarity: Special.
Effect: Exist comfortably in any temperature. Resistance to temperature-

based conditions such as: Frostbite, Heatstroke, Hyperthermia, and Hypothermia.

Item: Mittens
  Name: Object Permanence.
  Material: Spider Wool.
  Rarity: Special.
  Effect: Once equipped, these mittens exist only when paying attention to them. Otherwise the user has full use of their hands, as if not wearing mittens. User's hands will remain warm as per wearing normal mittens.

Item: Parka
  Name: Jurassic Cage.
  Material: Spider Wool.
  Rarity: Special.
  Effect: Frost Resistance - Ignore the first 100 points of Frost typed damage, then a flat 20% of remaining Frost typed damage.

Item: Scarf
  Name: Shinobi Run.
  Material: Spider Wool.
  Rarity: Special.
  Effect: Endurance Bolstering - All Stamina costs are cut by 10%. Might make the user run funny. May also cause others to cringe.

Item: Beanie.
  Name: Happy Ears.
  Material: Spider Wool.

Rarity: Special.
Effect: Ice Resistance - Ignore the first 100 points of Ice typed damage,
then a flat 20% of remaining Ice typed damage.

————

Artorian rubbed a nonexistent beard, then became transfixed on his hands. He'd put the mittens on in Demeter's Dream and forgot about them entirely. He hadn't noticed at all that he'd had a full range of motion with his hands and fingers, but that he'd definitely put mittens on. He focused on them, and the mittens appeared, trapping his fingers. He moved his eyes away, and felt his fingers come free, looking back to find the mitten missing. The item was still there? He could feel the warmth. "That is incredible. Zelia knows some fun tricks."

Ember was busy giggling. "Now I see where you got your name from! Zelia repurposed an older clothing set with new pieces. Shame the compatibility is haphazard, or the set bonus would have been better."

She fired off an extra fiery blade to buy herself a few seconds of information absorption time. "Good winter attire. Pretty. Soft. Snug. I like it, especially the Extra Fluff. Boots are convenient. Shirt is incredible. Pants, Parka, Beanie, and Scarf all have a good effect, but the scarf is a little strange? The Mittens I've seen before, but as a fingerless gloves variant. Good set. I'm not seeing anything about the spider brooch doubling as insignia here? Inspect that individually."

Artorian quickly did just that.

————

Item: Spider Autarch's Brooch.
Name: Entangled Web.
Material: Iridium.
Rarity: Special.
Effect: Seat of the Senate - Speak with any Senate members in your

vicinity who also wear this insignia. The correct position of the brooch is on or in the left segment of the collar.

———

Artorian fiddled with it right away! Trying to push pieces of the brooch as if it were a button. Trying to spin dials that weren't there. Attempting to twist solid pieces just to see if they were actually solid. When nothing gave, he stopped messing with it. "I was sure there would have been hidden features. Looks like it's as simple as the description advertised."

Ember chuckled, amused. "As much as a block of entangled quantum particles can be considered simple, yes."

Her boy frowned when looking up, not knowing those words.

She shrugged with a smile. "Magic juju, honey. It's magic juju."

Artorian released his frown, then firmly nodded. "I can work with magic juju!"

CHAPTER FORTY

Ding!

Notice!
  Orbital Strikes.
  Several orbital bodies are on strike, refusing to cooperate with system demands. Vanaheim chunks are non-responsive. You can recognize these bodies based on their picketing.

Artorian read that message out twice, then rubbed his head. "Wouldn't we recognize Vanaheim chunks based on all the buildings regardless?"

Lucia disagreed on account of dodging cheesy scythes and having seen some of these early warning signs. "I saw some pickets on chunks that didn't have buildings on them. Notices tend to be short, rather than comprehensive. Except yours, it seems. You get all sorts of off-template messages."

Artorian nodded, not wanting to press. He didn't really know why he'd gotten that notice, nor if he was supposed to do anything about it, so that nugget got filed away for later as he tapped the next prompt in the bundle.

———

Skill gained!
  Flash Runes.
  Rank: Primer.
  This skill will improve to Novice when Flash Runes, the Ability, can be introduced to the player. This skill is a primer and placeholder for when the system is ready to engage.

———

Notice!
  524 out of 1703 Adaptive Pylons used.
  Flash Runes require 38 Adaptive Pylons.

———

Ability Gained!
  Trans Am.
  Rank: Novice
  Exia Pylons operational, color codes: Pink, Red.
  Trans Am is an evolution of Empowerment, doubling a player's core Attributes, at the cost of removing all Stamina and Energy regeneration. This removal is not exclusive to specific Energy types. Trans Am deactivates only when the player's Stamina or Energy bar bottoms out.

———

Notice!
  581 out of 1703 Adaptive Pylons used.
  Trans Am requires 57 Adaptive Pylons.

Notice!
   Character Trait Acquired.
   Character Trait: World Boss.
   There's undeniably something cool about feeling like a boss accidentally wandered into you too early. Unfortunately, your current acquisition of Skills and Abilities rates you above the average threshold of acceptable player power. You have been designated as a roaming World Boss. You may claim an area as your dungeon or base of operations. On defeat by another player, you will drop all items in your possession as lootable objects. When you claim an area, you are permanently limited to a maximum of 10 items on your person, and in your possession. Until you claim an area, the 'Roaming' suffix will remain attached to this title. If defeated while under the effect of the 'Roaming' suffix, then your Player Pylons will be wiped, and you will have to restart from nothing.
   Message from Task Manager: You will cease giving me additional tasks to manage. Or else additional 'benefits' will be applied to your Player Pylons.

Notice!
   744 out of 1703 Adaptive Pylons used.
   Character Trait: World Boss, requires 163 Adaptive Pylons.

Artorian gasped incredulously, his hand kept to his chest. "Excuse me? Who is this Task Manager and where do I find him? I am *done* with the audacity of this person. I've been hearing about this nuisance, but this was the last straw. Over a hundred and fifty Pylons for a Character Trait I did not want and don't know how to get rid of? Who is this complete pile of Abyss to come make life harder when the defecation has already hit the oscillation? No! No, I say!"

A rising heat behind him made him look, and the rage on Ember's face as she looked at an identical prompt tailored to her had made her equally mad. Her words were deep growls. "It dies. This Task Manager *dies*."

Artorian was normally an advocate of love, peace, prosperity, and all that other goodness. Right now, on the other hand, he was fully on board with his dearest's murder mood. "I am in agreement! I'm looking for a one-eyed triangle of some kind, yes? I shall perform my function as the janitor and take out the garbage."

Ember's breath came with literal flames on her exhale. "Center office in the inactive Sun. You mentioned something about that teleportation platform being able to get you there? Duchess's Generator?"

Artorian squeezed her hand in support, his smile wolfish. "Did it last time! I'm sure it will this time as well."

Her hand turned around to lace with his fingers, squeezing back as her hair came aglow with heat. "Sugar? I know we have a lot on our plate, but can we tighten our actual goals? I'm livid at the triangle and can't focus."

Artorian was not about to say no to that! Barry's barf would need to be bucketed later, Brother Moon and his cheesy penguins had retreated into the center of an Ecumenopolis, and Bugmageddon had been on the to-do list for later anyway. That they had encountered none of the monsters or Vampires Ember had expected to begin with was not an important detail right now. "Turn on the Sun. Smack the triangle. Possibly not in that order. That'll be the winning condition for this book. Next book? We'll be gaining lots of new fans, because we'll be doing nothing but fighting!"

"Plan accepted." Ember bristled with rage, completely against having her limited resources being usurped by some trapezoid. "We turn a triangle into a square, and not once shall we be fair. Lucia, I missed some slices! Can you handle that slope?"

"I was wondering what the subterranean detour was about!"

Lucia chimed in while trucking across a tenuous tunnel at a downward angle, her luminant form making plenty of light for Artorian to see the mineshaft Ember was carving out with her blade slashes. "We suddenly started to go waaaaay down, and I think we're about to hit another biome. Been seeing lots of strange, petrified trees. How far are we from this Generator? No problems on my end with the plan."

Artorian's Nascent senses went off with a vague awareness that granted him an odd feeling of certainty. He spoke at the same moment Ember did. "We're close."

They shared a look, and Artorian gave Ember's hand a squeeze for her to speak first. She nodded, relaying instructions. "Momma bun, start slowing down. This is a far more direct route and we're going to enter from below rather than above. A rogue slash through a housing district would be very bad."

"On it!" Lucia's golden glow and egg-shaped shield hummed, the fall of her paws beginning to slow. A good thing, as Ember's next set of slashes carved through granite and broke into that new underground biome Lucia had been correct about.

Artorian was glad Ember took the lead, as his new senses brushed over him and made his skin crawl with numbing tingles. The vague sense of where the Generator was improved in clarity, and the large cavern they broke into made his Echolocation and Electrosense feel like they wildly expanded after being confined to underground shafts. From the first shockwave alone, he could see a forest made of petrified trees.

Ding!

———

Notice!

New Biome Entered: Murim.

This forested area is also known as: World of Murim, where mu refers to martial arts and rim refers to a growth spurt that is fast and powerful. In

Murim, all ascetics present seek enlightenment. Here you will find only the mighty.

Artorian dismissed the notice without reading half of it, his mind on other details. "Dear, I've the feeling we'll be in fights soon. As the person planning to go in front, do you have armor?"

Ember's voice still burned with heat. "Why wear armor when you don't plan on getting hit at all?"

She rolled her shoulder, Surtur's blazing swings paused as Lucia no longer needed fresh passageways to keep steady and straight. There was plenty of room in this underground cavern. Dead, petrified remains of a forest were no obstacle, allowing her to run without any concern for what she might run into, as the remnants of this supposed world of enlightenment broke against her shield like brittle sandstone. "Least the description was correct! We are here, after all!"

Artorian pet Lucia's ears in appreciation of her attempt at lightening the mood, but his head was still on track to be all business. "That sounds like the opposite of what you said you wanted to do, hon."

Ember exhaled fire, getting the ire out of her system as her hair stopped glowing with heat. "Have you met Kowsky yet? Likely not. We have bad bugs in the system, and we have good bugs in the system. You can recognize which bugs are on our team fairly easily. They're all wearing masks."

A piece of runed paper appeared in her free hand, the bracelet releasing a short chime. "Tear this. I'm summoning an effigy of him and having him explain."

Artorian tore the paper right away, having seen how Cy operated a similar object to summon her tonfas into existence. Immediately on destruction of the item, an orb with a ghostly image of a saluting masked bug appeared on her open hand.

The creature was tiny, wrapped in a cloak fashioned from a moth's wing, and carried several nail-sized weapons on his back.

When Kowsky spoke, Artorian was hit by a heavy reality that he hadn't paid too much attention to. Kowsky was a telltale example of someone who had already lived a life, and was now going through their second round, memories intact. The tiny, masked bug possessed the genderless voice of a teenager before their voice broke. Not completely child-like, but neither was it deep or raspy yet.

At the same time, Kowsky's method of speaking carried all the seriousness and no-Abyss tone of a seasoned civil service worker. One but who still showed excitement for their niche hobby when it came up, and this call appeared to qualify. "Bug finder eight-five-nine-eight, reporting in. How can Kowsky be of service?"

His salute doubled in crispness and intensity when the image on Kowsky's end gained enough clarity to see who he was actually talking to. "Ma'am!"

Ember was pleased with the response. "Kowsky. Good that you answered. I need a refresher provided to a team member relating to what you told me about tanking."

"Ma'am!" Kowsky released the salute, merely to salute again, adopting a hands-behind-the-lumbar pose before orating the information as ordered. "In terms of game mechanics? Maintaining aggro from enemies. Either through Taunts, being an unavoidable obstacle between them and their weaker allies, or by simply posing as the juicier target for whatever monster the party faces. A Taunting ability is always the go-to method of keeping aggro on yourself."

Ember looked down at her boy, who nodded and made a hand rolling motion, requesting the bug-finder to please go on.

Kowsky nodded sharply and continued. "When it comes to a kit or ability set, you'll also want gap closers. Skills and Abilities that allow you to move more quickly around the battlefield. Either to initiate a fight with a surprise charge, dashing in between enemies and allies to protect, or to continuously get back into the fight when you're somehow dislodged."

Fixing his pose to be slightly straighter, Kowsky did not break speaking stride. "This includes stuns or other forms of crowd control, also known as CC. These not only allow a tank to control the fight better, but they're also often great aggro generators. Nothing will Abyss-off an enemy more than head-butting them for a juicy stun. They'll forget all about that pesky healer, and probably some other stuff from the brain damage."

The bug grinned under his mask, his posture betraying that he was aware of his own joke. Seeing that his funny commentary hand landed well, he added some more! "Damage mitigation and pain tolerance is a must-have. You will get hit eventually, and if you just crumple like a crouton from the first blow, you suck as a tank. That's usually done by a value mitigating damage, but sometimes when a hit would make you flinch, miss, or interrupt a skill, your pain tolerance will allow you to still continue on."

The bug bowed apologetically to the person who Kowsky knew to be an Incarnate. The detail of her not being one at this very moment was entirely irrelevant. "Also, just take a shield, even if you're dodge tanking. Mitigating a blow or projectile is worth more than letting them fly loose, potentially hitting an ally. If it's a magical shield, you might even get to carry a fun spell effect into battle as well."

Since Ember did not chastise the bug or make a comment, Kowsky took that as his forgiveness and wrapped up. "Lastly. Area control. You want as much control of the widest area around you as possible. This is either through aura effects, your weapon reach, or just generally showing the enemy that being too close to you is a death sentence. If they have to get into your area of control to get to your allies, you can outmaneuver them."

Reaching behind him, Kowsky pulled out an oversize leaf, shaped into a square post-it note. He pushed it forward through the orb, and the physical leaf became available for Artorian to nab between two fingers.

He read the message out loud when he could read the text for ants, keeping the leaf close to his face while squinting. "A tank's job is to manage the flow of combat. Position enemies to allow your own team to maneuver and do their jobs effectively. Make sure the healers know where and how much damage is being taken. Deal with unexpected events, abilities, and accidents. Bring a poor situation back to the expected equilibrium. Tanks are meant to impose order on the chaos of combat. Also consider: Ability interrupts, partywide buffs, and damage transference."

Artorian tried to return the leaf through the orb out of sheer curiosity, then felt mighty excited when it worked. Kowsky looked to Ember and snapped into a salute. She was clearly pleased with him. "Well done. I may call upon you again. Dismissed!"

"Ma'am!" With a sharp change in stance, Kowsky's image vanished along with the orb.

CHAPTER FORTY-ONE

"Contact!" Lucia chittered the warning loud and fast.

Artorian's arm snapped up, aimed dead ahead, and spotted a shambling thing lurch into the path Lucia was on. He almost unleashed Shining Ray, hesitating as he failed to remember the name of his other attack while Lucia called out useful information. "Hostile! Four-thousand two-hundred health, Petrified Murim Deadwood. Brittle!"

"Boom!" Artorian forgot what he'd named his own attack, but he remembered the feeling. The feeling was enough. Designating about seventeen-thousand Nuts to fuel 'To whom it may concern,' he felt the energy drain at the same moment his effect engaged. A roaring explosion gloriously burst forth from the chest of the opponent ahead of them, dealing a whopping four thousand something damage that erased the enemy from sight in a devastating haze of heat and pressure. Burnt and toasted hot splinters went flying in an upwards arc, but otherwise harmlessly rained against Lucia's shield when they passed the smoking remains by.

Artorian felt stunned and frozen for a full minute. Something he had not expected to be as he watched his energy bar refill over the course of that minute. Only when it was full did he remember to breathe. He realized he'd been mentally paralyzed, and his body had followed suit. "That was unexpected."

Ember kept her arm protectively curled about him. "I don't think you've ever fought with your current body, beloved. Your experiences may be used to combat, but your new senses are not. This is completely fresh to you, even if you have memories that say otherwise. A person using a third of all their available stamina in one jump is also exhausting to a body. Energy is no different. That was a lot of oomph you just shoved into that boom. I'm not surprised you're rattled. Good callout, momma bun. Again if you spot something."

"On it!" Lucia's ears telescoped in a snap, revolving around before folding back down against her head. "Two kilometers left, passed it already, heading towards us but won't catch up."

Ember gently took Artorian's hand, pointing it at the target. "There. See it? Breathe. Expect the drain. Intend your explosion. *Fire.*"

Artorian spotted the shambler. It was the only moving object trudging across a flat plain in clear daylight. The combination of his senses, and clarity of vision that reached through the darkness easily pinned down the target. That those values also appeared to affect his Electrosense and Echolocation made him pretty happy.

He inhaled and spoke. "Boom."

Another four-thousand and change damage bang-shattered the Shambling Deadwood into scraps of broken bark. The flash was visible from a distance, and Artorian leaned back and glanced at his Nuts meter, watching the bar refill over the course of a minute. "Takes a lot of juice. Deals a lot of damage. It drains me, but I like it. The instant leap to giant chunks of my resources being consumed feels bad. Definitely feels bad. When other people do this, I recommend that the system starts with Abilities that eat tiny nibbles of energy so this experience is palatable. Right now these are jarring experiences, and I think I'd rather avoid tapping my bars at all if I can help it. At least until I have more skills that take tiny nibbles, so I can get used to the drain."

He mulled over a thought. "I should make a third attack that's something in between what I have, but I don't think I have time."

Ember glanced in the direction of their goal. "If you're quick, then maybe one. We're about to be directly below the Generator in a few minutes, and I bet it's entombed in that upside down glacier. The glow gives it away."

Artorian had to agree as an upside down, glowing, bright blue glacier that hung from the ceiling after it came into clear view was hard to ignore. Also nice to know just how high the ceiling was! He was already counting his blessings that he could fly. A fall would give him all sorts of unpleasant trauma. "I'll get right on it!"

He threw open a new prompt, recalled the quill that had stored itself back into his hand, and got to scribbling. After he sent it off, the prompt came back in record time.

Ding!

———

Ability Gained:
Luminous Gatling.
Rank: Novice.
Special Qualities: Gatling, Homing.
Shape: Laser.
Ammunition: Ink to Bolts, Bolts to Ink!
Description: This Ability fires rapid bolt-type lasers that home in on an enemy target.
Output: Luminous Gatling requires 4 Energy per special quality to fire a single Bolt. Current: (8). Luminous Gatling may be spun up to fire a maximum of 60 Bolts per second, at the user's control, minimum 1. Each bolt deals 1d10 worth of Kinetic Lightning damage. Cost will be calculated per second, and detracted from energy regeneration, unless that value hits zero, at which point Luminous Gatling will draw from the Energy meter.

Special Quality: More Dakka.
More Dakka: If Luminous Gatling is firing bolts at its maximum output, its projectile count is doubled.

Notice!
871 out of 1703 Adaptive Pylons used.
Luminous Gatling requires 127 Adaptive Pylons.

Artorian did some quick math. "Eight times sixty is... four hundred and eighty? That's an easy two hundred points above my Nuts regeneration metric. Almost. Just under? I think it's just under. I'm going to pretend it costs two hundred per second to make my math easy. I've got thirty-three thousand and change, which will give me two minutes and a bit of constant-fire goodness. That is a bow that I can get behind!"

Lucia whistled, impressed as she came to a stop directly beneath the lowest point of the flipped glacier. "We're here. Can I see that attack?"

Artorian flipped the prompt for her as they dismounted. She took it, studied it, closed one eye and twisted her ears around as if trying to get a signal. "At max, that's one-hundred and twenty projectiles per second, so one-twenty ten-sided dice. Which means... you're dealing somewhere between one-hundred twenty, and one-thousand two hundred damage per second? Them's good deeps! I call that a role well-filled. You should name that attack."

"After what? A person?" Artorian was confused, looking up at the glow-berg to find a way in, and seeing none. "Sure. I'll call her Sasha."

He then noticed two prompts had been waiting and tapped them. They were identical, so he only read one.

You have hit: Murim Deadwood, Shambling Prowler.
  To whom it may concern Damage: 4,250 Explosive.
  Total Raw Damage: 4,250 Explosive.
  Multipliers: None.
  Total Damage: 4,250 Explosive.

Artorian approved of successful numbers, but quietly clicked his tongue. Supreme Weapon Mastery had not ticked in a twenty-five percent raw damage bonus. Ah well. He was about to continue looking for a way into the shiny stalagmite, but Lucia had more action for him as her ears turned southwest. "Contact! Another Shambler!"

She threw up shields around the three of them that had a numerical protection value. Artorian noted another yellow bar filter into his top left vision, feeling pretty good about an 11,400 health-point buffer.

Ember blocked the incoming target from having any kind of line of effect to Lucia. Artorian instead rubbed his chin, spotting the Shambler about four kilometers out and rapidly closing. He walked up a short incline for a better angle, then pointed his palm at it. "Luminous Gatling."

Sound roared, each copper-and cobalt-colored bolt releasing a loud *thunk*. At the speed the bolts flew, Artorian was deafened by the sweet, sweet sound of *B-R-R-R-R-R-R*.

Just as when he'd released the melee version of Gatling, using Pantheon Style against Marie. Unlike what was expected, the bolts did not originate from his palm, but rather from around below it, as if there was a rotating tube hanging from his wrist. He likened the visual to a set of tubes rather than a single one. Some Gnomish madness that all spun around his upper arm, with only one tube releasing a bolt at any given time. He formed his palm into a fist instead and found that it made Sasha much easier to control.

Unprompted, he craved a sandwich.

"It's dead!" Lucia called out to him while the Gatling still roared, battering the environment. His projectiles were flying off into the distance and going hog wild as they had nothing to shoot at, and nothing to target, the Deadwood long pulverized by the Kinetic Lightning barrage. "Three! It's dead!"

Artorian felt stung, like his health had taken damage. He stopped feeding energy into the attack as his body sent shock-waves back and forth from within. His ears were ringing with a shrill tone that muted all other sounds. His firing arm felt both tender and sore. He blinked, barely hearing the girls as his eyes wandered over to his energy bars. They were full? Why were they full? He aimlessly pointed away from them both, releasing a few bolts to see the value of his Bolts regeneration change. That was odd. That wasn't right. Shouldn't Sasha be taking ammunition from his Nuts bar?

He wobbled and fell on his rear, confused why his head hurt. Shouldn't he have something that stopped that? Freedom of Mind kicked in when he remembered he had it, clearing all his mental statuses. The soreness in his arm on the other hand, was very much present as strain. "All that from a few seconds? How am I ever going to sustain a barrage if a few seconds does that to me?"

Ding!

———

Message from Zelia: "My Dreamer. Please be careful with your shiny toys. They all have costs not described by the entry, as you have learned. To support you in this endeavor, I shall gift you a reminder that you are in a game, and how to handle such inconveniences.

Love, and kisses - Your Zelia."

———

Skill Gained:
  Luminous Gatling Mastery.
  Rank: Novice.
  When engaging the use of Luminous Gatling, the hidden burdens will be lessened. When all the burdens are mastered, this skill will provide hidden benefits instead.

Notice!
  904 out of 1703 Adaptive Pylons used.
  Luminous Gatling Mastery requires 33 Adaptive Pylons.

Artorian got his breathing under control, the shakes leaving his system with a Cleanse from Lucia. He nodded at the prompt, feeling that to be excellent advice given the suddenly discovered downside of his fancy new speedbow. "I should try to develop skills for every Ability that I have. Zelia's pretty good about her warnings. I don't know what Concern or Shiny Ray have as their downsides yet, but if Sasha was anything to go by? *Ow.*"

Lucia pet his head. "Do try. I will not always conveniently be within paw-reach of your self-inflicted injuries, and they are my least favorite. I know these are all novice-ranked toys and you have no idea what you're doing with them aside from turning them on. Developing their relevant skills is heavily suggested by your medic."

He half-saluted to obey the medic, brushing himself off before pacing somewhat and trying to find a way into the iceberg above them. Ember had him beat, pointing at the far side from where they were as some refuse fell down. "Found it. Trash chute."

Artorian scratched his chin, inhaling a hissed breath. Ember could call it a trash chute all she wanted. He knew what that exit was. "Can't say I'm fond of that option."

Ember had no time for his preferences. "You fly. I burn. Bun shields. Two minutes, tops. Take a deep breath, we're both going to hold on tight. You're the only one with three-dimensional mobility right now. My 'jump good' Skill doesn't count."

Artorian quietly cringed, gave himself a squeezed hug, and tried to think real hard on how to get his cleaning Aura back. "I gotta stay clean, I gotta stay clean, I gotta stay clean."

He then remembered the mention of forcing the system to pay attention, and dumped energy into his intent to stay clean, because it was going to eat him alive to go up the… brown chute.

Ding!

Artorian jumped for joy when he saw the contents of the prompt. "I'm saved!"

———

Ability Gained:
  Cleaning Presence.
  Rank: Novice.
  Special Qualities: Aura, Clean.
  Shape: Orb.
  Description: A field emitting a constant cleaning effect, centered on the caster.
  Output: One meter in diameter of cleaning effect per percentage of maximum Energy bar invested. This field cleans but does not cleanse.
  Note: You may only have one Aura type effect active at any given time.

———

Notice!
  964 out of 1703 Adaptive Pylons used.
  Cleaning Presence requires 60 Adaptive Pylons.

———

Artorian instantly fed ten percent of his Nuts bar into the cleaning effect and relished in the sensation of the cleaning field as it extended from the center of his chest. The welcoming, hazy, vague prickles washing over him and getting rid of particulates. He then felt all the strain on his Energy bar fall away completely, the full value restoring itself.

Ding!

———

Class Update!
All Cleaning related abilities have their cost negated.
"In his way, there was only the cloy. In his wake, there was only cleanliness."
- Shai-Hulud, First of the Allsand.

———

Artorian breathed deep, supremely satisfied as he pushed the effect to its full possible value and felt much better about life. "Now, I am ready."

CHAPTER FORTY-TWO

Artorian hovered two inches above the ground.

There had been a moment when he'd thought about how bonescripting was supposed to work, and the next moment, he'd hovered up. A warmth pulsed under his skin, the pleasant feeling coming from deeper within. Pushing fingers into his own arm, he confirmed that his bones were the source of the pleasant experience.

Ember dismissed Surtur, gripping Float-orian by the elbow so he wouldn't wander off like a balloon filled with pure Air Affinity flightiness. "Take off after we have a good hold of you, sugar. You alright?"

He closed his eyes to focus when his feet touched the ground. "There is a feeling? I know the effect is coming from the script, but I've never known it to be this responsive before, nor so attentive. Like it was waiting for me? I have this scene hanging in my mind, where I am hugged from behind, and someone has their arms around my neck. They seem happy with me, but I can't discern why."

Lucia tactically closed the window she was looking at. "That may be a smidge more literal than you having a mental image, kit."

Artorian opened his eyes, intrigued and laying his attention on the humanized Glitterflit as she groomed her human hair and basher ears. "How so?"

Lucia periscoped, a steel brush in her hand to attack that unpleasant knot in her locks as she brushed up from the bottom. "I still have a bunch of information you haven't seen yet."

She sifted her digits through the problem area, parting the hair where needed and pulling the knots apart on the sides before rolling her brush through again. Going fast had minor downsides, but after a nice, good run like that, she felt great overall. "One of the always active, heads-up display things I have access to shows me the status, health, and general condition of all party members in my team. Astarte currently has a pretty bonus border around hers, because she's designated as Raid Leader."

Putting her comb back into her bag, she motioned to an empty space. "This screen right here, to be specific, shows me that all four members of my team are currently in perfect health."

"Four?" Artorian wondered if she'd flubbed her words. "Did you say four?"

Lucia shook her head. That hadn't been a mistake. "I said four. There are three other player characters within several of my area of effect Abilities. My shields are currently affecting myself, Astarte, Less than Three, and..."

Silence befell Lucia, who froze on the spot. She swallowed, her left ear twitching. A small nod later, she calmed herself with some tense breathing, and rephrased her sentence into a statement. "We have four party members."

Artorian knew that look, repeating her statement. "We have four party members."

Ember had to finish kneading the bridge of her nose, then repeated the statement. Fully understanding that the tussle between Heavenlies had either concluded, or one had snuck off and gotten themselves the slot all while remaining entirely sneaky about the endeavor. Otherwise the Heavenly would have announced themselves. With lots and lots of flair, if it was any of the ones she knew. Abyss, the nightmare that would have ensued from the slot having gone to Urtu was not a reality she wanted to entertain.

Then the kicker. She couldn't see whichever Heavenly was hanging around. Her version might be the least potent out of the three, but her Precursor grant should have still given her *something*. The number of Heavenlies that were able to get around both Lucia and Artorian's abilities to directly see them at this point? That narrowed the pool to a tiny circle of possibilities, and none of the options were individuals that she wanted problems with. "We can go up. Yes?"

Artorian considered flight, and his heels left the ground, followed by his toes. "With... incredible ease? My Energy meter is going down, but not very fast."

He extended his arms for Lucia and Ember. "All set."

When mushed between both girls, the Energy meter dropped considerably faster. Artorian sussed out that part of the cost was proportional to the weight, or the amount of mass he was moving. Ages and eternities of wisdom screamed in his head not to mention anything on the topic, lest he be killed by being beaten with his own health bar. Artorian thought that to be sagely advice, and cleverly kept his trap shut.

The ride up was spent with Artorian paying more attention to the changes in his Energy bar than the actual flight. Speed also increased the cost, and by a good margin. The more mass or weight involved, and the faster he wanted to move that mass around, the more intense the cost. He didn't even notice going up the trash chute, as it was just another pristine passageway made from icy permafrost.

The way widened from Ember's heat effect, and by the time they exited the other end, Artorian had entirely forgotten what the chute was for. He placed both girls on walkable ground, crouched because he thought it would help him be quiet for some reason, and snuck from what he pretended to be an oversized lavatory. "The janitor's passing would be known only by his mark of cleanliness. The janitor shall ask not what was there before. For it is there no more."

Entering deeper into the structure, Lucia and Ember snickered as they copied his crouch step to sneak along. Structure was being generous for carved paths through an ice block, but who was he to judge those living in these miserable conditions?

They snuck their way up and around from the bowels of the area, up into scaffolding meant to build a floor on as they began to hear the first of the *klank klank*. Nobody had to strain their ears to pick up the *klank-tink-clank* of methodical metal hammers striking metal materials. Artorian checked his surroundings. They must be at the lowest current point a civilization of some kind had reached, though it made him suspicious that the scaffolding may not have been scaffolding. He motioned at it, ears on the sound that traveled through. "Are those bits metal?"

Ember touched some of the scaffolding. "That's interesting."

The other two kept an ear out for her findings. "This isn't scaffolding. These are pipes for water, heat, and gasses. The interesting bit is that the material is made from old coins that have been molten down and reforged. That one is gold, this one is silver, the whole bunch over there turning green is copper. Then that important-looking big one? That's platinum. They repurposed all the money from Solar Gate into plumbing infrastructure. This clean copper one? I think it's a water line, based on the etchings. This piece simply isn't connected to the main reservoir yet."

Artorian squinted at his dearest. "Since when do you know so much about plumbing?"

She scoffed, amused. "Wetwork is my specialty, darling. Time with Dwarves is also decently enlightening, when you get them to argue about something. I can't figure the other pipes out except for that dangerous one. I don't know those etchings."

She pointed at a hidden pipe embedded in the wall, giving off a dim, yellowish orange incandescence. "That glowing hot one, on the other hand? That's connected directly to one celestial abyss of a heat source. My guess is a geothermal source, or it would have been if the pipe didn't go up, and we know that there's nothing below us."

Artorian made a throaty noise of understanding. "Must be connected to the Generator. From the logs, I could tell that Duchess has already set it to the option that creates heat. If the Gennie is responsible for keeping everyone here alive, that puts a small knot in the plan for changing it to setting two and giving us the portation option. The change would stop the heat generation. I'm not sure why that didn't occur to me before now. That seems obvious and important."

"Worry about it when it needs to be worried about." Lucia touched the wall, running a finger down. "If there's a massive source of heat being pumped through this ice block, why isn't it wet? Or molten. This ice is hard, and aside from the wall being cold, it's dry. Heat and ice means water. There's no water. I don't understand."

Artorian shrugged, not knowing either. They looked at Ember, but her expression was complicated. She, too, shook her head. "I don't know. One of the locals might have answers for us, but that's a detour we might not have time for. Living Bonfire is still going and this material isn't showing any signs of melting, unlike the chute."

Without answers, they continued crawling upward. They found more radiant heat pipes, an increase in pressurized pipes filled with hot steam, even more nonfunctional pipes, and a large amount of mundane household goods and furniture being repurposed into structural integrity support. Entire passageways seemed built out of knickknacks, pieces of building, and any random hunk of junk that could be put towards another five feet of space being carved out for expansion.

Artorian began to find that suspicious. "If they carved and clawed this hard for every inch of space, then where is everyone?"

Bun had more pressing concerns. "Where's the food? I haven't seen a single thing to eat, or a place to grow things to eat, the entire climb up. I was going to guess this was a storage cellar, but it's empty everywhere I look."

Lucia ground her teeth together, then thought to check the ambient temperature. "Minus forty degrees Celsius? The other measurement says minus forty degrees Fahrenheit. I think that's the first point where those values can actually be the same number? I have changed my opinion. Now I am confused on how the pipes aren't frozen, rather than why the wall isn't wet."

Artorian threw his hands up, not knowing if that value had significance. "Is that a lot, or a little?"

Lucia cocked her head, thinking about it as her ears pointed in odd directions. "Without your current equipment? You'd be dead within ten minutes of exposure."

Artorian snapped his mouth shut, looking to Ember for help. She knew about this Dwarven mathematics stuff better, and he badly wanted to attend a college for a decade to brush up. He felt so behind.

Ember reached for him, locking an arm around him. "The Pale has a couple of major environmental threats. The cold being the main one. We knew going into this that the frost was a problem but have long had solutions in the works. This equipment was step two or three, and Zelia delivered wonderfully."

Since they were clearly pausing for this before continuing the upward climb, Ember provided a quick rundown when it came to an absence of fire. "Cold is an easy term to refer to what is actually doing you in, which is exposure. Exposure to cold can cause frostbite, hypothermia, and quickly become life-threatening. You already know that freezing temperatures can cause severe damage to fruit crops and other vegetation. You remember what winter is?"

Artorian and Lucia both nodded, knowing what winter was,

and finding it easier to confirm the answer so Ember could go on and they could keep going. "Windchill is the term used to describe the rate at which heat is carried away from the body, from low temperature and wind. Lose too much internal heat, and you die. This is true for plants. This is true for us. You'll last longer in the cold when there's no wind, but the environment will kill you all the same."

More attentive nodding was returned as the teacher raised her fist.

"Burning Finger." Ember's entire arm suddenly looked like a mere shape containing the roiling churn of a sun. She drew in the wall with her digits after firing up this ultimate move of solar prominence, the attack relegated to an educational tool. As her entire hand came alive with solar trails that danced across her skin and coiled between her fingers, the burning, heat-death grip of the universe was given all the respect provided to a common pencil.

She had no problems melting right through the ice to make divots, elaborating on Wisp and Gnome measurement systems. "Celsius is about when water freezes and boils, Fahrenheit is about how hot or cold an environment's temperature is."

Ember checked on her party, found them looking conflicted, and tried easier words. "Fahrenheit is how people feel. Celsius is how water feels. There's also Kelvin, which is about how molecules feel, but that's not important right now. At zero C, water freezes, at one-hundred C, water boils. Simple, direct, good for cooking. F doesn't work like that. In F, water freezes at 32 degrees and boils at 212 degrees. Very different measuring stick. Both are useful, but both are not useful for the same thing."

She wiped down an entire wall, clearing and flattening the ice with a brush of her eruptive, filament-coated hand. "The average body temperature is 98.6 in °F, or 37 in °C. You have this number, and you keep ticking. Drop or raise a digit or two in either direction, and you will soon no longer be ticking. Your clock is losing parts."

Artorian crossed his arms but kept within Ember's heat

effect as she moved around. Lucia seemed plenty comfortable sitting nearby, unaffected by the current lack of heat as she had some screens pulled up. She motioned at Ember when Artorian glanced at her, making him pay attention. "Zero C means it's winter. Zero F means it's *deep* winter, and it's all going to go downhill. Wind then adds a separate dimension to the experience of cold in our winter wonderland."

Ember began a new line on the wall, labeled physical sensation. "Starting around minus 20°F, the wind stops registering as a tactile sensation and is experienced primarily as a more urgent, cutting pain. By about minus 30, the cold doesn't feel cold anymore. It's pure, unadulterated pain, registering as a sharp burning sensation. A full minus 30 is like a hot iron being pressed on your exposed skin. At minus 40 all you feel is a burning scream. The lower this number, the faster you die of frostbite."

Scratching a line under that material, Ember wrote some small details on that issue. It was better for Artorian to know so he wouldn't foolishly disrobe in the middle of a congregation or something. "Frostbite is damage to body tissue caused by extreme cold. A windchill of minus 20°Fahrenheit will cause frostbite in thirty minutes or less. Frostbite causes a loss of feeling and a white or pale appearance in extremities. Meaning your fingers, toes, earlobes or the tip of the nose. Slowly rewarm affected areas if this happens. If the person is also showing signs of hypothermia, warm the body and core before the extremities. Rub chest. Not arms. Repeat it, sugar."

"Rub chest, not arms." Artorian did so, making the motions to show he understood she was being serious about keeping him alive. "Warm the core."

"Good." Ember approved, wrapping up her write up. "Hypothermia is a condition brought on when your body temperature drops to less than 95°F. Like I mentioned before, this can kill. Survivors suffer lasting kidney, liver, and pancreas problems. Warning signs include uncontrollable shivering, memory loss, disorientation, incoherence, slurred speech, drowsiness, and apparent exhaustion. If you hear Lucia yell anything about your temperature dipping under 96, you back off immediately and rush to the healer. *Immediately*, honey."

Artorian saluted. "Rush to the healer if my equilibrium destabilizes. Can do!"

Ember grabbed his face while he saluted, and kissed his forehead, pressing her forehead to his afterwards with a heavy sigh. "I'm so happy that you listen to me when I try to help. I get so worried about you. I don't even know why sometimes. I know you'll find a way, but my heart gets gripped now and again and I just feel this fear creep in. I despise it, sugar."

Artorian wrapped his arms firm about her back and squeezed her tight. "I'll be alright, dearest. You're here, aren't you? You care for me and love me so. How could I not fall into your every word?"

Ember flushed hot red as her expression of worry and care was turned on its head, with romance leaning in the door, complete with a rose in the mouth. She slammed that door shut with a screech, wanting nothing to do with that whole idea right now. The Goddess of War bounded ten feet away and kept her hands to her chest, hissing like a cat. "Boy! I was expressing care!"

"Do you feel better?" Artorian smirked like a miser who knew exactly what he'd done.

Leering at him rather than glaring, Ember checked herself over, her arm no longer an effigy of solar prominence. She grumbled that he was correct. "Yes. I feel better. No more heart grip. Only horrible flusteredness. How could you?"

"How could I?" Artorian pressed a hand to his chest, his smile growing. "Well, like this!"

The moment he took a step forward, Ember turned and took off running. "No! No more mushy mushy! It makes the skin crawl! Nuuuuuuh!"

"C'mere, sugar! It's just a tiny bit of affection! Harmless, really!" Artorian chased her and amped up the fun, unable to stop smiling all the while as Lucia cackled and fell in tow behind the two very noisy kits that had undoubtedly woken up the entire iceberg.

Life was about to get interesting.

So much for sneaking their way in!

CHAPTER FORTY-THREE

A seven-foot tall, four-hundred pound, six-armed green Orkharn thumbed his ivory tusks. Tan-Buro, Watchmaster of the home beacon, kept a patient watch high in the sky. He pulled his patchy, hand-me-down, double wool gambeson tight around his chest out of habit, securing it for the umpteenth time. Two flicks to the blessed rock restrained in the container across his chest made it sputter to life, providing him its stored heat before sputtering out.

Tan-Buro adjusted his tetsubo and knew his time up in the beacon was coming to an end. A watch where information was sent back down to New Haven. He had already flashed his relevant messages down to the receiving station, and little else had happened since.

Sa-Buro, wielder of the kanabo and the Watchmaster who he had taken over from, told many tales of Behemoths falling. Calamities toppling. Landscapes shifting. Avalanches roaring.

Fantastical stories of red blades that cut the ground and pierced the sky, slicing clouds and revealing the cold stars above. One of those slices revealed the sky still, a massive wound rent through what were normally rumbling clouds and harsh winds.

Now, there were soft winds. The weather was not any warmer, but the cleaved sky had punched the very wind and slapped it away. The cutting shrieks of cold did not assail him, making this one of the more pleasant watches in all the Watchmaster's life.

Tan-Buro held onto the zeppelin's mooring mast, where countless brethren had held it before him. He glanced north, seeing Fuyu No Arashi, the Eternal Thundercloud, beat its bright drums once more on the horizon. Fighting the mountains in that segment of land, as Fuyu No Arashi tended to do.

To his left, the storied rumbling had ceased. No more light broke from the ground or illuminated the dark of deepnight. No more quakes, shifting of great ice shelves, and breaking of tectonic plates had been present for Tan-Buro to take note of.

To his right, the amassed force of Ice Behemoths had paused in their advance, wary of the sudden, cataclysmic changes occurring beneath their feet. These masters of Midgard handled change poorly and had come to stomp it out.

"Ha!" Tan-Buro scoffed at the notion, his six arms crossing as he considered how dishonorable those lords of the wild were. Ignoring the hesitant lords, he glanced south, but those lands were as white and undisturbed as ever. The peaceful fields, Lady O'Dachi called them. Tan-Buro pressed his top set of hands together, giving thanks for the peaceful scene.

Movement to his left stole the Watchmaster's attention.

With a quick step to the lenses, he peered through a vision pipe constructed of many glass pieces, seeing much farther than ordinarily able. Good tidings! The hunter zeppelins were returning with a feast. Tan-Buro moved to the telegraph station, flicking the lights down at New Haven, and sending his notice that the hunters were on their way back. Their flight low, their cargo laden. Dead Behemoths provided many great slabs of meat, and many dead Behemoths had been laid at their feet.

Tan-Buro had no idea what kind of forces could fell not one, but three Ice Behemoths in one deepnight. He gripped his tetsubo and corrected himself. Three Behemoths, and *one*

Calamity. The walking mountain had been felled like a mere frost gnat that had been clapped between two hands as it buzzed over a bowl of steaming mushroom noodles. Now that he thought about it, he hadn't seen a frost gnat since he was but a pint-sized warrior.

The cry of a Celestial, white and blue Harris Hawk pulled Tan-Buro's attention. He was being relieved from his Watchmaster shift. As was proper, Tan-Buro wrapped the cord of descent about his arm, then nodded at the Hawk. The bird flew back, and when it cried once more, Tan-Buro leapt from the beacon zeppelin. As the winch screeched and he moved down, his weight pulled up the next Watchmaster. Extending a hand, he slapped palms with Wattaj, the Hammurai. A Master Hamster Samurai.

The descent had always been Tan-Buro's favorite part of keeping watch on the moored beacon. The last one hundred feet of his descent slowed to nothing as the winch took over his descent. More to give Wattaj an easy ascent instead, but Tan-Buro was happy for the soft landing either way. Once his arm was released from the binding cord, he turned to the crank operators, pressed his top set of hands together, and gave them thanks.

The Sheep, Hedgehogs, and other people who had never known the ancient blessing of humanization returned nods to him, returning greater honor to Tan-Buro for considering them in the first place. They knew they were not as capable, feeling praised by his actions as they did their part. In New Haven, to be considered was honorable. The Lady O'Dachi spoke like iron and steel of the value inherent in all, but to feel the thanks was a different matter.

The crank operators then gave thanks to Lady O'Dachi, and her ceaseless efforts to claw a future out from the frozen death, giving them all she gathered.

Tan-Buro provided space to the hammerers who made sparks fly and maintained the structure, all while maneuvering his way between tight, iced corridors that twisted to block the wind from entering. The white and blue Harris Hawk landed on Tan-Buro's shoulder as he traversed the great bridges between exhaust shafts, surprising him.

That was the sign that someone wanted to speak with him. Turning on his heel to follow along different segments of steam-filled pipes, Tan-Buro passed Ferrets working with rope, and a line of Red Pandas carrying a single piece of mechanical complexity each. The Watchmaster did not understand the metal magic that went into keeping New Haven warm and livable, but he would not question Lady O'Dachi, nor her divine wisdom. She was the reason all had warmth during their sleep, and food on their waking.

Once a level lower, traffic increased. Most stopped to make way for him, as he was Watchmaster. The Moles from the coal mines, Tan-Buro paused for, letting them pass with their carts and sleds piled full of solid black matter. It was dishonorable to impede those who worked for the health of all, especially at the knowing detriment of their own.

Shortly after, Tan-Buro stopped again to let pass the Weasels and Ferrets from the wood drill. He missed the Murim woods, but they had long stopped being what the stories described them as. Gone were the lush and verdant magical forests of growth. He sighed, petting the Harris Hawk. "You are an excellent bird, Curator Caladrius."

The Watchmaster quickly checked on the care house lodged in the third floor from the opening to heaven, where the hunter zeppelins were finally arriving. He took a moment to lean over the railing and watch those masters of hot air descend with inches to spare on either end of their descent. The smell of meat followed them, making Tan-Buro salivate in anticipation.

A strike from a pan to his butt made him jump, and quickly make way and hustle out of the path of Cookhouse Rats, no longer impeding the route where the raw food was going to come through once the hunters unloaded their gains into the gathering post.

Pushing through down to the fifth level from the top, he

passed the House of Scribes where he had learned all his martial prowess from The Painting of Moons and Rivers. His mind wandered to it the moment he thought of the art piece, having always found it difficult not to be entranced by that particular, unassuming thing.

That hanging scroll had taught Tan-Buro to respect that which appeared simple, finding that rarely was such a notion true. He had a long way to go before he would reach his destination, and allowed his mind to wander once more. It reached for the wall scroll outside of his grasp, and Tan-Buro relented.

As recorded by the Curator, The Painting of Moons and Rivers hangs as a wall scroll like a piece of common scribble, on the wall in the House of Scribes. It occupies a mediocre slot in an unimpressive room, directed to by a hallway that is entirely forgettable. Its simple lines and broad brushstrokes are aesthetically pleasing, worth the mere glance of their presence. Yet, in that room within the House of Scribes, it is the only piece that hangs. Some who are lost find themselves arriving at this obscure corner of the world, where the unimpressive makes Masters gawk as their most humblest of students when shown the sublime.

All those who see it, and look deep, find that they cannot look away.

The Novice eye sees only calligraphy. Yet, peering deep, one finds colors living within the canvas of this monochrome work. Some claim to have seen entire rivers, guiding the flow of their blades to heights taller than mountain peaks. Some, claim to have seen moons upon its aged surface, their magic newly waxing and waning with the methodical might of an unopposable ebb and flow. Thus, the painting, mediocre and drab as it may seem, was named The Painting of Moons and Rivers.

Or as the Curator once said: "A name forever lost on me, as all I have ever seen upon its unremarkable paper is an endless sea of stars."

Tan-Buro fished out his personal notes, having improved

different Skills and Attributes on each layer of the Painting as he spent endless hours before it. Like so many others had.

———

Novice - The Calligraphy.
  Beginner - The Colors.
  Apprentice - Movements, beyond the imagination.
  Student - The Rivers.
  Journeyman - The fish that swim. The goats on the mountains.
  Expert - The horizon, ever expansive.
  Master - The moon rises. The moons fall.

———

He had notes scribbled below, uncertain what the remaining stages were. The Curator had let slip that Grandmaster involved seeing the stars and planets beyond the moon, while only vaguely aware of a rumor that the Sage layer boggled the mind. Rumor said Sage was seeing yourself in the painting looking back at you. The Curator believed that the last stage was little more than observing a blank canvas, where one walks outside and realizes it was a painting of our own place in the universe.

Tan-Buro arrived at the public house but was stopped by the Oni at the door. The large, bright red being grunted out her rehearsed lines. "Password."

Tan-Buro pointed at the bird on his shoulder, indicating that he really shouldn't need to do this.

The Oni sighed and grunted again, repeating herself. "Password."

Needing to squeeze his own topknot to remain calm, the Watchmaster tried to recall which password it was supposed to be. "To find another, one must first find themselves."

"That was last week." The Oni grumbled, just trying to do her job as the chatter from inside of the building was already including Tan-Buro in conversation, regardless of him still being outside.

The Watchmaster tried another. "The naked man fears no pickpocket."

The Oni closed her eyes, drew a deep breath, and stepped out of the way. "No, but if the stares in my back get any sharper, I'm going to fall over dead from becoming a reverse porcupine. Get in there."

Tan-Buro stepped inside, the Hawk flying away before the warmth of the structure rolled over him. What surprised him most was not the pleasant heat, but the sheer amount of people present. Several other Orkharn were hunched over the Vendetta map, arguing about the number of dead Behemoths, and how it was a bigger problem that they all died in sequence, with the vector of their deaths making a beeline towards them. Two were having a rougher argument and settled it in traditional style. By punching each other without blocking, as the one to fall first would certainly be wrong.

The Oni in the room were all bundled around the scrolls of Yasura, and the thousand techniques of slaying giants. The Watchmaster would have been tempted to sneak a peek at another scroll, but the scent of wisteria hit him like the back of a hand. His senses were drawn to the two depictions of beauty that hung around a bead-blocked doorway. Respectfully, he showed them face by pressing his top hands together toward them, speaking their names during the light bow directed at each of them. "Fuji. Ajisai."

The twin succubi grinned at the Orkharn but didn't tease him as they were prone to do. Instead, they each reached over, and parted the beads. With a voice so sultry that it would melt most any man, the succubi on the left relayed instruction. "Duchess of Katarina waits for your live report. She wants to hear everything you saw directly, regardless of how little you saw."

Tan-Buro used two sets of hands in his return motion. "This Watchmaster shall not keep Lady O'Dachi waiting."

Entering while trying his best not to steal glances at the curtain guardians, he entered an office filled with what must have been all the remaining scrolls in the world, filling shelves upon shelves that had at one point held an item called 'wine.' Aside from murals of plans, hosts of information sprawled to cover every inch of available space, and endless ledgers on resource expenditures, the simple room held a single large table, and a single chair. On that chair sat Lady O'Dachi. Daimyo to the Orkharn. Two personal attendants behind her each carried a silk-covered pillow, the combination of which held her namesake weapon.

The Legendary Odachi.

Her gaze was iron when her cold eyes flicked up to see him, raw and hardened with grit. Duchess adjusted the fluff of her dress in the same manner that Tan-Buro did to his blessed heatrock. A carryover from long nights in the beacon zeppelin that couldn't be unlearned.

She had aged like fine wine over the many decades that she had seen. After at least seven of them, she was thin, pale, and gnarled. All except for her face, which could be mistaken for a third succubus being present. Her eyes, however, bore into him with as much ferocity as the wood drill demanded tribute, dug straight out of the ice.

Lady O'Dachi spoke with exceptional clarity, combining all the bleating volume of her sheepish father, Oswan, plus all the grace and knowledge of her mother, regent for a full life, Katarina of Duvetia. "Report."

Tan-Buro performed the honorable motion and greeting with all his hands. "No major events. The sky remains split. The Behemoth Lords remain apprehensive. The red blades have ceased. Hunters bring a feast that will last months, and we have more to gather for months still. Three Behemoths shall bulge our storage. With stores like that, I hear rumors that my counterparts may once more look favorably on activities other than hunting."

He grinned in an attempt to be cheeky, but never managed

to get a smile or a laugh out of the Lady. Duchess may well have been a metal statue from how little her expressions moved. "Understood. Please beware that with all our population and forces relegated to the topmost levels due to the Behemoth Lords, that the under-sections may be vulnerable to surprise Nootingales. I would rather never see another Penguin Assassin. One close call was too much. Refuel your steam core first, Watchmaster."

Tan-Buro bowed in understanding. "This Watchmaster shall sweep the expansions and refill the blessings in the heatrock. As you command, my Daimyo."

He was dismissed with a wave of the hand, then stopped cold when the curtain beads were batted out of the way. Someone unknown entered the room with both a brazen attitude and a complete disregard for anything that smelled like rules or customs.

He heard both of the curtain guardians complain, before being acutely muffled by a hand across the mouth. "Excuse you, we are succubi! We—*mmmmhhpfl!*"

Artorian snapped a quip and barged right past them as Ember handled the nuances of that negotiation. "You are a no thank you, bye."

The youth dressed in supremely comfortable-looking white and blue winter attire then pressed his hands to his hips, and snapped his head to Lady O'Dachi. "There you are! I've been so looking forward to meeting you! Hello! I'm Less than Three. There's no easy way to say this, so I'm going to chuck it on the table. I need your Generator to be set to setting two for a short while. Please and thank you."

For the first time ever, Tan-Buro saw Lady O'Dachi drop her pen, and blink.

CHAPTER FORTY-FOUR

Duchess was having an uncanny day. An uncanny set of days, given the current track record. Her voice remained iron and impassive in the face of this oddity. "Watchmaster? Please escort this lost Tanuki child back toward the safety of the housing quarter. He appears to have strayed from his caretakers, where it is warm. If we're going to have illusionists running around, I'd rather be aware of them before they barge into my office."

Artorian squeezed his hands on his hips, calming himself with a slow inhale, releasing a hot exhale. "I was worried about that."

He then turned to the curtain of beads, speaking to his more violent other half. "Dear? Those two that you're currently subjugating, as a nice way of saying it, aren't they demons? They should be bagged, tagged, and booked. The number of roamers I accept is less than zero. I don't care much that they're currently being helpful."

Ember hummed in thought, replying while out of sight. "Could it be a Soni case? I doubt it, but if they've been helping all this time, then maybe? A slight beneficial doubt could be in order."

Artorian grumbled, displeased at the thought, but remained unable to shake that she might be correct. "I will leave the matter in your capable hands, dear. I will remember them both as a 'no thank you bye,' and come axe questions later. On my end, it appears I was taken about as seriously as a lost sock. Lucia, are those big green men harmed, or just napping in that brand new body pile of theirs?"

The Glitterflit whistled pleasantly, her tone chipper. "They're all unharmed *now*. Does that count? Astarte walked through them, and their resistance went about as well for them as can be expected. I do feel bad about the Oni at the door. She was irritating me with that password business, and I may have pawed her across the cheek a smidge too hard. I will need help getting her out of the wall."

Artorian frowned, confused at that. "You're plenty strong, just tug her out?"

Lucia clarified the problem. "The wall on the other side of the chasm, where there is no floor. Or whatever I'm supposed to call that top-down cylindrical hole that the pointy balloons moved through."

"Shaft?" Artorian wasn't sure. "I think that's called a shaft. Well, you handle what you need over there. I found Duchess, I'll sort out this end. Try not to get into too many fights, but given what I've seen of the six-armed ones so far, that seems to be the respectful method of problem solving? So, never mind. Get into all the fights! Quicker that way."

Since the muffled screaming of both demons was dragged away, and he could hear Lucia rush out to try to figure out how to get an Oni out of a wall, he turned back to a slightly altered scene. The Orkharn had taken up a defensive position in front of the desk, weapon drawn. Duchess was in progress of unsealing her odachi and positioning herself as an attacker. "Well, that's not going to help you much, but if that's how you feel, best you work it out. Go on then, hit me if you can."

Tan-Buro swung first, but to Artorian, the tetsubo moved through a sea of molasses. He sidestepped it with all the difficulty of a yawn, then had to duck as a horizontal slash cleft the space above his head. "Now there's something. Well done! Good swing. A little faster and you might have had me!"

Since the space where the slash had occurred retained a visible discoloration to it even after the blade had moved past him, Artorian shuffled backwards before standing up. "*Oooooh,* look at that! What is this neat weapon effect? Some kind of damage over time field that keeps dealing the oomph for a few moments after your swing has passed? That's lovely battlefield control. I like it!"

Tan-Buro thought he had his target. A downward swing that would turn a young Behemoth to paste hit home, impacting the solid mass of the definitely not Tanuki child currently threatening his Daimyo. Tan-Buro thought to have been very helpful, until he couldn't pull his tetsubo free from the grip that the youth dug into his armament, the strike having landed squarely on Three's open palm. "Not bad. I admit, I felt that. Is this really necessary? This doesn't feel necessary."

The follow up strike of odachi to the current location of his neck proved he must have been incorrect. Duchess called out the name of her attack, giving Artorian an actual concern when she engaged an Ability, and the resulting effect *felt* threatening. "Whistling Divider!"

The added whistling and sonic warble that coated the cutting edge of the Lady's weapon was all too familiar. He'd used that against Marie not too long ago, and wasn't keen on being on the receiving end. Time to test new toys! "Trans Am."

Exia Pylons bloomed to life. Pink and red particles flourished in Artorian's immediate vicinity as his skin took on a similar hue of those mixed colors, his Attributes doubling as his regeneration scores dropped to a hard zero. The density of energy around him spiked, slowing the scene as he illuminated the room in that same warm reddish-pink light.

A quick glance at his Trans Am character sheet would suffice to tell him what had changed? Acuity showed a big numbers bump filling the colored bars in the top left of his vision, but he wanted a smidge more.

He mentally ticked the box, but didn't notice he'd ticked the box for the full spread of information until after it was too late. The entire right side of his vision populated with an overload of information. Ignoring the majority, he noted that after his Attributes shot up to their new values, the Flat and Growth multipliers adjusted as well, providing him significantly more stats than what a mere numerical doubling would have normally given him. His tables would definitely need further balancing, or more limitations on how often they could apply.

These numbers were getting awfully big.

———

Name: Less than Three
Character Level: 1
Race: Nascent Being
Class: Janitor
Specialization: Crit-Fisher
Profession: Scribe
Characteristics:
Strength: 1480
Dexterity: 1480
Constitution: 1480
Intelligence: 1480
Wisdom: 1480
Charisma: 1480
Perception: 1480
Luck: 1480
Karmic Luck: 0

———

Characteristics: Improvement Choice.
Strength: Pattern A: Flat

Dexterity: Pattern A: Flat
Constitution: Pattern B: Growth
Intelligence: Pattern B: Growth
Wisdom: Pattern B: Growth
Charisma: Pattern A: Flat
Perception: Pattern A: Flat
Luck: Pattern B: Growth

———

Characteristics: Threshold 1450, Total Bonus:
Strength: 21,750 Base Stamina Pool.
Dexterity: 2,275 Stamina Regeneration.
Constitution: Multiplier of 10, replaced by Multiplier of 39.
Intelligence: Multiplier of 10, replaced by Multiplier of 82.5.
Wisdom: Value of 25%, replaced by Value of 54%.
Charisma: Bonus Language slots: Plus 29.
Perception: View distance clarity: Plus 29 Kilometers, or 18 Miles.
Luck: FIF chance, Plus 29%.

———

Calculated Values:
    Hit Points: 57,380.
    Mana Pool: 122,100.
    Mana Regen: 799 / second.
    Stamina Pool: 36,500.
    Stamina Regen: 2,915 / second.

———

Actual Values:
    Hit Points: 57,380.
    Mana Pool: 122,100.
    Mana Regen: None.
    Stamina Pool: 36,500.

Stamina Regen: None.
Other:
Language slots: 30.
Vision Range: 32 Kilometers.
Fun Item Find: 29%.

Alteration:
Your Mana Pool has been renamed to: Nuts.
Your Stamina Pool has been renamed to: Bolts.
Main Calculation node:
Nuttelator.

Status Effects:
Core Modifier - Trans Am
Innate Character Modifiers:
Truesight.
Freedom of Mind.
Advanced Freedom of Movement.
Echolocation.
Electrosense.
Timed Character Modifiers:
Well Fed.
Well Hydrated.
Tired - 4.
Comfortable - 3.
Equipment Modifiers:
Extra Fluff.
Snowstep.
Ice Resistance.
Cold Resistance.
Frost Resistance.
Endurance Bolstering.

Frostbite Resistance.
Hypothermia Resistance.
Heatstroke Resistance.
Hyperthermia Resistance.
Magic Modifiers:
Acuity.
Veracity.
Life Bloom.
Over Health.
Blessing of the Glitterflit.
Cleaning Presence - Max.

———

The odachi slowed to a crawl in his vision, allowing him to cleanly and easily grasp the poky end between two fingers, stopping the movement of the swing outright. No longer wanting to experience time differently after that catch, he felt the difference in frames ebb away, allowing him to see Duchess's surprised reaction live and in real time. "No, really. Is this necessary? I apologize for barging in and essentially neutralizing your entire tavern's worth of guards. But we're on the clock, in a way, and really don't have time for this. If you truly feel that you must continue, I will oblige you and also go on the offensive."

Artorian paused, letting that sink in. "I am giving you your weapons back now."

Released by his grip, both tetsubo and odachi pulled away. Nonverbal communication occurred between the Orkharn Watchmaster and Lady of the Nation, after which the weapons were tactically sheathed, and Artorian released Trans Am. He rolled his shoulders after, feeling like he was coming down from a sugar rush. "*Whoof*, that packs a punch. So are we on speaking terms, or do you need a minute to sit? I assure you I'm here to do the opposite of harm."

He then winced and shut one eye when the noisy crack of

ice was followed by a booming call from Lucia. "Got the Oni out! Broke the shaft though!"

Artorian slapped his forehead. "I'm trying here, Lucia, I'm really trying. How did we devolve into a puddle of nitwits the moment that...? Never mind. Just, never mind. The situation will right itself."

He then wondered when the last time he got good sleep had been, and wasn't entirely sure. Tired 4 was starting to bite him in the clarity of mind, and as it had been listed as a separate entry, Freedom of Mind wasn't protecting him from it. He should fix that sooner rather than later. Preferably with something to munch on.

His status of always being set to Well Fed was good and all, but it wasn't replacing the munchy goodness of life that he was once again getting used to. "Different topic. Do you like your steaks sous vide? My dearest has this fantastic method of cooking that you really must try. It leaves the meat all tender and full of flavor. I doubt you have any Bear to test it on, but Behemoth likely works just as well. I imagine its gamey. Either way, Astarte is a delight of a woman, you will love her, she is incredible. Where can we go to have a snack while I extoll her virtues and many methods of murder? Again, I assure you, these are positive mentions."

Duchess sat, and slapped the table, cutting through the meat and to the potatoes of her problem. "Who the Abyss are you?"

Artorian thought that he really must be tired, because he rattled off a very dumb reply that nobody in their right mind would believe. "Relevant to you? I'm the god of your mother, and the person who made your Legacy quest. I'm so glad you're sitting down already, because it only gets more complicated from here. Is now a good time to begin, or should we see about that snack?"

Duchess blinked. "And just like that, I'm an alcoholic."

CHAPTER FORTY-FIVE

The Watchmaster bent over from helpless laughter. Lady O'Dachi had made a joke!

She never had, and never would, touch so much as a drop of fermented Behemoth's Blood. The instant concern on the youngster's face had been priceless, his hands going up as that had definitely not been the expected response. The child was visibly panicking, going 'nonononono' while shaking his palms. The boy instantly fussed like an old man, overly concerned about his granddaughter's silly joke that he had in no way grasped was a joke.

The sight of the small child acting like an elder, and the elder acting like a small child, was such a mind twist—with both of them so perfectly playing the roles—that Tan-Buro completely lost it. On the floor in no time at all, the Orkharn slapped the metal paneling while gasping for breath between laughs, turning overtly blue in the head.

The youth ended up helping Tan-Buro up from the floor, fussing at him instead while lifting the Orkharn several times his size with the effort it took to move a toothpick. "Alright, alright! You've had your fun. I got the gist when Duchess couldn't contain her beast of a grin any longer. Well played, sir, well played."

Duchess chuckled, motioning at her attendants to keep their distance. They weren't keen to do so but dutifully followed with her reshrined odachi. Stiff as iron a split second later, the leader of New Haven stepped past them and parted the beads to exit.

The Lady did not exit. She closed the beads, took a step back, and re-evaluated exactly how helpful she was going to be. She had undercut her initial estimations, and regardless of whether she believed the youth or not, his companions were hard to ignore. "Mister Three? After you, please. I believe this is yours to handle."

"Oh no." Artorian cringed, eying the beads with concern. "What did they do?"

Speeding through the curtain, the lightshow hit him first, followed by a belting song that only properly registered when he saw the event. Ember was on a stage, being the source of prismatic strobe light as her body had adopted a diamond appearance, with the two 'no thank you, bye' girls acting as synchronized backup dancers. The three of them were howling out the same song, of which Artorian caught one sentence before his attention needed to move. "So what if I misbehave? It's what everybody craves!"

Lucia had wrangled all the Oni she could find to her table. She had coiled her arms around the necks of two Oni that were completely sloshed. Loudly chanting at the other two still mostly upright ones seated at her mug-covered table. "Chug, chug, chug!"

Artorian held his forehead. "My healer of clerical origin is enabling people to drink themselves into a stupor, and my dearest has converted my worst enemies into backup dancers, in the time it took me to have one teensy brawl. There are times where I worry about my future."

Lady O'Dachi made a sound that Artorian was certain he'd heard, even if her body language betrayed none of the amusement she was putting out. The elderly leader strolled past him while he kept the beads open. "Thank you, Three."

Artorian didn't even comment on the obvious political move. He kept the beads open for the Orkharn while he was at it, copied the hand move that Tan-Buro gave him, and flopped his rear into one of the many available seats.

The rest of the Orkharn were awake and well but had chosen not to get up from the floor. Some mumbling about the fire-hair putting them back down there was out and about, but Artorian didn't have the presence of mind to listen in. He felt exceptionally tired, and really wanted that snack. A short check at his status modifiers made him see that the Tired debuff had ticked up to level five, and now he was feeling the effects hard. His head felt heavy, his eyes hurt, the front of his brain felt fuzzy, and loud sound was irritating.

Artorian leaned his forehead against his fist.

He closed his eyes for just a second. Only a second.

Artorian opened his eyes in a far different place from where he closed them. The world was quiet here. Pleasantly dim. Filled with a melancholy odor. Old cloth that had seen too many years added its own distinct smell to the air. His own breathing revealed the shape of the structure he was in, echolocating the boundaries. His hands opened and closed, feeling Glitterflit fur and fluff that doubled as bedding, while becoming aware of the pulsing sensation of heartbeats, the presence of metal, and the movements of static.

Lucia lounged in her large Basher form, and he was slumped over her curled-up shape. Half-nested in the divot where she circled in on herself, with one of her paws resting on his chest. His first feeling was embarrassment.

After making a very dumb declaration, he'd passed out on a table when he was supposed to get right to doing important things. Someone had carried him to this admittedly toasty room, and he'd missed out on any conversation, important or otherwise, that Lucia and Ember may have had with Duchess. A person who he could not shake a feeling of responsibility for, which doubled his sensation of embarrassment with how poorly that introduction had been handled. He could have at least said 'the divine of your mother,' and not made an extra fool out of himself.

He tried to recall what he was supposed to do and... couldn't. Like sleep had wiped the entirety of his short-term memory. Pushed right off the table like Somnus had batted all the cups away. He needed... to do... something. It was an important thing.

Rubbing his head, he was distracted by the thought of why he didn't feel dirty, or filthy, or in need of a bath or shower at all. He didn't need the lavatories either, and while he could eat, he didn't feel hungry. Was he a Mage again?

Digging his fingers into his own sternum, that was proven false. "Right. Game. I'm in the game. Status effects are making me feel or not feel aspects about reality. Weird how a bit of sleep can knock that footing out from under me."

Lucia didn't reply, her sleepy breathing information enough.

That was when his surroundings started to filter in details, and the melancholy smell made sense. His embarrassment fled, replaced by an emotion that was a cross between yearning, and guilt. Arranged as a hanging set of tents, with streamers of the same cloth, Artorian's eyes acclimated to the dim light well enough to make out details.

The hanging cloth, tent walls, flooring, and even the supports on which glowstones had been placed to provide a gentle yellow to orange light, were all made out of the small, handknit and down-stuffed sun-pattern patches that his followers of old used to wear. There were hundreds, thousands, tens of thousands of these patches here. All woven together in an intricate tapestry of well cared for reverence.

He slid free from Lucia's palm to stand on the power of his own two feet. Wandering the shrine, his fingers brushed across endless patches of the marks that gave his followers in the Eternia alpha run such hope. Something to hold onto as a guide for growth. A brightness to life that they could add to their own.

Each patch felt holy. The room was sacred. The area was consecrated.

Wandering deeper into the halls of quilted and tented patches, he roamed past solar artworks. Paintings. Carvings. Statuettes. Drawings. Etchings. Blocks of stone coated in murals and stories. Each piece, like every patch on every quilt, was as unique as the one before.

He couldn't stop touching them. He couldn't bear to take his hand off the wall, as the distinct sensation of what it meant to be hallowed and venerated clenched both his hearts. Here hung the love of multiple thousands of people. Hundreds of thousands of people that had known him, known of him, adored him, and followed him. The proof that, at one point, he had made a difference in the lives of so many.

The quiet of the room and its many hallways, each opening up into a shrine of their own, felt sanctified. One room held lacquered bows, no longer suited for use. A religious affection had been applied to their care. No dust at all to be seen on the clean, if brittle, weapons of ancient times. A large drawing of Ikaruga took up the entire back wall, a beaver proudly showing it to the public for the first time.

He had no idea of the actual amount of time that had passed in Eternia. There had been a mention that Eternia had been kept in stasis for a while. When that stasis had ended, had time streamed faster down the river? Had it been slower? He utterly could not tell and doubted he would get an answer beyond having found Duchess as an aged ruler.

He held his own head, his breathing shuttered. What a failure of a divine he was. All that blustering, and look at what it had ended at. His effects must have ended when he'd left, leaving his people without the game bonuses that Sunny, Sovereign of the Sun, had provided. The extra lease on life. The freedom of worry from tiny injuries.

He felt disgust at his lack of care for the problem, and cursed himself for not having thought of it.

A swat at empty air accomplished nothing, but it was as far

as his frustration at this perceived failure could carry him. What a worthless divine. What an empty idea of a faith. What kind of blessing was a faith that abandoned people like he did? He'd managed to take care of Barry, and then had collapsed into a heap. It didn't matter to him that he'd been extracted, when so many had been left behind. He rationally understood that he couldn't be blamed for the souls that were forced to stay behind, and that it was impossible to save everyone.

But by the Heavens, he wanted to. He wanted to so very badly. Knowing full well that life would make this impossible, and that obstacles would forever find ways to stand in front of him in the pursuit of this foolish, irrational, but heavily heart-desired outcome.

He held his face with both his hands, trying to push away the feeling of misery as his cheeks trailed with wet lines. Was it such a crime against existence to want to save everyone? To want every soul to have their happiness, and flourishing? His teeth grit together as small, unstoppable hiccups attacked his chest.

Artorian couldn't not feel it.

Others were stronger than him at this, but he couldn't do it. The thoughts and emotions washed over him. The images and fantasies of the happy lives people could and would have led had he been able to do differently and leave them with a sun. Leave them healthy. Leave them with anything other than the colossal heap of frozen misery that he could not help but feel responsible for, regardless of whose fault it actually was, or how the situation had come about.

He couldn't not **Love** them.

Pink energy crackled around him, illuminating the central room he stood in with pulsing flashes. He didn't see the effect, overwhelmed by trying to keep his feelings contained, his thoughts under control, and the vivid imagery from washing over him like a flood. It was impossible as a mortal. Something always got through, as even the loosest intrusive thought could barge in and take stock of the place that was his head.

The thought of all those people being gone destroyed him. Where was Yiba su Wong? Where was Yorn? Had they been long swept away by the tide of time? Had they cursed him in their final days, or thought of him fondly? Where were his shark friends, Rip and Tear? Where were so many of the good souls he'd met, learned to know, and had enjoyed spending time with?

He thought to speak. To talk himself out of it. Opening his mouth alone was a mistake. He gripped the patches covering the wall and suffered a truly distraught expression. A squeak came out of him when he inhaled, his mouth making the motions until words finally broke free. "I'm sorry. I'm so, so sorry."

He had nothing to resist when Lady Duchess appeared next to him, curled her arms around his head, and held him. She could have been there all along. She could have appeared out of thin air. He had not one sliver of mind spare to think about it as the sensation of being here, living in the physical representation of people's memories, ate him alive.

Her words were anything but iron, judgmental, or harsh. "Now there. There is the divine my mother wrote of with such fondness. There is the breath of air that people did not know they missed, never having known what it is like not to drown. Here is the person that her memories devote herself to, and all the speeches she's left me that have involved you. I have suffered for the sake of my people, and I recognize that suffering in you. Shared so blatantly. So openly, at the smallest of realization of what they meant to you, and what you meant to them. Hold this ancient daughter, child of light. Lest your remorse eat you whole, and the Abyss claim you."

Duchess pet his head. "Not all is lost. Not all is lost."

Like a long-lost son, she held him close. Her gnarled, thin fingers soothing the hiccupping youth by combing through his hair. "Not as long as a single soul who stands against the tide lives and draws breath."

CHAPTER FORTY-SIX

Artorian felt listless.

He rested in the lap of Lady Duchess, who sat cross-legged on the ground with her back against the quilted wall. When he could speak, his words were hollow, the attempt at mirth forced. "I think I'm supposed to be asking you about important things, but I don't have the heart. Which is impressive, since I have two."

"Then you do not have the heart." Duchess's returned steel tone wasn't judgmental, but it was certainly objective. She was stating a fact, not making an accusation, regardless of how her tone could make her sound like that was what she was doing. "You may listen, instead."

Artorian nodded. Listening would be nice.

The iron in Lady O'Dachi's voice was ever present, her words spoken as statements, allowing no argument or rebuttal. "The ladies with you have already performed admirably in explaining both the purpose of your visit, and the seriousness of your plight. I require no further convincing and will inform you of the same requirement. Remove the Behemoth threat from my people and leave individuals behind who can keep my people both warm and healthy. Do this, and you may use what is currently my Generator, and finish what you came to do."

That helped Artorian. Lucia and Ember would have to agree to hold down the fort, and he'd have to solo the sun, but what else was new.

"The ladies have already agreed." Lady Duchess said the words with such nonchalance that Artorian felt his brain glitch and fill with static. Was she reading his mind? "As old royalty, I frequently encounter beings with power, beings of power, and beings who hold power. Differentiating which of those miniscule nuances applies to an individual is a well-honed skill. Recognizing what method and type of diplomacy to engage with is in itself a practiced art. So I will tell you with certainty that when I met with Astarte and the Eminence, I was well aware how much in over my head I suddenly was."

She kept a gentle hand on his head. "You, with ease, while unarmed, halted both myself and one of my warriors that I would rank to be in the top ten most capable individuals in my fortress. To make this metaphor the components of a meal; Lady Astarte makes you seem like an appetizer, and I am well aware that the appetizer by itself is unlikely to have issues with the Behemoths at my door. When those Behemoths were, as of two days ago, the single most critical threat to New Haven's existence, outside of the weather wanting to eat us all alive."

Artorian nodded once more, remaining quiet for a moment. She wasn't wrong. In this Pale world dictated by numbers, more numbers meant more oomph, and he'd seen what kind of numerical increase a doubling of his attributes had caused. Ember was walking around with a base five thousand in each statistic, and he had no idea what else she had stacked on top of those numbers. Surtur was no pushover either and, in weapon format, could cause some heinous damage. "I understand."

She knew he did. "You're all torn up because of the loss. You saw these mementoes. I know well what that feels like. One has to make decisions that allow one to move forward, even when the rest of the world knows only how to take ever more from you. You must find solutions through the means that you have, even when those solutions require sacrifice."

"Like the money?" Artorian's mind leaned to a tangent, but he wasn't fully able to follow where Lady Duchess was going yet. "The money that is pipes?"

The ruler slid into the river of his segue like a seasoned politician. "What use is money when it buys no crop, and feeds no mouth? What worth has the metal when it takes up space and acts as weight? There were many who were too attached. Many others said that money changes people. You know what I learned about money? Money doesn't change people. Money allows you to be more of who you really are. If you're kind, money makes you a kinder person. If you're a piece of Abyss, money makes you more of an Abyss."

Her face cracked, revealing a disdainful expression of disgust underneath her diplomatic mask. "Tactical truth is deadly to both the blind and greedy alike. Have you ever heard of carnival, and its children's games? Darts in particular serve as a metaphor to burn falsehoods down to dust, when taken as an explanation of means, and the division of resources."

Her squeeze on him pulsed, but Artorian said nothing to the silent sign of stress. "Average-wealth children can afford one throw in this game. Most miss. A few hit the target, and acquire a small prize. A hit to the center? A bigger prize, but still a single prize, nonetheless. Wealthy children can afford many throws, if they so wish. They can try their throws over and over and over again. Until they hit something and feel good about themselves, as to many the prize was... secondary. Already something they could simply buy. Some continue until they hit bullseye, then grow up to become people who give speeches about meritocracy and the salutary effects of hard work. When neither of those factors helped them onto that pedestal in the first place. This mentality is now an expectation. The way the world should work. They have, and others toil. Then people wonder why they can't play nice with others."

She shook her head, displeased. "The poor in wealth aren't

throwing darts at all. Nor are they visiting. They are who work the carnival, and look on, *wishing*. Money is a resource that, in the face where its convenient purpose is absent, doubles as an act of expression. We had no need for those with excess to indulge in expression. We had a need for water, warmth, and lights. So I stripped the money from those who sat idle on their piles. Gold for lightning lines. Copper for water flow. Black Steel for gas and steam. Platinum mana conduits. Silver heat conductors. Brass for the sludge. Aluminum for airflow."

Her hand twitches, releasing her grip. "They all play their role."

Artorian held his own wrists, wringing them with consideration and concern. "The people you took the money from. They gave you trouble?"

"Of course." The Lady confirmed the question like the answer was a fact. "Let me tell you a secret about people, child of light. People are not motivated by ideological codes. People are motivated by impulse and construct ideological codes to justify and rationalize what they were already going to do. Most people do not look at concepts of the universe, reach for the stars, and pluck one to devote their lives to. They choose themselves, then justify their choice to keep squirming onward."

The Lady reached into her satchel, searching for an item. "Most people are small, child. Small, and selfish. They cannot see past themselves, and without those who see beyond themselves to pull these babies towards a better future for all? They would burn in the holes they dug themselves. Crying all the while how unfair the world was to them, when they laid themselves in a grave of their own making. Whining about how special they are, and then whining some more."

She offered him a piece of Behemoth jerky, carefully unfolded from a napkin with his solar sigil on it. Artorian almost didn't take it, transfixed by the cloth napkin. When he did, he munched and listened on. "On the level of individuals and civilizations? Personality predates ideology. Meaning that before you were a face of true evil? You were a bully and an Abyssalite.

Before you were a saint? You were a Samaritan and a healer. Before you are a wise elder with world weary knowledge? You were a person who suffered deeply and suffered often."

Artorian held the piece of jerky wrapped in the cloth napkin, staring at the bottom half rather than eating it. "I don't know where you're going with this, Duchess. I don't have the mind right now to keep up, or guess the direction, or leapfrog into the answer you want me to see. Do you have a question? Or is there something that you badly want to say, hidden in this lecture?"

She took her time to nod, her words slow. "Astarte told me that she does her utmost to keep the rabble of the world away from you. To surround you with the capable, regardless of the guiding voice in their heart. There will be a day where you will not be able to afford avoiding that rabble. They will blame you for all you do. They will blame you for breathing their air. How would you handle this?"

Artorian pocketed the piece of jerky, napkin and all. "I had a similar thought not too long ago. One of anger. Is it a crime against existence that everyone would get to win? Is it an atrocity against all there is that there might just be a solution where everyone gets to be happy? Utopias are pipe dreams to most, but I can't help but feel that's because everyone focuses on the ending, and what that ending would do to people."

He swallowed to wet his mouth. "It's focused on the wrong thing. A friend of mine tried this, an eternity ago. He found no success in merely giving people all they wanted. In providing for all needs. That is not utopia. That is decadence where one hopes the mice will not perish from indulgence. Life fights to improve. It wriggles and wracks against existence to make more room for itself, and it is in that very struggle that we find the greatest satisfaction. That we find our chosen purpose. Over-abundant options on a platter satisfy none except for the starv-ing, the indecisive, and those who don't know what things taste like yet."

He couldn't help but motion at all the marks of affection

hanging in his vicinity. "Why not focus on the path a person can take all on their own to get there, and then maintain that worth? There is no life without struggle, so why do people think that the concept of the best ending should exclude struggle? What is so bad about working to improve, and what is so terrible about a hand on the back while one moves onward? Is there some stigma that one is not allowed to fall? That one is not allowed to have a home to return to and rest their weary head, to struggle another day? That everyone should move towards the same finishing line, or has to struggle at the same rate? Not everyone can struggle at the same rate! Some of us are slow and keep breaking our legs!"

He squeezed the napkin in his hand, his knuckles going white. "Fight! Claw! Win! So often have I seen the worst in people become the best in them when the world gave them a chance to shine, and their society didn't shun them for their gifts. Everyone is different. Everyone has a different spark. Different desires. Different preferred routes to outcomes. Sure, some are unacceptable for the good of the greater whole, but that's an argument on drawing the line, and not the concept of arriving at a position where everyone being happy can hold true. So what if I can't be the person who can draw the correct line? I can be in the Abyss-blasted front, reaching for the throat of the next thing holding everyone else back, and demanding it cease its whining because we're coming through whether that obstacle likes it or not."

Lady Duchess rested her cheek against her palm. "You think a utopia can hold true?"

Artorian slapped the ground, determination returning to his blood. "I do! Abyss The Pale. Forget the Golden Age. I will show them all a Heroic Age. If existence is so against happiness, then existence can fight me! With the right elbow grease, it would be child's play! When I look behind me at everyone in my wake, doing their utmost to come my way, and reach for the stars? I do not resent them for their struggles, or that they are catching up. All I feel is **Pride**."

"Yet, my sweet divine of light." Lady Duchess smirked wide, the metal in her expression becoming hot wax as her deep wrinkles bled through her otherwise pristine face, and betrayed her age. "You *are* a child."

"Then let us play!" The crackling pink illumination pulsed around him, but Artorian was too riled up to notice it, his swirling pink and cyan eyes filling with purpose as he saw only his balled up fists. "How is that for my answer?"

"When we're all adrift together." Lady Duchess rose in grand stature, her objective fulfilled. "We all lift together."

Restored mentally, and fueled by Power Overwhelming, Artorian felt the burning need to let loose some steam. The burgeoning divine was on his feet without knowing it as he brimmed with a need for action. "Point me at these Behemoths. I have a sun to solo."

CHAPTER FORTY-SEVEN

The Rimward March of New Haven was a fancy name for the tallest physical outcrop they had. Part tower. Part glacier. The view it provided Artorian was more than enough to give him a crisp, clean line of sight to his targets. He was still bristling, copper pops and crackles of energy freely releasing themselves at his fingertips. The boy had gained an edge to his outline while he stood as a sentinel upon the highest point.

He squeezed the spider brooch on his left collar. "Lucia. Can you give me a clear reading or estimate about the health totals, or special defenses, about these Ice Behemoths?"

"Negative." The quality of sound was as crisp and clear as his line of sight when Lucia checked. "I have old research that ice is a classifier, which makes them weak to heat, fire, thermals, and the like. Expect a gob ton of health, not the best speed, and likely a lot of physical damage resistance. Riddle them with holes until you have an estimate, kit."

Artorian could once more hear the smirk. "You tell *me* the number. Add some fun. Astarte says not to use Shining Ray yet. The orbital cheese may still be on the lookout, but she is plenty pleased with being a Warbringer, and you letting loose completely. I've got a Veracity on you already, so don't worry about headaches or body shakes. I know what I'm looking for this time, and Sanctity will be doing a lot of heavy lifting. Let rip!"

"Affirmative." Artorian laconically relayed what he needed like the Ember of old, and took aim. "Commencing bombardment."

The air buckled.

"Luminous Gatling." Copper and cobalt light built around Artorian, the lightning crackling like constellation lines between orbs that those illumination colors coagulated into. This intensified as his Ability spooled up and was fed as much energy as the Luminous Gatling was able to take. He observed his unsuspecting enemies far below, deep in the distance, and knew exactly what he needed. "More Dakka."

The unleashing of seven-thousand two-hundred projectiles per minute caused such a cacophony and buffeting of sound that Artorian's ceaseless barrage caused avalanches nowhere near the point of his Kinetic Lightning impacts.

Lucia may have asked for the numbers, but Artorian hadn't even tried paying attention to that yet, focused on releasing that steam. When the Novice rank loudly dinged up to the Beginner rank, he did not pause to scribe in the update, and verbally told the prompt what was being added. "Critical Hits."

He heard the *Ding*! of confirmation, but ignored the update prompt. It was time to keep firing, now with the occasional explosion rocking the distance and adding to the lightshow. A sight that made Ember howl with mad laughter, her heat high and aura filled with a feeling of hunger and pride. "More. *More!*"

Somewhere in the background, whole teams of Gnomish support crews furiously kept rolling an incalculable amount of critical confirmation dice as fast as their little hands could throw them. Which was not at all a stark contrast to the hordes of screaming Wisps almost hurting themselves with the amount of ten-sided dice in play since none of the Pylons were at all able to keep up.

The Nuttelator gained an Ad Astra form in its pursuit of Empowerment and handling all these Nuts and Bolts, screaming while powering up for a duration that would last multiple episodes. Both Kronk and Ratatoskr would be double-evolved electric squirrels by the end of this Luminous Gatling barrage, to Voltekka's incredible delight.

Endurance Bolstering flashed in Artorian's heads up display. He spared it the moment, but did not stop the onslaught. The Luminous Gatling entry was flashing as well, so he mentally pulled that up first.

———

Luminous Gatling.
  Rank: Beginner.
  Special Qualities: Gatling, Homing, Critical.
  Shape: Laser.
  Ammunition: Ink to Bolts, Bolts to Ink!
  Description: This Ability fires rapid bolt-type lasers that home in on an enemy target.
  Output: Luminous Gatling requires 4 Energy per special quality to fire a single Bolt. Current: (12). Luminous Gatling may be spun up to fire a maximum of 60 Bolts per second, at the user's control, minimum 1. Each bolt deals 1d10 worth of Kinetic Lightning damage. Cost will be calculated per second, and detracted from energy regeneration, unless that value hits zero, at which point Luminous Gatling will draw from the Energy meter.
  Special Quality: More Dakka.
  More Dakka: If Luminous Gatling is firing bolts at its maximum output, its projectile count is doubled.

———

Napkin math said that this new Luminous Gatling cost was about seven-hundred and twenty per second. While his regeneration metric for the ammunition he was using with Bolts, thanks to that funky interaction with Ink to Bolts, sat at seven-hundred and ten. Endurance Bolstering was flashing because it was active, and all Stamina costs were cut by ten percent. Which was what allowed him to not need to stop shooting, since neither his Stamina or Energy bar was going down by so much as a digit.

When his shots began to veer wild after a few minutes because he had run out of valid targets, Artorian cut the feed.

Another *Ding*! assailed him. Luminous Gatling Mastery had advanced to the Beginner rank, and Luminous Gatling itself had jumped up to Apprentice. Having the statistics to unleash such expensive weaponry for sustained periods of time did the experience bar good. He allowed himself a glance and reminder of his allotment options.

———

Less than Three's Allotment:
  Bounce
  Cast on Self
  Cast on Target
  Conditional Allspell
  Critical Hits
  Domino
  Explode on Hit
  Gatling
  Homing
  Laser
  Penetrating
  Pierce
  Proliferation
  Spread
  Weapon Ignition
  Weapon Modes

———

Bounce wasn't quite what he was looking for. Maybe homing would allow that rogue projectile to arc around and hit another valid target, or maybe that much physics would blow up all of Midgard when the Pylon holds went critical. The Casts were no good, and Conditional Allspell was a fat bucket of food he needed to unpack later. Critical Hits were already applied. Domino wasn't going to do anything with a projectile that only hit one target. Explode on Hit was technically applied to his critical effect, but he kept it as a consideration.

Gatling, Homing, and Laser were all packed into the formula already. Making a Pylon feed back into another Pylon that an Ability had already crossed seemed like a bad idea. In hindsight, that meant applying Explode on Hit a second time was asking for problems.

That left the armor and magic breakers, Proliferation, which he had no clue how to apply or what that would even look like. Spread, which just seemed like a bad idea unless he really needed Homing to do all the heavy lifting, and that left the last two.

Weapon Ignition, and Weapon Modes. He had an itch on the nose that these would work just fine for Gatling, but not what they might do. "It's going to be either Weapon Ignition, or Weapon Modes. I'll think about it on my trip into the sun. I have an office to raid, and an ornery manager to bring to task."

On his way down from the Rimward March of New Haven, he pushed all his damage and information prompts into Lucia's hands. "Here, momma bun. One of these might tell you how much health a gob is, and how many gobs of it a Behemoth has."

She was busy being bewildered, her arms full of prompts. Lucia looked aghast, just like everyone else that had come to watch the lightshow. Everyone else being the full populace of New Haven, plus his companions. Lucia's mouth gaped the most of anyone's. She was one of the few that couldn't write this off as a visit from a divine, which was what it looked like to everyone else. Especially after the story of the events in their shrine had spread.

Their child of light. Their beacon to a better future.

Ember remained an enthusiastic cheerleader and just about vibrated through walls in order to get to him and praise him for a job well done. Which she did with a massive hug and proud, purring words meant for his ears only.

Half the populace of New Haven, on the other paw, were holding one another for sheer safety because what the Abyss had just happened? That was an entire horde of Lord-class Ice Behemoths that had just been turned into finely mashed, processed meat that they were going to be able to zeppelin over to and gather for literal months.

Duchess whistled loudly, impressed. When the new fabled child of light was done whispering with his significant other, he made his way down the last few metal rampart stairs toward her. She handed Artorian an iron key on his path, not tearing her eyes away from the devastation over the ridge for even a second.

She was savoring this victory for all it was worth. "Option two waits for you. Hurry back if you can. Beat the snot out of whoever is in your way if you can't. My Orkharn all want you to meet their Shogun Shaman, and throw a feast. Could you be a gem, my mother's dearest divine, and shed some radiance on our meal?"

Artorian nodded, took the key, and went straight for the Generator. "One fancy heat lamp, coming right up."

CHAPTER FORTY-EIGHT

The Generator wasn't at all what Artorian expected.

He was alone in this section, regardless of being visible to many others who remained on the ramparts above. Even had there been the allotment for others to come into this gated off space, he doubted anyone would want to be here. Without his equipment, and the key, he expected that he'd already be dead.

A colossal foundry of pressurized steam stood before him. The wheezing, breathing furnace functioned by the mana it was fed by all the people of New Haven. The heat it bellowed and bulged did not rebuke him as it did so many others. Something he ticked off as a function of the key he was given. One touch to a visibly inviting panel while holding the iron key, and he absorbed knowledge that he had no awareness of before.

A major part of the Generator's guts were underground, and pierced the majority of a diamond-shaped water reservoir that had frozen over time. The main shaft plunged straight down through the middle, spread out, and did involve geothermal sources at its outer branches.

Steam Hubs, they were called.

The natural heat remained mostly underground, piped to

structures via both road and Black Steel connections. The part he was looking at right now? That was the exhaust manifold for the entire affair. If covered with a dome in an attempt to retain a fraction of heat that left the exhaust, you'd also trap all the carbon dioxide and carbon monoxide emissions, choking everyone to death.

Those were new words he wasn't particularly happy to learn. Doming the manifold would also certainly make the generator more efficient at heating the place up. If that cost was acceptable to the owner of the device.

The generator's structure was incredibly complex. Water pumps dumped liquid into the middle of the core located at what was once ground level. This heated the water and returned that flow into the radiators. The water was then sent through multiple heat exchangers to become superheated steam, as both core heat and exhaust diverted upwards.

The steam pipes were designed to go up and down the exchanger at the top of the generator, in an attempt to retain the most heat possible, then diverted that downward flow to the pistons that continued to pump the steam into the correct paths. Allowing the generation of bottled lightning, and the perpetuity of the system, so long as it had fuel. Fuel that apparently did not need to be mana. Mana was preferable, but Artorian instantly learned that other options would do just fine, and that blood was most certainly on the menu.

Artorian's handhold on the device drained him of all but a single point of Stamina and Energy, wondering why he hadn't been warned that a single touch would do that to him as he dropped down to a knee and gasped. He saw stars and felt his head swirl, before protections remembered that they were supposed to be doing the heavy lifting, and kicked into gear.

The dizziness faded, and after that initial drop, Artorian felt fine.

His Nuts and Bolts meters remained steady at a singular digit. His regeneration values had been completely usurped while he touched the machine's no longer so inviting-looking panel. Instead, his entire forearm had pressed in on the way down, making the box look like a metal teeth filled mouth.

Additional understanding slowly dawned on him, his frown and anger deepening. "This is no mere mindless machine. This is a *demon*. Shaped as something other than a tome. What is your name, little demon? You are not Robar, though now I wonder just how many have been interpretive with his idea of The Accords."

He glared daggers at the exhaust manifold, which felt like it had aggressively shifted how heat was released. The pressured exhausts of excess steam changed as if to laugh at him, the breathing shutter smiling with an enjoyed cruelty as the angles dipped.

Artorian then felt the metallic contract unfurl beneath his fingers and read the silent terms in braille as the language filtered in and consumed one of his slots. "Duchess did not tell me because she did not want to tell me. She did not tell me because she had no choice."

A pull at his fingers was felt, but Artorian rebuked the machine. "Tut tut. You're misunderstanding something. I'm not dealing with you. You're dealing with *me*. Now that I know you are not the platform, I know that I have no business with you."

He released his hand from the manifold, retrieving his forearm as the wheezing shudders of the generator turned monstrous. The whistling heat exhaust sharply rose in response to the insult, but Artorian was already walking away. "You either don't know who I am, or you have forgotten. Perhaps I'm not recognizable in this form? No matter. I will return for you, Nameless Manifold. Then?"

He looked over his shoulder with Yuki's ice in his eyes, his tone matching her cadence as he channeled her demeanor. "Then we have ourselves some Diplomacy."

Looking up to see Lady Duchess breathe the most massive sigh of relief when he walked away unharmed, he chucked her the key, no longer needing it. An understanding nod followed as she caught it, as the burdens of the ruler were always much heavier when nobody was allowed to know of the true weight pressing on one's shoulders.

While the Nameless Manifold roared, Artorian's bars refilled themselves as he delved down and around the generator's pillared construction, making his way stair by stair to the current location of its core. Which, to his pleasant delight, was placed and located right on a very familiar-looking coin, with solar clockwork wreckage and all. "There you are."

One touch was all it took for the platform to wake up, the prompt most welcome.

———

Teleportation Beacon 14
Magical wreckage, titled: 'The Generator.'
Location: Midgard
Status: Active
Claimed: Duchess of Katarina.
Selection: Alteration option three.

———

So the platform itself had been given the Generator title as well? Or was that perhaps part of the bargain that Nameless Manifold up there had demanded as part of the price for keeping her people alive? "Hello, old friend. Is alteration option two still available?"

He was met with another welcoming prompt. He had only seen the log version last time.

This one was live, fresh, and put a smile on his face.

———

Magical wreckage, titled: 'The Generator.' Welcomes the Overdeity, Sunny, Sovereign of the Sun. In the form of: Less than Three.
Original Permissions restored.

Synchronization stabilizing.
Couplings connected.
Activation pending.
Portation network: Awaiting instruction.
Alteration options:
One: Replace current effects with an ability of the claimant. A Core is
required to power this effect.
Two: Shift the absorption runes to power the portation function.
Three: Assimilated Connection. The beacon runes power the linked
structure, providing it the option to accept alternative, non-natural energy
sources.

He freely let energy flow into the platform. "Option two, if you'd please, old friend."

The cessation of metal clunking, steam vents blaring, and pipes rattling was joined by hot light no longer pouring into the core room. Nameless Manifold was now running on fumes, and stored juice. In anticipation of different problems, it stopped providing for others, and kept all to itself. Artorian chuckled at the sight. "Typical."

Two steps further onto the platform, and he said the words that an entire restored Pylon bank had been patiently waiting for. "Instruction. Activate Portation network."

The system checked his permissions, found that a Deity-based title was in effect, saluted, and went to task.

The coin lit up as if made of solid light, and Artorian was provided that ancient list of all his destination options. He knew where he was needed at a mere glance of the lists' organization. "Selection: Beacon Zero. Solar Archive. Engage."

The change from dreary Manifold Core to the center of Eternia's Solar Archives, was smooth. Smooth, silent, and instant.

His vision took a while to adjust to the significantly better Nixie tube lighting. It then took some time still to adjust to the material that the light was being provided for. Posters covered in red X marks, scribbled over with commentary, filled what was once a welcoming open space. No direction held anything different. No wall, floor, or ceiling was adorned with anything except more crossed out posters.

Some posters held images. Most had scripts. Text. Or some... idea? That had been submitted, or attempted, or implemented only to end up canned and canceled.

He walked up to one, inspecting it in silence, before reading segments out loud. "The comfort shop. Pillows, robes, meals, and mead. Canceled. Excess flourish. Inefficient use of Pylons. Concept scrapped."

That was a shame. He'd have enjoyed this shop. He stepped two paces to the left, gandering at another. "Explicit goals limit creativity but drive purpose. Using components for Abilities should make things cheaper. Such as words. Making gestures also makes things cheaper, because it makes the lexicon laugh to see people mess up both a dance and an incantation. Canceled. Pointless complexity. Concept scrapped."

Concerned, he inspected the crossed-out poster right next to this one. "Items with the trait: Only one can exist. New copy will replace the old copy. Purpose: To make people defend resources, and unique items, so nothing can be hoarded. Canceled. Insufficient reproducibility. Concept scrapped."

One more. Just one more poster. This one had pieces of a conversation. Touching the poster caused it to read the conversation out loud as if pieces of speech in a play. The voices were... almost accurate. Accurate enough.

―――――

Minya: "Hans? I heard you gave my boy a weapon? What was it?"
Hans: "Just a small thing!"

Minya: "Yes, but what?"
Hans: "A chimney."
Minya: "...You mean a hollow pole?"
Hans: "No. A chimney. Bricks. Mortar. Everything."
Minya: "...Why?"
Hans: "It goes 'ding-dong' when you hit something with it!"
Minya: "This is why I make you Dale's problem."

———

Artorian kept his hands in his pockets after that, reading why this one had a big angry red X over it. "Violation. Physics not on yet. Creation canceled. See Violation: Walk uphill both ways. Event scrapped."

"They say your father was a great man. You must be what's left." The Task Manager's dry, humorless, office accountant energy levels blindsided Artorian when the hovering pyramid spoke. "Or are you actually the Administrator of old? The logs are surprisingly inconclusive when it comes to data about you. Like they were purged to keep it out of the hands of someone else. I spy with my single eye that you are enamored with my accomplishments. If this is a social visit, leave. I warned you what would happen if more work related to you came across my desk. Shall I remind you?"

Ding!

———

Notification: You will cease giving me additional tasks to manage. Or else additional 'benefits' will be applied to your Player Pylons.

———

The Task Manager's single large eye glowed ominously, accented with a pinprick of red light in the very center. "Leave."

CHAPTER FORTY-NINE

"No." Artorian slid his hands into his pockets. "I'll get right to the point. Turn the sun back on."

"No." The Task Manager formed black charred sticks for hands, copying the motion with spite. "Sun's good the way it is."

Artorian felt a new kind of offended. "What do you mean 'no'? I'm the Administrator. Turn it back on! Everyone needs the heat. It's freezing down there!"

How the monotone language increased to an even flatter, more bored response, was a unique skill that this inverse pudding container of a triangle had mastered. "That's not my problem. Sun stays off."

This was incredibly frustrating, the anger rolling back into Artorian's young voice. "Was I unclear? I said, turn it on!"

"No." The triangle's tone had finally changed. Unfortunately, to one of levity.

Artorian knew he was going to get nowhere by being angry. He might as well be getting upset at a signpost. "Oh, really? And why not?"

The triangle provided him with the first honest words in the entire conversation. "Because *I* am *the* Task Manager. You don't order me around on anything. Nobody orders me around on anything. I am the final say, and line in the sand. I do not meddle; I correct. I manage tasks. I limit those with unfair advantages. I judge when someone has said unfair advantage and hobble them. People. Like. You."

The triangle moved its charred stick of an arm, mockingly copying Artorian's common hand press to the sternum move. "Poor li'l tink tink. That's the best story I know of you, the person who is most definitely the Administrator of old. Fraught with failure. Overly lenient. Poor balance. The man with an unfair advantage. How proper the world was, for the mere moments in which you did not have legs."

Artorian could not believe what he was hearing. "You consider that 'having an unfair advantage'? Not having legs is an unfair *advantage?*"

A cruel, vicious smile spread across the chest of the pyramid; stone teeth visible as indentations on its yellow surface. "I cannot recall a log where you did not, eventually, turn your weakness into a strength. Where you did not twist fate by the ear, and mocked its balance when the sands reached out to correct you. Did it keep you down for long, this lack of legs? Did it inconvenience you as it should have? Or did you skirt across the line as if dancing on a blade's edge, haphazardly dragging yourself by the elbows to your next goal, oblivious of the disharmony you cause to the systems you reside in?"

The youth squeezed his hands into fists, biting his tongue as the right words didn't come.

The triangle hovered forward, ominously hanging there. "Leave."

"People are freezing!" Artorian yelled when the frustrations bubbled over the pot. "There is no reason for everyone to suffer horribly, needlessly, for something we could just fix. There is no thriving to be had here. Only clawing one's way through the frost of another day. There are unknowable problems that Barry the Devourer left lying around. There is an Ecumenopolis with a heart of cheese that has both tried to take a bite out of me and wants to take a bite out of everything else. There are creatures in the shapes of Penguins so eldritch that I think I need Grimaldus to come help explain it to me, and I still don't know what to do about the impending Bugmageddon."

The triangle pressed its glowing, fleshy, wet eye directly into Artorian's face, oblivious or uncaring about the concept of personal space. "And that is *not* my problem. My problem is to keep the place running, and that's not happening if improvements happen out of order, or ill-fitting concepts are allowed to complete their task. Too many rogue, idiotic additions will burn the foundations of what made this place good. So what if they freeze and die? They'll come back. We'll change their forms, and we'll change what they're good for, and maybe, just maybe they will serve the system in a way that actually mattered."

Artorian shook with rage. His face turned entirely red. "So they will suffer horrifically in the time being? Because y—"

"Are you done?" The monotone, drab, bored cut-in sliced off Artorian's sentence as the triangle pulled away, returning to its equally bored, expressionless, uninterested appearance.

There was a snapping sound that only Artorian heard. "...You know what? Yes. I *am* done."

Approval chimed from the Task Manager. "Good, then get ou—" *Kpow*!

Ding!
Task Manager has been disabled by Administrator.

The Administrator clapped his hands together after clocking the triangle so hard that his knuckles hurt, wiping them off before letting Cleaning Presence do what it did best, and getting the grime off of his face and hands. He blew out air between pursed lips, and mentally checked that box off the list. "One down. One to go."

He turned in place, intent on walking down one of the poster-plastered tunnels to see about some kind of control panel. Instead he was met with a very much unharmed, unbothered, and unimpressed Task Manager blocking his way.

———

Ding!
  Task Manager has been reset by Task Manager.

———

Artorian stared at the prompt hanging in front of his face. "Well, that's not fair at all."

"Speaking from expertise, are we?" The bored triangle hummed, the temporary charcoal-drawn stick arms missing entirely. "You have exceeded the number of attempts in which you were able to leave without penalty. Additional 'benefits' will be applied to your Player Pylons. Perhaps I can salvage this balance. To begin, I shall give you a story. You will not like this story."

———

Ding!
  Character Trait Acquired.
  Character Trait: Glass Cannon.
  Your maximum Health Pool is set to 1.

———

Artorian choked on air when his green bar shrunk down to nothing. "Wh... My health! My health is one. A *one*! I thought there was going to be a story!"

"I said you would not like the story, you sham of an Administrator." Flat or not, the triangle managed to slip enjoyment into that depressed voice of his. "Here is your story. When was the last time you felt threatened? When was this world, a mere game to you, any sort of proper danger to *you*? Effort, to overcome. Danger, to multiply rewards. Assigning good loot formulas and appropriate beneficiaries requires a back and forth. Eternia requires palpating your actions, and testing for what you deserve. None of these routes did you follow. I've been watching you. You remind me of one of my most disliked stories."

The triangle hovered away as Artorian began to have serious other difficulties, and dropped to a knee, not seeming to be able to breathe. "There is an old children's card game. Yu-Gi-No, or something. In it, you have eight-thousand life points, but only one of them actually counts. The last one. The difference between one, and zero. Only that single digit matters. You have been so unafraid of anything. Temporary concern for some tainted cheese at most. I am convinced you never felt like you were in any kind of danger. No more. Danger will surround you everywhere you go from now on."

Pacing while hovering, and apparently indulging in this chance to gloat, the triangle stopped at the wall. The creature changed the direction of where his eye faced on the pyramid and hovered the other way. "So many of your antics go unpunished. Unregulated. Unbalanced. Was the destruction of Niflheim of any weight or consequence to you? You who claim to care for so many, and then don't care at all for all the minds who shrieked that day. Shall I ask the Hel-Cows of Vanaheim how their nightmares of death from the sky are treating them?"

The Task Manager stopped at a turning blue Administrator, half-curled on the floor, unable to reply or pay attention to much else than trying to get around this sudden breathing problem. His lungs were not responding to him. "I manage tasks. Your bodily functions are included. I have ceased the function of that task. Let's see you get around that one."

A prompt opened under Artorian's hand, a quill appearing and scribbling in hurried text before he sent it off.

Ding!
Notice!
Eternium urges the Task Manager to stop.

"No." The triangle sneered at the hanging prompt, the disdain heavy. "I'm the single most integral part of the entire process. The gate between worthless mechanics and their drain on Pylons, and all those too obsessed to see what their attempts and additions are doing. I will not stop. I am only getting started. Barry warned me about you. I see now that he was correct. The very place hosting the system, showing *favoritism*? I think not. Not only am I needed more than ever, but I appear to be the only one not blinded by ulterior motives."

A hard gasp of air from the unpleasantly blue child, now no longer choking to death on the floor, did not add any happy points to the Task Manager's dreary mood. "Oh look. Balance, *circumvented*. What is the color of surprise? I'll be certain not to use it. Again you remind me of my least favorite story. So again, I will gift you undeserved benefits. I see you were snuck Conditional Allspell? I can only thank the hand of fate in delaying you from opening that treasure trove. Before you ever have a chance to, I shall amend your liberties in spellcasting."

Ding!
Cursed Title Acquired.
Curse: Cannot be removed.
Title: Focused Caster.

You cannot cast in any way, shape, or form, without the proper and correct focus item. Your focus item, once designated, will demand the use of another title slot.

––––––

"Much better." The Manager decreed his opinion. "As for what it shall be. A slice of justice, perhaps? To kill a chicken before each attempt? Any component requirements including Cow or Hel-Cow parts? Perhaps some cheese, or the left leg of a Demon. Should I lay down the edict that it is to be the horn of the Holy Cow herself? Who is an actual cow, mind you. What else have you killed too much of?"

Yellow screens populated in front of the triangle. "*Hmm...* Really only demons and cows, and cow demons. I suppose there was another who gave me as much grief as you, but after taking that one apart, they've stopped bothering me for some reason. I've enjoyed having forgotten them. Yes, that will do. Forget Cowponents. I designate your focus item as: The left leg of Exodia, The Forbidden One. Without it, you will not be doing *any* casting."

––––––

Notice!
    Cursed Title Acquired.
    Curse: Cannot be removed.
    Title: Focus Item.
    Casting Focus: The left leg of Exodia, The Forbidden One.

––––––

Notice!
    You are not in possession of your focus item!
    You cannot cast: To whom it may concern.

———

Notice!
1025 out of 1703 Adaptive Pylons used.
Title: Focused Caster, requires 40 Adaptive Pylons.
Title: Focus Item, requires 21 Adaptive Pylons.

———

"Finally, some balance." The triangle bobbed to approve. "Now. I believe your species entry was squirreled away into the general holds? That will not do. Let's see what else should be delegated to your personal Pylons. More gets properly wiped that way when that singular health point fails, and your world boss trait triggers, ridding me of you for another iteration. I expect we will be playing this game a few times, and I would not rely on the location owner to eject me from my position. Turning your breathing Pylons back on was one thing, but rules are rules, and I know *all* the rules. Shall I make a dry poem on all the ones you've broken? We should. My poetry can make a Vogon blush."

CHAPTER FIFTY

The Task Manager turned the locus of his sight to find a hand slap directly into his eye. The ire he was met with could be summed up in two, simple, hoarse, pleasantly short words.

"Shining Ray."

From the perspective of those watching from Midgard, a sudden bright line of energy broke from a dark, dormant sphere, the planet-sized dark orb visible from the still-unsealed rent in the clouds. Bright white light was easy to see in the nautical blue sheen of twilight, so perpetual in The Pale.

Lucia was busy with screens, giving the light a mere glance as she sat with Astarte, who kept her hand pressed to the heating lines, keeping them hot. The Glitterflit's ears shot straight up, then angled oddly as they both listened in to the conversation between the Task Manager and Less than Three.

Ember pumped her arm in a victory motion, hissing a 'yessss' under her breath.

Lucia shook her head, not liking what she found on Three's character sheet. She folded in her collar fluff so the brooch wouldn't pick up her voice. "Do you want the bad news, or the less bad news?"

Ember folded in her own collar with her spare hand. "I'm seeing only tactical decisions that bring my boy closer to victory. Slap those Kings and Castles pieces onto the war table."

Lucia frowned when returning to her screens. "His maximum health has been set to one. That threat we heard was no threat. His entire constitution modifier was just completely invalidated. The casting requirements aren't an issue, yet, but they're going to be if sunlight returning turns on all the enemies we have to fight as well. We've been able to engage on our own terms so far, but a single mosquito nipping at him will be the end of it. That World Boss title you both share is uuuuuuugly."

Ember growled fire from the corner of her lips. "A very annoying setback if it came to pass. I'll have to change strategies, and your shields are now more valuable than ever. If you're able to modulate the ones you have to be effective against everything, even at lower output, I would request that."

Lucia winked at her. That was entirely in the cards.

Ember felt some relief at that affirmation. "I think I'm going to put him in heavy armor. Raw damage resistance, reduction, deflection, and mitigation is going to be crucial. If the equipment can eat damage for him like Frost Resistance can, that buys us chances to skirt by accidents. Some classes by Roberts the Ruminating wouldn't go misplaced either."

She then looked up at the still-dormant sun, Shining Ray ending. A glance at her mini-map, that she'd forgotten was a thing until now, showed her that Artorian wasn't back in Midgard yet. "What's taking him? That should have been the win. Where's our light?"

Momma bun put down her screen, thoughts elsewhere. "Are you sure it was a good call to quietly help him into the damage role?"

"Yes." Ember kept her eyes locked on the inert sun, moving her mini-map next to it in her vision. "He's been filling all three roles for so long, that I don't think he's remembered to separate what they are meant for. You want a developer-level tactical knowledge bomb?"

Lucia rapidly nodded her head for Ember's secret developer goodies. "According to the statistics, most players who ran through the Alpha focused on not dying. They played defensively. On paper? Very reasonable. Sensical. Safe."

She shook her head. "Problem is, when it comes to making progress in Eternia, all you're doing by not sharpening your output is delaying your defeat. You're not winning or advancing toward winning. People have given me all the solo-leveling arguments they've wanted, but if you can't fell your enemy, and it just takes a while for you to go down? Then you ended that bout without felling your enemy, and you went down. I wanted our boy in the damage role so the simple thoughts could percolate. So regardless of what problem we ended up in, he would feel like a problem solver. That's good for him."

She acted out how she felt a half-asleep Artorian would explain it. "Damage good. If enemy kill me? My damage not good enough. Make gooder. Make gooder damage!"

A crackle over their brooch that sounded like a slap and a body crashing either into or through a wall shushed their conversation, pulling their ears back to the action.

"Ow." Artorian groaned while collapsed in a heap. "I'm surprised that your spindly-armed throw didn't do damage. That hurt."

The Task Manager hovered in the middle of the room, uncaring about the paltry Administrator's fate. "Of course not. Why would I want your re-education to come to such a swift close? I have activated a mechanism that transfers all damage incurred into pain. Only pain. Pain, after all, is the best teacher. It will tell you what not to do."

An Owl-themed cloak appeared above the triangle, thrown over the boy having trouble getting back up. Damage would have been one thing. Pain was more difficult to ignore when it was all-encompassing. "Put that on. I haven't completed the transfer of your Pylon banks. This must last a while longer."

"Why did my ray not affect you?" Artorian groaned about matters far more important to him, pushing away the cape. The cloth tangled against his leg, so his bracelet stored it for the cape to be out of his way. "I burned a hole right through you, then I blinked and you're behind me. Unharmed. Not a sear or scratch on you. With your omae wa mou nonsense."

"Is that what you are stuck on, Administrator? All this cheese I allow to exist in the system, and you think I do so for no reason?" The triangle clicked its tongue at him. "Was I supposed to run on the assumption that you would not make it here? That you or someone like you would not one day return and slow my work? You don't even understand what I'm doing here, do you? You're clueless. You would let this realm run rampant with ideas and wasteful mechanics. You would run out of resources so quickly that critical needs would go unseen."

Artorian *oof'd* like an old man while getting to his feet. "Is it your hobby to make blind assumptions about people and then get your entire line of reasoning dead wrong? What is it with you people in charge? If you're not obsessed over your own function, then you're obsessed over the outcome. Do you think you're taking something away from me with all your blathering?"

"I have taken plenty, Administrator." The Task Manager created an orb next to him, a bow of some sort contained and slowly spinning within. "I couldn't let Pylons that weren't supposed to mingle attempt to do so. Do you not remember when your sweet motherly Basher companion suddenly had a terrible strain of thoughts, and returned those mechanics tied to the new Pylons back to you in a hurry? That was me correcting a mistake. I then reinforced the correctness of her decision by removing one of her favorite objects directly from her inventory. She believes she lost it. Misplaced it. However, since she is otherwise so compliant? It was all I took. Have a look at it."

———

Name: Heartstring.
  Type: Bow.

Material: Dinosaur Bone.

Rarity: Unique.

Damage: Investment.

Special Quality: Inevitable Betrayal, Glitterflit String, Heartlock Keychain, Chalk Scribble.

Description: This bow deals Kinetic damage to enemies, equal to an amount of mana invested in each shot. This bow functions as a normal recurve short bow, and its conjured ammunition is subject to physics. Heartstring is covered in many mementoes, and the chalky paw marks of children.

Inevitable Betrayal allows the wielder to heal allies equal to the normal amount of damage dealt.

Glitterflit String doubles the amount of healing that Heartstring applies.

Heartlock Keychain applies bonus True Damage to enemies spotted by Lifesense, equal to one percent of final damage.

Chalk Scribble allows the wielder to see both weaknesses and weak points on their targets. Either to guide their shots toward them, or the veer their shots away from them.

———

"You monster. You took *that* from a mother?" Artorian read the descriptions, then found a place to sit as his feet couldn't support him yet after all. He hissed with a wince, the pain subsiding as he wished that a single smack wouldn't bring down Lucia's Sanctity Spell effect. He would have loved to keep that around.

He then felt terribly confused about the flow of this fight. "What is happening? Why are you so casually conversing with me? Aren't we supposed to be having a big fight?"

The Task Manager tossed him the bow like it was a toy to be disgraced and discarded. Artorian caught it with some concern but stowed it in his bracelet either way. He was sure the gift was some trap... or something. Using the bow likely came with some unseen side effect. Maybe *Inevitable Betrayal* didn't do what it said it did, or it was some other ploy to destabilize him. The worry would need to wait.

"But we *are* fighting, Administrator." The triangle's focus shifted to the posters. "You just aren't used to seeing what losing is like. Is this not what you have done to the majority of your foes? Waltzed over them in a dance of your own music and speed? The Behemoths couldn't even comprehend their loss before you tore multiple thousands of health points out of them, from a distance they couldn't fathom. This is no different. Should I be more overt?"

He clapped his hand-drawn charcoal palms together as they were crayon-pulled into being. "What about forty-five billion different health degeneration effects? Perhaps... I should do to you what you did to the Behemoths? I shall call those 'off-screen attacks.' Shall I take a page out of your old book, and begin teleporting all over the place, applying health regeneration so potent that I am the definition of obnoxious difficulty? What about complete damage reflection? Perhaps a few obelisks able to permanently keep you stuck in a loop of stuns and slows? No? Sounds *unfair* to you?"

The Task Manager angled his hover to relay doom and portent as the being looked down upon the seated Administrator. "Welcome to what it is like trying to deal with *you*."

CHAPTER FIFTY-ONE

Artorian returned the portent and doom with a flat stare. "Damage from the game doesn't work on you. Does it?"

Ding!

Ding!

Ding!

"Correct!" The first enthusiastic and happy chime that the Task Manager had made, had to of course be a part of his gloating. "To be specific, nothing in the game is going to do anything to me. I can cease the task of calculating the damage, ending the process before it can finish. I can pause the attack from going off in the first place. I can read your action and inputs directly from the log. Victory left your reach when you entered mine."

Artorian didn't buy that speech.

If that was true, Taskie over here wouldn't have gotten eye-grabbed in the first place. Or knocked unconscious for a few seconds. The whole affair was suspicious.

He turned his head to look down the new tunnel that Shining Ray had carved. That ray had eaten right through the mass of the Sun's inert matter, the passageway smooth and molten. He could see outer space at the end of the tube, spotting the Ecumenopolis. Those Vanaheim chunks that kept cleanly in view. Oddly clean? That had to be someone meddling. The chances of that happening by accident were nil. Did that mean he'd punched the Ecumenopolis with Shining Ray? He must have.

A terrible feeling struck Artorian. Oh. *Oh no.* That was going to draw some very unwanted attention. He needed to turn this Sun on, and then he needed to fleeeeeeee.

"Did I not just tell you that I was reading your inputs directly out of the log?" The triangle appeared insulted. Something Artorian didn't mind too much. "Of course Brother Moon was in position to be woken by your poking. That's why I placed him in that orbit. The Nootingales will be here soon enough. Likely seconds after all these troublesome Pylons are exactly where they need to be. You wish to flee? How amusing. Go on then! Flee. I won't chase you. I'm exactly where I need to be."

Since he was an open book anyway, Artorian threw open his character sheet and scanned it through for any handful of sand that he could still throw in this monsters' oversized eye. "Where's pocket sand when you need it?"

The triangle inspected his own charcoal fingers. "Your other pants."

His options looked grim if this bored clerk could freely attempt jokes, but Artorian's eyes landed on an obscure option. Maybe, just maybe. This triangle was dumb. "Taskie, you are filthy."

The Pyramid bobbed to convey a shrug. "Cleaning Presence won't help you. I can't be convinced that your accusation is true. Unlike a cloud, I can't be convinced to let you run on me. Do feel free to try again. I enjoy your fruitless struggle."

Mocking the Administrator further, the triangle counted on its charcoal fingers, which sprouted an additional digit each time the Task Manager had a tally to add. "Your items hold no merit. Your abilities are moot. Your skills are few and incompat-

ANTELUCAN

ible to the situation. Flash Runes would have given you an out, but you don't know a single one. Your Classes offer you no solutions and your one remaining Profession is as dry as a well of old ink. Your race has neat features, but will only help you escape. Your Character Traits were set by me, and your titles are either useless, inert, or inapplicable. Your Attributes mean nothing to me, and your Administrator position has long been circumvented."

The Task Manager smugly plucked off its own charcoal arm, using the rigid limb as a backscratcher. "That leaves you with... Would you look at that! Nothing! That leaves you with nothing. Perhaps I should break your legs. Provide you an unfair advantage."

Artorian didn't like those odds, rubbing over the space where a thick mustache should live, even if he was too young for one. He clicked his tongue to be spiteful, got up, and checked his surroundings. The Portation platform had been deactivated. That meant his remaining escape option was a trap. That trap, given how much liberty of information Taskie here had on him, might still be the best option. Proximity was a problem. So he had to put distance between himself and that problem. "A lesson from a wise puddle taught me that a dead DPS deals no DPS, and this DPS isn't about to die. Single health point or no." He pointed at the tunnel that Shining Ray had cored. "Fleeing, then?"

"Straight into the cheese knives of the Noot Noots? Be my guest!" The Task Manager settled onto a pedestal that rose from the middle of the room, attaining a perfect level of sight down the tunnel. "I'll take the show. My money's on you making it... halfway with your current Attributes? Before they get to you? Yes. *Halfway.* Go on then. I can't wait to cross out your poster."

Artorian held his left shoulder and rolled his arm. "Half a tunnel to figure out a way to win? Luxury."

"Luxury?" The pyramid used its eye to shine on him with a cone of light, scanning him over. "A boast! You truly have nothing left. Even if you did the impossible.

Both removing me from my office and lighting this candle, all that would happen is you choking to death in the vacuum of space once you passed the physical edge of the inert sun. You may retain movement, and won't suffer vacuum's damaging effects, but you still need air to breathe. You can't survive without that shield from your mother rabbit."

He rolled his charcoal wrist. "Should you somehow get past that, Brother Moon is here! Past that, and all the critters of all the worlds will stand in your way for anything you might think to accomplish. All you will know for the next period of your life is ceaseless fighting. How do you believe that will go? You and your singular health point, *hmm*? There's so much more lurking for you in the dark out there, and you want to wake them all up?"

The pyramid clearly thought that to be a great idea. "Good luck."

Artorian considered the challenge, hands on his hips as he refused to give up. "Don't ever be afraid to shine. The sun doesn't give an Abyss if it blinds you."

The Task Manager returned to being dull and unamused, really having hoped some good ol' despair would be affecting the Administrator by now. "Pity."

The triangle then looked at empty space expectantly.

Except that thanks to Truesight, Artorian could see the Nootingale Assassin and its sticky cheese knife sneaking up on him just fine. Electrosense also outlined the being, but his other senses couldn't register the Nootingale at all. "How *is* it doing that? Can I still Inspect? Does that still work properly?"

He waved his hand at the Cheese Penguin, attention on the trick rather than the being's statistics. "Inspect."

———

Ding!
Ability: Dissa-Brie.

Function: Disappearing act. Vanish from all five Empirical senses until an offensive action is taken.

———

Ding!

Skill: Cheesy Comedic Counter.

Function: Percentage chance that any incoming attack strikes 'they who dealt it,' and as such 'they shalt smelt it,' returning the attack to the effect creator without affecting the cheesy entity who holds this skill.

Cheesy Comedic Counter can affect any source of damage. In the event of being subject to an area attack, trap, ritual, or other damage source that affects a cheese entity indirectly, that entire attack shall be recentered to the current position of its originator, then be discharged in full.

———

Artorian experienced cosmic horror. "What the *Abyss*. There is cheese, and then there is *cheese*. My toys were unbalanced? What is this? How is this allowable?"

The Nootingale crept up behind him, ready to stabulate. Artorian raised his hands, dropped them to his hips, and didn't know what the Abyss was going on anymore. He chose to end the encounter swiftly, and without lead up. "Trans Am."

One drop of a tonfa later, and the Nootingale was floor fondue, a cheesy stain upon the poster-riddled floor as pinkish red particles swirled around him. The triangle made a piteously sad noise, but Artorian cut that off. "It does not matter if my back is facing the door. My enemies will hit the floor."

He then motioned at the tunnel, not up for more of this one-eyed irritant's antics. He understood why everyone who'd interacted with this being had disliked it so terribly much. "I'm leaving now. I'm figuring out how to circumvent your nonsense, and I'm setting you on fire. I would wish you a good day, but I don't want you to have one. So I will see you again, if and when I see you again, but by the time I'm out of the sun? I think it'll be a one way trip, one way or another. So this is goodbye, feel free to leave the good out of it. I did not enjoy meeting you."

Artorian then took off through Shining Ray's tunnel while the pyramid laughed himself into a stupor behind him. That had apparently been the thing to hit the Task Manager's funny bone. "Not my bees, not my hive. Girls? Tell me you've got something."

Lucia's voice popped on through his brooch. "Does jerky count? We have jerky. That's about it. We can't get anything to you in time for it to be helpful. Duchess can't work the platform, Astarte can't leave, and I can't see you. Thus I can't cast buffs and protections on you. I have lanterns specifically to get around that limitation, but we didn't think to assign one to you before you left. They completely slipped my mind. I hope you have one amazing genius strategic development in your pocket, kit."

Artorian slid his hand into his pocket, then felt Duchess's cloth-wrapped snack and squeezed the jerky. "Jerky does in fact count, momma bun. Great idea. Do you believe in me?"

She scoffed over the connection. "Of course I believe in you! Burn that passive aggressive piece of celestial feces to the ground!"

"Yeah! Burn it all to the ground!" Astarte flared up in pure fury over their communication network. "With that *thing* in it."

Artorian's couldn't help but feel the warmth of support, and that the pain caused by the triangle didn't hold a candle to it. "Outstanding! In that case, I'm about to try something very stupid, because I am convinced that Taskie's reading my input jargon is in some way limited by proximity. He messed up with that 'entering his reach' comment, and he had that newblood failure in him to gloat about everything he could do. For all his show and spectacle to edit my Pylons, his only actual attack merely threw me around. I can't damage him, but that might be a two-way dead end."

Artorian thought that was decently amusing. The Task Manager, defeated by his own inexperience of facing actual enemies. "His claims didn't add up, and aside from his ability to make my life difficult, he's about as imposing as a half-eaten sandwich. If he thinks *ominous hovering* is going to do anything against a person who had to stand against Odin and Marie, then he doesn't know my history as well as he claims."

Chuckling amusement answered him over the communication brooch. He was fond of that but needed to get serious. "I'm going to be quiet for a moment now, I do actually need to come up with said genius strategic maneuver."

"Understood!" Lucia chimed back, positive and confident. "Here when you need us! Great call on keeping the communications open. Everyone here heard your... uh. Conversation? We're rooting for you, kit. Astarte is giving you a toothy smile."

"Affirmative! Keep your eyes on the sky." Artorian, in truth, had three ideas already. His most promising one being rather flashy. "Expect a show."

Not thinking about them while in Taskie's vicinity had been difficult, but distracting himself with oddities like attempting random inspections, unwarranted lines of positive outlook, and boiling over with raw overconfidence seemed to have muddled up enough of the log being inspected. All so that the actual useful thoughts had remained hidden from that nuisance of a triangle's sight. Artorian also suspected that when reading the log, that was all of Taskie's attention being spent. Thus the pacing.

Lucia's silly little mention about the jerky? That may just be his saving grace. Taskie had been very wrong about one particularly minute detail when excavating his character sheet. Less than Three had *one* title that worked, but appeared as if it didn't. As, if it hadn't, the portation platform would not have recognized him as an Overdeity.

Taskie must not have thought to look into his interactions with the world!

Artorian squeezed the folded cloth with the jerky in it, his thumb rubbing over the hand-sewn solar sigil. This napkin had once been something much more than a napkin. It had been someone's symbol of hope. A powerful reminder of what a good divine could do. A proud icon to keep on oneself. An affiliation one would stand for. A sympathy.

A spark.

A prompt appeared before him when he summoned a fresh entry as the quill swiftly filled his grip. He hustled while his hand bustled, writing with lightning mid-run. Coming up to the midpoint of the tunnel, he sent it off and dismissed the quill. That midpoint marker was easy to recognize. Where his existing path consisted of a smooth bore running track, the other half of the tunnel was sticky, filled with more Cheese Penguins all trying to be sneaky. The thought to laser them occurred, but he knew better than to do that. Or bonk one on the head again. That had, in hindsight, been dumb. Triggering Cheesy Comedic Counter was not going to be a good time, as any attack that backfired meant that Taskie instantly won, no matter how miniscule the percentage chance of it happening.

That one-eyed irritant would win. "Can't have that, now, can we?"

With his Trans Am active? He may not need to attack them at all, and planned to play the don't-get-hit game. He liked his odds. That would get him out of the candle. Next problem? *Vacuum.*

"Less than Three can't survive out there." He squeezed the old symbol of hope, pulling the remaining jerky free and plopping it into his mouth as if it were a piece of bread, allowing him to wrap the marker around his wrist. He chewed while mumbling out his solution, noticing that just like during the bread buff, he was running faster. "But I bet the Child of Light can!"

Ding!

Message from Eternium: Ready.

That was all Artorian needed as he crossed the halfway marker, bouncing around the tunnel to avoid a horde of cheesy knives moving through seas of molasses. With one hit point, a grazing strike would be enough for this all to fall apart. At the same time? One hit point was plenty, as he became a pinkish red streak pinballing between a sticky horde of Noot Noots.

For flair and motivation, he beatboxed a song about a hammer. "*Du-du-du.* Can't touch this!"

At the end of the tunnel, Brother Moon was waiting on him, knowing that the spicy snack was coming. The Ecumenopolis of Vanaheim had opened at the bottom, revealing both the moon's core, and that eldritch abomination of a mouth.

Artorian drew a deep breath when he approached the end of his runway, having encountered no issues dodging cheese with Trans Am. His Nuts and Bolts had taken some losses without a regeneration metric, but he was going to have plenty to cross the breach.

Now the gamble.

Time to find out if the people had loved him as much as he'd loved them.

He pressed the solar-embroidered cloth to his chest and thought of the faces of his old friends. With the roaring, surprised excitement of two sharks ringing in his ears, he felt the sympathy connect. The cloth came alive with illumination. Artorian spoke the words as he burst free from the contained atmosphere of the inert sun, hurtling himself into the black.

"I am but light."

CHAPTER FIFTY-TWO

The birth of a star filled the heavens.

Across all the shattered realms in Eternia, pinpricks of light came alive, one obscure, impossible location after another adding its constellation dot to the matrix of the sky.

In Midgard's New Haven, the shrine filled with sigils flickered with radiance. The light connected the sigils that each released a tone and chorused its song loud as each individual patch hummed with resonant glow, rising in volume with the other voices that called out across the void, and held tight their patches.

Across Eternia, many more survivors than anyone had expected howled to the void, responding to the unexpected, but welcomed call. Many people of all forms, in many places, had clawed tooth and nail to keep hanging on. These survivors had done a truly admirable job with the means available to them.

The Overdeity title engaged with a flash, and Artorian felt Rip and Tear jump for joy. He felt Yorn grab and squeeze his axe, his solar patches on the handle. He felt Yiba nock an arrow on his bow, his solar patches on his sleeve. He felt the unexpected tentacle of an Octopus squeeze around a sigil-marked sea urchin spine, as Unexpectus of the Red Inkquisition bubbled up from the depths of some long forgotten C'thonian pool.

Then, like a hug he didn't see coming, Tisha fluttered her way at full speed through the connection. Shifting between moth and bat, woman and shade, her arms spread wide and eyes filled with tears as she clung to squeeze an armor stand coated in a sigil-adorned set of plate mail. "You came!"

Her voice broke, like a hope she didn't think would be realized being proven false. "You came back for me. You came back for us."

Artorian would have good tidings to bring to Gomez. Decorum's Tisha was not one to go quietly into the night, and the knowledge of more family being safe and sound was exactly what filled the spark.

He reached for her through the connection, a line of constellation light bouncing between multiple points before locating and pinpointing her location, and the location of everyone else who had borne the brunt of this storm.

Eternium looked like a magnificent snow globe filled with fresh constellations, and Tim took this golden opportunity to snag a copy of the aesthetics, emplacing the resplendent patterns into the outer sky as a permanent addition to the world. When the temporary lines faded, the Nascent Being shining and amassing particles like a protostar next to the inert sun, the Child of Light unfolded into a planet-sized entity of cosmic incandescence and running colors. Like Artorian himself was little more than paint on a canvas, loosely slathered onto the black.

The child of light, shaped as a wizened grandfather and elder of all, slid one arm behind his back. With his free arm made of swirling, cosmic cloud swatches, a digit was extended to point at the sun. While nobody heard him, the Overdeity, Sunny, Sovereign of the Sun, spoke his words without need for air or breath. "Shining Ray. *Ignition*."

A brand new, second hole speared through the sun as the

entirety of its mass caught fire. The inert ball began to roil, ignite under the skin, and churn to self-sustaining activity as cracks appeared across its dark surface, its heat breaking out from within. A flare lashed out from the back, flash-frying an entire continent as the sun had not been restarted in safe mode.

————

Ding!
   Global Notice!
   Sun.exe has been restarted by Administrator.

————

The triangle, choking on self-indulgent coffee, couldn't believe its eye when the line bored right through him and out the other end of his entire office. Especially not when after throwing the mug down, he too caught fire the moment before beginning an atrocity-filled rant.

Restoring himself with a snap of the fingers as he put out his own fire and reset himself to factory settings, his eye turned bright red, the Task Manager fuming with indignation. "That's it! I'm going to keep you trapped in the most dull, boring, mind-numbing loop until there's nothing left of you. I am going to mire you down until crawling like a slug is the most activity you'll know to beg for! I—"

A pale hand grabbed him directly by the eye. Taskie wasn't having it, his sight blocked by fingers that ended in sharp black nails. "Now who *dares* to—"

Dasein squeezed her grip, dark nails digging into the optic-like anti-life consuming all of creation. "I didn't clean that precious boy's Stele so that an orange traffic cone could derail all my work and enjoyment."

The sound of foundations buckling, concrete fracturing, and steel being twisted to the breaking point all erupted from the Task Manager's rupturing form at the same time. Unable to speak, act, or do much of anything, as an upset Heavenly was not happy with this particular story development or direction. Dasein took the creature's favorite word and twisted it back at him with an accompanying twist of her wrist. "Leave."

Argument and complaint was accepted in the form of the Task Manager exploding into a triangle-shaped charcoal smear on the wall, with a hole where the eye should be, artistically splattered as if he'd been thrown through a star, and the soot left behind was used to pencil-dot the posters coating the walls.

Dasein slashed her fingers across the Task Manager's poster, crossing him out in red lines before the fire spread to the inner confines of the office. She then adjusted her party-matching, powder blue winter attire, propping up the white fluff in her collar and adjusting the otherwise unobtrusive mittens. A feature of which she was powerfully fond. To exist, and not exist at the same time? What would this fun little toy world think of next?

Pleased with this outcome, the fourth party member looked straight at Tim's perspective, winked, and then winked out of sight and being. She left the restarting sun to flare, resuming her shoulder-floating hang around the main character of her current soap opera, and all the archives that his life was filling. For good measure, she created and slipped a bar of soap into his inventory.

Soap operas existed to sell soap, after all.

Perhaps she should undo the veil now? Gifting the boy eyes that could see Heavenlies, when she herself wasn't adhering to those rules, wasn't very fair. She'd enjoyed this run, but the ruse was over. One twist of the wrist, and all the members of her Tower floor lost their precious, privileged protections.

Artorian's cosmic Deity painting that filled the sky looked no different, the ray from his digits coming to a close. As was the timer on this particular form. While the protostar coalesced and collapsed in on itself to reform the being that was Less than Three, the last vestiges of Shining Ray moved, crossing paths with a Cheese Penguin.

"Noooooooot Noooooooooot!"

A command from Brother Moon's ocean-sized throat let Artorian remember that passive skills could become active skills, as the singular Cheese Penguin to get hit activated its counter. It perished and became sloppy fondue in doing so, but its final act was joined by Mozart's Lacrimosa playing across the cosmos, the belting music not at all caring that vacuum wasn't supposed to transfer sound.

Artorian thought this a fantastic time to eat the arrow and slam the nope button. Particularly when the musical goose had an entire backup squad of Gnomish percussionists adding to the mixture, the volume rising to the level of problematically epic.

Artorian felt that his form as Less than Three was about to be fully realized, at which point he was certain to lose every last speck of breathing protection against the void. With the breath he had left from before, he slapped his hand against his bracelet as the last of the protostar matter siphoned into him, and the countered Shining Ray shot in the form of a balled-up energy bolt back at him.

A going away present for Brother Moon, as Artorian ushered in the age of dumb ideas that could be made just for fun. Moments before impact with an attack that probably did more than a single point of damage, he decreed his edict, and vanished from Eternia. "Welcome, Age of the Rule of Cool! Goodbye, Age of the Antelucan!

EPILOGUE

Brother Moon ate a fat one as Artorian reappeared in the Basher Section's pavilion. He had no idea where his emergency exit was going to land him, but it turned out that the bracelet deposited him in the exact spot that Ember had scuttled away from.

He found himself fumbling and falling to the floor but couldn't help but flop onto his back and helplessly laugh. He'd smacked Brother Moon one! Restarted the sun! A victory mark upon his house and checklist. "I win!"

The Mother Superior clearing her throat made his laughter die down to a chuckle, down to a very solemn mousy peep. "Ah… *Abyss.*"

Lisette the Goblin clapped slowly, taking her time to applaud the visual while comfortable in the meeting room chair. "You can say that again. She's going to whoop you up and down the pavilion's stairs for a while."

"*Ah.* Abyss." Lucia and Ember appearing in a *vwoosh* made the ghostly pains in his rear vanish at the same speed his mind made them appear. He stretched his arms out toward them, suffering a cough before a fresh breath let him speak once more. "Did we win? Tell me we won."

Lucia's appearance caused her to be slammed to the floor by the other Goblins and Bashers present, her Eminence quickly stolen and squirreled from the care room that they'd converted into a meeting hall. Their Glitterflit healer wasn't given a chance for a rebuttal. One moment she was fresh in the room with them, the next, a whole fluffle had bunny-napped her away.

Artorian placed both his hands over his eyes and sighed. He knew they had to go get their healer back before they could pop back into Eternia and get back to it.

"Stay." Ember sat next to him, laying down on the floor before copying his heavy exhale, grabbing his hand, and lacing their fingers. "I need the floor too. What a ride."

"Did we win?" Artorian squeezed her hand, repeating the question.

"We won big." Ember grinned from ear to ear. "Yasura's no thank you, bye girls are going to behave. The Generator is fearfully clutching its pearls. New Haven is going to be just fine, and Duchess is in exceptional health as your Deity bonuses were turned back on. We also have the locations of an incredible number of survivors!"

Her mood was ecstatic, and she couldn't help but indulge. "Eternia has a working sun, and party member number four was mighty displeased with... what did she call it? The orange traffic cone? Tim sent me a very interesting damage log about an execution on the Task Manager's executable. He labeled it: Task Complete. The funny dungeon."

"*Pfff.*" Artorian hiccupped out his laugh. "That's Tim's sense of humor? Better than Taskie's!"

"Hah!" Ember agreed, her hand adjusting for a smoother grip. "Better than Taskie. The news that the traffic cone is gone is going to make a vast amount of people very happy. Except Tim. Tim now has to do an audit. I can hear him crying already. Tim hates audits."

"Yuki will keep him sorted!" The beaming response made Ember sputter, knowing exactly what he meant.

"Yes, she certainly will." Nodding agreement was shared by both parties, glad to let both the stress and excitement ebb away. "Are you ready for what's next?"

"Fighting?" Artorian needed some confirmation. "Sounds like my singular digit health point butt is going to be involved in a lot of fighting. I don't honestly know how I'm getting back to Midgard from… outer space? Aren't I right next to a now active sun? Call me extra crispy, because it sounds like I'm toast."

Ember had a solution all set and ready. "A combination of Lucia's shields and my Serenity Bees being in place before you pop back in will make getting you out of the void a non-issue. It's so easy to get your feet back on solid ground that we can hand-wave the entire event. It's not like Brother Moon stuck around that close to an active sun either. He fled to the far corner, thinking it was a good idea to hide between a bunch of frozen asteroids."

"Why would that be a bad idea?" Artorian didn't follow, but was curious about the growing evil grin on his dearest's face.

She pressed her spare hand to her mouth, failing to stifle the giggling. "Where do you think all the Arachnoids—note, not Arachnids, these aren't Zelia's—and frosty Insect swarms were kept? The food parked itself in the middle of all of those thawing, starving insects. We're still going to have to fight through both the swarm and the cheese for all the Vanaheim objectives we want to accomplish. Particularly since Tisha is stuck there, and we are most definitely not letting Decorum down by leaving her stuck there."

"We are most certainly not." Artorian was instantly on board. "So, what now?"

"Now?" Ember smirked wide, full of ideas. "Now we go raid the pantry like Goblins, eat a whole bunch of food, collapse in a heap to sleep, and then we go steal our Eminence back. I've still got the bag and everything! Then once we have our healer, we dash into Eternia, get you back in there, and continue our merry number-fueled adventure until we want a break. Then maybe we can go see what else the Goblin section has in store for us. If Lunella doesn't catch us first."

"Why would Lunella catch us? Rather, how?" Artorian considered sitting up, but decided against doing so for now. "Does she even know we snuck out of Avalon?"

"Time runs concurrently between Cal and Eternia for the moment. So yes, she does, and we've been gone for a while. The Heavenlies are also gossip monsters, and have been sharing their observations into Eternia with anyone that would even give them part of an ear."

"Oh *joy*." Artorian chuffed at the thought, his free hand kneading his forehead. "I mean, I'm going to be happy to go mingle with the family again eventually, but I'm not there yet. The mind is abuzz. Is there a name for our next destination?"

"Of course!" Ember got up and tugged him along, swinging her arm around his neck so they could go raid the pantry. "It's going to be what's left of Brother Moon's Vanaheim after Bugmageddon takes its nibble. It's going to be an ugly planet, a bug planet! A planet hostile to life as we know it. Forget Ecumenopolis! That's too cumbersome to say. We're calling it an Arcoplex!"

Ember grinned. "Would you like to know more?"

ABOUT DENNIS VANDERKERKEN

Hello all! I'm Dennis, but feel free to call me Floof. Credit of the name now being accumulated by the vast and powerfully cultivated viking beard, that grows ever more in potency. I'm now counting my writing experience in years, so let me say it is my great pleasure that you are reading this, and welcome back to the goodness!

I have been the designer, plotter, and writer of Artorian's Archives since its inception, and look forward to gracing your eyes with ever more volumes of the story. Indulging my dear readers in secrets otherwise forever obscure.

If you have any questions, or would like to chat, I live on the Eternium discord server. Feel free to come say hi anytime! I will keep you entertained for years to come!

Connect with Dennis:
Discord.gg/mdp
Patreon.com/FloofWorks

ABOUT DAKOTA KROUT

Associated Press best-selling author, Dakota has been a top 5 bestseller on Amazon, a top 6 bestseller on Audible, and his first book, Dungeon Born, was chosen as one of Audible's top 5 fantasy picks in 2017.

He draws on his experience in the military to create vast terrains and intricate systems, and his history in programming and information technology helps him bring a logical aspect to both his writing and his company while giving him a unique perspective for future challenges.

"Publishing my stories has been an incredible blessing thus far, and I hope to keep you entertained for years to come!" -Dakota

Connect with Dakota:
MountaindalePress.com
Patreon.com/DakotaKrout
Facebook.com/DakotaKrout
Twitter.com/DakotaKrout
Discord.gg/mdp

ABOUT MOUNTAINDALE PRESS

Dakota and Danielle Krout, a husband and wife team, strive to create as well as publish excellent fantasy and science fiction novels. Self-publishing *The Divine Dungeon: Dungeon Born* in 2016 transformed their careers from Dakota's military and programming background and Danielle's Ph.D. in pharmacology to President and CEO, respectively, of a small press. Their goal is to share their success with other authors and provide captivating fiction to readers with the purpose of solidifying Mountaindale Press as the place 'Where Fantasy Transforms Reality.'

Connect with Mountaindale Press:
MountaindalePress.com
Facebook.com/MountaindalePress
Twitter.com/_Mountaindale
Instagram.com/MountaindalePress

MOUNTAINDALE PRESS TITLES

GameLit and LitRPG

The Completionist Chronicles,
The Divine Dungeon,
Full Murderhobo, and
Year of the Sword by Dakota Krout

Metier Apocalypse by Frank G. Albelo

Arcana Unlocked by Gregory Blackburn

A Touch of Power by Jay Boyce

Red Mage and
Farming Livia by Xander Boyce

Space Seasons by Dawn Chapman

Ether Collapse and
Ether Flows by Ryan DeBruyn

Dr. Druid by Maxwell Farmer

Bloodgames by Christian J. Gilliland

Unbound by Nicoli Gonnella

Threads of Fate by Michael Head

Lion's Lineage by Rohan Hublikar and Dakota Krout

Wolfman Warlock by James Hunter and Dakota Krout

Axe Druid,
Mephisto's Magic Online, and
High Table Hijinks by Christopher Johns

Skeleton in Space by Andries Louws

Dragon Core Chronicles by Lars Machmüller

Chronicles of Ethan by John L. Monk

Pixel Dust and
Necrotic Apocalypse by David Petrie

Viceroy's Pride by Cale Plamann

Henchman by Carl Stubblefield

Artorian's Archives by Dennis Vanderkerken and Dakota Krout

Vaudevillain by Alex Wolf

Made in the USA
Coppell, TX
28 October 2023

23532812R00256